Mozart Studies

Mozart Studies

Edited by
CLIFF EISEN

CLARENDON PRESS · OXFORD
1991

Oxford University Press, Walton Street, Oxford OX2 6DP
Oxford New York Toronto
Delhi Bombay Calcutta Madras Karachi
Petaling Jaya Singapore Hong Kong Tokyo
Nairobi Dar es Salaam Cape Town
Melbourne Auckland
and associated companies in
Berlin Ibadan

Oxford is a trade mark of Oxford University Press

Published in the United States
by Oxford University Press, New York

British Library Cataloguing in Publication Data
Data available

Library of Congress Cataloging in Publication Data
Mozart studies/edited by Cliff Eisen.
Includes bibliographical references and index.
1. *Mozart, Wolfgang Amadeus, 1756–1791—Criticism and interpretation.* I. *Eisen, Cliff, 1952–* .
ML410.M9M73 1991 780'.92—dc20 91-33961

ISBN 0-19-816191-3

Typeset by Joshua Associates Limited, Oxford
Printed in Great Britain by
St Edmundsbury Press, Bury St Edmunds

Preface

FOR about thirty-five years now—by no accident, almost exactly Mozart's life-span—the dominant thrust of Mozart scholarship has been the completion of a modern, critical edition of his works, the *Neue Mozart-Ausgabe*. While the primary goal of this venture was to produce new and better texts for the composer's works, it also could not fail to broaden the horizons of Mozart scholarship in many other areas. The by-products of the work on the *NMA* include the discovery of numerous new sources, a revised chronology for Mozart's works, a re-evaluation of the historical contexts in which the works were composed and performed, insights into contemporary performance practice, and, more practically, modern editions of the complete family letters and a comprehensive documentary biography.

Yet even as the *NMA* approaches completion, it is clear that the edition does not represent the conclusion of a particular phase of Mozart scholarship. On the contrary, its large and strikingly diverse body of results has served to stimulate Mozart scholarship in new, more probing directions, many of which have been pursued by English-language scholars. The Mozart bicentennial is a fitting time not only to review this recent scholarship, but also to strike out again in still newer directions.

The essays in this volume are concerned with biography, analysis and criticism, and source studies. In his biographical article, Maynard Solomon discusses Johann Friedrich Rochlitz's anecdotes of Mozart, first published in the *Allgemeine musikalische Zeitung* between October 1798 and May 1801. This crucial biographical source—so crucial, in fact, that by constant repetition the anecdotes are often taken for granted as unadulterated truth—receives here not only its first complete translation, but also its first critical evaluation, demonstrating that the anecdotes are in large part fiction. The analytical and critical articles include those by Christoph Wolff, James Webster, Neal Zaslaw, and Carl Schachter. Christoph Wolff writes on the Requiem, reviewing the work's complicated history and suggesting that, whatever the faults of Süssmayr's completion may be, it nevertheless represents the source that is as likely as any to bring us close to the work as Mozart originally conceived it. James Webster discusses Mozart's arias, setting out on a new path in Mozart opera analysis, which previously has concentrated chiefly on the composer's ensembles and finales. His is an attempt not merely to analyse these works, but, more importantly, to establish a new critical methodology for understanding them. Neal Zaslaw discusses a striking feature of Mozart's orchestral scoring, the use of both flute and oboes, which may have implications for the intended venues and purposes of the symphonies K. 184 and 385 ('Haffner'). And Carl Schachter analyses the similar tonal plans of the first movements of Mozart's 'Jupiter' symphony and Beethoven's first symphony, arguing that the similarity is more than coincidental.

The source articles include Albi Rosenthal's description of Leopold Mozart's previously unknown *Handexemplar* of the *Versuch einer gründlichen Violinschule* (1756), a work central to discussions of later eighteenth-century performance practice. Almost certainly, this source, with its expanded music examples, was the basis for the second edition (1769–70) of the work. Alan Tyson reviews his pioneering work on the paper types in Mozart's autographs of the Vienna years, summarizing his conclusions in a revised chronology of Mozart's output during the final decade of the composer's life. My own article identifies the Mozarts' Salzburg copyists and discusses the implications of their work for questions of attribution, chronology, text, performance practice, and the development of Mozart's style.

In addition to the several libraries that provided plates, or permission to publish extracts from manuscripts, my thanks are also due to Dale Rejtmar and Karl Kugle, who helped in the preparation of this volume. I am especially grateful to Bruce Phillips and his colleagues at Oxford University Press for their unflagging encouragement and help.

C. E.

New York
February 1991

Contents

Notes on Contributors

MAYNARD SOLOMON has written extensively on Beethoven, including *Beethoven* (1977) and *Beethoven Essays* (1988), winner of the American Musicological Society's Kinkeldey Award for most distinguished book. He has been a Visiting Professor at State University of New York at Stony Brook and Columbia University, and in 1992 will be a Visiting Professor at Harvard University. He is currently writing a biography of Mozart.

CHRISTOPH WOLFF is William Powell Mason Professor of Music at Harvard University. He has published widely on the history of music from the fifteenth to the twentieth centuries, especially on Bach and Mozart. His most recent books are *Bach: Essays on His Life and Music* (Harvard University Press, Cambridge and London, 1991); and *Mozart's Requiem* (Bärenreiter/DTV: Kassel and Munich, 1991). Professor Wolff is a contributing editor of the *Neue Mozart-Ausgabe* and a member of the Zentralinstitut für Mozart-Forschung in Salzburg.

ALBI ROSENTHAL is a music scholar and antiquarian bookseller. He discovered and published the earliest long obituary of Mozart, and is the organizer of the 1991 Mozart exhibition at the Bodleian Library.

JAMES WEBSTER is Professor of Music at Cornell University. He is the author of *Haydn's 'Farewell' Symphony and the Idea of Classical Style: Through-Composition and Cyclic Integration in his Instrumental Music* (Cambridge, 1991), and co-editor of *Haydn Studies* (Norton, 1981), and of a volume of string quartets in *Joseph Haydn: Werke* (Henle, forthcoming). He has published widely on Haydn, Mozart (especially his operas), Beethoven, Schubert, Brahms, chamber music in the Classical period, and musical form.

NEAL ZASLAW has recently published four books: *Mozart's Symphonies: Context, Performance Practice, Reception* (Oxford, 1989), *Man & Music: The Classical Eras from the 1740s to the End of the 18th Century* (Macmillan/Prentice Hall, 1989), *The Compleat Mozart: A Guide to the Musical Works of Wolfgang Amadeus Mozart* (Norton, 1990), and *The Mozart Repertory* (Cornell, 1991). Neal Zaslaw has been professor of music at Cornell University since 1970 and in 1991–2 served as the musicological adviser to the Mozart Bicentennial at the Lincoln Center.

ALAN TYSON has been a Fellow of All Souls College, Oxford, since 1952, and a Senior Research Fellow, working on musicology, since 1971. He is the author of Harvard University Press's *Mozart: Studies of the Autograph Scores* (Cambridge, Mass., 1987). He has also written the introductions to the following facsimiles: *Mozart, The Six 'Haydn' String Quartets*, *Mozart, The Late Chamber Works for Strings*, and, with Albi Rosenthal, *Mozart's Thematic Catalogue* (The British Library, 1980, 1985, and 1990), and *Mozart, Piano Concerto No. 26 in D Major ('Coronation') K. 537* (The Pierpont Morgan Library and Dover

Publications, New York, 1991). He has also prepared, for publication in two volumes in the *Neue Mozart-Ausgabe*, a catalogue of the watermarks in the many music papers that Mozart used at different times.

CARL SCHACHTER is Professor of Music at Queens College, City University of New York and is also on the faculty of CUNY Graduate School. For many years he has maintained an association with the Mannes College of Music, and he continues to teach there part-time. Professor Schachter is the co-author of *Counterpoint in Composition* (with Felix Salzer) and *Harmony and Voice Leading* (with Edward Aldwell) as well as the author of many articles on music theory and analysis.

CLIFF EISEN (New York University) has taught at the University of Western Ontario, Cornell University, and New York University. His articles on Mozart have been published in *The Musical Times, The Journal of the Royal Musical Association, Music and Letters, The Journal of the American Musicological Society, Early Music*, and the *Mozart-Jahrbuch* among others. He has edited symphonies by Mozart and his father, and published a documentary study of Mozart, *New Mozart Documents* (Macmillan, 1991). His forthcoming books include a study of Mozart's Salzburg symphonies and an edited volume on Mozart's string quintets.

Abbreviations

Abert	Hermann Abert, *W. A. Mozart*, 2 vols. (Leipzig, 1919–21: repr. 1956)
AmZ	*Allgemeine musikalische Zeitung*
B&H	Breitkopf & Härtel
Briefe	Wilhelm A. Bauer. Otto Erich Deutsch, and Joseph Heinz Eibl (eds.), *Wolfgang Amadeus Mozart: Briefe und Aufzeichnungen. Gesamtausgabe*, 7 vols. (Kassel, 1962–75)
Dokumente	Otto Erich Deutsch (ed.), *Mozart: Die Dokumente seines Lebens (Neue Mozart-Ausgabe*, X/34) (Kassel, 1961). English trans. Eric Blom, Peter Branscombe, and Jeremy Noble as *Mozart: A Documentary Biography* (London, 1965; 2nd edn., 1966)
Jahn	Otto Jahn, *W. A. Mozart*, 4th edn., ed. and enl. by Hermann Deiters, 2 vols. (Leipzig, 1905–7); trans. Pauline D. Townsend, *The Life of Mozart*, 3 vols. (London, 1882)
K.	L. von Köchel, *Chronologisch-thematisches Verzeichnis der Werke W. A. Mozarts* (Leipzig, 1862)
K^6	L. von Köchel, *Chronologisch-thematisches Verzeichnis sämtlicher Tonwerke Wolfgang Amadè Mozarts nebst Angabe der verlorengegangenen, angefangenen, von fremder Hand bearbeiteten, zweifelhaften und unterschobenen Kompositionen*, 6th edn. by F. Giegling, A. Weinmann, and G. Sievers (Wiesbaden, 1964)
Letters	Emily Anderson (trans. and ed.), *The Letters of Mozart and His Family, Chronologically Arranged, Translated, and Edited with an Introduction, Notes and Indices*, 2 vols. (2nd edn., London, 1966; 3rd edn. rev. Stanley Sadie and Fiona Smart, London, 1985)
The New Grove	Stanley Sadie (ed.), *The New Grove Dictionary of Music and Musicians*, 20 vols. (London, 1980)
NMA	*Wolfgang Amadeus Mozart: Neue Ausgabe sämtlicher Werke* (Kassel, 1955–)

The Rochlitz Anecdotes: Issues of Authenticity in Early Mozart Biography

MAYNARD SOLOMON

THE gathering and publication of information about Mozart's life was still in its very earliest stages when editor Friedrich Rochlitz set out to fill the pages of the first volume of Breitkopf & Härtel's *Allgemeine musikalische Zeitung* (henceforth *AmZ*), founded in 1798. Friedrich Schlichtegroll had published a professional and reliable obituary of Mozart in his *Nekrolog* (1793), utilizing materials provided by Mozart's sister from the family archives, along with her own and court-trumpeter Johann Andreas Schachtner's reminiscences of Mozart's childhood.[1] Franz Niemetschek's well-crafted and affecting biography of Mozart, which appeared in 1798, made good use of Schlichtegroll's data for the early years, to which were added the author's own observations of the composer, whom he had met during his last visit to Prague, and supplemented by rich materials furnished by Constanze Mozart.[2] Beyond these there existed only a handful of ephemeral journalistic reports, most of which originated in the period just after Mozart's death.[3]

Because the paucity of materials on Mozart's life could not satisfy music-lovers' hunger for such information, Rochlitz's twenty-seven colourful anecdotes, entitled 'Authentic Anecdotes from Wolfgang Gottlieb Mozart's Life: A Contribution to the More Accurate Knowledge of this Man, both as Human Being and Artist (*Verbürgte Anekdoten aus Wolfgang Gottlieb Mozarts Leben: Ein Beitrag zur richtigeren Kenntnis dieses Mannes, als Mensch und Künstler*)', whose publication in the *AmZ* commenced on 10 October 1798, were extraordinarily influential. They were reprinted, reworded, expanded, and elaborated in the numerous early anecdotal biographies of Mozart—by Cramer, Winckler, Arnold, Suard, Stendhal, Schlosser, and others—and thereby gained wide currency as authentic sources.[4] As such they became firmly embedded in the biographical literature and played

[1] Friedrich Schlichtegroll, 'Johannes Chrysostomus Wolfgang Gottlieb Mozart', in *Nekrolog auf das Jahr 1791* (Gotha, 1793), ii. 82–112 (entry for 5 Dec.). For data on Schlichtegroll's biography and its reprints and translations, see Rudolph Angermüller, '"Das musikalische Kind Mozart": Ein Beitrag zur Biographie Mozarts im ausgehenden 18. Jahrhundert', *Wiener Figaro. Mitteilungen der Mozartgemeinde Wien*, 42 (1975), 28–35.

[2] Franz Xaver Niemetschek, *Leben des k. k. Kapellmeisters Wolfgang Gottlieb Mozart, nach Originalquellen beschrieben* (Prague, 1798) cited hereinafter from Niemetschek, *Life of Mozart*, trans. Helen Mautner (London, 1956).

[3] Otto Erich Deutsch (ed.), *Mozart: Die Dokumente seines Lebens* (Kassel, 1961), *passim*; Deutsch, *Mozart: A Documentary Biography*, trans. Eric Blom, Peter Branscombe, and Jeremy Noble (London, 1966), *passim*.

[4] Carl Friedrich Cramer, *Anecdotes sur W. G. Mozart* (Paris and Hamburg, 1801); Théophile Frédéric Winckler, *Notice bibliographique sur Jean-Chrysostome-Wolfgang-Théophile Mozart* (Paris, 1801); Ignaz Ferdinand Cajetan Arnold, *Mozarts Geist* (Erfurt, 1803); Jean-Baptiste-Antoine Suard, 'Anecdotes sur Mozart', *Mélanges*

FIG. 1. Friedrich Rochlitz. Lithograph by C. Lange, after a portrait in oils by A. Böhme. Österreichische Nationalbibliothek, Vienna.

a crucial role in shaping perceptions of Mozart's personality for subsequent generations, down to the present day. Those seeking to understand the psychological sources of Mozart's protean creativity were quick to attach themselves to whatever materials were at hand, and Rochlitz's fragmentary anecdotes became nuclei around which global characterizations of Mozart began to condense. Rochlitz provided significant materials to support the belief that Mozart was the archetypal unappreciated Viennese artist, neglected by aristocratic and imperial patrons, the object of cabals by envious composers, exploited or cheated by impresarios and publishers, living on the edge of impoverishment. According to Rochlitz, Mozart faced these difficulties with an equanimity compounded of equal parts of an aloof disdain and a Parsifal-like innocence: he could not bear to leave his beloved Emperor Joseph to accept a well-remunerated post in Berlin; despite his own economic plight, he was careless of money matters, generous to a fault, a soft touch for friends and musicians in need; towards the end, enfeebled and death-haunted, he retreated from the agonies of the real world into his art.

de littérature, 10 (1804), 337–47; Louis-Alexandre-César Bombet [pseud. of Henri Beyle = Stendhal], *Lettres écrites de Vienne en Autriche, sur le célèbre compositeur Joseph Haydn, suivies d'une vie de Mozart*... (Paris, 1814); Johann Aloys Schlosser, *W. A. Mozarts Biographie* (Prague, 1828).

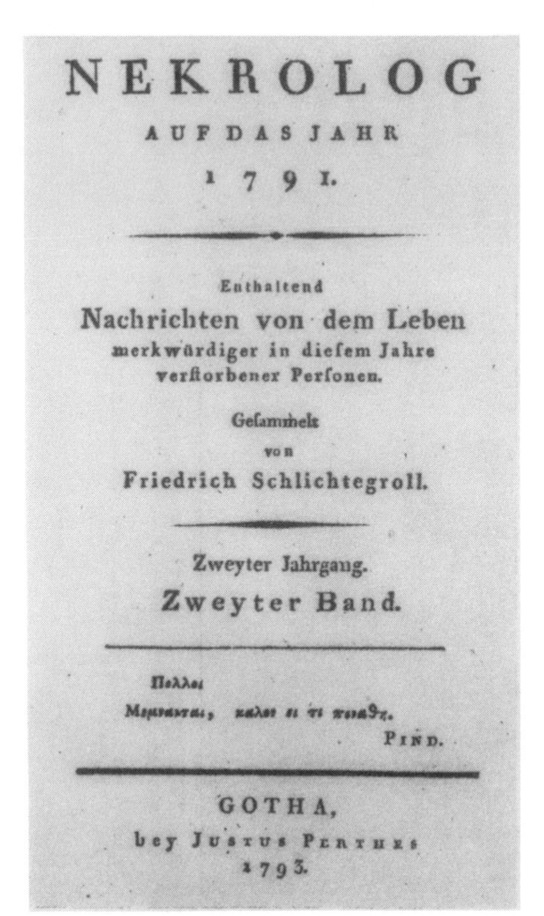

NEKROLOG

AUF DAS JAHR

1791.

Enthaltend

Nachrichten von dem Leben

merkwürdiger in diesem Jahre

verstorbener Personen.

Gesammelt

von

Friedrich Schlichtegroll.

Zweyter Jahrgang.

Zweyter Band.

Πολλοι

Μεμνανται, καλον ει τι ποναθῃ.

PIND.

GOTHA,

bey Justus Perthes

1793.

FIG. 2. Title-page of Friedrich Schlichtegroll, *Nekrolog auf das Jahr 1791* (Gotha, 1793).

From Rochlitz one could also learn a good deal about Mozart's musical thought—his opinions of a wide variety of composers, from Johann Sebastian Bach and Handel to Haydn, Paisiello, and Jommelli; his favourites among his own operas; even the connection between one of his operas and his courtship of Constanze Weber. Mozart was said to be contemptuous of inattentive audiences, to dislike virtuosity for its own sake, to insist on correct tempos and to demand a high level of performance. One even learns from Rochlitz about Mozart's prodigious creativity, especially his ability to write masterpieces at breakneck speed, shaking them out of his sleeve without apparent effort. And several anecdotes offer detailed descriptions of events apparently witnessed by Rochlitz during Mozart's stay in Leipzig in 1789: improvisations on the Thomaskirche organ, reading through scores of Bach's motets there, his Akademie at the Gewandhaus on 12 May; the writing of a memorable farewell canon for Cantor Johann Friedrich Doles.

Rochlitz did not hesitate to warrant the authenticity of his materials: 'I therefore ratify with my signature and make reference thereby that I personally came to know Mozart

ALLGEMEINE
MUSIKALISCHE ZEITUNG.

Den 10ten October | No. 2. | 1798.

BIOGRAPHIEEN.

Verbürgte Anekdoten aus Wolfgang Gottlieb Mozarts Leben, ein Beytrag zur richtigern Kenntnis dieses Mannes, als Mensch und Künstler.

Es ist das Schicksal der ausgezeichnetsten Männer von jeher gewesen, dafs sich der Haufe gemeiner von allen Seiten beschränkter Geister gleichsam in Masse gegen sie vereinigt, um, wenn es ihnen nicht gelingt, jenen Genie's das Verdienstliche und Ausgezeichnete ihrer Werke wegzudemonstriren oder wegzuwitzeln — wenigstens irgend eine schwache Seite, die jeder grofse Mann, da er doch immer Mensch bleibt, hat, hervorzusuchen, aufzustutzen, hier und da manches aus eignem Schatz des Herzens hinzuzuthun, nun das Ganze emsig bekannt zu machen und dann zu stehen und lächelnd oder prahlend auszurufen: Adam ist worden wie unser Einer! So ging es auch besonders dem wackern Mozart, so lange er lebte, und so gehet es ihm grofstentheils noch. Man hört seine vortrefflichen Kompositionen, kann dem gewaltigen Eindruck derselben nicht widerstehen, kann diesen Eindruck sich selbst und Andern nicht ableugnen; bricht defshalb allenfalls in ein allgemeines Lob und gleichfalls im Allgemeinen hin und her gezerretes Geschwätz darüber aus — welches beydes Mozart selbst fast so bitter, wie Schurkerey, hafste; — knüpft aber immer und ewig Bemerkungen daran, wie: sollte man's glauben, dafs ein solcher Mann doch übrigens zeitlebens ein Kind war, und dergl. Freylich gab Mozart bey seinem liberalen Leben, bey seinem nur allzuoffnen Charakter, bey seiner Verachtung alles Geschwätzes über ihn — eine Verachtung, welche zu tief war, als dafs er jemals etwas anders hätte thun, als darüber lachen sollen — Gelegenheit genug zu solchen Urtheilen.

Seit einigen Jahren hat die Biographie Mozarts in Schlichtegrolls Nekrolog, wo es denn doch gewifs Zeit und Ort gewesen wäre, den Mann ganz, und zwar mehr in seinem öffentlichen als Privatleben darzustellen — noch mehr zur Verbreitung solcher kleinlicher Anekdoten beygetragen und diesen sogar eine dauerhafte Haltung und ziemliche Autorität verschafft: indefs Mozarts künstlerische Verdienste fast einzig mit einem allgemeinen himmelhohen Lobe abgefertigt werden. Dieses ist nicht gegen den wackern Herausgeber jenes Werks gesagt: ich weifs es — dieser thut alles, um sein Institut seinem Zwecke so nahe zu bringen, als es — in Deutschland möglich ist: sondern gegen Mozarts nähere Bekannte und gegen Kenner und Verehrer seiner Verdienste spreche ich, die dem Herausgeber des Nekrologs nichts weiter gaben und geben wollten. Ich behaupte hiermit nicht, dafs die kleine Sammlung zusammengereiheter Anekdoten, welche dort die Stelle einer Biographie des Künstlers einnimmt, offenbare Unwahrheiten enthalte (über seine frühere Jugend bin ich nicht unterrichtet): aber wie viel kömmt nicht auf die Art der Darstellung selbst solcher kleinen Züge an? auf den Zweck des Erzählers — blos zu unterhalten, oder zu belehren, u. s. w.? Man braucht wahrlich einen Mann nicht vorsätzlich verleumden zu wollen: ja man braucht sogar der Wahrheit der Thatsachen kein Jota wissentlich zu vergeben: und kann dennoch aus weifs — wenn auch nicht schwarz, doch schmuziggrau machen. Und dann — was eine Hauptsache ist: sind denn Anekdoten aus dem Privatleben eines Mannes für die Welt, eines grossen Künstlers, das wichtigste, was man von

1798. 2

FIG. 3. *Allgemeine musikalische Zeitung*, 10 October 1798.

during his stay in Leipzig; that I was present there at most of the social occasions which he attended . . . and that I later on made the personal acquaintance of his widow and of assorted trusted friends of Mozart and spoke often with them at great length about the deceased and everything that I knew about him was confirmed, corrected, or contradicted . . .'.[5] In 1825, Rochlitz varied this story in several important details in order to affirm his bona fides, asserting: 'I conceived and immediately wrote [the anecdotes] down during the weeks when (in the third year before his death) it was my luck to be near him . . . Some of the more significant ones were personally communicated to me by his widow, soon after his death.'[6]

In these claims and in several of the anecdotes themselves Rochlitz more than once implied that his materials had Constanze Mozart's endorsement. However, it can fairly

[5] *AmZ* 1 (1798), 19–20.

[6] 'Ein guter Rath Mozarts', in Rochlitz, *Für Freunde der Tonkunst*, 4 vols. (Leipzig, 1824–32), ii. 282 n. In the corresponding footnote to the first publication of his article, Rochlitz did not claim to have written the anecdotes down in 1789 or to have met Constanze Mozart 'soon' after Mozart's death. *AmZ* 22 (1820), 297–8 n.

be concluded from her correspondence with Breitkopf & Härtel that Constanze Mozart had nothing to do with any of the anecdotes which appeared in the *AmZ* between 10 October and 19 December 1798. On 27 October 1798, responding to a request by Breitkopf & Härtel, she promised to furnish them with 'new materials and unknown anecdotes' for the eventual purpose of preparing a comprehensive new biography of Mozart;[7] Breitkopf & Härtel sent her a reminder on 10 November 1798 and she responded on 5 December 1798: 'Concerning anecdotes and materials for a biography, I am working on these with a friend . . .'.[8] Thus, nothing had been sent in time to use in preparing any of the first twenty-two of Rochlitz's anecdotes. Furthermore, in a subsequent letter summarizing her transmittal of anecdotes to the Leipzig firm, she specifically mentions only those which were published under her own name.[9] Nowhere in the correspondence is there the slightest hint that she had co-operated in the preparation of Rochlitz's anecdotes. Nor is there any correspondence or supporting evidence of direct contact between her and Rochlitz. Thus, it is clear that she provided no materials to Rochlitz for use in preparing the first twenty-two anecdotes. Nor, from their content, was she involved in the remaining anecdotes, Nos. 23–7.

Even more tellingly, however, she would not vouch for Rochlitz's anecdotes at the time of their first publication. In a letter of 18 May 1799, Breitkopf & Härtel's representative Georg August Griesinger reported to the owner, Gottfried Christoph Härtel that he had been told that 'Mozart's widow would not be willing to guarantee the authenticity of the anecdotes which are published' in the *AmZ*.[10] Apparently, Härtel had asked him to approach her on this issue. However, perhaps because she did not wish to offend the *AmZ* or its publisher, the issue was never publicized. Thus, it remained for Mozart's great biographer, Otto Jahn, to be the first publicly to point out that Rochlitz's anecdotes contained a substantial admixture of invention. In the preface to his *W. A. Mozart*, Jahn wrote:

> I could not fail to observe that those particulars of Mozart's life which Rochlitz gives us as the result of his own observation or as narrated to him by Mozart, are peculiar to himself in form and colouring, and that many of the circumstances which he relates with absolute certainty are manifestly untrue.[11]

[7] Constanze Mozart to Breitkopf & Härtel (henceforth B&H), 27 Oct. 1798, in Wilhelm A. Bauer, Otto Erich Deutsch, and Joseph Heinz Eibl (eds.), *Wolfgang Amadeus Mozart: Briefe und Aufzeichnungen: Gesamtausgabe*, 7 vols. (Kassel, 1962–75), iv. 219; not in Emily Anderson (trans. and ed.), *The Letters of Mozart and His Family*, 2 vols. (2nd edn., London, 1966). Citations from the Mozart correspondence will give *Briefe* first, followed by *Letters* except where no English translation is available.

[8] B&H to Constanze Mozart, 10 Nov. 1798; *Briefe*, iv. 219; Constanze Mozart to B&H, 5 Dec. 1798; *Briefe*, iv. 223.

[9] Constanze Mozart to B&H, 17 Nov. 1799; *Briefe*, iv. 295.

[10] 'Man sagte mir, daß die Wittwe Mozart die Aechtheit der Anecdoten, welche in der Music-Zeitung stehen nicht verbürgen möchte.' G. Thomas, 'Griesingers Briefe über Haydn', *Haydn-Studien*, 1 (1966), 49–114 at 54; '*Eben komme ich von Haydn . . .*': *Georg August Griesingers Korrespondenz mit Joseph Haydns Verleger Breitkopf & Härtel 1799–1819*, ed. Otto Biba (Zurich, 1987), 24.

[11] Otto Jahn, *W. A. Mozart*, 4th edn., ed. and enl. by Hermann Deiters, 2 vols. (Leipzig, 1905–7), i, p. x; *The Life of Mozart*, trans. Pauline D. Townsend, 3 vols. (London, 1882), i, p. iv.

Elsewhere, he observed wryly that when on a much later occasion Rochlitz 'speaks of a visit paid by Mozart to [C. P. E.] Bach in Hamburg, shortly before he went to Leipzig (1789), he forgets that Bach died in 1788, and Mozart was never in Hamburg'.[12] And with some dismay he disclosed that an unpublished manuscript by Rochlitz contained deliberate falsifications of biographical data pertaining to Mozart's courtship and marriage:

> All the statements of Rochlitz as to time, place, persons, and events are completely false . . . [N]o poetical license could account for it; unpleasant as it is, I consider it my duty to expose the affair, partly that it may teach caution, and partly that tedious and vexatious discussion may be avoided, should the narrative in question ever be printed.[13]

However, Jahn's consternation was insufficient to lead him to reject the Rochlitz anecdotes altogether; instead, he utilized most of them, while occasionally calling attention to clear factual contradictions. And, although Jahn was the first to label as a forgery the famous undated letter by Mozart to 'Baron von . . .', with its fascinating portrayal of the composer's effortless creative process, he did not charge Rochlitz with its fabrication, although it was Rochlitz who 'discovered' the letter, annotated it with what he termed 'diplomatic exactitude', and attested to the authenticity of this hitherto unknown document when he published it in the *AmZ* for 1815.[14] In part, Jahn may have acted out of discretion; and in part he may have had a biographer's natural hesitation to dispense with such interesting materials. Jahn's posthumous editor, Hermann Abert, was extremely sceptical of Rochlitz's accounts, subjecting several of them to close scrutiny and repeatedly calling attention to Rochlitz's 'well-known decorative manner', but he, too, continued to cite most of the anecdotes approvingly, picking and choosing among them according to his sense of which appeared to be authentic.[15]

Recently, Rochlitz's reliability has again been called into question. In 1980, Joseph Heinz Eibl concluded that Rochlitz probably forged the 'letter' to the 'Baron von . . .' and showed that the vivid descriptions of Mozart's somnambulistic creative process in that letter were embroideries of several passages in Niemetschek's book.[16] In that same year I published a paper that stressed Rochlitz's role in the forgery of Mozart's 'letter' to the 'Baron von . . .' and for the first time demonstrated that the Leipzig editor's famous account of his three meetings with Beethoven during the summer of 1822 had been

[12] Jahn, ii. 157 n. 3; Eng. trans. ii. 442 n. 2. The account of Mozart's imaginary visit to Hamburg includes several realistic details: of Bach improvising for Mozart several times on a Silbermann organ, of Bach's delight in Mozart's own organ-playing. Rochlitz, *Für Freunde der Tonkunst*, iv. 308 n.

[13] Jahn, i, pp. x–xi; Eng. trans., i, pp. iv–v. A recent paper mistakenly asserts that this passage represents Jahn's judgement of all of the Rochlitz Mozart anecdotes. Carsten E. Hatting, 'Anmerkungen zu Mozarts Biographie', *Mitteilungen der Internationalen Stiftung Mozarteums*, 37 (1989), 137–60 at 147.

[14] *AmZ* 17 (1814–15), 561–6.

[15] Hermann Abert, *W. A. Mozart*, 3 vols. (repr. of 7th edn., Leipzig, 1983), ii. 519 and *passim*. For his critical remarks, see i. 155, 638, 824–5; ii. 410, 519, 521; for some of his approving citations, see i. 837, 838; ii. 41, 43, 44, 45, 46, 54, 69, 113, 114, 158, 519, 521, 522, 523.

[16] Joseph Heinz Eibl, 'Ein Brief Mozarts über seine Schaffensweise?', *Österreichische Musikzeitschrift*, 35 (1980), 578–93 at 584–5, 591.

invented; indeed, it seemed probable from the evidence that Rochlitz had never even met Beethoven.[17] Therefore, the pattern of fabrication and falsification in Rochlitz's writings is so extensive that the prudent scholar may already have good reason to exclude the whole from use as authentic biographical sources. However, as in the very similar case of Beethoven's biographer Anton Schindler, where fabrications are intertwined with genuine materials, a careful evaluation is in order, for one does not want to discard stories which may be based on direct observation, or on reports transmitted to their author by third persons, or derived by him from authentic sources. Thus, a re-examination of the Rochlitz anecdotes is very much on the agenda of Mozart studies.

Rochlitz wrote twenty-seven Mozart anecdotes for the *AmZ*, published in eleven instalments of vols. 1–3, dating from 10 October 1798 to 27 May 1801.[18] Twenty-two of these appeared under his byline in six issues through 19 December 1798, preceded by an introduction; one unsigned anecdote appeared in the issue for 4 April 1799; and four unsigned anecdotes in the issues for 25 March 1801, 15 April 1801, and 27 May 1801, headed 'Several Additional Bagatelles from Mozart's Life (*Noch einige Kleinigkeiten aus Mozarts Leben*)', the last being of article length and promising a continuation, which was not forthcoming.[19] The following is the first complete English edition of the Rochlitz anecdotes, translated from their original printings in the *AmZ*.

Anecdote 1 (10 October 1798, cols. 20–2): When Mozart was last in Berlin, he arrived towards evening. He had hardly arrived when he asked the innkeeper, who did not know him, 'Is there any music here this evening?' 'O yes,' said the man, 'a German opera will be presented.' 'Which?' '*Die Entführung aus dem Serail*'. 'Charming', called Mozart, laughing. 'Yes,' continued the man, 'it is a very pretty piece. It was composed by—what was his name?' Mozart, who was in his greatcoat, set off at once. He stood at the entrance of the parterre, meaning to listen without being seen. But at one moment he too much enjoyed the execution of certain passages, at another he was unhappy with the tempos or found that the singers were adding too many ornaments, or *Schnörkeleyen*, as he called them. In brief, his interest was increasingly stimulated and

[17] Solomon, 'On Beethoven's Creative Process: A Two-Part Invention', *Music and Letters*, 61 (1980), 272–83 (= Solomon, *Beethoven Essays* (Cambridge, Mass., 1988), 126–38).

[18] Rochlitz's other writings on Mozart include 'Raphael und Mozart', *AmZ* 2 (1799–1800), 641–51, and 'Ein guter Rath Mozart's. Betrachtung,' *AmZ* 22 (1820), 297–307, enlarged in *Für Freunde der Tonkunst*, ii. 281–304.

[19] See *Briefe*, vi. 492, which mistakenly lists the first instalment of Constanze Mozart's anecdotes (see below) as by Rochlitz; and Rudolph Angermüller and Otto Schneider (eds.), *Mozart Bibliographie*, in *Mozart-Jahrbuch 1975*, 242 (No. 4888), which mistakenly includes the instalments of Constanze Mozart's as well as Niemetschek's anecdotes (see below). In addition to his own, Rochlitz published in *AmZ* anecdotes by others: three excerpted from Niemetschek's biography were appended to his own in the issue of 19 Dec. 1798, 180–3; seven 'Anecdotes from Mozart's Life, Told to us by his Widow' appeared in the issue of 6 Feb. 1799, 289–91; three more by Constanze Mozart headed 'Several Further Bagatelles from Mozart's Life, Related by his Widow' in the issue of 11 Sept. 1799, 854–6; and four by Maria Anna (Nannerl) Mozart headed 'Several More Anecdotes from Mozart's Childhood Years', in the issue of 22 Jan. 1800, 300–1; see *Dokumente*, 426–7; *Documentary Biography*, 493–4. Abridged German editions of Rochlitz's anecdotes appeared in Ludwig Nohl, *Mozart nach den Schilderungen seiner Zeitgenossen* (Leipzig, 1880), 345–73, and Albert Leitzmann, *Mozarts Persönlichkeit: Urteile der Zeitgenossen* (Leipzig, 1914), 113–53.

unconsciously he moved ever closer and closer to the orchestra, now humming and murmuring this tune, now that, now soft, now loud. Seeing the small homely man in the worn overcoat, people began to laugh, of which, of course, he was unaware. Finally they came to Pedrillo's aria—'Frisch zum Kampfe, frisch zum Streite' etc. The management either had a defective score or wanted to improve it by substituting a D♯ for a D for the second violins at the oft-repeated words 'Nur ein feiger Tropf verzagt'. Here Mozart could no longer contain himself: he called out in a loud voice in his usual forceful language: 'Confound it!—it must be a D!' Everyone looked around, including several members of the orchestra. Several of the musicians recognized him and the word spread like wildfire through the orchestra and the theatre: Mozart is here! Several of the actors, particularly the esteemed singer Madame B, who played 'Blonde' (Blondchen), didn't want to come back on stage. This news quickly reached the attention of the music director; in his embarrassment he told Mozart, who had now come up close behind him. In a flash he was in the wings: 'Madam,' he said to her, 'why do you carry on so? You have sung magnificently, and so that you can do even better another time, I will rehearse the role with you!'

Mozart was indeed in Berlin on 19 May 1789, a day on which *Die Entführung aus dem Serail* was performed (under the title *Belmonte und Constanze*); and there was a 'Madame B'—soprano Henriette Baranius—who played Blonde. A sequel to Rochlitz's account is provided by 'an old campaigner', who decades later reported that when Mozart returned to the theatre to apologize for his disturbance and to praise the singers, he became entangled with Madame Baranius, so that it cost his Berlin friends much effort and skill to bring 'these hidden and forbidden perfect fifths to a resolution'.[20] The anecdote as a whole presumably is derived from a report by an unidentified third person, for Rochlitz himself nowhere claims to have accompanied Mozart from Leipzig to Berlin. Notices of the opera production published in the *Chronik von Berlin* and the *Theater-Zeitung für Deutschland* fail to mention Mozart's presence, but these appear to pertain to April performances, preceding his arrival in Berlin.[21] However, the notice in the Weimar *Journal des Luxus und der Moden* is of the 19 May performance and it, too, neglects to note that Mozart was there. Reports about Mozart appearing anonymously in a theatre and subsequently being recognized proliferated, becoming almost a biographical trope. Hummel's widow told Jahn in 1855 of a Berlin concert that her husband gave, 'without being aware of Mozart's presence'; afterwards they embraced with the 'tenderest expressions of joy'.[22] Ludwig Tieck's memoirs described his 1789 encounter in a Berlin opera house with 'an unprepossessing figure in a grey overcoat' who turned out to be Mozart.[23] The actor Wilhelm Backhaus recalled a very similar story connected with

[20] 'Ein alter Veteran', 'Zur Säcularfeier Mozart's in Berlin', *Neue Berliner Musik Zeitung* (1856), 34–6 at 36. 'Mozart', writes Jahn, 'became so deeply involved with her that it cost his friends much trouble to extricate him' (ii. 491; Eng. trans., iii. 234).

[21] Deutsch, *Dokumente*, 301; *Documentary Biography*, 343; Cliff Eisen (ed.), *New Mozart Documents* (London, 1991), Doc. 92.

[22] Jahn, ii. 492; Eng. trans., iii. 235.

[23] Rudolf Köpke, *Ludwig Tieck: Erinnerungen aus dem Leben des Dichters nach dessen mündlichen und schriftlichen Mitteilungen*, 2 vols. (Leipzig, 1855), i. 86; see *Dokumente*, 476–7; *Documentary Biography*, 562; see also Erich Valentin, 'Es war Mozart selbst gewesen', *Acta Mozartiana*, 36 (1989), 21–6. For sceptical views of Tieck's belated report, see Gernot Gruber, *Mozart und die Nachwelt* (Salzburg and Vienna, 1985), 95, and Jahn, ii. 492; Eng. trans., iii. 235.

Mozart's visit to Mannheim in 1790: 'I got into great disgrace with Mozart. I was standing at the door while our rehearsal [of *Le nozze di Figaro*] was going on. He came and asked me about it, and whether he might hear it. I took him for a little journeyman tailor, and refused to let him in. "You will surely allow Kapellmeister Mozart to hear the rehearsal?"[24] E. T. A. Hoffmann's tale 'Ritter Gluck' is a variant of this Gothic trope.

Anecdote 2 (10 October 1787, cols. 22–3). When it became known in Berlin that Mozart was there, everyone, particularly also Frederick William II, received him with great pleasure. This prince not only treasured and patronized music, but really was in truth, if not a connoisseur, a tasteful music-lover. Almost every day, Mozart was required, so long as he was in Berlin, to improvise for him; in the King's chamber, he often performed quartets with several court musicians. Once, when he and the King were alone together, the King asked him what he thought of the Berlin court orchestra. Mozart, to whom nothing was more alien than flattery, answered: 'You have the greatest collection of virtuosos in the world, and I have never heard such a quartet as here, but when they all play as an ensemble, they could still do better.' Frederick William rejoiced at this sincerity; he responded, laughing:

'Stay here with me—you could make them do better! I will give you 3,000 Taler a year as a salary.'

'Should I wholly abandon my good Emperor?' said the worthy Mozart, remaining silently moved and lost in thought. One may recall that the good Emperor, whom Mozart did not want to abandon, was still leaving him to starve. The King, too, was moved and after a while continued: 'Think about it—I'll keep my word, even if you first decide to come a year and a day from now!'

In a footnote, Rochlitz explains how he came by this story: 'The king afterwards related this little conversation to various people, among whom was Mozart's wife, when she came to Berlin four years ago, and was assisted so nicely by the patrons of her late husband.'[25] Thus, anticipating the objection that he could scarcely have been privy to the King's private offer, Rochlitz hints—but carefully avoids claiming outright—that he had the story from Constanze Mozart, a suggestion that needs to be weighed against her refusal to vouch for his anecdotes. Both the anecdote and the footnote appear to be an imaginative expansion of Niemetschek's account: 'The King of Prussia, that generous patron and lover of music, was quite taken with him and gave him excellent proof of his respect. How genuine and lasting this was is proved by the royal generosity with which the monarch in later years befriended and supported Mozart's widow in Berlin.'[26] Inasmuch as Niemetschek, who is a reliable source of information from Mozart's wife, mentions no offer of a post, it seems probable that Rochlitz's story of such an offer did not originate with her. The 'excellent proof of his respect' was surely the King's present to Mozart of 100 Friedrichs d'or and the request that he compose some quartets for him.

Jahn accepted the story despite his inability to confirm it: 'My researches in the Royal Library and archives for some trace of negotiations accompanying this offer have proved

[24] Backhaus's *Tagebuch der Mannheimer Schaubühne*, cit. from Ludwig Nohl, *Musikalisches Skizzenbuch* (Munich, 1866), 190, by Jahn, ii. 551; Eng. trans., iii. 278.

[25] *AmZ* 1 (1798–9), 23.

[26] Niemetschek, *Leben*, 38–9; see also 51–2.

fruitless. It must therefore have been at once refused at Mozart's personal interview with the King; the way in which Mozart writes to his wife, that she has cause to be satisfied with the favour in which he stands with the King, seems to refer to some definite proposal.'[27] However, there is no mention of any such offer in Mozart's letters (unfortunately, four letters written between 22 April and 9 May are missing, including two from Potsdam); on 10 April he wrote from Prague of a report that the King was concerned lest Mozart not come to Berlin: 'Judging by this, my affairs ought to be fairly successful.'[28] However, on 23 May he wrote that inasmuch as the King was disinclined to sponsor a concert for him, he considered himself 'fortunate enough to be enjoying the King's favour' at all, a remark which scarcely can be squared with an offer of a major post.[29] In all probability, Mozart went to Potsdam precisely in quest of a position or, at least, in the hope that he might use an offer as a lever to better his situation in Vienna. Abert assigns this anecdote to 'the domain of legend' and presents a thoroughgoing critique of it.[30] Schenk concludes that this tale is 'based upon no evidence whatsoever', and is 'completely made up of thin air'.[31]

In the last analysis, this and the following anecdote may be read as pedagogic exemplary legends in praise of benevolent monarchs, especially the one closest at hand to Leipzig. Predictably, Emperor Joseph comes off second-best to the King of Prussia. Rochlitz comments, in an aside: 'One may recall that the good Emperor, whom Mozart did not want to abandon, was still leaving him to starve.' But Joseph nevertheless remains a good, if misguided, emperor. Reading Mozart's supposed remark, 'I cannot leave my good Emperor', in the year 1798, during the anti-Jacobin repression, not very long after Beethoven was impelled to write, 'You dare not raise his voice here or the police will take you into custody', involved its own special set of ironies.[32]

Anecdote 3 (10 October 1798, col. 23). Mozart returned to Vienna, pondering this proposal. He knew that in Vienna he could only continue to expect envy, cabals of various sorts, oppression, lack of appreciation, and poverty (for at that time he had no certainty of receiving anything from the Emperor). His friends encouraged him, but he became desperate. A certain circumstance—which I cannot relate because I don't want to harm anyone on whom Mozart himself didn't choose to seek vengeance—finally decided him. He went to the Emperor and asked for his release. Joseph, that ruler so often underestimated, so often reviled, whose faults were really forced and pressed upon him by his subjects—Joseph had a heartfelt love of music and particularly to Mozart's music. He heard Mozart out and then replied:

[27] Jahn, ii. 487 n. 30; Eng. trans., iii. 231 n. 35. For all documentary materials pertaining to Mozart's Berlin visit, see Ernst Friedländer, 'Mozarts Beziehungen zu Berlin', in *Mitteilungen für die Mozartgemeinde in Berlin*, 1 (1897), 115–21.

[28] Mozart to Constanze Mozart, 10 Apr. 1789; *Briefe*, iv. 80; *Letters*, ii. 921.

[29] Mozart to Constanze Mozart, 23 May 1789; *Briefe*, iv. 90; *Letters*, ii. 928. On Mozart's arrival in Potsdam, the King referred him to his director of chamber music, Jean Pierre Duport, who was ill disposed towards Mozart. See Ernst Friedländer, 'Mozart's Beziehungen zu Berlin', 1, 118–19, 121.

[30] Abert, i. 824–5; ii. 521.

[31] Erich Schenk, *Mozart and his Times*, trans. Richard and Clara Winston (New York, 1959), 416.

[32] Beethoven to Nikolaus Simrock, 2 Aug. 1794; Emily Anderson, *The Letters of Beethoven*, 3 vols. (London, 1961), i. 18.

'Dear Mozart—You know what I think of the Italians: and do you want to abandon me all the same?'

Mozart looked at his expressive face and said, moved: 'Your Majesty—I—commend myself to Your Grace—I will remain!'

And with that he went home.

'But Mozart,' his friends said when they met him and he told them what had taken place, 'why didn't you use that moment at least to demand a firm salary?'

'Only the devil can think of that at such times!' said Mozart indignant.

Excellent, dear estimable man!

Rochlitz's understanding of Mozart's relationship to the Imperial Court is hopelessly confused. He incorrectly assumes that Mozart was an unsalaried employee of the Court; otherwise, there would be no reason to ask for his discharge. But he is wholly unaware here (and in No. 4) that, prior to 1789, the date of this anecdote, Mozart had already been appointed Imperial Chamber Composer, at an annual salary of 800 florins. One needs to contrast the attitude of humble devotion towards Emperor Joseph expressed here with Mozart's markedly independent, even defiant attitude towards authority—including not only Salzburg Archbishop Hieronymus Colloredo and members of the Viennese nobility, but Emperor Joseph II as well—that is documented in his correspondence. For example, in a letter to his father, Mozart wrote:

The Viennese gentry, and in particular the Emperor, must not imagine that I am on this earth solely for the sake of Vienna. There is no monarch in the world whom I should be more glad to serve than the Emperor, but I refuse to beg for any post. I believe that I am capable of doing credit to any court. If Germany . . . will not accept me, then in God's name let France or England become the richer by another talented German, to the disgrace of the German nation.[33]

Nor was Mozart willing to work for little or nothing, let alone out of love for the Emperor: 'The Emperor is a skinflint', he wrote; 'If he wants me he must pay me, for the honour alone of serving him is not enough. Indeed, if he were to offer me 1,000 Gulden and some Count were to offer 2,000, I should decline the former proposal with thanks . . .'.[34] Rochlitz does not explain how he learned of Mozart's conversation with the Emperor.

Joseph's remark, 'You know what I think of the Italians', seems fabricated, for Italian composers and musical personnel were given the leading role at the Viennese court by his own choice, and Italian opera, despite several challenges from German opera and *Singspiel* during the decade, achieved dominance in Vienna under his aegis. Probably, however, Rochlitz elaborated this remark from Niemetschek's comment: 'Emperor Joseph II had the idea, so worthy of a German Emperor, of suppressing the taste for Italian opera by supporting German operettas and singers, and by giving more support to the music of the Fatherland.'[35]

[33] Letter of 17 Aug. 1782; *Briefe*, iii. 220; *Letters*, ii. 814.

[34] Letter of 10 Apr. 1782; *Briefe*, iii. 201; *Letters*, ii. 799–800. Translation amended.

[35] Niemetschek, *Leben*, 32.

Anecdote 4 (10 October 1798, cols. 23–4). Emperor Joseph himself had the idea that Mozart, who until then only had the prospect of a salaried post and a title, ought at least to be given a tolerable salary, and he asked a certain person about it, who on this matter was the last person he should have asked. In answer to the question from the Emperor, who, like any great lord, was ignorant of an ordinary citizen's needs and in whose mind one zero more or less was little more than zero—to this question, how much to direct for Mozart, that gentleman suggested 800 florins annually. The Emperor was pleased with this and the matter was settled. Mozart thus now received 800 florins annually—in Vienna! If I reckon correctly, this was barely enough to cover his rent. And thus he remained as before with Joseph and said no further word on this matter.

This and No. 3 are surely elaborations of Niemetschek's account:

[N]o thought was given to rewarding or supporting him . . . He therefore decided to leave the city . . . He was on the point of departure [for England] when Emperor Joseph conferred on him the title of Imperial Chamber Composer with an annual salary of 800 florins, and the promise that his future would be assured . . . Mozart swallowed his pride, accepted the offer and remained.[36]

As already noted, Rochlitz mistakenly believed Mozart to have obtained his appointment following his return from Berlin in June 1789, whereas he actually was granted the post as of 1 December 1787.[37] The error derived from a hasty reading of Niemetschek, who in his narrative somewhat confusingly mingled his discussion of the appointment with a description of Mozart's return from Berlin. Nissen amplified the anecdote, noting that Mozart's annual rent in 1785 was 460 florins;[38] more relevant, his rent in 1789–91 averaged about 300 florins per year.[39]

Anecdote 5 (*Anekdoten aus Mozarts Leben. (Fortsetzung)*, 24 October 1798, cols. 49–51). Hardly any virtuoso in the world was less prone than Mozart to indulge in the all-too-common capriciousness of virtuosos who will perform only after extravagant requests and pleas. On the contrary, a great many fine gentlemen, especially in Vienna, held it against him that he was willing to perform for anyone who wanted to hear him. However, his greatest complaint in that respect, one which he frequently bemoaned, was that, as a rule, people wanted to *see* him perform mechanical wizardries and juggling acrobatics were expected and desired from his performances on his instrument; but there were few ready or willing to follow the lofty flight of his imagination and his mighty ideas. When Mozart visited the town of N—* [I indicate this and several other names by letters with which they do *not* begin, for the reason already stated] the art-loving X—invited a numerous assembly of the pillars of the community in order to give them the pleasure of hearing Mozart, who had promised to join the assembly and to play on that occasion. Mozart naturally assumed that the audience of ladies and gentlemen, of whom he scarcely knew two, was made up of connoisseurs, or at least educated music-lovers; so he began as usual in a slow tempo, with a simple melody and even simpler harmony, which was to become gradually

[36] Niemetschek, *Leben*, 39.

[37] *Dokumente*, 269–70; *Documentary Biography*, 305–6.

[38] Georg Nikolaus Nissen, *Biographie W. A. Mozart's*, ed. Constanze Nissen (Leipzig, 1828 [1829]), 537.

[39] See Carl Bär, 'Er war . . . —kein guter Wirth': Eine Studie über Mozarts Verhältnis zum Geld', *Acta Mozartiana*, 25 (1978), 30–53 at 39–40.

more interesting—in part to elevate his own mood, in part to carry the spirits of the listeners upwards with him. The people sat in a half-circle of the magnificent room and found that to be ordinary fare. Mozart now became more fiery; they found this quite agreeable. Then he became both solemn and fiery, with particularly striking harmonies, exalted and somewhat difficult: that, to most, appeared boring. A number of women began to whisper to each other, probably some short criticism, several others joined in, and before long perhaps half of the people were speaking; the host—who truly loved music—became more and more embarrassed. Now Mozart noticed the effect of his music upon the assembly. In general, he was easily irritated and now, because of the performance, was even more sensitive than usual. Rather than abandoning his main theme on the fortepiano, he started to develop it with an intensity probably corresponding to that of the blood then coursing through his veins. When that was not noticed, he began to abuse his audience—first softly but then increasingly loudly—in the most merciless fashion. Luckily, the language which first came to his tongue was Italian (there was certainly no other reason) and only a few of the members of the society understood it well enough that they might have been able to understand the thundering apostrophes of the performer, who never stopped playing. However, they took notice of what was happening and fell silent, ashamed. Mozart, who continued improvising without interruption, must have secretly been laughing at himself now that his rage had blown over; he now gave his ideas a more *galant* direction and finally began to play the melody of the Liedchen, 'Ich klage dir', which was sung everywhere at that time. This he presented more elegantly, varied it ten or twelve times, alternately with digital wizardry or affected sweetness, and came to a conclusion with it. Everyone was wholly enchanted and only a few realized how cruelly he was mocking these people. Mozart himself left the house at once, meanwhile inviting his host and several of the old town musicians to come together; they had an evening meal and, in response to their shy request, he improvised for the old ones with pleasure until after midnight.

Rochlitz offers no information as to time, place, or circumstances, thus making it impossible to check the veracity of this engaging anecdote, which is surely a fanciful embroidery of several paragraphs in Niemetschek and Schlichtegroll describing Mozart's impatience with audiences. Niemetschek wrote:

Occasionally, even in the presence of people of the highest rank, he could not be persuaded to play; or he would merely play trifles, if he saw that they were neither connoisseurs nor lovers of music. But Mozart was the most obliging man in the world when he saw that one possessed real feeling for his art; then he would often play for hours to someone quite unknown and unimportant.[40]

Niemetschek also reported that, as a boy, Mozart had 'contempt for all praise from the nobility and a certain diffidence about playing to them, if they were not, at the same time, knowledgeable people. When compelled to do so nevertheless, he would play nothing but trivial pieces, dances, etc.—unimportant trifles. But when experts were present he was all fire and enthusiasm'.[41] The latter passage is closely derived from Nannerl Mozart's memoirs of her brother which she furnished to Schlichtegroll: 'The praise of the great never made him arrogant, for he always played with more fire and attentiveness when he knew that he was playing for connoisseurs. Already as a child he would play

[40] Niemetschek, *Leben*, 69.
[41] Ibid. 16.

nothing but trifles when he played for people who didn't understand music.'[42] Finally, Niemetschek wrote: 'Nothing annoyed him more than restlessness, fuss, or chatter while music was being played. Then this quiet, friendly man would become extremely annoyed, and showed it in no uncertain way. It is well known that once in the middle of playing he got up, though with reluctance, and left the inattentive audience.'[43] Mozart himself related such an instance in a letter to his father from Paris, describing his resentment at being forced by an inconsiderate audience 'to play to the chairs, tables, and walls'; he wrote: 'Give me the best clavier in Europe with an audience who understand nothing, or don't want to understand and who do not feel with me in what I am playing, and I shall cease to feel any pleasure.'[44] Mozart never wrote variations on the lied, 'Ich klage dir, o Echo, dir die Leiden meiner Brust' (author unknown).[45]

In 1812 Rochlitz published another anecdote along similar lines, relating how, following his public concert in Leipzig, Mozart invited the violinist Carl Gottlieb Berger to his room and played for him until midnight, saying, 'Come with me, good Berger! I will play for you for a while. You understand things much better than most of those who now applaud me.'[46]

Anecdote 6 (24 October 1798, cols. 51–2). Of all his operas, Mozart esteemed none higher than *Idomeneo* and *Don Giovanni*. To be sure, I know that the authors of excellent works of all kinds are not always the best judge of their value: they may consider first and foremost the amount of labour they put into a work, whereas the art critic concerns himself only with judging the artwork in itself; or they created one or another of their works under circumstances of particular interest or value to them, the memory of which, when they think about the work itself, somehow stirs their emotions—obscurely and often unconsciously—bonding itself to the very idea of the work. And there are other, similar circumstances, as a result of which Titian, for example, remained indifferent to some of his most accomplished works of his later years, while placing a greater value on other, much less accomplished works of his youth. But if, in determining the value of a work of art, we emphasize in particular the extent to which it represents the greatest personal individuality, the purest and strongest qualities of its author's genius, then Mozart's judgement concerning those two operas is incontestably the most correct that could be passed. However, his opinion of them was not frequently voiced—as a rule he seldom spoke, and then only briefly, about his works—but he did say so occasionally. Of *Idomeneo* later. Concerning *Don Giovanni* he said: 'This opera was not written for the Viennese, but rather for Prague, and most of all for myself and my friends.' It is almost incomprehensible but nevertheless true that he wrote the Overture to this opera—which is recognized as the most distinguished of all those he wrote—in one night, and indeed in the night preceding the first public performance, so that the copyists could scarcely complete their work until the hour of the performance and the orchestra had to play it without rehearsal. At first, *Don Giovanni* did not particularly please in Vienna. After a couple of performances there, the well-known art-loving Prince R—— had a large company at his residence. Most

[42] Nannerl Mozart, sketch for a 1792 letter addressed to Albert von Mölk, intended to be forwarded to Schlichtegroll through B&H; *Briefe*, iv. 201; Schlichtegroll, 'Mozart', 91.

[43] Niemetschek, *Leben*, 65.

[44] Letter of 1 May 1778; *Briefe*, ii. 344; *Letters*, ii. 531–2.

[45] Max Friedländer, *Das deutsche Lied im 18. Jahrhundert* (Stuttgart, 1902), ii. 311–13.

[46] *AmZ* 14 (1812), 106; Eisen, *New Mozart Documents*, Doc. 96; Nissen, *Biographie*, 660.

of the music connoisseurs of the Imperial City were present, including Joseph Haydn. Mozart was not there. There was much talk about the new production. After the fine ladies and gentlemen had chattered about it some connoisseurs took the floor. All agreed that it was a work of great merit, an incomparable fantasy, rich in genius; but everyone voiced some objection: one found it excessive, another too chaotic, a third too unmelodious, a fourth too unevenly worked out, and so forth. In general one couldn't gainsay that there was something of the truth in each of these judgements. Everyone had now spoken except—father Haydn. Finally the modest composer was asked to give his judgement. He said with his accustomed circumspection: 'I cannot settle this issue—but I do know this,' he asserted with great animation, 'that Mozart is the greatest composer that the world now possesses!' Thereupon, the ladies and gentlemen fell silent.

Rochlitz, who does not cite his authority, is the only source to claim that Mozart set especial store by *Idomeneo*.[47] (See also No. 8.) Mozart's comment about *Don Giovanni* is expanded from Niemetschek, who quoted him as saying, '*Don Giovanni* was written for Prague.'[48] The story of the composition of the Overture is also lifted outright from Niemetschek: 'On the evening before the day of the first performance . . . he went into his room towards midnight, began writing, and in a few hours had completed this admirable masterpiece . . . The copyists were only just ready in time for the performance and the opera orchestra . . . played it excellently *prima vista* . . .'.[49] *Don Giovanni* received fifteen performances in Vienna between 7 May and 15 December 1788. While it was not the success of *Die Entführung*, *Le nozze di Figaro*, or *Die Zauberflöte*, it was far from a failure, notwithstanding Emperor Joseph's remark, 'Mozart's music is certainly too difficult for the singers.'[50] The story of Haydn's defence of Mozart is probably pure invention, based on Rochlitz's mistaken assumption (see No. 7) that both men lived in Vienna at the time (*beyde an einem Orte lebten*). It cannot be confirmed that Haydn, who rarely visited Vienna in the 1780s, was there for an early performance of *Don Giovanni*. Landon, seeking to accommodate Rochlitz's anecdote, speculates that Haydn managed 'to escape for a day or two to Vienna in order to hear *Don Giovanni*'.[51] However, such a visit is very unlikely, for the Esterházy archives indicate that in 1788, in addition to his other duties, Haydn prepared, rehearsed, and conducted no fewer than 108 opera performances of seventeen different operas, including seven premières; in May—when the *Don Giovanni* Vienna premiere took place—Haydn presented no fewer than eleven days of opera performances at Esterháza.[52] As late as 1790 Haydn openly complained to Frau Genzinger: 'Your Haydn, who, often as his Prince absents himself from Estoras, cannot go to Vienna

[47] Jahn, i. 660; Eng. trans., ii. 141–2.

[48] Niemetschek, *Leben*, 37.

[49] Ibid. 63–4; see also Constanze Mozart, *AmZ* 1 (1798–1799), 19–20 (Anecdote No. 3).

[50] *Dokumente*, 277; *Documentary Biography*, 315.

[51] H. C. Robbins Landon, *Haydn: Chronicle and Works*, 5 vols. (Bloomington, Ind., and London, 1976–80), ii. 708; see also 700. Cf. Jahn, who observed: 'Haydn sometimes obtained leave of absence for a flying visit to Vienna, but the Prince always gave it unwillingly' (ii. 46; Eng. trans., ii. 351). On Haydn's fear of offending Prince Esterházy by absences from his post, see Th. G. von Karajan, 'J. Haydn in London 1791 und 1792', *Jahrbuch für vaterländische Geschichte*, 1 (Vienna, 1861), 47–166 at 65–6.

[52] Janos Harich, 'Das Repertoire des Opernkapellmeisters Joseph Haydn in Esterháza (1780–1790)', *Haydn Year Book*, 1 (1962), 9–110 at 18, 78–84.

even for 24 hours; it's scarcely credible, and yet the refusal is always couched in such polite terms . . .'.[53]

Anecdote 7 (24 October 1798, cols. 52–3). Mozart behaved the same way towards Haydn. As is known, he dedicated to him a collection of his most beautiful quartets. They belong among the most superlative, not only of those that Mozart wrote but which exist in this genre in general. His later quartets are more *galant*, more in a *concertante* style: in these, however, every note is thought through; they must therefore be executed exactly as written, no figure may be altered. His dedication is a beautiful indication of his inner veneration for the great Haydn. 'This was a debt,' remarked Mozart, 'for it was from Haydn that I first learned how to write quartets.'

Mozart always spoke of the master with the liveliest regard, notwithstanding that both lived in one place and that reasons for mutual jealousy were not lacking on either side. A certain composer who at that time was first becoming known and only subsequently has acquired something more of a reputation, an industrious composer who is not without skill but pretty well devoid of genius, was rankled—then and probably now as well—by Haydn's fame. He frequently caught up with Mozart, bringing him scores of Haydn's symphonies or quartets, and each time he would triumphantly demonstrate some small stylistic fault which had, no matter how seldom, escaped that artist's attention. Mozart avoided or broke off these conversations. Finally, however, it became too irritating for him:

'Sir,' he said rather vehemently, 'if the two of us were put together we'd be nowhere near one Haydn!'

Thus have great men always given other great men their due. Only when one secretly feels weak does one seek to find a weakness in those who are superior, to pull down one whom one is incapable of surpassing.

Rochlitz does not reveal how he learned this story or to whom Mozart's words were addressed. A similar anecdote in Niemetschek probably was Rochlitz's source: When Haydn was criticized by another composer, Mozart 'could bear it no longer and when the conceited fault-finder again declared: "I would not have done that", Mozart retorted: "Neither would I, but do you know why? Because neither of us could have thought of anything so appropriate".'[54] The famous quotation about learning to write quartets from Haydn is original with Rochlitz.

Anecdote 8 (24 October 1798, cols. 53–5). *Idomeneo* was written under extremely favourable circumstances, destined for the then outstanding Munich Theatre. The Elector ordered it and gave him indications of his regard, including payment. In Munich, Mozart composed for one of the finest orchestras in the world, of which he could expect a lot, so that he could give free rein to the flights of his fantasy without external constraints. He was in the most beautiful flowering of his life, aged twenty-five, with broad achievements and an incandescent love for his art; with his quick light physique, his mighty youthful imagination; and—what was a major factor—with the wings he was lent by his deeply requited love for his wife-to-be; a love which managed to overcome all obstacles

[53] Haydn to Marianne von Genzinger, 30 May 1790, in H. C. Robbins Landon (ed.), *The Collected Correspondence and London Notebooks of Joseph Haydn* (London, 1959), 102; Landon, *Chronicle and Works*, ii. 741.

[54] Niemetschek, *Leben*, 69. Another possible source is a report of Mozart's defence of a 'trifling' composition of Haydn's, published in the *Wiener Schriftsteller und Kunstler Lexikon* for 1793, cited in H. C. Robbins Landon, 'Two Orchestral Works Wrongly Attributed to Mozart', *Music Review*, 17 (1956), 29–34.

placed by his beloved's side of the family and thereby gained even more interest for Mozart. How should such a reputable family have wanted its daughter to be united with a young, constantly travelling, light-hearted artist, and one who had no steady position? That these notions even greatly magnified Mozart's ambition, and gave him strength to work with all his might to establish his name and thereby to win his beloved girl and to revenge himself upon those who estimated him so meanly—all that is self-evident. That an artist, even if he were by no means a Mozart, should want under these circumstances to supply something excellent; that Mozart should be especially fond of a work born under such auspices, even if it had not the high value that it had, is even more readily self-evident. His preference for this child is further attested by the fact that he took several of its main themes as the basis—almost even more than just that—for some of his best later works. In order to understand this one may compare the Overture to *Idomeneo* with, for example, the Overture to *Clemenza di T.*; the incomparable scene, 'Volgi intorno lo sguardo, o sire', with the also wholly excellent finale of the first act of *Clemenza di T.*; the moving aria of the first act, 'Se il padre perdei'; with the aria, 'dies Bildnis is bezaubernd schön', and the Andante of the aria, 'Zum Leiden bin ich auserkohren' of *Die Zauberflöte*; the march of the third act of *Idomeneo* with the beginning of the second act of *Die Zauberflöte*, and so forth. He has been reproached for this; unjustly, I believe. Mozart could justly make use of his earlier work, not only because it was so excellent, but particularly also because, as along as he lived, it lay hidden like a buried treasure.

This defective account of Mozart's courtship is clear proof that Rochlitz did not have access to information from Constanze Mozart in the preparation of his anecdotes, let alone that she 'confirmed, corrected, or contradicted' them before publication. Far from opposing the match, Constanze Weber's mother was anxious to assure that the marriage take place. It was Mozart's family that was opposed to the marriage. As for a possible autobiographical significance of Mozart's operas, Rochlitz here once again appears to have read Niemetschek too hastily, for the latter, doubtless on the authority of Constanze Mozart, connected Mozart's courtship of his future wife not with *Idomeneo* but with *Die Entführung aus dem Serail*, which was composed between 30 July 1781 and the end of May 1782. Again, no doubt following Constanze Mozart's lead, Niemetschek wrote: 'The influence of the romantic mood on the composition of this opera is there for all to hear . . .'.[55] *Idomeneo*, however, was composed between October 1780 and January 1781 and had its first performance on 29 January 1781, several months before Mozart moved to Vienna, where he took up lodgings in Frau Weber's home in early May 1781. Nissen writes: 'The assumption that *Idomeneo* fell in the period of Mozart's love-affair with Constanze is entirely false, since this love relationship first began in Vienna.'[56] Although Mozart sometimes reused existing materials for later works—for example, the reworking of the unfinished Mass in C minor, K. 427 (417a) as *Davidde Penitente*, K. 469—the charge that he cannibalized *Idomeneo* in his later operas is unfounded.

Anecdote 9 (7 November 1798, cols. 81–2). Mozart was often condemned for his carelessness and frivolity in money matters. The matter is indeed as true as the fact that it cannot be separated from such a man's individuality. But since people still tell only stories about how he either spent

[55] Niemetschek, *Leben*, 32.
[56] Nissen, *Biographie*, 464.

money foolishly or threw it away, permit me to relate several different ones in which he gave, indeed with accustomed liberality, but so straightforwardly, with so much good nature and purity, and so completely without the refined self-interest that often accompanied generosity. True, these are only bagatelles, but they were observed by me in just the few days of his stay in Leipzig and probably far more occasions escaped me even in those few days. When he was visiting the Leipzig Thomasschule and the choir sang some eight-voice motets in his honour, he avowed: 'We have such a choir in Vienna, but not in Berlin and Prague.' Among the crowd of at least forty singers he noticed particularly a bass, who pleased him very much. He had a short conversation with him and, without any of us present noticing it, he pressed a considerable present into the young man's hand.

An old honoured piano tuner tuned some of the strings on his borrowed instrument:

'Dear old man,' said Mozart, 'what do I owe you for your efforts? Tomorrow I leave here.' The old man, who was constantly embarrassed whenever he spoke with anyone, stuttered:

'Your imperial majesty—I'd like to say—Your imperial majesty, Sir Kapellmeister—I have indeed been here on several different occasions—I ask nevertheless—one Taler.'

'One Taler? That is not enough to pay such a good man, even for only one visit.' And thereupon he pressed into his hand several ducats.

'Your imperial majesty', began the startled man.

'Farewell, dear old man! Farewell!' called Mozart, and rapidly went into another room.

He was asked to give public concerts in Leipzig and he was willing to do so. Nevertheless, I know not why, the assembly was not very numerous, and almost half of those present had free tickets, for everyone who knew him received them. Because he was giving no chorus, the rather numerous choral singers were forbidden free entrance. Several came and said to the ticket seller, 'I was invited by the Kapellmeister.' 'Oh let them in! Let them come in!' answered Mozart, 'Who has to be so exact in such things?'

This is the first of Rochlitz's Leipzig anecdotes, presumably based on personal observation, for he was a native of Leipzig, where he studied music at the Thomasschule under Cantor Johann Friedrich Doles (1714–97). Although Rochlitz's name does not appear in Mozart's letters and the two men were never in correspondence, Rochlitz was in a position to have met Mozart—at least, to have seen or heard him—during April and May 1789. Mozart arrived in Leipzig on 20 April 1789, remaining for about three days before his departure for Potsdam. On 22 April he improvised on the Thomaskirche organ in the presence of Doles and the organist Karl Friedrich Görner. He returned to Leipzig on 8 May and remained until the morning of 17 May. The main event of his stay was the 12 May concert at the Gewandhaus, which is referred to here as well as in Nos. 12 and 13. Rochlitz's comment that the audience was small is confirmed in Mozart's letter to his wife: 'From the point of view of applause and glory this concert was absolutely magnificent, but the profits were wretchedly meagre.'[57] A few days later, he wrote again: 'my concert at Leipzig was a failure . . .'.[58] According to Nissen, the hall was 'almost empty'.[59]

[57] Letter of 16 May 1789; *Briefe*, iv. 86; *Letters*, ii. 925.
[58] Letter of 23 May 1789; *Briefe*, iv. 90; *Letters*, ii. 928.
[59] Nissen, *Biographie*, 530.

Reichardt writes that Mozart was 'famous for his thoughtfulness . . . And he was not parsimonious, giving free tickets for his concert to friends of music who were without means.'[60] Rochlitz's other examples of Mozart's generosity and his high opinion of the Thomasschule choir are not otherwise confirmed, but could be based on personal observation. It is true that Mozart often spent money freely. His alleged carelessness with money was a source of friction with his father and is mentioned by Schlichtegroll, Niemetschek, and others. Niemetschek called him imprudent. 'It is true, he should have been more careful with his money; but is a genius not allowed any weaknesses?'[61]

Anecdote 10 (7 November 1798, col. 83). No one abused this carelessness concerning money more than music dealers and theatre directors. Most of his piano compositions, for example, didn't even bring in a penny. He obligingly wrote them for acquaintances so that they might have an autograph, and indeed for their own use. Concerning the latter, one might ask why more than a few of these, particularly solo piano pieces, are unworthy of him. He must have prepared them according to the mental capacity, the fancies, and the abilities and technical preparedness of the amateurs for whom they were tossed off. Those venturesome gentlemen subsequently found ways to procure manuscript copies for themselves and set about printing them right away. In particular a certain rather famous music dealer printed a variety of such creations, and a variety of Mozart's compositions were printed and sold without asking the master about it. Once a friend came to him:

'The firm of A— again has published a set of variations for piano by you: do you know about it?'

'No!'

'Why won't you step forward and put an end to his trade, once and for all?'

'What's the point of so much talk about it? He is a scoundrel!'

'But it is not just a matter of money, it's also a question of your honour!'

'Now—he who judges me by such Bagatelles is also a scoundrel. Let's not hear anything more about this!'

There are multiple inaccuracies here. It is untrue that Mozart earned nothing from his piano compositions, that many of them were casually tossed off, or that he habitually wrote them as gifts for acquaintances. The piano sonatas, variations, and concertos were written primarily for his own use in his very numerous, lucrative concert and salon appearances. Furthermore, publishers (and presumably copyists as well) paid substantial sums to Mozart for the rights to sell his works in engraved or manuscript form.[62] It is true that Mozart, like other composers whose works were in demand, had good reason to fear unauthorized publications of his works: according to A. Hyatt King, of 144 publications during Mozart's lifetime 30 were not authorized by Mozart, most of these being reprint editions.[63] Leopold Mozart reported on 16 December 1785 that a clavier arrangement of

[60] *Berlinische musikalische Zeitung*, 1 (1805), 132.

[61] Niemetschek, *Leben*, 50.

[62] Otto Erich Deutsch, 'Mozarts Verleger', *Mozart-Jahrbuch 1955*, 49–55 at 52; Otto Erich Deutsch and Cecil B. Oldman, 'Mozart-Drucke. Eine bibliographische Ergänzung zu Köchels Werkverzeichnis', *Zeitschrift für Musikwissenschaft*, 14 (1931–2), 135–50, 337–51 at 137.

[63] A. Hyatt King, *Mozart in Retrospect: Studies in Criticism and Bibliography* (London, 1955), 9; Haberkamp lists 131 authentic works in 78 editions published during Mozart's lifetime; she does not, however, clearly differentiate between authentic and pirated editions. Gertraut Haberkamp, *Die Erstdrucke der Werke von Wolfgang Amadeus Mozart*, 2 vols. (Tutzing, 1986), 13 and *passim*.

Die Entführung aus dem Serail had been published by an Augsburg bookseller in advance of Mozart's own arrangement, which Torricella was in process of publishing.[64] Mozart himself took precautions to prevent copyists from stealing his works (see No. 13); and he was concerned that printers might cheat him: 'If I have some work printed or engraved at my own expense, how can I protect myself from being cheated by the engraver? For surely he can print off as many copies as he likes and therefore swindle me.'[65] And, in competition with the music dealers, Mozart on occasion offered for sale manuscript copies of certain works. However, there is no evidence to support Rochlitz's statements about systematic or widespread piracy of Mozart's keyboard compositions. 'A' presumably designates the Viennese firm of Artaria and Co., which, far from pirating Mozart's works, was his leading source of publishing income during his Vienna years and paid him substantial fees at least equal to those received by Haydn, Dittersdorf, and other popular composers. In 1785, Artaria paid him 75 florins each for the six 'Haydn' String Quartets; for comparison, in 1784, Artaria paid Haydn 50 florins per string quartet; earlier, the publisher paid him 22 florins 50 Kreuzer for each of six overtures, an amount identical with what Mozart received from Johann Sieber of Paris for each of the six Sonatas for Violin and Piano, K. 301–6.[66] Dittersdorf was satisfied that Mozart was being paid well, for in 1788 he offered Artaria six quartets at 'the same price which you have paid for those by Mozart'.[67] Artaria had 25 separate publications of Mozart's works during his last decade, comprising 48 separate Köchel numbers.[68] In papers filed in connection with a lawsuit against Cappi & Diabelli in 1818, Artaria claimed that, although it had no specific contractual assignment of rights from Mozart, its rights to its publications of his works could be confirmed by witnesses and by the firm's account-books, which reflected fees paid to him for major works. As for minor works, the brief stated that 'Mozart was much too generous to accept or to request anything for such bagatelles.'[69] Rochlitz's reference to publications of piano works unworthy of Mozart may derive in part from the following passage in Niemetschek, which refers to posthumous publications: '[Mozart] is saddled with many spurious works quite unworthy of his genius, and what is worse, often incompetent adapters patch together piano pieces from his larger works and sell them as though they were originals, which are obviously not in the same class as his genuine piano compositions'.[70]

Anecdote 11 (7 November 1798, cols. 83–4). A certain theatre manager, who certainly deserves to be mentioned, went completely under, partly through his own fault, partly through lack of public

[64] Leopold Mozart to Nannerl Mozart; *Briefe*, iii. 471; *Letters*, ii. 895.

[65] Mozart to Leopold Mozart, 20 Feb. 1784; *Briefe*, iii. 302; *Letters*, ii. 868.

[66] Landon (ed.), *Collected Correspondence*, 45, 37, 38 (letters to Artaria of 5 Apr. 1784, 16 Aug. 1782, and 29 Sept. 1782).

[67] Eisen, *New Mozart Documents*, Doc. 86.

[68] Deutsch, 'Mozarts Verleger,' 50–1. There is no reason to share Haberkamp's opinion—circularly based on the present Rochlitz anecdote—that any of these were unauthorized; Haberkamp, i. 18; see also 21.

[69] Otto Erich Deutsch, 'Mozarts Verlagshonorare', in *Börsenblatt für den Deutschen Buchhandel*, No. 86 (11 Apr. 1933), 263. The account-books do not survive. Artaria's application to enforce its claim to exclusive rights was rejected.

[70] Niemetschek, *Leben*, 79.

support. Half in confusion he went to Mozart, told him of his circumstances, and ended by saying that only he could help.

'I? How?'

'Write an opera for me, wholly to the taste of the modern audience in—; you may serve both the connoisseurs and your reputation in doing so, but above all be sure to provide for humble people of every social status. I will provide the text, create the scenery, and so forth, I'll take care of everything that needs doing.'

'Good, I'll undertake it!'

'What will you accept for an honorarium?'

'You have no money! Therefore we'll arrange things so that you will be helped and I won't be deprived of all the profits. I'll give you and you alone my score; give me for it what you will, but under the condition that you warrant to me that it will not be copied. If the opera makes a stir, I will sell it to another management, and that will be my payment.'

The theatre manager concluded the contract with delight and sacred vows. Mozart wrote diligently, valiantly, and wholly in accordance with the man's instructions. The opera was produced and had a great reception; its acclaim spread through all Germany and after a few weeks it was already being given at the out-of-town theatres, without a single one of Mozart's scores being obtained!

Early biographers were quick to promote this legend—which Rochlitz originated and for which he remains the only source—about Mozart's financial arrangements with Emanuel Schikaneder for the composition of *Die Zauberflöte*. (For a further reference, see No. 17.) Nissen reprinted Rochlitz's anecdote, preserving all his essential details,[71] and Jahn elaborated it, adding a colourful description of Schikaneder as a licentious, thieving, parasitical adventurer who was extricated from his financial difficulties by Mozart's naïve intervention.[72] Jahn wrote: 'Schikaneder took care to keep the composer in good humour by frequent invitations to his table, where both eating and drinking were of the best, and by introductions to the jovial and free-living society in which he himself moved . . . Folly and dissipation were the inevitable accompaniments of such an existence . . .'.[73] However, according to Komorzynski, far from facing bankruptcy, Schikaneder's Freihaus Theater (the Theater auf der Wieden) was 'going brilliantly' in the first years after he took it over in 1789, mounting numerous productions of plays, operas, and Singspiele, including several major popular hits.[74] Far from attempting to save a composer's fee, he spared 'no expense with his new productions', and, according to a contemporary theatre journal, his production of *Die Zauberflöte* 'is said to have amounted to 5,000 fl.'.[75] His often extravagant productions were underwritten, first by Joseph von Bauernfeld and then by Bartholomäus Zitterbarth, and it was only towards the end of the 1790s that he fell into

[71] Nissen, *Biographie*, 548–9.

[72] Jahn, ii. 565–9; Eng. trans., iii. 283–5.

[73] Jahn, ii. 569; Eng. trans., iii. 285.

[74] See Egon Komorzynski, *Der Vater der Zauberflöte: Emanuel Schikaneder* (Vienna, 1948), 130; Volkmar Braunbehrens, *Mozart in Vienna* (New York, 1990), 377–8.

[75] *Allgemeines Theaterjournal* (Frankfurt and Mainz, 1792), i. 149 f.; cit. *Dokumente*, 381; *Documentary Biography*, 433–4.

heavy debt and was forced to sell the theatre.[76] Rochlitz may have been aware of Schikaneder's later embarrassments.

Mozart customarily received 100 to 200 ducats for an opera and for *Così fan tutte* and *La clemenza di Tito*, the two operas which preceded *Die Zauberflöte*, it is thought that he received 200 ducats each.[77] These fees were quite in line with contemporary payments to other composers.[78] Mozart was well aware of the possibilities of large profits from productions of his operas and had long been determined to obtain his fair share, and even to produce his own works. As early as 1782 he wrote: 'I am willing to write an opera, but not to look on with a hundred ducats in my pocket and see the theatre making four times as much in a fortnight. I intend to produce my opera at my own expense, I shall clear at least 1,200 gulden by three performances and then the management may have it for fifty ducats.'[79] A letter to his wife from Prague in 1789 confirms that he hoped to receive 200 ducats plus 50 ducats in travelling expenses from Domenico Guardasoni for an opera.[80] It is unthinkable that the financially pressed author of the letters to Michael Puchberg could have been so negligent as to waive his fee. And it seems self-evident that Mozart would scarcely have participated in the production and première performances of *Die Zauberflöte* with such whole-hearted enthusiasm if he had not shared in its fortunes. Braunbehrens asks, 'When was Mozart ever prepared to write a large work without receiving appropriate payment?' and Landon also recognizes the difficulties of Rochlitz's anecdote, calling it a 'very unlikely story', for, 'in the spring of 1791, Mozart was hardly in a position to take several months off to write a huge opera "on speculation"'.[81] Mozart's wife was then both pregnant and ailing, and his letters of this period reflect his anxieties about money matters. A letter to Puchberg dated 25 June 1791 tells of Mozart's expectation that he would receive 2,000 florins—a sum equivalent to about 450 ducats—within 'a few days'; the source of this money is not known, but a connection with the delivery of his opera, which is dated 'July' in his *Verzeichnis*, cannot be ruled out.[82] Alternatively, I think it feasible that Mozart was Schikaneder's partner in the enterprise, perhaps taking a reduced advance fee in exchange for a share of the profits. This would tally with the report by the usually reliable Ignaz von Seyfried—who studied with Mozart and who had an opera produced at the Freihaus Theater during the period in question—that Schikaneder paid Mozart 100 ducats for the opera and later paid all net

[76] Komorzynski, *Vater*, 204–5; Anton Bauer, *150 Jahre Theater an der Wien* (Zurich, Leipzig, and Vienna, 1952), 23–6.

[77] See e.g. Bär, 'Er war . . . —kein guter Wirth', 51, but Steptoe questions the reliability of the evidence for this. Andrew Steptoe, *The Mozart–Da Ponte Operas* (Oxford, 1988), 59–60.

[78] For example, Dittersdorf recounts that Stephani commissioned *Doctor und Apotheker* 'on the usual terms of 100 ducats'. A single benefit performance of the same opera in Vienna brought him an additional 200 ducats. *Autobiography of Karl von Dittersdorf, Dictated to his Son*, trans. A. D. Coleridge (London, 1896; repr. New York, 1970), 256, 257–8.

[79] Mozart to Leopold Mozart, 5 Oct. 1782; *Briefe*, iii. 236; *Letters*, ii. 826.

[80] Mozart to Constanze Mozart, 10 Apr. 1789; *Briefe*, iv. 80; *Letters*, ii. 920.

[81] Braunbehrens, *Mozart in Vienna*, 381; H. C. Robbins Landon, *1791: Mozart's Last Year* (New York, 1988), 125.

[82] *Briefe*, iv. 140; *Letters*, ii. 957.

profits from the sale of the score to the widow.[83] The tone of Mozart's last letters to his wife, reporting on 'the splendid reception of my German opera', suggests that his financial worries had been mitigated: 'I am anxious, as far as possible, to avoid all risk of *money difficulties*. For the most pleasant thing of all is if one can live peacefully. To achieve this, however, one must work hard; and I like hard work.'[84]

According to Abert, it was usual in the Italian theatres for a composer's opera score 'to remain in the possession of the impresario, who in favourable circumstances permitted his copyists to make and sell copies'; and even in the German court theatres, where the composer usually kept the score for his own disposition, it was not uncommon for the impresario to retain these rights.[85]

Die Zauberflöte was indeed produced everywhere (and widely imitated), but not within 'a few weeks', as Rochlitz asserts here and assumes in No. 17. The earliest productions outside of Vienna were in Lemberg (September 1792), Prague (25 October 1792), Frankfurt (16 August 1793), Munich (11 July 1793), Hamburg (15 November 1793), and Berlin (12 May 1794). Thus, Mozart was dead well before any unauthorized productions of his opera were mounted and therefore could not have made the comment about Schikaneder—'the scoundrel!'—attributed to him by Rochlitz in No. 17.

Anecdote 12 (7 November 1798, cols. 84–6). But Mozart never complained more vehemently than about the 'botching' of his compositions at public performances, mainly through exaggerated tempos.

'They think it is going to make it fiery, but if there is no fire in the composition itself', he said, 'it will not really be brought in by excessive speed.'

He was particularly unhappy with most of the new Italian singers:

'They race or trill and over-ornament', he said, 'because they don't study hard and can't hold the pitch!'

The evening before the rehearsal of his public concert in Leipzig, I heard him declaiming in a very lively manner on precisely this point. When I went to the rehearsal the next day I observed to my amazement that he took the first movement to be rehearsed—it was the Allegro of one of his symphonies—very, very fast. Scarcely twenty bars were played and—it was easy to predict—the orchestra lagged behind the proper tempo, dragging. Mozart stopped, pointed out how they were at fault, called 'Ancora' and began once again just as fast. The result was the same. He did everything to hold the tempo steady; once he pounded out the beat so powerfully that one of his magnificently worked steel shoe-buckles broke in pieces; but it was all in vain. He laughed at his accident, let the buckle lie, called 'Ancora' again, and for the third time started in the same tempo. The musicians were indignant at the deathly pale little man who was vexing them; they went hard at it in embittered mood, and this time it worked. All that followed he took *moderato*. I must confess—I could not help but consider that he insisted on this rather rushed tempo not so

[83] [Ignaz von Seyfried], 'Commentar zur Erzählung: Johann Schenk, von J. P. Lyser,' *Neue Zeitschrift für Musik*, 12 (2 June 1840), 180. See Jahn, i. 834; Eng. trans. ii. 296. According to Gräffer's published account, allegedly taken down from Schikaneder's own remarks, Mozart asked for and received 100 ducats for the opera. Franz Gräffer, *Kleine Wiener Memoiren und Wiener Dosenstücke*, ed. Anton Schlossar und Gustav Gugitz, 2 vols. (Munich, 1918), ii. 5.

[84] Letter of 7 and 8 Oct. 1791; *Briefe*, iv. 157–8; *Letters*, ii. 967–8. Translation amended.

[85] Abert, i. 839–40.

much out of obstinacy as in order not to compromise his authority. After the rehearsal, however, he said privately to several connoisseurs:

'Don't be surprised; it was not capricious; I saw, however, that most of the musicians were rather advanced in age. There would have been no end to the dragging if I had not first driven them into a passion and made them angry. Out of pure irritation they then did their best.'

As Mozart had never heard this orchestra play, this certainly reveals no small understanding of people; therefore, he was not a child in everything that was not music, as is often said and written.

[In a footnote to No. 22 (19 December 1798, cols. 179–80), Rochlitz wrote that 'through an oversight . . . the following paragraph was omitted from Anecdote 10' [*sic*]]:

Still more. The worthy man now wanted once again to earn the love of the exasperated orchestra, without, however, forfeiting the good effect of his enthusiasm. He therefore now praised the accompaniment and said that if the gentlemen were able to play this way, it would not be necessary to rehearse for his concertos—for, he said, the parts are correctly written, you play correctly, and so do I—what more can one want from an accompaniment! And at the performance the orchestra really did accompany him without any rehearsal in the extremely difficult and complex [C major] concerto, and indeed perfectly—for it played with reverence towards Mozart—and with the greatest delicacy—for it played out of love for him.

Mozart's 12 May 1789 concert at the Gewandhaus is the subject of this anecdote (see also Nos. 9 and 13). Jahn found confirmation of the story: 'The scene made such an impression that a viola-player marked the place on his part where Mozart stamped the time till his shoe-buckle snapped. Griel, the old orchestra attendant at Leipzig, had picked it up and showed it as a token.'[86] Mozart's widow told the Novellos that 'occasionally [he] would stamp with his foot when impatient, or things do not go correctly in the orchestra', and that at a performance of *Die Entführung*, when the orchestra 'took the time of one of the movements too fast—he became quite impatient and called out to the orchestra without seeming to fear or to be aware of the presence of the audience'.[87] (See also No. 1.) Nannerl Mozart and Schlichtegroll promoted the view that Mozart was a child in all things; Mozart's sister wrote: 'Apart from his music he was almost always a child, and thus he remained: and this is a main feature of his character on the dark side.'[88] Schlichtegroll cited Nannerl Mozart's formulation in his *Nekrolog* for 1792, from whence it made its way into many influential contemporary writings about Mozart.[89]

Anecdote 13 (21 November 1798, cols. 113–14). At this concert he performed nothing except compositions of his own which at that time existed only in manuscript. Madame Duschek from Prague, that well-known and worthy singer, was present and she sang the now fairly familiar, extremely difficult *Szena* with fortepiano obbligato which had actually been written especially for her. In the second half, he played the Concerto in C major, the most magnificent and difficult of

[86] Jahn, ii. 489 n. 36; Eng. trans., iii. 232 n. 29.

[87] Nerina Medici di Marignano (transcriber and compiler), *A Mozart Pilgrimage: Being the Travel Diaries of Vincent and Mary Novello in the Year 1829*, ed. Rosemary Hughes (London, 1955), 113.

[88] Postscript to Nannerl Mozart's Reminiscences, in *Dokumente*, 405; *Documentary Biography*, 462.

[89] Schlichtegroll, *Nekrolog*, 109; see also Suard in *Dokumente*, 429; *Documentary Biography*, 498; Nissen, *Biographie*, 529.

all his hitherto known concertos, which his wife published after his death. This may be the most magnificent of all the concertos which have ever been written. Never more can I forget that heavenly enjoyment, created in part through the spirit of those works, partly through the brilliance, and again through the heart-melting tenderness of his performance. In order to prevent the usual theft of his compositions—at least of his concertos—he played from a piano part which had a peculiar appearance. It contained nothing except a figured bass, over which were written out only the main ideas; the figures, passages and such things were only lightly indicated. He could presume to do this because he could rely as much on his memory as on his feeling. At the end of the whole concert, some people wanted to hear him play solo; and this obliging man, who had already played two concertos and an obbligato *Szena*, and moreover had accompanied for almost two hours, was ready for it; he promptly sat down and played in order to satisfy everyone. He began simply, freely, and solemnly in C minor—but it would be absurd to attempt to describe such a feat as his. Since he had initially been addressing himself more to the connoisseurs, he now gradually curtailed the flight of his fantasy and closed with the published variations in E flat major, which are printed in the Collection of Mozart's Works by Breitkopf and Härtel, vol. II, pages 45–6.

According to the program of the Gewandhaus concert of 12 May 1789, Mozart conducted two symphonies (unidentified), and performed two piano concertos and a Fantasy for piano (presumably the C minor Fantasy, K. 475).[90] In addition, the program lists soprano Josepha Duschek in two Scenes, probably the Scene with Rondo, 'Ch'io mi scordi di te'—'Non temer, amato bene', K. 505, and perhaps the Scene, 'Bella mia fiamma'—'Resta, o cara', K. 528. (The former was actually written for Anna [Nancy] Storace.) The E flat major Variations are not listed on the program: the Breitkopf & Härtel edition includes two sets of variations in that key, K. 353 and 354. Rochlitz here identifies one of the concertos as the Concerto in C major, K. 503, and in a later publication he identifies the other as the Concerto in B flat major, K. 456.[91] For the story of the figured bass, he appears to have appropriated Niemetschek's Prague report: 'As his works were in unbelievable demand, he was never quite sure whether a new work of his, even while it was being copied, had not been stolen. So he generally wrote only a line for one hand in his piano concertos and played the rest from memory.'[92] However, the autographs of the piano concertos do not bear out Niemetschek's assertion: only a few passages of the concertos are incompletely notated, the significant exception being the

[90] *Dokumente*, 300; *Documentary Biography*, 342.

[91] Rochlitz, *Für Freunde der Tonkunst*, ii. 284 n. (at 287). 'At his Leipzig Akademie, three years before his death, he played two concertos: the cheerful and delightful B flat major with the G minor variations, which was engraved shortly thereafter, and the brilliant, glorious C major, which was published after his death.' Rochlitz then elaborates the story of Mozart playing from a figured bass, claiming that this was Mozart's universal practice when he was on the road, and adding a direct explanatory quotation from the composer: 'The solo parts, he said, are closely guarded in Vienna. I must do it thus when I am travelling: otherwise they steal copies and publish them immediately.' Ibid. Suard relates that Emperor Joseph, 'happening to glance at the music paper which Mozart appeared to be following, was astonished to see on it nothing but staves without notes, and [he] said to him: "Where is your part?" "There", said Mozart, putting his hand to his forehead.' *Dokumente*, 429–30; *Documentary Biography*, 499.

[92] Niemetschek, *Leben*, 64–5.

Concerto in D major, K. 537, which is partially unnotated for the left hand in the Larghetto and Allegretto; Mozart performed it on 14 April in Dresden and may have repeated it in Leipzig. If Rochlitz's identification of the concertos is accurate, it would have been pointless to protect those concertos in such a manner, for neither was a new work; moreover, a manuscript copy of the Concerto in B flat major, K. 456, had been available for sale since 1785; and the Concerto in C major, K. 503, was written in 1786 and may even have been publicly performed by Marianne Willmann in March 1787.[93] Mozart did express concern about copyists to his father: 'I do ask you to have the four concertos copied at home, for the Salzburg copyists are as little to be trusted as the Viennese ... And as no one but myself possesses these new concertos in B♭ and D, and no one but *myself* and Fräulein von Ployer (for whom I composed them) those in E♭ and G, the only way in which they could fall into other hands is by that kind of cheating. I myself have everything copied in my room and in my presence.'[94] The closing line of the anecdote shows that Rochlitz was quick to promote the interests of his employer, Breitkopf & Härtel, who was then commencing the publication of Mozart's complete works, advertisements for which appeared in the *AmZ*.

Anecdote 14 (21 November 1798, cols. 114–16). Mozart was often reproached, as are many of today's philosophers, that he busied himself only with his own works and didn't trouble himself, or know about, what others also worthy of respect were accomplishing in his art. If this reproach is confined within reasonable limits one cannot wholly absolve M— of it. The fault for this lies less with him than with his circumstances, for he was almost constantly travelling or composing, and could only hear and get to know what was new or his own. Where, however, he happened upon something really good, whether it was old or new, then he was filled with joy and knew that it was to be treasured. But he was a sworn enemy of popular mediocrity, mindless imitations, thoughtless and empty mannerisms. He would exclaim, 'There is nothing in it!' of a work that had no spirit of its own. But he would not overlook anything in which there was even a faint spark of genius; he took young talented artists under his protection and did what he could for their education, recommendation, and pay. I could give many examples, were it not that, precisely because of their number, I believe that they must be well enough known. The ingratitude of so many of those from whom he deserved better did not discourage him in this; he overlooked the evil that was done to him as quickly as they did the favours he had extended to them. He was—if not the very first, one of the first who liberated Germans from the prejudice that the seat of true music was still to be found in Italy. Rather, he often declaimed against most new Italian composers, still more against Italian virtuosi, even more against Italian singers in Germany, and most of all against the current ruling Italianate musical taste in the capital cities—all that, after encountering these things on the spot. But music critics do him a great injustice when they assume that he valued only artful harmonies or learned work above all else. He approved of the most transparent music, if only it possessed a modicum of imagination and originality. For example, I heard him speak very favorably about Paisiello, whose works were very

[93] See *Dokumente*, 227, 252; *Documentary Biography*, 258, 286; Moreover, the B flat Concerto probably was written for Marie Theresia Paradies to perform. *Dokumente*, 210; *Documentary Biography*, 236–7. The Concerto in E flat major, K. 482, is incompletely notated in the 3rd movement, mm. 164–72.

[94] Mozart to Leopold Mozart, 15 May 1784; *Briefe*, iii. 313; *Letters*, ii. 876–7.

well known to him. For those who seek only light pleasures in music, one cannot surpass this man's compositions, he said. Among the older composers he particularly valued several of the older Italians, who are unfortunately now long forgotten; but he ranked Handel highest of all. He had such a thorough knowledge of the finest works by this in some fields still unsurpassed master—as if he had served all his life as director of the Academy for the Preservation of Ancient Music in London.

'Handel knew better than any of us what will make an effect', I heard him say once; 'where he wants to he strikes like a thunderstorm.'

This love for Handel went so far that he wrote many things in his style—which, however, he didn't permit to become known. Among his surviving papers there must be such works to be found. Indeed, in this respect he went even further than most of our contemporary connoisseurs would go: he treasured and loved not only Handel's choruses, but also many of his arias and solos.

'Although he sometimes rambles on, as was the style in his time,' he said, 'there is always something in it!' He fancied that he would set an aria in his own *Don Giovanni* in the manner of Handel and frankly inscribe this on his score. So far as I know, it was left out wherever the opera was performed. He seemed to have less regard for Hasse and Graun than these men deserved; perhaps he didn't know most of their works. Jomelli he valued very highly:

'This man is brilliant in his field', he said; 'That is why we'll probably have to give up trying to dislodge him among those who know something about it. But he shouldn't have gone beyond it and, for example, written church music in the archaic style.'

Of Martín y Soler, who at the time Mozart was in Leipzig had begun to enchant all music lovers, he judged, 'Much of his stuff is really very pretty: but in ten years no one will take any more notice of him.' A prophecy, which has almost exactly come true.

'However,' he added, 'nobody can do everything—joke and stagger, stimulate both laughter and deep feeling—and do everything equally well, as Joseph Haydn.'

Rochlitz does not explain under what circumstances he was so fortunate as to elicit this unique survey of Mozart's musical opinions. There is no reason to believe that Mozart actually voiced any of these views, which doubtless are Rochlitz's own. No special knowledge was needed for most of the vague details presented here. It was well known that Mozart, in addition to his aristocratic pupils, taught or encouraged such virtuosi as Barbara von Ployer, Johann Nepomuk Hummel, and (probably) Joseph Wölffl and such composers as Thomas Attwood, Joseph Eybler, and Franz Xaver Süssmayr.[95] The mutual hostility between Mozart and exponents of the dominant Italian style in Vienna is also well documented, as is Mozart's zeal for German opera. Rochlitz probably deduced these facts from Niemetschek, who repeatedly expressed an anti-Italian bias; for example, of the great stir created by *Die Entführung aus dem Serail*, he wrote that 'the cunning Italians soon realized that such a man might be a menace to their childish tinkling. Jealousy now reared its head with typical Italian venom'; and he praised Mozart because he 'dared to defy the Italian singers and to forbid all unnecessary embellishments, ornamentations, and trills'.[96] It is not true that Mozart wrote, but kept secret,

[95] See Heinz Wolfgang Hamann, 'Mozarts Schülerkreis: Versuch einer chronologischen Ordnung', *Mozart-Jahrbuch 1962/63*, 115–39.

[96] Niemetschek, *Leben*, 32, 58.

many works in the Handelian style; clearly, Rochlitz was unaware of Mozart's arrangements of major choral works by Handel. The 'Handelian' aria for *Don Giovanni* may be Elvira's Aria, 'Ah fuggi il traditor' (No. 8), but the story about a superscription on the score is invented. Vicente Martín y Soler (1754–1806) was a competitor of Mozart's in Vienna, where Da Ponte collaborated with him on three successful operas. Mozart quoted a tune from Martín's 'Una cosa rara' in the second finale of *Don Giovanni*: 'O quanto un sì bel giubilo'.

Anecdote 15 (21 November 1798, cols. 116–17). At the instigation of the late Doles, the then Cantor of the Leipzig Thomasschule, the choir surprised Mozart by a performance of the motet for double choir 'Singet dem Herrn ein neues Lied', by the father of German music, Sebastian Bach. Mozart knew this Albrecht Dürer of German music more by hearsay than by his own rarely available works. The choir had scarcely sung a few measures, when Mozart started; a few more, and he called out, 'What is this?' A few more measures and his entire soul seemed to be concentrated in his ears. When the singing ended, he called out with great delight: 'That is indeed something that one can take a lesson from!' He was told that this school, of which Sebastian Bach had formerly been Cantor, possessed the complete collection of his motets and had preserved them as a kind of relic. 'That's good, that is proper', he exclaimed, 'Show them to me!' Since they didn't have any scores for these vocal works, he read them from the transcribed parts—and now the hushed onlookers joyfully observed how eagerly Mozart sat down, spread the parts all around him, in both of his hands, on his knees, on the adjoining chairs, and how, forgetting everything else, he didn't rise again until he had looked through everything of Sebastian Bach's that was there. He asked for a copy, cherished it highly and—if I am not very much mistaken, the connoisseurs of Bach's compositions and of the Mozart Requiem (of which more in what follows)—particularly the great fugue Christe eleison—not fail to observe how Mozart's all-capable mind studied, valued, and fully understood the mind of that ancient contrapuntist.

Mozart's earlier knowledge of Johann Sebastian Bach was more extensive than Rochlitz believed, extending, perhaps, from his keyboard improvisations and performances of fugues and other 'difficult pieces' as a child to his merger of Bachian counterpoint and the sonata style in several of his Viennese masterworks.[97] He wrote to his father on 10 April 1782 of his regular attendance at Baron van Swieten's Sunday musicales, where 'nothing is played but Handel and Bach', and he wrote that he was 'collecting' fugues by members of the Bach family.[98] In his following letter he announced that van Swieten 'gave me all the works of Handel and Sebastian Bach to take home with me (after I had played them to him)'.[99] The musicales featured vocal as well as instrumental music and Mozart regularly 'accompanied at the fortepiano'.[100] Mozart's *Nachlaß* contained a copy of the *Clavierübung*, part II, including the Italian Concerto and the

[97] *Dokumente*, 41; *Documentary Biography*, 41. According to Mozart's sister, Mozart encountered 'various difficult works' in the older style in Paris and in London; *Dokumente*, 400; *Documentary Biography*, 456. For a thorough discussion, see Warren Kirkendale, *Fugue and Fugato in Rococo and Classical Chamber Music* (Durham, NC, 1979), 152–81.

[98] Letter of 10 Apr. 1782; *Briefe*, iii. 201; *Letters*, ii. 800.

[99] Letter of 20 Apr. 1782; *Briefe*, iii. 202; *Letters*, ii. 801.

[100] Joseph Weigl's autobiography, cited *Dokumente*, 446; *Documentary Biography*, 519.

French Overture in B major, along with the probably inauthentic 'Kleines harmonisches Labyrinth', BWV 591.[101] Nevertheless, it is doubtful that he knew many of Bach's choral works, such as the cantatas or motets. For performance at van Swieten's concerts in 1782, Mozart arranged five fugues from Bach's *Well-Tempered Clavier* for two violins, viola, and bass, K. 405.[102] The existence of a copy of Bach's motet 'Singet dem Herrn', BWV 225, with a notation in Mozart's hand, has been taken as confirmation of the essence of this anecdote.[103] It is assumed that Rochlitz was present at the Thomasschule on this occasion. Curiously, however, none of the anecdotes describes one of the highlights of Mozart's sojourn in Leipzig, his extended improvisation of the Thomaskirche organ before a large audience on 22 April.[104] In 1832, in a tardy attempt to repair his omission, Rochlitz suddenly remembered 'the liveliest, totally unanimous request' by Cantor Doles's house guests to hear Mozart play the organ, a request that 'he fulfilled the following afternoon at St Thomas's: one of the most beautiful memories of my entire life!'[105]

Anecdote 16 (5 December 1798, col. 145). Concerning those of his works which he himself valued, he was more severe than is customarily believed; perhaps also more severe than he wished others to be with them. Thus, for example, his judgement on the rightly much-loved *Entführung aus dem Serail*, which he wrote in his youthful years: in later years, he undertook a severe revision of this work in which he changed and especially abridged many things. I heard him play Konstanze's main aria in both versions and lamented some of the deleted passages:

'At the piano, it may go thus,' he said, 'but not at the theatre. When I wrote this, I enjoyed listening to myself too much and could never find a conclusion for it.'

Objections, even censure, he accepted gladly; only to one kind was he very sensitive and that was the kind that he most often ran into—censure for a too fiery spirit, an excessive fantasy. This sensitivity was also very natural: for if this censure was well founded, the individuality and excellence of his works was not worthwhile, and they lost all value in his eyes.

[101] *Dokumente*, 499; *Documentary Biography*, 590.

[102] Mozart's authorship of the string trio arrangements of six additional Bach fugues, K. 404a, is questioned in Kirkendale, *Fugue and Fugato*, 162.

[103] Ernst Fritz Schmid, 'Zu Mozarts Leipziger Bach-Erlebnis', *Neue Zeitschrift für Musik*, 111 (1950), 297–303 at 298. The notation reads: 'NB müßte ein ganzes orchestre dazu gesezt werden.' The manuscript is in the Bach holdings of the Gesellschaft der Musikfreunde in Vienna. Mozart's handwriting was confirmed by Alfred Einstein. A copy of Telemann's motet 'Jauchzet dem Herrn, alle Welt', BWV Anhang 160, formerly attributed to Bach, also belongs here, for it is by the same copyist and on the same paper. Schmid assumes that both manuscripts were 'remembrances of Mozart's stay in Leipzig'; ibid. 301. The notation suggests another possibility: that Mozart had the scores in connection with his work as an arranger for van Swieten's ancient-music society.

[104] Johann Friedrich Reichardt has left an account of this recital: 'On 22 April, without a prior announcement and without payment, he permitted everyone to hear him play the organ of the Thomaskirche. For a full hour he played beautifully and artfully for a large audience. The then organist, Görner, and the late Cantor Doles sat alongside him and pulled the stops. I myself saw him, a young modishly dressed man of medium size. Doles was wholly delighted by the performance and declared that . . . the old Sebastian Bach (his teacher) had risen again. With very good grace, and with the greatest agility, Mozart brought to bear all the arts of harmony, improvising magnificently on themes—among others on the chorale "Jesu meine Zuversicht"'; [Reichardt], 'Erinnerung an Mozarts Aufenthalt zu Leipzig', *Berlinische musikalische Zeitung*, 1 (1805), 132. See Jahn, ii. 484. Kirkendale, *Fugue and Fugato*, 161, attributes this unsigned anecdote to C. F. Michaelis.

[105] Rochlitz, *Für Freunde der Tonkunst*, iv. 308 n.

This tale of a revised version of *Die Entführung* is wholly fabricated. There is no reason to credit Rochlitz's account of Mozart's self-critical attitude; Jahn, who reprints the anecdote without addressing the issue of its accuracy, comments: 'This is the only instance known of such hypercriticism on Mozart's part.'[106]

Anecdote 17 (5 December 1798, cols. 146–7). I have often heard, even from people who claimed to have known Mozart, that he was not interested in anything in the world except music. Whether this accusation is a mortification for the artist I don't know; but I know this, that—it is not true. It arises from a superficial observation about his nature and it therefore rests on a misunderstanding, whose basis is that, for example, the beauties of nature and of arts other than his own etc., presented themselves to him and were absorbed by him only, so to speak, in the form of his own art.

Indeed, he was quite soon finished with the satisfaction, or rather the completion, of his physical needs of all sorts, without ceremonies and formalities; moreover, he tended to overlook their satisfaction, or rather dispatch indeed more so than was good for him. But what a beautiful and unselfish sense he had of friendship, benevolence, and so forth. In that regard several things have already been mentioned and considerably more could still be adduced if I were not concerned of being too prolix and if I had permission from the other individuals who are involved.

How much he worked out of pure kindness for mere acquaintances! how much more for his friends! How often did he sacrifice himself for poor travelling virtuosos! How often did he write concertos, of which he retained no copy, so that they would get a good reception and could find assistance! How often did he share bed and board etc. with them, if they came without money and acquaintances to Vienna. Ingratitude did not bother him; he would be indignant about it for just a few minutes. When he heard about the fraud committed by that stage manager whom I introduced in No. 11, all he said was: 'The scoundrel!'—and with that it was forgotten. What I pictured above, perhaps in overly obscure terms, about his individual but, I believe, true artist's—way of enjoying the beauties of nature and similar things, will become clear through this small character trait. When he travelled with his wife through beautiful country, he was attentive and silent as he gazed on the surrounding world without; his expression usually absent-minded and thoughtful, rather than cheerful and open, brightened by degrees and finally he began—to sing, or rather to hum, until finally he burst out:

'If I could only put this melody on paper!'

And when she said to him that that was probably possible, he responded:

'Yes, all worked out—, of course! It is a foolish thing that we must hatch our work indoors!'

I think that this small character trait is not wholly without significance for understanding the meaning of art.

This anecdote is primarily an unacknowledged gloss and commentary on a passage in Niemetschek: 'Music was his chief and favourite interest in life—and his whole thoughts and feelings were centred on it; all the powers he had acquired were directed to this one end. Is it surprising if he devoted too little attention to other matters? . . . Who can draw the line of his genius so exactly as to declare that Mozart had no talent or ability for anything but his music?'[107] There is no known instance of Mozart writing concertos to assist

[106] Jahn, i. 766 n. 54; Eng. trans., ii. 236 n. 53.
[107] Niemetschek, *Leben*, 66.

'poor travelling virtuosos'. We need not accept Rochlitz's implication that the story of Mozart's desire to represent nature in his music derives from Constanze Mozart. Einstein, who is one of the few biographers entirely to reject Rochlitz's anecdotes, describes this as 'just a well-meaning but irresponsible hoax, like the other anecdotes this inventive chatterer of Leipzig put into circulation after Mozart's death'.[108] Otherwise, this anecdote is composed of clichés and bland assertions.

Anecdote 18 (5 December 1798, 147–8). At the end of his life, when he already was suffering from a sick body and particularly from an extreme irritability of the nerves—which can, in my opinion, be easily accounted for on psychological grounds—he was generally very fearful, particularly disquieted by thoughts of death. Now he worked so much, so fast, therefore indeed at times also so carelessly, that it appeared he wanted to flee from the agonies of the real world into the creations of his spirit. His exertions often went so far that he not only forgot the entire world around him but, sank down totally enfeebled, and had to be brought to rest. Everyone saw that if things continued in this way he would soon be worn out. All the warnings of his wife and friends did not help, all attempts at diversion even less. To please his loved ones, he went with them on carriage rides and so forth; but he couldn't really participate in anything, rather he lived constantly in his fantasies, from which he occasionally awakened with a shudder in the face of death, which had already begun to squeeze his bones. His wife often secretly asked people whom he loved to visit him; they had to appear to surprise him when he was again sunk so deeply and so unremittingly in his works; he rejoiced, but remained sitting and working. They now had to make idle chatter, his wife joined in—but he didn't hear anything; they directed the conversation to him; he wasn't annoyed, he said a few words, but always continued writing.

For commentary, see No. 22.

Anecdote 19 (5 December 1798, cols. 148–9). At this time, he wrote his *Zauberflöte*, his *Clemenza di Tito*, his heavenly Requiem, and many smaller things, which are less familiar or even unknown. While he was writing the first-named of these works, day and night were the same to him when he was gripped by inspiration—he often suffered from weakness and fainting spells lasting several minutes. He liked the music to this opera, although he laughed about many passages that were most applauded.* It was, as everyone knows, performed in Vienna almost as often as Beaumarchais's *Marriage of Figaro* had been in Paris. However, because he was so enfeebled he could conduct it himself only about ten times. When it was impossible for him to be in the theatre himself, he would—so sadly—place his watch beside him and hear the music in his mind.

'Now the first act is ending—now the passage, "Dir, große Königin der Nacht", etc.', he would say. Then he was again gripped by the thought that soon it would all be over for him, and he shuddered.

* Note. With permission, I shall mention a trifle. Several reviews have called attention to the curious song of the armoured men, in particular the peculiar, eccentric transitions and especially the closing strains of the melody, heard while the pious hero, Tamino, leads his Pamina through fire and water; however, I have not yet found a review revealing the real point of this caprice, on which these strange things depend. For, to the sombre, melancholy accompaniment, the black-armoured men sing the ancient hymn: 'Aus tiefer Noth ich schrey' zu dir', note for note. [Corrected in note to No. 22: 'Ach Gott von Himmel sieh darein und laß sich doch erbarmen!]

For commentary, see No. 22.

[108] Albert Einstein, *Mozart: His Character, His Work* (London, New York, and Toronto, 1945), 15.

Anecdote 20 (5 December 1798, cols. 149–51). One day, as he sat lost in his melancholy fantasies, a carriage arrived and a stranger announced himself. He was shown in. An elderly, serious, stately man, of very dignified appearance, known neither to Mozart nor his wife, entered. The man began:

'I come to you as the messenger of a very distinguished man.'

'From whom do you come?' asked Mozart.

'The man does not wish to make himself known.'

'All right—what does he want of me?'

'Someone has died who was very dear to him and who will remain eternally so; he desires each year to celebrate the day of that person's death, and he asks you to compose for him a Requiem for that purpose.'

Mozart was deeply affected by this speech, by the shadow of mystery that was cast over the entire matter, by the solemnity with which the man spoke, by his own present frame of mind, and he promised to undertake the commission. The man continued:

'Work with all possible diligence: the man is a connoisseur.'

'So much the better.'

'There are no time restrictions.'

'Excellent.'

'How long will you require?'

Mozart, who was rarely in the habit of calculating time and money, replied:

'About four weeks.'

'I shall return at that time and fetch the score. How much do you want as your fee?'

Mozart answered him lightly:

'A hundred ducats.'

'Here they are', said the man; he placed the money on the table and departed. Mozart once again remained sunk in deep thought, did not hear what his wife said to him, and at last asked for pen, ink, and paper. He immediately began to work on the commission. With each measure his interest in the matter increased; he wrote day and night. His body could not endure the strain, and several times he collapsed in a faint from his labours. All exhortations to moderate his work were fruitless. After several days his wife took him to the Prater. He remained constantly quiet and turned inward. Finally he could deny it no longer—he was certain that he was writing this work for his own funeral. He could not rid himself of this idea; he worked, therefore, like Raphael on his *Transfiguration*, with the constant sense of his approaching death, and, like him, he himself made this declaration. And he spoke very curious thoughts about the unusual appearance and commission of this unknown man. If one tried to talk him out of these, he would fall silent, unconvinced.

For commentary, see No. 22.

Anecdote 21 (5 December 1798, cols. 151–2). Meanwhile the time neared for Leopold's departure to Prague for his coronation. Only rather late did the opera management think to turn to Mozart for a new opera to express the exuberant abundance of the celebrations and festivals. His wife and his friends were pleased by this, for it would provide him with distraction. Through their urging and because he was flattered by the honour, he undertook the composition of the proposed opera: *Clemenza di Tito* by Metastasio. The libretto was chosen by the Bohemian Estates. The time was, however, so short, that he was not able to write the unaccompanied recitatives himself, and had to deliver each section and have the voice-parts scored as soon as it was ready, so that he could not even revise it. He saw himself forced not being God, either to deliver such a wholly mediocre work or to rework only the main sections properly, the less interesting ones superficially and in accordance with the prevailing taste of the great mass. He rightly took the second approach. In doing so, he gave an indication of the soundness of his taste and of his knowledge of theatre and public alike, cutting the endlessly extended substitution plot by which Metastasio had filled almost the entire middle act, thereby speeding up the action, making the piece as a whole more concentrated and, therefore, more interesting by being completed in two acts of moderate length. In addition, in order to lend more variety to the monotonous, unchanging alternation of arias and recitatives, he melded together several such sections towards the end of the first act, and created out of them the great masterpiece, the finale of the first act—a composition which, as noted above, is modelled after a scene from his *Idomeneo*, but which displays so unmistakably and with such hair-raising intensity Mozart's Shakespearian, omnipotent power for the grand, the magnificent, the terrifying, the monstrous, the staggering, scarcely matched by the celebrated Finale of the first act of his *Don Giovanni*.

For commentary, see No. 22.

Anecdote 22 (19 December 1798, cols. 177–80). Ailing greatly, he travelled to Prague. The abundance of work stimulated the powers of his mind once again and focused them upon one point. The many diversions reanimated his courage, his senses were brightened to an easy gaiety—the little lamp flamed up once more before its brightness was extinguished. But these very efforts debilitated him and he was even sicker when he returned to Vienna, and now, completely satiated with the pomp and wastefulness, he was ravenous to take up the interrupted work on his Requiem. The four weeks, which he himself had specified, had in the mean time fled by, and hardly had he returned when the strange man appeared once more.

'I have not been able to keep my word', said Mozart.

'I know that', was the answer, 'You were right not to bind yourself. How much more time do you need?'

'Another four weeks—the work has become ever more interesting to me; it has led me much further than I had originally desired.'

'Very good. In that case you must also receive a greater payment. Here are another hundred ducats.'

'Sir, who has sent you?'

'The man wants to remain unknown.'

'Who are *you*?'

'That is unimportant. In four weeks I will be with you once again.'

With that he departed. Mozart tried to take note of where he went; but the people who were sent after him were either too careless or they were misled. In brief, they didn't succeed. Now Mozart was firmly convinced (I must confess this) that the man with the noble demeanour must have been an unusual being, one who stood in close connection with the world beyond, or who had been sent to him to announce his death. He decided now very seriously to establish a worthy monument to his name. With this idea in mind he kept on working and it is hardly any wonder that he brought such a perfect work to completion. During this work he often was overcome by lassitude and fainting spells. Even before the four weeks were over, he was finished, but he had also passed away.

From this work one can see that Mozart, like so many other great men, was unable to find a place for himself during his lifetime. It was he who sought to raise up religious music, which is presently debased, to where it belonged—on the throne above all other music. In this field he became the leading artist in the world—for those who have heard his last work, according to the unanimous judgement of all connoisseurs, even those who are not particularly fond of Mozart, place it among the most perfect that the most recent art has produced. His existing masses are mostly early works which he himself made nothing of and which he, justly for the most part, would rather have forgotten. I would gladly furnish a closer analysis of that masterpiece, but apart from the fact that such dissections are inadequate in themselves, because, for the most part, one is forced to adhere closely to the skeleton, at best to the flesh and the letter, whereas the spirit defies description because it is spirit and indescribable, I also fear that such representations might, like more extensive individual studies of Mozart's spirit in his works, of their idiosyncrasies and character, of the realms of his art where he rules brilliantly as a prince, and of others where he went astray, like an incautious pilgrim—such representations might fail to be of sufficient interest to a readership as diverse as one presupposes for a periodical. I therefore conclude for the time being the writing of these bagatelles which, if it is really desired, I can perhaps continue upon another occasion, with the hope that I have been successful in setting against the quantity of hateful, unkind, and revolting anecdotes still told of Mozart, even if people will not wholly give them up, several respectable ones, which, have the advantage of being true.*

* A footnote here contains a correction to No. 19 and restores a paragraph omitted from No. 12. These corrections have been noted at the appropriate places.

Anecdotes 18–22, inasmuch as they form a fairly connected narrative of events and compositions of Mozart's final year, may be considered as a unit. They include the most influential of Rochlitz's anecdotes, those dealing with the commission and composition of the Requiem. They tell a melodramatic story of Mozart's final illness and death, of an anonymous patron, his grey-clothed messenger, and of Mozart's belief that he was writing his own Requiem. Niemetschek had already given a detailed account of these same events, set down, he related, 'as he has often heard it from the lips of Mozart's widow . . .',[109] and Rochlitz's is nothing more than a melodramatic elaboration of the earlier account.[110] As usual, he avoids direct plagiarism, taking his source as a springboard, and adding numerous realistic touches for the sake of verisimilitude. Often, however, he makes errors of fact or of emphasis when he departs from his model, and these provide the clearest confirmation of the fictional method which he employed. Among these, we may cite the following examples:

1. Perhaps Rochlitz's most obvious blunder is his assertion that Mozart completed the Requiem before his death. And it may simply be set down to carelessness, for the fact that the Requiem had been completed by others after Mozart's death was an open secret,

[109] Niemetschek, *Leben*, 41–4, 44 n. 8.

[110] Jahn is mistaken to believe that they 'are both founded on statements by Frau Mozart'; Jahn ii. 570 n. 54; Eng. trans., iii. 286 n. 32. Jahn incorrectly asserts that Rochlitz claimed (in *AmZ* 1 (1798–1800), 178) to have 'questioned Mozart's widow at Leipzig in 1796 concerning the whole story of the Requiem . . .' (Jahn ii. 671; Eng. trans., iii. 366). Nissen reprints Niemetschek's rather than Rochlitz's account (Nissen, *Biographie*, 554–5, 563–4, 566).

known to many, including the composers who worked on it and the musicians who performed it at Jahn's Room in Vienna on 2 January 1793.[111] In that same year Schlichtegroll noted in print that Mozart had left it unfinished.[112] Moreover, Constanze Mozart did not try to deceive Niemetschek on this point; he reported: 'the messenger arrived and asked for the composition in its incomplete state, and it was given him'.[113]

2. Rochlitz asserts that Mozart received 200 ducats for the Requiem—an advance payment of 100 ducats and an additional 100 ducats as it neared completion. This would be equivalent to his highest fee for an opera. Niemetschek named no amount. According to Constanze Mozart, the 'purchase price' was 50 ducats.[114] It was not in her interest to exaggerate the amount of the honorarium, so she cannot be held responsible for Rochlitz's higher figure. Actually, Mozart was paid between 30 and 50 ducats as an advance; and, after his death, Constanze Mozart negotiated for herself a fee of 100 ducats, which reportedly was received from Count Walsegg upon delivery of the Requiem on 4 March 1792.[115]

3. Rochlitz pictures Mozart as ill, death-haunted, and suffering from weakness and fainting spells as early as when he started to write *Die Zauberflöte*, i.e., during the spring of 1791. But so simplified a view is belied both by Mozart's letters and his prodigious creativity during this period. His fatal illness commenced suddenly, on 20 November; according to Niemetschek, he also fell ill while in Prague, between 25 August and mid-September.[116] His notion that he had been poisoned postdates his return to Vienna.[117]

4. According to Rochlitz, Mozart began to write the Requiem before he started for Prague. However, it is reasonably clear, and was stated both by Niemetschek and Nissen (who presumably derived this information from Constanze Mozart), that the Requiem was begun only following his return from Prague. ('He was already sick in Prague', wrote

[111] Jahn, ii. 671; Eng. trans., iii. 366.

[112] Schlichtegroll, *Nekrolog*, 108.

[113] Niemetschek, *Leben*, 44.

[114] Constanze Mozart to B&H, 30 Jan. 1799; *Briefe*, iv. 310; Bauer-Deutsch-Eibl point out that this was 'solely the payment on account'; *Briefe*, vi. 514. In Jan. 1792, two newspapers reported that Mozart's fee was 60 ducats, one-half payable in advance and the remainder upon completion, which was agreed to take place within three months. See *Salzburger Intelligenzblatt* for 7 Jan. 1792, in Johannes Dalchow, Gunther Duda, and Dieter Kerner, *Mozarts Tod, 1791–1971* (Pähl, 1971), 78, and Eisen, *New Mozart Documents*, Doc. 119; *Zeitung für Damen und andere Frauenzimmer* for 18 Jan. 1792, *Dokumente*, 526; *Documentary Biography*, 439.

[115] Dalchow *et al.*, *Mozarts Tod*, 91, 109, and Anton Herzog's account, cited in *Mozart: Die Dokumente seines Lebens. Addenda und Corrigenda*, ed. Joseph Heinz Eibl (Kassel, 1978), 102; *Documentary Biography*, 552.

[116] 'While he was in Prague Mozart became ill and was continually receiving medical attention. He was pale and his expression was sad . . .'; Niemetschek, *Leben*, 43; it is only in the 1808 edition, following Rochlitz, that Niemetschek added a reference to Mozart's premonition of death: 'A foreboding sense of his approaching death seemed to have produced this melancholy mood—for at this time he already had the seed of the disease which was so soon to carry him off', cited in *Dokumente*, 439; *Documentary Biography*, 510. The earliest contemporary report reads: 'He returned home from Prague a sick man, and continued to get worse . . .' (*Musikalisches Wochenblatt* [Berlin] ?31 Dec. 1791, No. XII, 94, cited in *Dokumente*, 380; *Documentary Biography*, 432).

[117] Niemetschek, *Leben*, 43; Nissen, *Biographie*, 563. The Novellos, on the aged Constanze Mozart's authority, mistakenly place Mozart's idea that he had been poisoned 'some six months' before his death; *A Mozart Pilgrimage*, 125.

Nissen, 'before he worked on the Requiem . . .'.[118]) Plath's examination of the sketches and Tyson's analysis of the autograph's paper types do not contradict this assumption, Plath finding it 'highly probable that the first sketches fell in September 1791'.[119]

5. Rochlitz writes that Mozart conducted ten or more performances of *Die Zauberflöte*. He actually conducted it only twice: on 30 September and 1 October 1791.

6. Rochlitz attributes to Mozart the extensive revision of Metastasio's *La clemenza di Tito*. However, it was the Saxon court poet Caterino Mazzolà who reworked Metastasio's 1734 libretto.[120] Rochlitz probably relies on Niemetschek's account that the opera was written 'in the short space of eighteen days in Prague', and that most of the recitatives are 'in a pupil's hand'.[121] Niemetschek attributes the commission to the Bohemian Parliament, whereas Rochlitz attributes it to the opera management. In fact, impresario Domenico Guardasoni transmitted the commission from the Bohemian legislative assembly to Mozart.

One detail does imply that Rochlitz may have had an authentic source other than Niemetschek for his Requiem narrative: it is the messenger's remark that his employer wanted a Requiem to perform each year to commemorate the recent death of a beloved person. This detail, which is not in Niemetschek or any other published source, was eventually confirmed by an employee of Count Walsegg's.[122] If Constanze Mozart is to be believed, she did not know Walsegg's name, let alone anything about his motives for the commission. Perhaps she did know more than she allowed, but it is amply clear that she would not have revealed this knowledge either to Breitkopf & Härtel or to Rochlitz. In 1798 she even drafted an appeal to the anonymous patron to come forward, and it was only in January 1800, after Breitkopf & Härtel's announcement of its edition of the Requiem, that Count Walsegg actually revealed himself.[123] It seems likely that Rochlitz had no informant but was simply making a logical surmise.

In his footnote to No. 19, concerning the duet of the armoured men in *Die Zauberflöte* (Act II, sc. 26), Rochlitz misidentifies the Protestant chorale: it is actually 'Ach Gott, von Himmel sieh darein'. He himself corrects the error in a footnote to No. 22.

Anecdote [23] (April 1799, col. 480). The following little anecdote bears additional witness to how accurately Mozart, guided solely by his genius, viewed matters concerning the world of music. During his travels Mozart arrived at the house of the then —— von ——, who treasured music and whose now-famous son was a good piano player at the age of 12 or 13.

'But, Herr Kapellmeister,' said the boy, 'I myself would very much like to compose something; just tell me, how shall I begin?'

[118] Nissen, *Biographie*, 571.

[119] Wolfgang Plath, 'Über Skizzen zu Mozarts "Requiem"', *Bericht über den Internationalen Musikwissenschaftlichen Kongreß Kassel 1962*, ed. Georg Reichert and Martin Just (Kassel, 1963), 184–7 at 185; Alan Tyson, private communication cited in Richard Maunder, *Mozart's Requiem: On Preparing a New Edition* (Oxford, 1988), 206 n. 17.

[120] *Dokumente*, 354; *Documentary Biography*, 404; see also Jahn, ii. 575 and n. 2; Eng. trans., iii. 290 and n. 42.

[121] Niemetschek, *Leben*, 41, 82.

[122] Anton Herzog's account, cited in *Dokumente: Addenda und Corrigenda*, 102; *Documentary Biography*, 552.

[123] Constanze Mozart to B&H, 18 Oct. 1799 and 30 Jan 1800; *Briefe*, iv. 277–8, 309–10; *Dokumente*, 424; *Documentary Biography*, 488.

'No! No! You must wait!'

'But you were composing at an even younger age.'

'But I never asked! If you have the spirit to do it, it will drive you and torment you; one must simply do it and not ask anything about it.'

The boy was ashamed and sad at Mozart's harangue.

He said, 'I only mean, if you could suggest a book for me from which I could learn how to do it.'

Now Mozart answered in a friendlier tone, and stroked the boy's cheeks—'That doesn't amount to anything either! Here, here, and here (he pointed to his ear, head, and heart) is your school. If all is right there, then in God's name you will take pen in hand, and if it remains there—you may afterwards ask a knowledgeable person about it.'

This unsigned anecdote—which is not necessarily by Rochlitz—is obscure as to time and place as well as to the identity of the young musician. The samples of Mozart's advice to young musicians that are preserved in his correspondence scarcely resemble the shallow, sententious guidance offered here. 'Please give a special message to little Greta,' he writes his father in 1783, 'and tell her that when she sings she must not be so arch and coy . . . [O]nly silly asses are taken in by such devices'.[124]

Anecdote No. [24] (No. 1 of 'Anekdoten. Noch einige Kleinigkeiten aus Mozarts Leben,' March 1801, cols. 450–2). When he was in Leipzig, Mozart frequently and with great pleasure visited the house of Friedrich Doles, who was at that time Cantor of the Thomasschule in Leipzig, and his music-loving son. Here he completely relaxed and took nothing amiss, convinced that those present would in turn not be offended by him. He travelled from Leipzig to Dresden, intending to return from there after a few days. The evening before his departure he was dining with Doles and was in a very cheerful mood. His hosts were all the more saddened when it came time for Mozart to leave. 'Who knows if we will ever see each other again; leave me a line in your own handwriting.' Mozart, whose whole life was little but a succession of arrivals and leave-takings, and who therefore had become indifferent to both, made fun of what he called their 'sentimental' notion, and wanted to sleep, not write. At last, however he said: 'Now, papa, give me a piece of paper.' He tore it in half, sat down and wrote—for at most five or six minutes. Then he handed one half to the father and the other to the son. On the first sheet was a three-part canon in long notes, without words. We sang the music; the canon was excellent and very mournful. On the second sheet was similarly a three-part canon, also without words, but in quavers. We sang this and found it excellent and very droll. Now someone remarked that if the two were sung together, it would make up a six-voice whole. We rejoiced at this. 'Now the words', said Mozart, and he wrote under the first: 'Lebet wohl, wir sehn uns wieder' (Farewell, we shall meet again!) and under the second: 'Heult noch gar wie alte Weiber' (Go on howling like old women!). Thus we sang it through again, and one cannot describe what a funny and at the same time a deeply sublime-comic effect it had on us all. And, if I am not mistaken, upon him himself. Then with a somewhat wild mien he suddenly called out: 'Adieu, children!' and he was gone.

It is a shame that these pages should have been lost, since father and son soon died one after the other. I remember this bagatelle, not only because it gives us a new, small indication of the freedom with which his genius lived and moved in the abysses of harmony (for to solve such a prodigious arithmetical problem after a rich meal in only a few minutes means more than anyone

[124] Letter of 31 Oct. 1783; *Briefe*, iii. 292; *Letters*, ii. 860. 'Greta' was Margarethe Marchand.

can imagine who has not himself made a similar attempt), but also since it also permits us penetrate to a certain characteristic of his personality which I will have occasion to remark upon in what follows.

It is true, as Jahn phrased it, that Mozart 'was seized with a periodical canon-fever' and that he would often write comic multi-part canons 'on the spur of the moment'.[125] Unfortunately, however, the six-part double canon on the texts mentioned here does not survive in any form, although, solely on Rochlitz's authority, it has been graced with a sceptical Köchel listing K. Anh. 4 (572a). One would like to accept this delightful tale, but its author's scholarship has not earned for him the willing suspension of disbelief that one normally grants to sober eyewitnesses of important events even in the absence of supporting documentary evidence. Nevertheless, Jahn chose to believe that Rochlitz 'became intimate with [Mozart] at the house of their common friend Doles, and preserved a number of interesting traits, characteristic both of the man and the artist'.[126]

Anecdote No. [25] (No. 2 of 'Anekdoten. Noch einige Kleinigkeiten aus Mozarts Leben,' April 1801, cols. 493–4). In the same house there was an argument one evening, following Mozart's return, concerning the merit of several still living composers, particularly about one man, who had an obvious talent for comic opera, but had a post as a church composer. Father Doles, who in general was somewhat fonder of the operatic style in church music than might seem fair and justifiable, took that composer's part very vigorously against Mozart's persistent, 'There's nothing in it.' 'And I bet that you still haven't heard much of his music', answered Doles in an equally lively manner. 'You win', answered Mozart; 'but that isn't really the point; someone like that simply *cannot* produce anything decent of this sort! He has not the faintest idea about it. Lord, if the dear God had placed me in the church and with such an orchestra!' etc. 'Now, today you will look at one of his masses, and you will be reconciled to him.' Mozart took it with him and brought it back the following evening.

'Now, what do you say about the mass by —?'

'Very nice to listen to, but not in church! Don't take it badly, but I have set another text as far as the *Credo* in order to make it still better. No, no one needs to read it first. We will perform it straight away!'

He sat down at the fortepiano, passed out the parts for the four voices, and we had to sing while he accompanied. A more ludicrous performance of the mass had never been given. The main parts—Father Doles taking the alto, which he sang so excellently with a constant, earnest headshaking over the scandal of it; Mozart, his ten fingers fully occupied with the trumpet and drum parts, repeatedly said, 'Well, doesn't it go better like that?' And now the mischievous yet marvellously well-matched text, for example the brilliant Allegro of the Kyrie eleison: 'To hell with it; let's get on with it! (*Hol's der Geyer, das geht flink*)!' And at the close of the fugue of the Cum Sancto Spiritu in gloria Dei patris: 'These are stolen goods; the gentlemen shouldn't be offended! (*Das ist gestohlen Gut, ihr Herren nehmt's nicht übel*!).'

Although often free with praise of his colleagues, scathing references to music by other composers are not uncharacteristic of Mozart. A few examples: Clementi's sonatas 'are

[125] Jahn, ii. 64; Eng. trans., ii. 365.
[126] Jahn, ii. 483–4; iii. 228.

worthless'; Umlauf's opera is 'execrable'; Freyhold played 'a concerto of his own wretched composition'.[127] And, starting when he was a child, Mozart was known to mimic the idiosyncrasies of other composers.[128] The description of the prolific composer of operas who held a post as church composer more or less fits Dresden *Oberkapellmeister* Johann Gottlieb Naumann (1741–1801), who wrote numerous operas and was a prolific composer of church music; in the Dresden Court chapel on 13 April, a few days before arriving in Leipzig, Mozart heard a mass by Naumann, which he described as 'very mediocre'.[129]

Anecdote No. [26] (No. 3 of 'Anekdoten. Noch einige Kleinigkeiten aus Mozarts Leben,' April 1801, cols. 494–7). It lay in his excitable nature to be capricious and not uncommonly, in so far as his emotional states were concerned, to go from one extreme to the other in a matter of seconds. After continuing in such unfettered good humour for some time and speaking, as frequently, in so-called doggerel rhyme (*Knittelvers*),* he went to the window and—as was his habit—played the window-sill as though it were a keyboard, and daydreamed, giving only listless, almost unconscious answers to what was said to him. The conversation about church music grew more wide-ranging and more serious. What an infinite loss, someone said, that so many great musicians, especially of the past, have shared the fate of the old painters; that is, they were mostly obliged to direct the powers of their genius to Church-imposed subjects, which were not merely barren but spiritually deadening. Completely changed in mood and filled with sadness, Mozart at this point turned to the others and said (at least, this is the sense, if not the manner of it): This is some more of the usual mindless chatter about the arts! Perhaps for you *enlightened* Protestants, as you call yourselves when you remember your religion, there may be some truth in such a statement; I cannot say. But for us, it is a different matter. You have no conception of what it means: *Agnus Dei, qui tollis peccata mundi, dona nobis pacem*, etc. But if someone like myself, who from earliest childhood was introduced into the mystical sanctuary of our religion; if someone, not yet knowing where to go with his dark yet urgent feelings, full of heartfelt inner passion, sits through the holy service without really knowing what his purpose was, and leaves with his heart lightened and exalted without really knowing precisely what has happened to him; if you call blessed those who kneeled down to the touching sounds of the *Agnus Dei* and received communion, while the music at the same time spoke: *Benedictus qui venit* etc. joyfully and softly from the hearts of those kneeling, then it is a different matter. Of course, this admittedly tends to get lost as one goes through life on this earth; but—at least in my case—if one looks once again at those words heard a thousand times over with the intent of setting them to music, all of this revives and stands before you, and moves your soul.

He now went on to describe some scenes of that kind, dating from his earliest childhood years in Salzburg, followed by his first trip to Italy, and he dwelt with particular interest on the anecdote which tells of the Empress Maria Theresa asking him, as a 14-year-old youngster, to compose the *Te Deum* for the inauguration of—I do not remember, a large hospital or some similar charitable institution—and to direct its performance himself, leading the entire Imperial Chapel. Imagine how I felt!—imagine how I felt!—he exclaimed over and over again. Such things

[127] Letters of 7 June 1783, 5 Feb. 1783, and 20 Feb. 1784; *Briefe*, iii. 272, 254, 301; *Letters*, ii. 850, 839, 867.

[128] See, for example, Daines Barrington's 1769 'Account of a Very Remarkable Young Musician', *Dokumente*, 89; *Documentary Biography*, 98.

[129] Mozart to Constanze Mozart, 16 Apr. 1789; *Briefe*, iv. 82; *Letters*, ii. 922. Translation amended.

never come back! One drifts aimlessly through an empty, everyday existence. He continued, grew embittered, drank a lot of strong wine, and did not utter a coherent word for the remainder of the evening.

I mention this last, trusting that it will not be used against this worthy human being, but rather that it may provide a deeper insight into his whole personality, and particularly into the reasons for his way of life as an adult which admittedly helped to destroy him. The ideal dwelt in his bosom with powerful force and warmth, and it stirred in him that exalted, unceasing yearning and striving that tormented *him*; but also the sense of despair that one would never be able to find, because one had never previously found, that violent self-anaesthetizing because one nevertheless cannot kill one's need to find. His undirected mind believed it could attain the object of his longing, and could attain it *outside himself*; his spirit, left to itself, remained incapable of abandoning the dark ideas which make him a great artist yet a confused human being. Like all people endowed with an excessive amount of imagination and sensuality, he dreamed his own heaven (could such a thing exist here) in the bygone days of his childhood, without being able to raise himself to cling to the idea of a new and purer heaven in the future; and yet he was far too vigorous to stand still, as so many do, enjoying his laments and his sentimental lassitude while contemplating his loss; he wanted to arise and to ascend without knowing what or where; he went astray, felt himself deceived and repulsed. This made him so unhappy that he wanted to forget himself, unless it so happened at such moments that his art took him under her protective and soothing wings. That he thereby would almost everywhere be misunderstood is quite clear. How few can understand such things; and as far as the others are concerned, how many took the time and the trouble to reflect on the relationship between the often vulgar, disordered, and (why not say it outright?) foolish aspects of his behaviour, and the depth, greatness, and sublimity of his art?

For the rest, I do not think it also necessary to explain that in these remarks by Mozart about church music, etc., which I have abridged, and which it took a rather long conversation to extract from him, there lies much that is true and pure, much that might give rise to many and varied profound remarks, and that confirms once more that Mozart never really found his place, and, just when he was *perhaps* about to reach it, stern Fate cut his life's thread.

* This was one of the whimsies in which he readily and with quite extraordinary facility indulged, both in speech and in writing. Just as one who is entirely uncultivated in rhetoric will be apt, without being aware of it, to use all the so-called figures of speech in an animated conversation, so it went with him concerning the rules of versification, of which he was completely ignorant. For example, he would always change metre according to subject-matter and so on. His skills were so advanced that he could write entire letters *with an echo*. One such letter, extending over three quarto pages, can be found among those of his papers collected after his death. I would feel free to communicate it were it not as naughty as it is witty.

Rochlitz manages to achieve in a few lines what Leopold Mozart could not accomplish in a lifetime of written and spoken exhortation—to implant in Mozart an unswerving reverence for and conscientious observance of the Church's sacraments of confession and communion. Improbably, Rochlitz here has Mozart speaking in the language of emergent Romantic Catholicism *à la* Wackenroder, recalling 'the mystical sanctuary of our religion' and the 'dark, yet urgent feelings' of those blessed souls who received communion. Mozart was indeed a Catholic, and not infrequently an observant one, but neither in his correspondence with his father, which contains many references to religious matters, nor in reports by his contemporaries is there anything to suggest such extravagant notions. Rather, Mozart's Catholicism—like his father's—abjured both mysticism and superstitious reverence for ritual.[130] Rochlitz is not quite secure in his grasp of theological matters: neither the Agnus Dei nor the Benedictus are sung during communion.

Concerning Mozart's 'first trip to Italy' and his *Te Deum* for Empress Maria Theresa in 1768, Rochlitz need not have strained quite so hard to recall the details, for he got these from Schlichtegroll or from Schlichtegroll's source, Mozart's sister; the former wrote: 'For the inauguration of the Waisenhauskirche he was employed to compose the *Offertorium* and a trumpet concerto and although but twelve years of age [Rochlitz says he was fourteen by mistake and calls the work a *Te Deum* to assure us of his imperfect powers of recall], he conducted the solemn concert in the presence of the Imperial Court.'[131] This derives from Nannerl Mozart's Reminiscences: 'At the consecration of the Orphanage Church on the Landstrasse this 12-year-old boy conducted the service in the presence of the imperial court. (The son set the service, the offertory and a trumpet concerto for it.)'[132] The Orphanage Church was consecrated on 7 December 1768. There is some dispute about which works were composed for it; most probably they are the *Missa [solemnis]*, K. 47a/139, an *Offertorium*, K. 47b (lost), and a Trumpet Concerto, K. 47c (lost).

Rochlitz, who offers no details (except for the reference to Henriette Baranius in No. 1), seems to have derived his report about the 'vulgar, disordered, and (why not say it outright?) foolish aspects of [Mozart's] behaviour' from Schlichtegroll and Niemetschek, and perhaps even from the sensational press, which, in the years immediately following Mozart's death, published accounts of his alleged promiscuity and dissipation. In 1793, Schlichtegroll referred bluntly to Mozart's 'overwhelming sensuality and domestic disorder (*überwiegenden Sinnlichkeit und häuslichen Unordnung*)', and he described Constanze Mozart as 'a worthy wife, who tried to deter him from many follies and debaucheries (*Thorheiten und Ausschweifungen*)'.[133] Niemetschek took note of the 'many ugly tales of his frivolity and extravagance', attributing them to Mozart's enemies and to 'tainted sources'; but he referred opaquely to 'inclinations which are not found in ordinary persons', he was ready to acknowledge that 'Mozart was a man, therefore as liable to human failings as anyone else', and he told how Mozart confided to his wife 'even his petty sins' and how 'she forgave him with loving-kindness and tenderness'.[134] Presumably, these and similar tales circulated via the musical grape-vine as well. The related notion of self-destructive tendencies in Mozart—'his way of life as an adult which admittedly helped to destroy him'—is, I believe, original with Rochlitz here and in No. 18, where a despairing Mozart flees from life into fantasy and into his art.

[130] See, for example, Einstein, *Mozart*, 77–82; Karl Hammer, 'Mozarts geistige Welt', *Acta Mozartiana*, 13 (1966), 4–6; id., 'Kirche und Welt bei Mozart', *Acta Mozartiana*, 17 (1970), 7–17; Abert, ii. 19–20.

[131] Schlichtegroll, *Nekrolog*, 100.

[132] Nannerl Mozart's Reminiscences, in *Dokumente*, 402; *Documentary Biography*, 458.

[133] Schlichtegroll, *Nekrolog*, 110.

[134] Niemetschek, *Leben*, 71, 72.

By the time this anecdote was published Rochlitz already had access to materials sent by Constanze Mozart to Breitkopf & Härtel for use in the projected biography. That may explain the authentic references to the 'verses with an Echo'; to 'doggerel verses (*Knittelvers*)', and to Mozart's obscene letters. Re the latter, on 28 August 1799, Constanze alluded to 'the admittedly tasteless but very witty letters to his cousin', which, she believed, 'were deserving of mention' even if they 'couldn't be printed in their entirety'.[135] Re Mozart's poetic inclinations, Niemetschek wrote, 'He often wrote verse himself; mostly only of a humorous kind.'[136]

Anecdote No. [27] (No. 4 of 'Anekdoten. Noch einige Kleinigkeiten aus Mozarts Leben', May 1801, cols. 590–6). It is well known that benign Nature endowed Mozart with a generous supply of wit. That he often displayed this treasure in strange, not particularly well-chosen ways, was inevitable, for *apart* from his art and that with which it was immediately connected, he had an insufficiently diverse set of ideas, and hence, insufficient *material* from which to form, to sharpen and practise his wit. However, in his music—how rich was the outpouring from the fountain of merriment! When, for example, he improvised at the fortepiano: how easy it was for him to work a theme, first in a droll way, then with such pompousness, once again with biting virtuosity and breakneck speed, or, once again with such pleading and agony, and so on, that he was capable of doing whatever he wished with his audience—and that even when an unfavourable fate placed him in front of the most downright grumblers (but not quite lacking in musical culture)! That, specifically that, was perhaps never granted in such measure to any pianist, either before or after him. I know the playing of most of the excellent virtuosos on this instrument since Mozart (with the exception of Beethoven); I have heard so much excellent playing—but nothing even resembling that inexhaustible wit.

However, such things are not easily depicted in words. More to the purpose: not seldom, he was wont to satirize—without real malice—those other composers, virtuosi, and singers of note whom he considered to be destructive to art and good taste; his musical parody tended to exceed the bounds of playfulness when he came to certain Italian artists, along with composers who had written for them and in their style, who were at that time very highly praised. To be sure, some of them had indeed caused him considerable trouble. So, on the spur of the moment, he directed from his piano entire large-scale operatic scenes in the manner of this or that colleague, to which no one could remain indifferent! Mozart did not take the time to write such things down; however, he did commit at least one such grand bravura scene for the *prima donna* to paper. Probably this singular caricature piece is to be found among his posthumous papers, which have not yet been made known. It is an artfully woven and, at first glance, very seriously intended totality, concocted from favourite ideas of Messrs Alessandri, Gazzaniga, and whatever their names may be. The text was also written by Mozart himself. It consisted of an aggregation of those grandiloquent or mad flourishes and exclamations with which the Italian librettists love to heap on everything, and these gaudy beads were arranged in an extremely ludicrous way. *Dove, ahi dove son io?* called the noble princess, more or less. *Oh Dio! questa pena! o prince . . . o sorte . . . io tremo . . . io manco . . . io moro . . . O dolce morte . . .* At that point, like a bombshell in the house, the most out-of-the-way chord resounds, and the jolted fair one sings: *Ah, qual contrasto . . . barbare*

[135] Constanze Mozart to B&H, 28 Aug. 1799; *Briefe*, iv. 269.
[136] Niemetschek, *Leben*, 67.

stelle... traditor... carnefice... And so the piece proceeds over the collapsing bridges of *Imponendo, colla parte, vibrando, rinforzando, smorzando*, and so forth, with their multiple barbs and snags.

However, it might be of greater interest and at the same time increase the appreciation of Mozart's best-known works, if I added some examples from these in support of my contentions. I will not mention Leporello from *Don Juan*, that perfect creature of musical wit and of the most cheerful spirits, because no further allusion is needed, and, moreover, Leporello is all too well known. Considerably less well known, but hardly less perfected, is the musical character of Don Alfonso, the so-called philosopher in *Così fan tutte*. He, too, with all his amusing individuality, is such a well-rounded and consistent character that he is sufficient reason to regret that the work, as it stands, is hardly suited for the German stage. A German-speaking poet, highly knowledgeable in music, would need to go at it from scratch and, relying more on the music than on the Italian text, create something else in its place. The German public, no matter where, is too serious-minded and not sufficiently light-hearted to appreciate this kind of comedy; and most of our singers, male or female, are much too inadequate as actors, and, above all, do not possess the grace, clownishness, and bravado for the Italian burlesque genre, especially when it is pushed as far as it is here. As clearly defined as Don Alfonso is in the music, one is at a loss to explain in a comprehensible way what he represents in a few words: a quick, round, compact, nasty little man, who, through many years' experience, learned to laugh about many a great thing coveted by the world at large, and instead, with a certain kind of seriousness, turned his attention to various small things that are despised. To the spectator, this appears much less serious than comical. In conveying the latter feature, Mozart succeeded particularly well. It simply is not possible for the old man to be serious, and even when sharing the young woman's sorrow, or trying to appear scared to death at the end, it is and remains fun, so that his cry of *Misericordia*, towards the end, is truly no less amusing than his earlier, precocious *Amico, finem lauda*. To go into further detail is not possible precisely because the whole work is so well rounded. However, I should still like to point out a few additional relevant features from other roles of this opera. I have still another, special reason for mentioning the very first lines of the overture. One critic, not without merit and reputation, once wrote that this beginning was specifically a proof of the indiscriminate way in which Mozart understood his ideas: for here there was a noble invitation, followed immediately by a very commonplace little phrase that was to be played with everyday demeanour, followed in turn, and again without pause, by a merry, carefree Allegro, and so forth. What is really going on here? Well. The title: *Così fan tutte*, which is known to be a proverb, is here utilized as such. Two lovers are in a lively dispute with the philosopher because the eternal cynic refuses to concede that nothing on earth could cause the girls to be unfaithful to them. A plan is worked out, the experiment is successful, but it is the philosopher's advantage. The lovers are furious, the old man preaches a consoling sermon to them, succeeds in calming them down, restores their faith in humanity, and concludes in his earlier mood: *Ripete tel con me: così fan tutte*. As good humour overtakes them, they join in: *Così fan tutte*. Peace sets in, and the librettist aptly places this motto at the head of the entire work. Mozart does not lag behind. In the later spot, the proverb is sung in choral style, and earlier, in the overture, after a few imposing measures that lead the listener to expect something of the greatest significance, the melody—the signature of the entire work—appears, sung as bluntly as if it had been trumpeted from the tower. Can one fail to recognize this? Could it be done more prettily?

During the admirable first Finale of this opera, where the despairing lovers pretend to have taken poison, the stage is filled with buffoonery and the most comical wit; but I should have to provide a copy of the music to make this manifest. However, I might perhaps succeed, even without such a copy, if we turn to a scene from the second Finale. After peace has been re-established and everything restored *in integrum*, the men appropriately tease their damsels about what had happened. In particular, one of them impresses upon his beloved the scene where she accepted the first present from the second, disguised lover, and how Despina, posing as a physician, manipulated the poisoned ones back to health, and so forth. Mozart here takes the principal themes from the accompaniment, elaborates them further on in these scenes during the events, rearranges them in random order, and out of this creates a new, joyful section, in which the careful listener will remark once more all the music from those scenes, but now seen from the opposite perspective. If anyone fails to notice this, it is not Mozart's fault.

I should be delighted to present still more subtleties of this kind from that opera as well as from *Figaro*. However, I have to limit myself to just a few words about the latter. *Figaro*, as is well known, is no fit subject for opera, for the very reason that it is an excellent comedy. Taken by themselves, the characters of the Count and the Countess are, in my opinion, the most accomplished ones (from a musical point of view). Figaro, naturally, was destined to lose out in an art which cannot represent ideas. The same goes for Susanna. Cherubino's sweet, frivolous, quite tender nature was not *destined* to be diminished, but it did not quite fit with Mozart's individuality. Cherubino became more mature—if you will, more weighty; Susanna more serious, Figaro more German. But the way the composer succeeded in shaping the characters as they are *now*—particularly in the exceptionally rich and detailed ensembles: that is, and remains, an entirely masterful achievement. As an example of what I am referring to in particular, however, I shall limit myself to the small duet between Susanna and the Count (A minor: *Crudel, perchè finora*) from Act 3. The Countess had promised Susanna to sneak into the garden that evening wearing her (Susanna's) clothes, there to await her own husband. At this point, Susanna appears and responds to the Count, stating that she will yield to his wishes and meet him under the unfortunate chestnut trees. I will not mention the absolutely magnificent musical characterization of the Count in this brief passage, the mounting of his desire, how he accordingly presses the poor girl with ever greater urgency, and so on. That is not really our subject, and it is obvious to everyone who is sensitive to it. But so long as the Count asked her in a cunning and mistrustful tone, Susanna has been replying firmly, if a little bashfully, that she will come. Now, the Count can no longer conceal his burning impulses (Mozart switches to *major*), so the questions start anew. Now the girl becomes more anxious and pensive. To his insistent eagerness: *Dunque verrai?* a worried *No* escapes her lips. *No*?—explodes the count, and she, regaining her composure and correcting herself, responds: *Sì*, and so forth. But this once more confuses the oft-deceived Count. He starts again, with new suspicions: *Dunque verrai? non mancherai?* but his outburst has amused her; deliberately and flirtatiously, she roguishly imitates herself in response to the last question: *Sì. Sì*. Understandably, the Count erupts once more and Susanna, laughing, now reassures him. Of all this there is not a syllable in Beaumarchais, let alone in the Italian librettist. It is all Mozart's. It is not his fault that our average Susannas fail to understand him and that all this subtle wit usually is lost in ordinary performances. However, this reproach falls less upon those who sing Susanna than on those music directors of whom it is fair to ask that they understand such things and whose job it is to point out such things to singers during coaching and rehearsals.

The lengthiest of Rochlitz's anecdotes requires a brief commentary, for the author has run out of fuel, reduced to elaborating motifs from his own, earlier anecdotes. As in No. 5, we hear once again of Mozart's improvisatory powers; as in No. 25, we learn of his sharp sense of humour, his penchant for musical parody, his acerbic satires of colleagues, composers, and virtuosi, especially Italians (see No. 14). Needless to say, no trace of his 'grand bravura scene' *alla Italiana* has been located. The balance of the anecdote is given over to Rochlitz's opinions of *Don Giovanni*, *Figaro*, and *Così fan tutte*. Of Rochlitz's references to the latter opera, 'Misericordia' is in the second Finale (No. 31); 'Amico, finem lauda' is in the Quintet (No. 6); 'Ripete tel con me' is in the Cavatina (No. 30). The small duet from *Le nozze di Figaro*, 'Crudel, perchè finora', is in Act 3 (No. 16). The Italian librettist is Da Ponte.

As an addendum to his *Verbürgte Anekdoten*, Rochlitz for the first time made reference to Niemetschek's life of Mozart and reprinted three excerpts from it. He wrote:

Author's addendum (19 December 1798, cols. 180–1). I feel all the more justified to break off here, because, after part of these anecdotes had already appeared in print, a recently published book came into my hands:

Leben des K. K. Kapellmeisters Wolfgang Gottlieb Mozart, von Franz Niemtschek, Professor in Prag. Prag in der Herrlischen Buchhandlung 1798.

The author had the same primary intention as I did, and he worked from the same available sources—however, he apparently had no personal contact with Mozart, while he in turn had access to those surviving documents that were lacking to me. A few, but only a few, of the anecdotes published here can, as a matter of course, be found there as well. I subscribe for the most part to the author's judgement concerning Mozart's merit and individuality as an artist, although I am not wholly in agreement concerning the loftiness and grandeur, and even the excellence, that he regularly detects in the arias from *Clemenza* and similar works. Such differences of opinion over things naturally do not alter in the slightest the respect that I have for Herr N. For those of my readers who may not have an opportunity to read that little book, I select some anecdotes, citing them mostly in the words of their author, for they confirm what I myself have said about Mozart in the foregoing. Since it is the concern of the author to disseminate truth as widely as possible, I hope he will not be discontented about my having done so.[137]

Naturally, Niemetschek was not wholly pleased by this notice. Against all the evidence in Niemetschek's book, Rochlitz had asserted that Niemetschek was not personally acquainted with Mozart; he had failed to mention Constanze Mozart's close co-operation with the author; and he had tried to explain away the overlaps between Niemetschek's work and his own, without crediting the earlier book as his source. In a letter of 1799 Niemetschek took polite exception to Rochlitz's condescending under-valuation of his work: 'I am satisfied with Rochlitz's remarks about my biography,' he

[137] In cols. 181–3, Rochlitz reprints three passages from Niemetschek: (1) The story of Mozart and Thomas Linley; (2) Emperor Joseph's remark to Mozart, 'Zu schön für unsre Ohren, und gewaltig viel Noten, lieber Mozart!' along with the composer's response; (3) Haydn's (perhaps inauthentic) letter in praise of Mozart's genius to Herr Roth of Prague.

wrote to Gottfried Härtel, 'but I must say that I was indeed associated with Mozart, though not for a long time, during his last stay in Prague.'[138] His letter also called attention to several of Rochlitz's most blatant errors, namely his assumption that Mozart completed the Requiem and that *Idomeneo* was composed for Constanze Weber.[139] These corrections were never acknowledged in the *AmZ*.

In light of the clear evidence that a majority of Rochlitz's anecdotes derive or are elaborated from Niemetschek's biography of Mozart, the claim that the book became known to him only after he had commenced publication of the *Verbürgte Anekdoten* is disingenuous. Niemetschek's book had been published anonymously (as 'by N**') at Prague as early as 1797[140] and appeared under its author's full name, with a dedication to Joseph Haydn, in that same city in 1798. Moreover, Niemetschek was engaged by Härtel as an adviser to his ongoing Mozart edition and a lengthy correspondence between them started in September 1798 or earlier.[141] Lastly, on 6 October 1798, Härtel referred to Niemetschek in a letter to Constanze Mozart: 'We ask you to please let us know if, apart from Herr Niemetschek in Prague, there is anyone else busy writing the biography of your husband.'[142] Thus, Breitkopf & Härtel—and surely, therefore, Rochlitz, the editor of its house journal—knew of Niemetschek's work before the series of anecdotes was published. (To complicate matters somewhat, Hitzig mistakenly assumed that Rochlitz actually used anecdotes furnished by Niemetschek in the preparation of the *Verbürgte Anekdoten*; but this assumption is contradicted by the clear derivation of so many anecdotes from Niemetschek's published book and by Niemetschek's corrections of Rochlitz.[143])

Niemetschek's book was of prime utility to Rochlitz, for he did not use documentary sources. There is not a single citation from a letter, written memoir, autograph score, or other original document in any of the *Verbürgte Anekdoten*. Further, he names no informants and in some instances even avoids telling us when or where the events allegedly occurred. This gives an impressive Gothic cast to several of the anecdotes but does little to enhance our confidence in their reliability. So persuasive did Rochlitz find Niemetschek's ideas and descriptions that it remained virtually the exclusive published source of inspiration for his Mozart journalism, here as well as in the supposed letter from Mozart to 'Baron von . . .' about his creative process. Although he knew and discussed Schlichtegroll's *Nekrolog*, Rochlitz did not favour it as a source of material: only

[138] Letter of 1799, cited in Wilhelm Hitzig, 'Die Briefe Franz Xaver Niemetscheks und der Marianne Mozarts an Breitkopf & Härtel', *Der Bär: Jahrbuch von Breitkopf & Härtel auf das Jahr 1927* (Leipzig, 1928), 101–13 at 106.

[139] Ibid. 105.

[140] 'N**', *Lebensbeschreibung des k. k. Kapellmeisters Wolfg. Amad. Mozart* (Prague, 1797).

[141] Hitzig, 'Die Briefe', 101–10.

[142] B&H to Constanze Mozart, 6 Oct. 1798; *Briefe*, iv. 215. She replied that there is 'nothing, outside of my friend Niemetschek's and the *Nekrolog*, the latter of which I am not pleased with'. Letter of 27 Oct. 1798; *Briefe*, iv. 219.

[143] Hitzig, 'Die Briefe', 105. This issue cannot wholly be settled because the correspondence was destroyed during World War II.

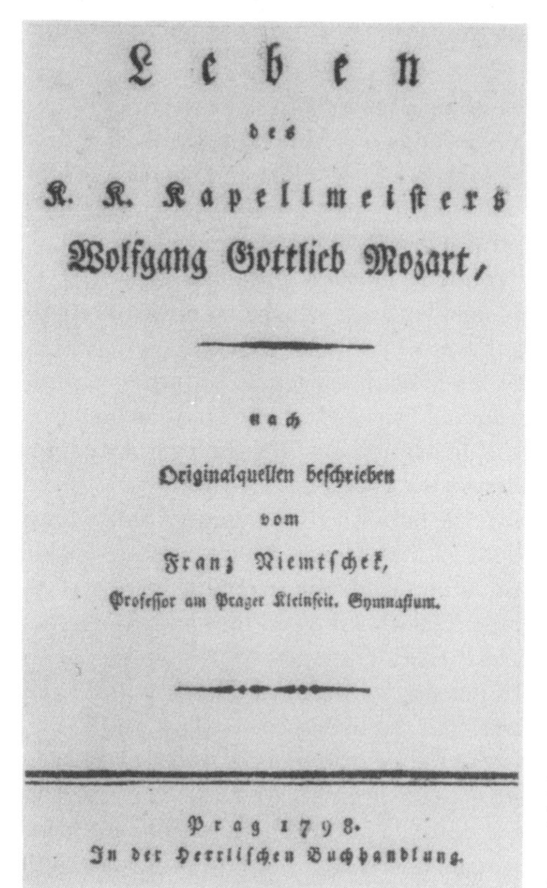

Leben

des

K. K. Kapellmeisters

Wolfgang Gottlieb Mozart,

nach

Originalquellen beschrieben

vom

Franz Niemtschek,

Professor am Prager Kleinseit. Gymnasium.

Prag 1798.

In der Herrlischen Buchhandlung.

FIG. 4. Title-page of Franz Niemetschek, *Leben des k. k. Kapellmeisters Wolfgang Gottlieb Mozart* (Prague, 1798).

two or three passages—Mozart's anger at a restless audience in No. 5, the reference to Mozart as a child at the end of No. 12, and his role in connection with the 1768 dedication of the Orphanage Hospital in No. 26—appear to be derived from it. In the introduction to his *Verbürgte Anekdoten*, Rochlitz adopted a critical, even hostile attitude towards the *Nekrolog*. Without offering details, he made reference to the 'apparent falsehoods in such books', raising questions about the 'method of presentation' and 'the goal of the narrator—whether simply to entertain or to instruct'.[144] Schlichtegroll's sober recital perhaps did not buttress or lend itself to Rochlitz's sentimental and melodramatic views of Mozart; furthermore, it dealt primarily with Mozart's childhood and youth, having little to say about his Vienna years, his death, and late masterworks, all of which were of greatest interest to Rochlitz. And, inasmuch as Breitkopf & Härtel was then in negotiation with Constanze Mozart for the publication of Mozart's music and wanted her co-operation in the preparation of a biography as well, Rochlitz may have wanted to avoid

[144] *AmZ* 1 (1798–9), 10 Oct. 1798, 18.

using a book which frankly adopted the viewpoint of Mozart's father and sister and which contained a personal criticism of Mozart's wife.[145]

To recapitulate, the Rochlitz Mozart anecdotes fall into several distinct categories. In the first group are the many which patently are reworkings of Niemetschek or which take Niemetschek's material as a point of departure for more or less imaginative elaboration. These carry with them whatever degree of authenticity may attach to Niemetschek's original presentation; however, we need to strip away Rochlitz's colourful accretions, elaborations, and disguises, for it is surely prudent in such instances to revert to Niemetschek's earlier account. A second group includes those which contain gross errors or inconsistencies. These may be presumed to have been fabricated, except where they are misreadings of existing materials, and may safely be discarded. In a third group are those which have no apparent prior source, including those which may have been based on personal observation or transmitted to Rochlitz by others. The Leipzig anecdotes describing events at the Thomaskirche, rehearsals, the Akademie of 12 May 1789, and friendly gatherings at private homes in his honour, fall into this category. As we have seen, at least one of them—the story in Anecdote 12 that Mozart broke his shoe-buckle while stamping out the tempo for the orchestra—is confirmed by an independent source, unless Jahn was taken in by the old Leipzig musician who showed him a broken shoe-buckle that he said he had preserved as a Mozart relic. These anecdotes often contain quite specific details—Mozart reading Bach, conversing with Cantor Doles, writing and performing musical spoofs, rehearsing musicians, and the like.

Rochlitz may actually have been present on the public occasions of Mozart's Leipzig visit, or he may have spoken to others who were actually present. We know that Rochlitz (born 1769, the son of a Leipzig tailor) had been enrolled at the Thomasschule from the fall of 1782; there he studied singing, clavier, organ, and composition under Doles until he underwent a career crisis in 1788–9 and opted to abandon music in favour of theology.[146] His memoirs fix the date upon which 'he gave up music [and] sold his instrument' as 'Easter 1789', that is, just before Mozart's arrival in Leipzig. (In 1789, Easter Day fell on 12 April; Mozart arrived eight days later, on 20 April, remained for a few days, and returned again on 8 May.) Curiously enough, he claimed that the direct impact of Mozart's presence persuaded him to change careers.[147] His decision to quit music could not have had Cantor Doles's approval: 'He vacillated, so to speak, between Cantor Doles and Rector Fischer, two very pronounced personalities who were for the most part at

[145] Constanze Mozart bought up 600 copies of the Graz 1794 reprint edition of the *Nekrolog*, 'so that I could at least destroy these, since I was not able to destroy the appendix to the *Nekrolog*', the appendix containing material highly offensive to her. Letter to B&H, 13 Aug. 1799; *Briefe*, iv. 263.

[146] In this and what follows I rely upon A. Dörffel, 'Friedrich Rochlitz: Sein Leben und Wirken', in Rochlitz, *Für Freunde der Tonkunst*, iv (3rd edn., Leipzig, 1868), 319–41.

[147] Ibid. 324, 329. Rochlitz's superficial hero-worship masked no little hostility towards Mozart. He belittled a good deal of Mozart's œuvre as pot-boilers and disparaged *La clemenza di Tito* and *Don Giovanni*. He portrayed Mozart as a fool who would give away his shirt to save a casual acquaintance from bankruptcy while his own family was falling perilously close to poverty.

odds with one another.'[148] Apparently, Doles lost the contest and thus may not have been content with his former pupil at the very moment of Mozart's arrival, causing one to wonder whether Rochlitz could have been a witness to events occurring in the privacy of Doles's home in April and May 1789. Prior to that time, Rochlitz certainly had been, as he claims in No. 24, a member of the Thomasschule choir, serving as first soprano for three years until 1786 and as tenor thereafter; whether he was still in the choir after his dramatic Easter-Day conversion to theology cannot be determined.

Although there is no objective evidence that Rochlitz became closely acquainted with Mozart or interviewed him during the Leipzig visit, one would like to believe that Rochlitz did not wholly fabricate these anecdotes. Of course, it is not very encouraging to find him, a quarter century later, continuing vividly to 'recall' verbatim additional remarks made by Mozart at Cantor Doles's house parties.[149] However, if he was not actually present on those occasions, it seems probable that he obtained at least some information from an actual eyewitness. Thus, we may reasonably conclude that the materials in the third group do contain a residue of possibly authentic materials, which, in light of Rochlitz's known penchant for outright fabrication or fictionalization, ought to be used with caution. There is surely no reason to accept the colourful details so characteristic of his hasty, journalistic style. And those passages in the anecdotes which presume to tell us what Mozart believed or felt may be discarded, along with all 'transcribed' conversation and direct quotations.

In addition, there are a substantial number of passages, especially in the later anecdotes, which are so general, vague, or imprecise that they can neither be confirmed nor disconfirmed. Little is lost if these materials remain in limbo, for they have not left a particularly strong imprint on Mozart biography.

Earlier, we noted Constanze Mozart's refusal to vouch for the authenticity of Rochlitz's anecdotes at the time of their publication. Even if one does not consider Rochlitz's numerous, blatant errors concerning Mozart's Vienna years, her refusal, by itself, might be sufficient to counter his claim that the anecdotes somehow had either her assistance or endorsement. However, it has been argued that by their inclusion in the massive *Biographie W. A. Mozarts*, authored by Georg Nikolaus Nissen and 'edited' by Constanze Nissen, Rochlitz's anecdotes were, in effect, validated by her.[150] This may be a reason why so many of the major biographers of Mozart—including Jahn, Nohl, Schurig, Abert, Schenk, and Paumgartner—have treated Rochlitz's anecdotes more respectfully than they merited.

A closer look at Nissen's book, its origin, and its editorial practices may clarify why Rochlitz's anecdotes were so extensively reprinted in it and why we need not make too much of the fact of those inclusions. On the editorial level, the book uncritically and indiscriminately reprinted all sorts of excerpts from previously published biographies and

[148] Ibid. 323.
[149] Rochlitz, *Für Freunde der Tonkunst*, iv. 308 n.; see also Jahn, ii. 157; Eng. trans., ii. 442.
[150] See, for example, Landon, *1791*, 74.

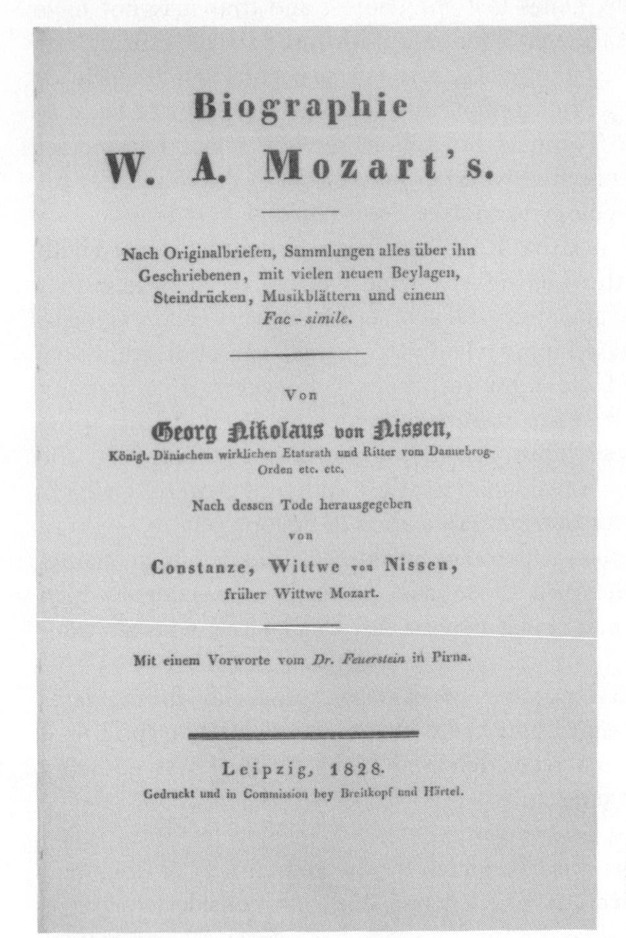
Biographie

W. A. Mozart's.

Nach Originalbriefen, Sammlungen alles über ihn Geschriebenen, mit vielen neuen Beylagen, Steindrücken, Musikblättern und einem *Fac-simile.*

Von

Georg Nikolaus von Nissen,

Königl. Dänischem wirklichen Etatsrath und Ritter vom Dannebrog-Orden etc. etc.

Nach dessen Tode herausgegeben

von

Constanze, Wittwe von Nissen,

früher Wittwe Mozart.

Mit einem Vorworte vom *Dr. Feuerstein* in Pirna.

Leipzig, 1828.

Gedruckt und in Commission bey Breitkopf und Härtel.

FIG. 5. Title-page of Georg Nikolaus von Nissen, *Biographie W. A. Mozart's* (Leipzig, 1828).

articles. These extracts are rarely evaluated, the occasional emendations being limited to obvious blunders, for example, *Idomeneo* as a courtship work, a non-existent revision of *Die Entführung*, or the predating by several months of Mozart's final illness. Often they are unidentified as well, a fault that has also resulted in some confusion; for example, the editors of *Mozart: Briefe und Aufzeichnungen* cite Nissen as the source of stories—especially those pertaining to Mozart in Leipzig—that were actually written by Rochlitz for the *AmZ*.[151] Indeed, the editorial control over Nissen's inclusions is so loose that the book often covers the same ground two, three, or more times: the story that the Overture to *Don Giovanni* was written in Prague during the night before the last rehearsal is related at least three times, each time from a different source.[152]

[151] See, for example, *Briefe*, vi. 383, 385.

[152] Nissen, *Biographie*, 510, 512, and 650–1.

Taken together, these curious duplications, the confused manner of presentation, and the numerous unattributed quotations from published sources add up to an editorial ineptitude unsurpassed in biographical annals. Ultimately, they lead one to question whether Nissen's book as published actually represents its author's intentions or considered judgement, for it is difficult to credit the apparently unlimited extent of Nissen's incompetence. However, a close look at the evidence suggests that Nissen may never actually have drafted a life of Mozart and that the book as we know it is merely an uncritical publication of his notes and interviews, the family correspondence, and his raw extracts from published sources, these having been assembled into a printer's manuscript almost wholly after his death.

Nissen's work on the biography was begun no earlier than 1823 or 1824 and had not reached an advanced stage of preparation when he died on 24 March 1826. His correspondence concerning the biography began only in 1825: late 1825 and early 1826 found him still seeking both documentary materials and personal reminiscences and aiming to achieve a high scholarly standard. On 28 September 1825 he wrote to Albert Stadler, 'My efforts have been rewarded without satisfying me, for many known items have still not reached me and many sources may still remain unknown.'[153] He was aware of how much still remained to be done; in a subsequent letter to Stadler, Nissen writes that 'I have already gathered together a great deal of material, whose most essential and largest lacunae fall in the years 1781–1791.'[154] According to his wife, the New Year found him 'sitting day and night buried in piles of his books and newspapers, within which he can barely be seen'.[155] And, writing under Constanze Nissen's name as late as 16 February, he confessed: 'I am not satisfied with the skeleton of my late husband's biography, which is full of gaps; together with my present life-companion, I busy myself trying to make a comprehensive whole by any possible means.'[156] A letter of 12 March shows that even on his deathbed he was still eagerly seeking a wide variety of Mozart documents and printed materials.[157]

Otto Jahn was right to lament that the published result was 'enough to drive one to absolute despair'; in its printed form, it well deserves his characterization as a 'confused and ill-proportioned mass', whose author had 'huddled together these heterogeneous fragments without design, connection, or explanation'.[158] One needs to add that, by its many unattributed quotations spanning paragraphs and pages, it often borders on plagiarism. But it is difficult to imagine such a result from Nissen, a professional diplomat whose letters reflect his tact, industriousness, and a precision of thought and language

[153] *Briefe*, iv. 466. This and subsequent letters show Nissen trying to obtain a copy of the anonymous (1797) edition of Niemetschek along with publications by Sonnleithner and Charles-Louis de Sévelinges. These books and numerous other materials arrived only after his death. (See Friedrich Dionys Weber to Constanze Nissen, 8 Apr. 1826; *Briefe*, iv. 486–8.)

[154] Letter of 23–4 Oct. 1825; *Briefe*, iv. 468.

[155] Constanze Nissen to Carl Thomas Mozart, 22 Jan. 1826; *Briefe*, iv. 474.

[156] Constanze Nissen to Benedikt Schack, 16 Feb. 1826; *Briefe*, iv. 475–6.

[157] Letter to Franz von Kandler, 12 Mar. 1826; *Briefe*, iv. 624.

[158] Jahn, i, p. iv; Eng. trans., i, pp. viii–ix.

wholly lacking in the life of Mozart that bears his name. It is much more likely that when death interrupted his labours Nissen had not got past the stage of gathering materials and establishing bibliographical control over his subject. The surviving rough draft consists of excerpts from the literature, a list of sources, and the names of Mozart's acquaintances and patrons whom Nissen still intended to consult; in addition there are manuscripts containing extracts from Schlichtegroll and Niemetschek; a list of Mozart's compositions which are mentioned in the correspondence; Nannerl Mozart's autograph letters and biographical notes; copies of the family correspondence; and excerpts from various articles devoted to Mozart.[159] No outlines or substantial drafts of the biography itself survive.

All of these anomalies may be clarified if we consider the implications of the fact that Nissen's book was 'completed' after his death by one Johann Heinrich Feuerstein, an eccentric young medical man without obvious qualifications or previous literary or musical publications, who was selected in preference to Nissen's friends Anton Jähndl and Maximilian Keller, who had earlier assisted his researches.[160] Feuerstein, who lived near Dresden, may have been recommended by the nearby firm of Breitkopf & Härtel as someone capable of bringing the project to rapid fruition. Indeed, he hastily assembled the work from Nissen's voluminous notes and extracts, which were furnished to him by Constanze Nissen, and delivered the indigestible mass that we now open with such trepidation for publication in the summer of 1828, in time to satisfy the almost 600 distinguished subscribers whose orders for 936 copies had been solicited earlier in the year. It is believed that, in addition to the foreword, Feuerstein actually wrote the 78-page culminating chapter, 'Mozart als Künstler and Mensch'.[161] So slapdash was his work that he printed as part of the Mozart correspondence Nissen's interpolated identifications of the names of individuals mentioned therein. Just as Nissen intended these pencilled notations for his own use, it surely was never Nissen's intention uncritically to reprint the huge chunks of materials from the earlier biographical literature which he had assembled for study purposes. It remains for a critical edition to sort matters out, to identify the printed sources for unattributed quotations, and to highlight those significant, original materials that derive from his interviews with Constanze Mozart or other survivors and from manuscript memoirs—such as Sophie Haibel's—which were solicited by him.

Thus, the inclusion in Nissen of Rochlitz's *Verbürgte Anekdoten* may not constitute an endorsement of them nor does it necessarily fairly represent Nissen's attitude towards Rochlitz. It is striking that in his unfinished introduction Nissen did not include Rochlitz

[159] Rudolph Angermüller, 'Nissens Kollektaneen für seine Mozartbiographie', *Mozart-Jahrbuch 1971/72*, 217–26; id., Foreword to fac. repr. of Nissen (Hildesheim, 1972), pp. vii–viii.

[160] Angermüller, Foreword to facs. repr. of Nissen, pp. ix–x. For Feuerstein, see *Briefe*, vi. 634–5; Angermüller, 'Feuerstein, Jähndl und das Ehepaar Nissen', *Wiener Figaro, Mitteilungsblatt der Mozartgemeinde Wien*, 39 (May 1971), 9–15. According to a letter from Feuerstein dated 28 Feb. 1826, Jähndl had worked on the Mozart biography for a time after Nissen's death (ibid. 13).

[161] Arthur Schurig, *Konstanze Mozart: Briefe, Aufzeichnungen, Dokumente. 1781–1842* (Dresden, 1922), p. xlvi; Angermüller, 'Nissens Kollektaneen', 218.

in his list of authentic sources, citing only Schlichtegroll, Niemetschek, and Arnold as writers who worked with documentary materials. Obviously, Rochlitz's materials were not considered essential by Nissen. However, when his work was rushed into print after his death, his implicit judgement had been contravened, for the first chapter actually opens with a four-page quotation from Rochlitz's introduction to the *Verbürgte Anekdoten*, followed by a testimonial to Rochlitz's veracity, stressing his personal acquaintance with Mozart and Mozart's widow. The testimonial is not identified either by quotation marks or otherwise for what it is—Rochlitz's own formulation, given in the precise words with which he had assured his readers in 1798 that his scholarship was beyond reproach. It strains credulity to believe that Nissen, who was well aware that his own access to the family correspondence and to memoirs by Mozart's family and friends had the potential to raise his book far above those of any of his predecessors, and whose goal was to create a definitive biography 'derived from the sources' ('*aus Quellen geschöpft*'), could have authorized or intended such a result.[162]

Even if Constanze Nissen's second husband can be absolved of responsibility for his *Biographie W. A. Mozarts*, she herself must take a large share of the blame for its defects. Apparently, she had excessive faith in Feuerstein, whom she appointed her 'authorized agent' in all affairs pertaining to the publication and sale of the book.[163] (Parenthetically, Feuerstein obtained a financial interest in the project, which was published on Constanze Mozart's account by Breitkopf & Härtel;[164] a substantial portion of the proceeds from the subscription sale came into his hands and he failed to pay Constanze Mozart all that was owed to her, leading to a fruitless litigation.[165]) She surely was daunted by the magnitude of the task, one which she could not herself undertake. And her main objective was to have the book published as expeditiously as possible, partly for financial reasons and partly because it was a project with great meaning for her. Upon its publication, she wrote enthusiastically in her diary: 'On the first of April 1829 I was so fortunate as to receive Mozart's biography, published through me in Leipzig by Breitkopf and Härtel. Praise and thanks to God that I have come so far!'[166] It is doubtful that she critically read Feuerstein's manuscript, let alone carefully edited it for content. Ultimately, it seems, she did not really care if the book contained embellished or suspect materials so long as it did not tell unsympathetic or prurient stories, or contradict the basic elements of the Mozart mythology which she herself had helped to crystallize.

[162] Nissen, *Biographie*, 4. Hausner remarks that many of the book's defects cannot be 'traced to [Nissen's] negligence'; he observes that Constanze Mozart pursued her own agenda, using the book to idealize her second husband and to promote her son's career. Henry H. Hausner, 'Gedanken zu Nissens Mozart-Biographie', *Mitteilungen der Internationalen Stiftung Mozarteums*, 25 (1977), 12–28.

[163] She referred to him as 'meinen Bevollmächtigten Dr. von Feuerstein'. Letter to Marie Céleste Spontini, 10 Oct. 1828; *Briefe*, iv. 497.

[164] *Briefe*, vi. 609. See also Angermüller, 'Aus dem Briefwechsel M. Kellers mit A. Jähndl. Neues zu Nissens Mozartbiographie', *Mitteilungen der Internationalen Stiftung Mozarteum*, 19 (1971), 18–28.

[165] See Constanze Nissen to Marie Céleste Spontini, 21 Apr. 1829; *Briefe*, iv. 503; Constanze Nissen to the Bavarian provincial deputy judge, Sattler, 30 Apr. 1835, in Ernst Fritz Schmid, 'Schicksale einer Mozart-Handschrift', *Mozart-Jahrbuch 1957*, 43–56 at 46–7; *Briefe*, vi. 635, 653; see also B&H to Constanze Nissen, 14 Apr. 1832, cited in Angermüller, Foreword, pp. x–xi.

[166] *Briefe*, iv. 502.

For Constanze Mozart did have a story to tell: it is of a devoted and loving couple, of their triumphs and their poverty, which they offset by music, love, and laughter until their marriage was cut short by Mozart's tragic early death. In general outline, and even in the details, this is not far from the truth. But she had an interest in stressing or exaggerating Mozart's reputed generosity, his naïveté about worldly matters, and especially his poverty, for she applied to the Emperor for a pension and for permission to put on benefit concerts to pay Mozart's remaining debts. In subsequent years she was to earn considerable sums exploiting her role as Mozart's poverty-stricken widow. 'Many noble benefactors are helping this unhappy woman', wrote one Viennese newspaper in 1793; after a Prague benefit, another paper reported that 'Mozart's widow and son both wept tears of grief at their loss and of gratitude towards a noble nation'.[167] In 1795, she continued to express her thanks to 'Vienna's noble citizens, [who] have always followed their favourite inclination: to do good, whenever it was a question of supporting widows and orphaned children'.[168] For several years she pursued further benefit performances in Graz, Linz, Dresden, Leipzig, and Berlin, winding up once more in Prague on 15 November 1797. Her earnings enabled her to lend the large sum of 3,500 florins at 6% interest in 1797 and to leave the considerable fortune of 27,191 florins in cash at her death.[169] Nissen wrote to her son Carl in 1810: 'By her tours, concert performances, as well as by the sale of your late father's original scores . . . your mother has been fortunate enough not only to pay the debts but also to amass a small capital.'[170] Under these circumstances, it would not do for her to acknowledge Mozart's extraordinarily large earnings during his Vienna years.

Thus, we need not be overly surprised if, despite her earlier rejection of the Rochlitz anecdotes, Constanze Mozart did not object to their use in Nissen's life of Mozart. She may well have been amenable to taking over from Rochlitz those anecdotes, however dressed up or falsified, which suited her purposes, such as those stressing Mozart's generosity, poverty, and lack of recognition, or those alleging that he was taken advantage of by impresarios, publishers, and fellow musicians, even where she knew these to be false or exaggerated. In particular, Rochlitz's fable about Mozart making an absurdly disadvantageous deal with Schikaneder for *Die Zauberflöte* ideally suited her purposes, just as it suited her to circulate and/or certify false accounts about the composition and completion of the Requiem. By the time Mary and Vincent Novello visited her in Salzburg in 1829, Constanze Mozart remembered that 'all Mozart's operas were either given, or stolen, the remainder of his music was sold for a mere trifle'; she recalled, as though she had herself been present, how Mozart, at a performance of *Die Entführung* in Berlin, had startled the audience by calling out a correction to the orchestra; and she

[167] *Magyar Hírmondó*, 4 Jan. 1793; *Prager Neue Zeitung*, ?9 Feb. 1794; *Dokumente*, 409, 411; *Documentary Biography*, 467, 470.

[168] *Wiener Zeitung*, 18 Mar. 1795; *Dokumente*, 414; *Documentary Biography*, 473.

[169] *Dokumente*, 422; *Documentary Biography*, 485; Erich Valentin, 'Das Testament der Constanze Mozart-Nissen', *Neues Mozart-Jahrbuch*, 2 (Regensburg, 1942), 128–75 at 137.

[170] Georg Nissen and Constanze Nissen to Carl Thomas Mozart, 13 June 1810; *Briefe*, iv. 454; *Dokumente*, 441; *Documentary Biography*, 513 (translation revised).

was ready to affirm that Mozart had 'refused an offer of the King of Prussia to reside at his court with a salary of 1,600 sequins because he would not leave [Emperor] Joseph', expressing the hope that 'this generous sacrifice will not go unrewarded to his family by the Austrian court'.[171] Earlier, even her friend Niemetschek observed that her evidence had to be treated judiciously; he wrote to Härtel: 'For the composition of the biography Frau Mozart gave me a great quantity of memoranda and letters; I could not use all of them, partly because of persons who were still alive, partly because I didn't believe everything that Frau Mozart said or indicated.'[172] Thus, Rochlitz's are not the only early biographical materials concerning Mozart which need to be evaluated.

Biography is a contest for possession. This is transparent in early Mozart biography, where the rival branches of his family contended to have their stories told. Nannerl Mozart furnished a set of materials to Schlichtegroll, aiming to buttress her father's view of Mozart, emphasizing his genius as a family enterprise, and picturing the early journeys as her brother's golden age. Constanze Mozart bought up and destroyed the entire second edition of Schlichtegroll's book because an offending passage portrayed her married life in a highly unfavourable light. She soon balanced the scales by using Niemetschek's biography to tell Mozart's story from her own standpoint, furnishing 'information, papers, and letters' to its author, who was her friend.[173]

Subsequently, Constanze Mozart engaged in a lengthy correspondence with Breitkopf & Härtel and provided the publisher with voluminous materials for the purpose of preparing a full-scale biography of her husband;[174] ten of her own anecdotes appeared in the *AmZ*;[175] and, in 1828, she published her second husband's massive life of Mozart. It is to her credit that she did not use any of these occasions to settle scores with her father-in-law or sister-in-law; apart from a poignant reference to Mozart having been refused permission to select something for his wife from among the many gifts he had received on his early journeys, there is scarcely a hint of rancour towards them in these writings.

Breitkopf & Härtel pursued a correspondence with Nannerl Mozart as well (particularly after it became clear that Constanze Mozart was not pleased with the publisher's paltry offers), enlisting her aid in supplying Mozart manuscripts as well as materials for the projected biography. She used the opportunity to promote her own proxy biographer: 'Concerning the biography of my brother,' she wrote, 'I find it remarkable that you have made no announcement of the *Nekrolog* of Professor Schlichtegroll, wherein is contained an authentic biography of my brother, for which, at the request of a friend, I

[171] *A Mozart Pilgrimage*, 97–8, 81, 113.

[172] Letter of 21 Mar. 1800, cited in Hitzig, 'Die Briefe', 110.

[173] Niemetschek, *Leben*, 87; see also 72.

[174] These materials, along with additional documents furnished by Nannerl Mozart, were retained in the B&H archives; they were reprinted in Gustav Nottebohm, *Mozartiana* (Leipzig, 1880). Rochlitz did not utilize any of these materials in the preparation of his *Anekdoten*. Frau Mozart's correspondence with the publisher does not clarify who was intended to write the biography; Nottebohm (v) and Jahn (i, pp. ix–x; Eng. trans., i, p. iv) thought it was Rochlitz, wrongly assuming that Constanze Mozart's letters to Härtel were equivalent to her writing to Rochlitz.

[175] See above, n. 14.

provided an article . . . as well as excerpts from letters and writings and epigrams, written with much spice and humour.'[176] She, too, wanted to be represented in *AmZ*: 'If you would like me to send you my article along with these writings, please let me know your pleasure.'[177] Soon, four of her own anecdotes appeared in the journal, telling, among other things, of the child Mozart's reign over his 'Königreich Rücken' and of his inexhaustible love for his father.[178]

Eventually, Mozart's widow and sister were reconciled to the biographies of Mozart which the other had shaped. When Constanze Mozart offered Breitkopf & Härtel access to the documents in her possession, she rightly pointed out that these, together with 'Niemetschek's work and the good part of [Schlichtegroll's] *Nekrolog* would permit one to make a whole'.[179] (The omission of Rochlitz's anecdotes in her list of authentic materials is another tacit indication of her opinion as to their value.) Her objective acknowledgement of Schlichtegroll's importance is matched by Nannerl Mozart's emotional reaction upon reading Niemetschek for the first time: 'Herr Prof. Niemetschek's *Biography* again so totally animated my sisterly feelings towards my so ardently beloved brother that I was often dissolved in tears, since it is only now that I became acquainted with the sad condition in which my brother found himself.'[180]

What had been a family affair became a matter of commerce when Breitkopf & Härtel commenced publication of its (*Œuvres complettes* of Mozart in 1798, an edition which was to become one of the more profitable ventures in the early history of serious music publishing and to establish the supremacy of Breitkopf & Härtel in its field. Both in scope and in speed, the Leipzig publisher outstripped its many competitors who sought to capitalize on the Mozart enthusiasm that commenced shortly after his death and was rapidly reaching a crest. Within eight years from the inception of the (*Œuvres complettes* in the autumn of 1798, Breitkopf & Härtel had placed on sale more than 225 separate works by Mozart, including comprehensive editions of his piano solos, piano duos, sonatas for violin and piano, and Lieder; in addition, 12 concert arias, 12 string quartets, and 20 piano concertos were published in parts, and the Requiem, 2 masses, and *Don Giovanni* in full score.[181]

Naturally, so ambitious a project as the rapid and orderly publication of Mozart's collected works called both for quick action and for a strong promotional campaign, particularly since a rival collected edition (from Brunswick publisher Johann Peter Spehr) was also in progress. The founding of Breitkopf & Härtel's house journal, the *AmZ*, provided outstanding promotional opportunities. Large advertisements for its Mozart edition were featured in the *Intelligenz-Blatt* supplements to many *AmZ* issues, repeatedly stressing the assistance of 'Mozarts Wittwe' in furnishing original scores. This

[176] Letter of 4 Aug. 1799; *Briefe*, iv. 259–60.
[177] Ibid.
[178] See above n. 14.
[179] Constanze Mozart to Breitkopf & Härtel, 13 Aug. 1799; *Briefe*, iv. 263.
[180] Letter of 8 Feb. 1800; *Briefe*, iv. 312.
[181] Köchel^6, Anhang D, 915–17.

was, of course, perfectly legitimate; but the *AmZ* was scarcely an objective journal on matters affecting its interests. Under Rochlitz's editorial guidance, it did not scruple to ridicule other publishers' offerings; in its issue of 30 October 1799 its reviewer was delighted to point out that Johann Anton André, the Offenbach publisher, had engraved the spurious Violin Concerto in E flat, K. 268/Anhang C 14.04;[182] naturally it never called attention to its own publication, in volume 6 of its edition, of two spurious sets of piano variations, K. Anh. 287 and 289. Also in October 1799, Rochlitz or his anonymous reviewer of André's edition of the Piano Concerto in B flat major, K. 450 (published in parts as Op. 67) pointed out various flaws, and concluded: 'Breitkopf & Härtel of Leipzig, who, in addition to the original score of this concerto, possess still other original manuscripts of hitherto unpublished and unengraved piano concertos by Mozart, would certainly give great joy to everyone who reveres Mozart—and especially to all performers of piano concertos—by an early publication of these treasures.'[183] Within a year, Breitkopf & Härtel indeed published parts for this concerto.

In a letter to André, Constanze Mozart found it 'most revolting to hear these gentlemen talking of the great expense they have not shrunk from incurring to honour Mozart in his grave, when one remembers that most of the pieces they have published so far have not been copied from the original manuscripts, but are only *reprints* which haven't cost them a penny, whilst the few works they have so copied have cost the merest trifle. Moreover, they did not even trouble to enquire into their authenticity'.[184] Later on, Beethoven's experience raised serious questions about the objectivity of notices in the *AmZ*: as a young composer he for the most part received negative reviews, if any, so long as he was published in Vienna; but after the Leipzig publisher applied to him for manuscripts, his notices improved considerably, culminating in the extraordinary series of reviews (of Breitkopf & Härtel imprints) commissioned from E. T. A. Hoffmann starting in 1810. In his last dozen years, after the close of his relationship with Breitkopf & Härtel, the *AmZ* variously reported that Beethoven was written out, doddering, and incomprehensible, even when it paid fulsome lip-service to his genius. Little wonder that Beethoven was wont to call Rochlitz 'Beelzebub' or 'Mephistopheles' and to hope that he would meet the same fate as Goethe's flea.

In support of his employer's ends, newly appointed editor Rochlitz undertook to write and publish anecdotes about Mozart which were calculated to increase public interest in his person and his music. This promotional aspect of Rochlitz's anecdotes is quite on the surface. In No. 10 Rochlitz derided rival publishers as larcenists who exploited and/or robbed Mozart. Buyers were warned that unscrupulous publishers often issued worthless editions and unauthentic materials. The unsubtle message was *caveat emptor*, advising music-lovers to buy Mozart only from the distinguished publisher of the journal they were holding in their hands. In his derogation of foreign—especially Viennese—publishers is hidden a shrewd appeal to Prussian nationalism, which was buttressed in

[182] *AmZ* 2 (1799–1800), 93–4.

[183] Ibid. 13–14.

[184] Letter of 29 Mar. 1800; *Briefe*, iv. 345; trans. Anderson, *The Letters of Mozart and His Family*, 3 vols. (London, 1938), iii, 1471.

the anecdotes that showed Prussian King Frederick William II to be far more sensitive to Mozart's worth than was Habsburg Emperor Joseph II. It is also worth noting that Rochlitz often praised those works which his employer was publishing, and felt free to criticize works, such as a *clemenza di Tito*, which Breitkopf & Härtel did not intend to publish. He even included at least one explicit commercial announcement, in No. 13, mentioning that a set of Variations in E flat (K. 353 or 354) was available in Breitkopf & Härtel's collected edition.

So successfully was this enterprise conducted that Breitkopf & Härtel achieved a pre-eminent position in the market for engraved classical music in the nineteenth century. Naturally, Rochlitz also furthered his own purposes—to enhance his personal reputation and to enlarge both the sales and the reputation of the journal which he edited. These goals were also accomplished: the *AmZ* dominated European music journals for a quarter of a century, until a group of rival publishers' journals, headed by editors more closely aligned with the new Romanticist attitudes, eroded its influence; and Rochlitz came to be regarded as the outstanding music-editor of his generation, a power to be courted and feared by composers and performers alike.

Breitkopf & Härtel did not conduct itself honourably in this undertaking. Its own historian, Wilhelm Hitzig, wrote: 'From the letters in its archive emerges the portrait of a downright unbelievable disorder, an incomprehensible confusion, and a professional falsification in every question connected with Mozart's artistic *Nachlaß*'.[185] The publisher was not interested in paying the composer's widow for his autograph scores wherever it had the less expensive alternative of reprinting from earlier engraved editions or manuscript copies in its collection, even where these were not always authentic; accordingly, it purchased from her for very small sums only those autographs not otherwise available to it. To persuade her to reach a disadvantageous agreement, Niemetschek was enlisted in Breitkopf & Härtel's camp, a circumstance which could scarcely have endeared him to Constanze Mozart: 'For a considerable time she no longer has written to me,' he wrote Härtel in early 1800, 'probably because I always seriously tried to get her to reach an accord with you.'[186]

It soon became evident to Constanze Mozart and her adviser, Georg Nissen, that Breitkopf & Härtel's main interest was in paying her the smallest possible amount of money while deriving the largest promotional benefit from the use of her name in connection with its Mozart publications. Thus, Gottfried Härtel should not have been so surprised when, early in 1800, she broke off her frustrating negotiations with him and instead sold her husband's manuscripts en bloc to André.[187] On 5 March 1800 Breitkopf & Härtel used the pages of its journal to publish a statement minimizing the importance

[185] Hitzig, 'Die Briefe', 104.

[186] Letter of 21 Mar. 1800, Hitzig, 'Die Briefe', 109; earlier, he wrote to Härtel: 'Someone is giving her false notions' (letter of 15 Nov. 1798; Hitzig, Die Briefe, 107). Niemetschek was paid for his services as adviser to B&H.

[187] See C. B. Oldman, introduction to his translation of Constanze Mozart's letters to Johann Anton André, in Anderson, *Letters of Mozart and His Family*, iii. 1454–8; Hitzig, 'Die Briefe', 101–16; Deutsch, 'Mozarts Nachlaß: Aus den Briefen Konstanzens an den Verlag André', *Mozart-Jahrbuch 1953*, 32–41.

of André's collection; on 13 March Constanze Mozart countered with a statement announcing André's purchase and depreciating what she had furnished to Breitkopf & Härtel, describing it as consisting in the main of smaller works.[188]

Both the circulation of Mozart's works and the financial health of Breitkopf & Härtel were well served by this campaign. However, biographical truth became a casualty of commercial enterprise and editorial vanity. To meet publication deadlines and to boost circulation, Rochlitz's *Verbürgte Anekdoten* were hastily assembled, mostly by rewriting a single previously published source, and carelessly rushed into print without any attempt to confirm their accuracy. Indeed, accuracy was a secondary issue where promotional journalism of this type was concerned. And, once launched, his anecdotes were quickly absorbed into both the folklore and the biographical literature on Wolfgang Amadeus Mozart. For Rochlitz had wrought better than could reasonably have been anticipated.

Part of the appeal of his fables lay in his ability to connect them with mythic undercurrents, playing upon our need to view Mozart through the prism of long-held beliefs about genius and creativity, to make of Mozart's life a twice-told tale. The mythic connection tends to overwhelm our resistances to these stories, for it suggests that they belong to a chain of ancient stories, tapping into archaic underlying truths. We want to believe that the great geniuses are themselves fated to be actors in predestined dramas. Thus we are not surprised to encounter mysterious strangers, anonymous messengers, Dionysian companions, sirens, enemies, cabals, good kings, misguided emperors—all of the paraphernalia of the legendary—in these anecdotes. Nor are recognition scenes lacking: like Pallas Athene or Zeus, Mozart materializes as a nameless stranger in a Berlin theatre; a grey-clothed messenger brings a summons from the underworld to prepare for an Appointment in Samarra. And Rochlitz knowingly improvises on a variety of biographical tropes which confirm our feeling that geniuses are childlike, divine vessels, amoral, decadent, neglected, doomed.

One ought have no illusions that a careful demonstration of the fraudulence or fabrication of biographical data inevitably leads to the rapid expunging of the offending materials from the literature. Schindler's, Schlösser's, and Rochlitz's Beethoven forgeries continue to be cited, even by scholars who are very well aware that the materials have been seriously thrown into question. Rochlitz's Mozart letter to 'Baron von . . .' and the anonymously forged letter to Da Ponte are repeatedly quoted in the literature of several disciplines. The memoirs of Berlioz, the autobiography of Wagner, and the 'memos' of Ives have not lost their fascination. We have a limited fund of good stories available to us in the manufacture of musical biographies, so it is not surprising that we want to hold on to them, especially when they reinforce our long-held beliefs, prejudies, and wishes. It will be a long time before Rochlitz's work will be undone.

[188] See *Dokumente*, 532; *Documentary Biography*, 495–6. According to Deutsch, her statement was published in the *Frankfurter Staats-Ristretto* for 4 Apr. 1800.

The Composition and Completion of Mozart's Requiem, 1791–1792

CHRISTOPH WOLFF

ONE of the most elegant, descriptive, and truthful titles in twentieth-century musicological literature was given by Paul Henry Lang to Friedrich Blume's important article on Mozart's Requiem: 'Requiem but no peace'.[1] This title emphatically sums up the open-ended nature of Blume's own conclusions regarding the problems surrounding the completion of Mozart's last, unfinished work. Blume was indeed unable to dispel, let alone put to rest, the manifold controversies that have plagued studies of the Requiem for nearly two hundred years, and the same is true of more recent attempts to do so—including, to be sure, the present essay. A cautionary note seems well in order, particularly in view of the unusual complexity of the problems. On the other hand, there is no reason to give up in the face of an apparently hopeless state of affairs marked by an unfortunate competitive juxtaposition of source studies and style criticism: the two methods—as Blume axiomatically states—'must complement one another'.[2]

Progress can be and has been made, as demonstrated especially in the studies of Wolfgang Plath (on the sketches and correspondence concerning the Requiem)[3] and Ernst Hess (on the style-critical evaluation of Süssmayr's compositional contributions.)[4] Moreover, Leopold Nowak, with his critical edition of the Requiem in the *Neue Mozart-Ausgabe*,[5] contributed significantly to a clarification of the issues by placing emphasis on the value of the primary musical sources and literary documents.[6] Most recently, Paul

[1] *Musical Quarterly*, 48 (1961), 147–69; reprinted (with postscript) in: Paul Henry Lang (ed.), *The Creative World of Mozart* (New York, 1963), 103–26. The German original was published afterwards in Friedrich Blume, *Syntagma musicologicum*, ed. M. Ruhnke (Kassel, 1963), 714–34.

[2] 'Requiem but no peace', 125.

[3] 'Über Skizzen zu Mozarts "Requiem"', *Bericht über den Internationalen Musikwissenschaftlichen Kongreß Kassel 1962*, ed. Georg Reichert and Martin Just (Kassel, 1963), 184–7; 'Requiem-Briefe. Aus der Korrespondenz Joh. Anton Andrés 1825–1831', *Mozart-Jahrbuch 1977/78*, 174–203; 'Noch ein Requiem-Brief', *Mitteilungen der Internationalen Stiftung Mozarteum*, 29 (1981), 96–101.

[4] 'Zur Ergänzung des Requiems von Mozart durch F. X. Süßmayr', *Mozart-Jahrbuch 1959*, 99–108.

[5] *NMA* I/1/2, vols. 1–2 (1965).

[6] My own research on the Requiem benefited considerably from the quality and commitment of Nowak's scholarship I encountered in preparing the Critical Report for the *NMA*, which I took over from him or, rather, for him. I am also indebted to some good friends, Wolfgang Plath (whom I consulted in scribal matters), Alan Tyson (who shared with me the results of his paper studies), and Robert Levin (whose musical judgement I hold in particularly high esteem), and last, but not least, a group of students at Harvard who came up with good points and helped sharpen my methods of inquiry in a graduate seminar on Mozart's Requiem a few years ago. The present chapter is a slightly modified version of a paper read at the Annual

Moseley presented a carefully researched account of the present state of affairs regarding the sources of the Requiem and the historical references.[7]

The principal issues will once again be debated here. It is, of course, beyond dispute that Mozart did not finish the Requiem, but precisely how far did he get? It is also well known that Franz Xaver Süssmayr assumed a primary role in completing the Requiem, but what exactly were his contributions and how did they come about? In addition to these two basic questions, one must consider some further, closely related problems. What was the chronological framework for the entire project? (When did Mozart begin and how did he proceed? What happened to the work after his death and when was the score actually completed?) Moreover, what are the compositional and stylistic premises of Mozart's Requiem, and to what extent were they understood and realized after his death? These historical, philological, and analytical questions largely determine the organization of the present essay. The discussion, however, must necessarily proceed in summary fashion and be limited to selected aspects and examples.

I

The authenticity problem or, more precisely, the question of who completed the Requiem, was at the centre of the controversy that arose from Gottfried Weber's fiercely polemical article, 'Über die Echtheit des Mozart'schen Requiem', published in 1825 in the periodical *Caecilia*.[8] Weber went so far as to consider the whole work a forgery that damaged the reputation of Mozart's genius, and his article prompted a series of responses in defence of the Requiem's authenticity, including a pamphlet by the Abbé Maximilian Stadler, *Vertheidigung der Echtheit des Mozart'schen Requiem* (Vienna, 1826),[9] and two critical editions by Johann Anton André (Offenbach, 1827 and 1829),[10] which aimed at differentiating—as far as was possible—between the Mozartian and non-Mozartian portions of the work (both editions included extensive prefatory materials). But the most important evidence to surface in Vienna during these years was two substantial portions of the autograph draft score: the Abbé Stadler came up with the portion containing the Sequence, from the 'Dies irae' on, but excluding the 'Lacrimosa', which he gave before 1831 to the Imperial Library in Vienna; while Joseph Eybler produced the 'Lacrimosa' and the two movements of the Offertory, 'Domine Jesu Christe' and 'Hostias', which he donated in 1833 to the same Library.[11] Curiously, neither

Meeting of the American Musicological Society, New Orleans, November 1987. See also my monograph *Mozarts Requiem: Geschichte—Musik—Dokumente—Partitur des Fragments* (Munich, 1991).

[7] 'Mozart's Requiem: A Revaluation of the Evidence', *Journal of the Royal Musical Association*, 114 (1989), 203–37. The following discussion takes a similar stand on the overall source situation.

[8] Vol. 3 (1825), 205–29.

[9] With two follow-ups: *Nachtrag* [and: *Zweiter und letzter*] *zur Vertheidigung der Echtheit des Mozartischen Requiem* (Vienna, 1827).

[10] See K[6] and Gertraut Haberkamp, *Die Erstdrucke der Werke von Wolfgang Amadeus Mozart*, 2 vols. (Tutzing, 1986).

[11] See Leopold Nowak, 'Die Erwerbung des Mozart-Requiem durch die k. k. Hofbibliothek im Jahre 1838', in J. Mayerhöfer and W. Ritzer (eds.), *Festschrift Josef Stummvoll* (Vienna, 1970), 295–310.

Stadler nor Eybler clearly stated where the material came from. Stadler referred merely to a somebody ('Jemand'), who himself had received the draft score portion as a gift and left it with Stadler on 22 March 1826;[12] Eybler, according to Stadler, was presumably given his portion by Georg Nikolaus Nissen, Constanze's second husband, sometime before Nissen's death in Salzburg on 26 March 1826.

The simmering public debate[13] took a new turn with the unexpected surfacing, in 1838, of the 'original' full score of the complete Requiem, formerly in the possession of Count Walsegg-Stuppach, who had commissioned the work from Mozart in 1791. This score was offered to, and immediately acquired by, the Imperial Library in Vienna, whose music librarian, Hofrat Ignaz von Mosel, immediately had it examined by a group of graphological experts.[14] Since they confirmed the involvement of at least two different hands in the supposedly autograph score (it was compared with Süssmayr manuscripts in Budapest), Mosel—with the backing of his superior, Count Dietrichstein—wrote a remarkably strongly-worded letter to Constanze in Salzburg,[15] asking her point-blank for a definitive answer concerning the extent of Mozart's and, possibly, others' participation in the Walsegg score. On previous occasions Constanze always balked and hedged, but her quick reply now was virtually useless. She simply observed that Süssmayr had indeed written into the original score and that he completed the piece, not too difficult a task since the main passages were all realized in such a way that he could not go astray ('die Hauptstellen alle ausgesetzt waren, und Süßm. nicht irre gehen könnt').[16] Not once since Mozart's death had she presented a non-contradictory statement, let alone a full account of the Requiem story. Constanze died in 1842, bringing to an end at least that part of the long controversy, the so-called 'Requiem-Streit', during which the key witnesses themselves could participate—and they all played their role well by involving everyone else in some sort of blind-man's buff.

It is interesting that the picture that finally emerged did not differ substantially from what had already become known at the time of the appearance of the first edition of the Requiem, published by Breitkopf & Härtel (Leipzig, 1800). In 1799, Breitkopf, well aware of the problems and potential trouble with publishing a work solely on the basis of a secondary copy (their copy had served for the performance in 1794 under the later Thomascantor Johann Gottfried Schicht), contacted Constanze (who was apparently unable to produce an original manuscript) and later Franz Xaver Süssmayr. Moreover, in the fall of 1800, at the Vienna office of Dr Sortschan, the lawyer of Count Walsegg, who claimed to have the sole rights to the work commissioned by him, a textual collation of original materials in Constanze's possession and the Breitkopf score took place. At that point, the Abbé Stadler, representing Constanze, identified as

[12] *Vertheidigung der Echtheit*, 8.

[13] Reflected in many literary references, for instance, in the correspondence between Goethe and Zelter. Cf. Karl Friedrich Zelter and Johann Wolfgang Goethe, *Briefwechsel: Eine Auswahl*, ed. H.-G. Ottenberg (Leipzig 1987), 331 ff.

[14] See Mosel's detailed report in *Über die Originalpartitur des Requiem von W. A. Mozart* (Vienna, 1839).

[15] Wolfgang Plath, 'Noch ein Requiem-Brief', 100 f.

[16] Ibid.

best as he could all non-Mozartian additions, thereby providing the foundation for André's critical score (published later on, in 1827), which differentiates between the Mozart and Süssmayr portions by use of capital letters, 'M' and 'S'—incidentally, the same method used by Brahms in his edition for the old Mozart *Gesamtausgabe*.

In a letter of 8 February 1800 to Breitkopf, Süssmayr himself had emphasized his rather inadequate contribution to Mozart's Requiem and specifically stated the following:[17] (1) That the completion of the work had been assigned by Constanze to several 'masters', some of whom could not undertake the project owing to other commitments, others of whom would not get involved because they did not want to mix their talents with Mozart's. (2) That, finally, he was approached because during Mozart's last months he had often played and sung through the finished pieces with the composer ('. . . öfters mit ihm durchgespielt und gesungen'), who had also frequently discussed with him the elaboration of the work ('. . . mit mir über die Ausarbeitung des Werkes sehr oft besprochen') and the method of, and reasons for, its instrumentation ('. . . mir den Gang und die Gründe seiner Instrumentirung mitgeteilt hatte'). (3) That Mozart had written out completely the four-part vocal score plus thorough-bass through the Offertory, except for the 'Lacrimosa', which he had set up to and including the verse 'qua resurget ex favilla', and that for the instrumentation Mozart had here and there indicated the 'motivum'. (4) That he, Süssmayr, had finished the 'Lacrimosa' from the text 'judicandus homo reus' on, and that the Sanctus, Benedictus, and Agnus Dei were newly composed by him ('ganz neu von mir verfertigt'). (5) Finally, that he took the liberty ('habe ich mir erlaubt') of repeating the Kyrie fugue with the verse 'cum sanctis tuis' in order to give the work greater unity ('um dem Werke mehr Einförmigkeit zu geben').

The Süssmayr letter to Breitkopf has long been recognized as the most important, and a basically reliable, statement regarding the completion of the Requiem and his own role in it. Süssmayr died shortly thereafter, in 1803, and thus had no chance to amplify, confirm, or change anything in view of the later debate. In the course of this paper, we shall give Süssmayr's letter a close reading—paying attention to what he says, what he does not say, and what other key players in the scenario evolving after Mozart's death have to say—in conjunction with a critical review of the surviving principal musical manuscripts. These main sources, which—perhaps like no other musical manuscripts—were subject to considerable manipulation by various parties in the decades following Mozart's death, are the same ones that today have to help us reconstruct and determine the actual course of events. All the sources are located in the Österreichische Nationalbibliothek, Vienna, except for the sketches discovered in 1961 by Wolfgang Plath in the Deutsche Staatsbibliothek, Berlin.

II

The autograph and Süssmayr parts of the Requiem materials in Vienna are somewhat confusingly combined under one call-number (Mus. Hs. 17561), but divided into Codex a

[17] Joseph Heinz Eibl, *Mozart-Dokumente: Addenda et Corrigenda*, (Kassel, 1978), 89.

and Codex b; for the sake of clarity of provenance I have subdivided both codices into two parts, with the numbering in square brackets (see Table 1).

Codex a as a whole represents the score given by Constanze Mozart to Count Walsegg, acquired in 1838 from the Count's heirs (see Table 1, col. 3). Codex a[1] is mainly in Mozart's hand and originally formed the first section of the autograph score (with an old foliation); Codex a[2] is completely in Süssmayr's hand. The first page of Codex a[1] bears the inscription: 'di me W: A: Mozart mpr. / 1792.' Until recently, this inscription was considered to be an autograph and deliberately post-dated signature, but it is actually a forgery in Süssmayr's hand.[18] His music hand resembles that of Mozart very closely (surely one major reason why Constanze had him prepare the Walsegg score), and in the Requiem score he actually made it a point to imitate Mozart's scribal features. It was probably Constanze who instigated the falsification of the signature in order to give the manuscript the stamp of unquestionable authenticity. Consider the emphasis on 'di me'—for Mozart utterly atypical—and, of course, the fact that Süssmayr's own name appears nowhere, which must have been according to prior agreement. Moreover, Süssmayr may well have imitated Mozart's signature in good conscience. After all, the Requiem was first and foremost Mozart's work, and Süssmayr clearly understood his role as subsidiary and quite modest—in his own words to Breitkopf, 'unworthy of the great man' ('. . . des grossen Mannes unwürdig'). Moreover, the date '1792' is nothing but the truth—everyone knew that Mozart did not live into 1792. The only completely false, and purposefully misleading, part of the inscription. then, consists in the 'manu propria' certification, underlining the fact that the whole thing was prompted by a curious combination of strong devotion and mildly devious conduct.

Codex b[1] (actually the continuation of fos. 1–10 of the autograph that had become the first section of the Walsegg score) came to the Library from the Abbé Stadler (see Table 1, col. 1). That it was available at the collation session in 1800 at the office of Walsegg's lawyer is shown by the lead pencil framings of the non-autograph portions, presumably drawn by Stadler (see Fig. 1). Codex b[2], the continuation of fos. 11–32 of the autograph score, i.e. Codex b[1], shows a distinctly different image: apart from mm. 9–10 in the soprano part of the 'Lacrimosa', it contains only entries in Mozart's hand (see Fig. 2).

The appearance of fos. 1–45 of the dismembered autograph score quite clearly confirms Süssmayr's description of what Mozart had written: a complete vocal scoring plus thorough-bass, as well as motivic portions of the instrumentation. It is particularly noteworthy that Süssmayr does not exclude from this description the full score of the Requiem and Kyrie movements, which have long been considered to be completely autograph. Nowak was able to show, however,[19] that the colla-parte accompaniment of the Kyrie fugue was not written by Mozart, but by another (though very similar) hand, which he identified as most likely that of Franz Jacob Freystädtler, a Mozart student (see Table 1, col. 2).

[18] See Johannes Dalchow *et al., Mozarts Tod 1791–1971* (Pähl, 1971), 284–7.

[19] 'Wer hat die Instrumentalstimmen in der Kyrie-Fuge des Requiems von W. A. Mozart geschrieben? Ein vorläufiger Bericht,' *Mozart-Jahrbuch 1974*, 191–201.

TABLE 1. *Original manuscript sources of the Requiem*

	Autograph score	Intermediate stages[a]	Score for Count Walsegg
	Österreichische Nationalbibliothek, MS 17561: Codex a[1]		*MS 17561: Codex a[1]* (= autograph score, fos. 1–10)
Requiem	fos. 1^r–5^v	Süssmayr inscription on fo. 1^r: *di me W: A: Mozart mpr. / 1792*	
Kyrie	fos. 5^v–9^r	Freystädtler and Süssmayr	
	fos. 9^v–10^r blank		
	MS 17561: Codex b[1]		*MS 17561: Codex a[2]*
Dies irae	fos. 11^r–15^v	Eybler	fos. 1^r–20^v (old): Süssmayr's copy and revision of Eybler's instrumentation
Tuba mirum	fos. 16^r–19^v	Eybler	
Rex tremendae[b]	fos. 20^r–22^r	Eybler	
Recordare	fos. 22^v–28^v	Eybler	
Confutatis	fos. 29^r–32^r	Eybler	
	fo. 32^v blank		
	MS 17561: Codex b[2]		
Lacrimosa[c]	fos. 33^{r-v}	Eybler also composed mm. 9–10	fos. 21^r–23^r: Süssmayr's instrumentation (mm. 1–8); composition (mm. 9–30); fo. 23^v blank
	fo. 34^r blank		
		MS 4375 A	
Domine Jesu	fos. 35^r–41^r fos. 41^v–42^v blank	fos. 1^r–6^r Stadler	fos. 24^r–33^v: Süssmayr's copy and revision of Stadler's instrumentation or Süssmayr's own instrumentation
Hostias	fos. 43^r–45^r	fos. 6^v–8^r Stadler	
	fo. 45^v blank		
[Sanctus-Hosanna-Benedictus]			fos. 1–19 (old): Süssmayr's composition (fair copy): fo. 20 blank
[Agnus Dei]			
[Lux aeterna]			

[a] Instrumentation in autograph score unless otherwise marked.

[b] Autograph sketches for mm. 7 ff. are preserved in Deutsche Staatsbibliothek, Akz. Nr. 1889.401.

[c] Autograph sketches for 16 measures of the 'Amen' are preserved in Deutsche Staatsbibliothek, Akz. Nr. 1889.401.

FIG. 1. Mozart, autograph score of Requiem (Österreichische Nationalbibliothek, Vienna; Mus. Hs. 17561a), fo. 11ʳ: Dies irae (supplemental instrumentation by Joseph Eybler).

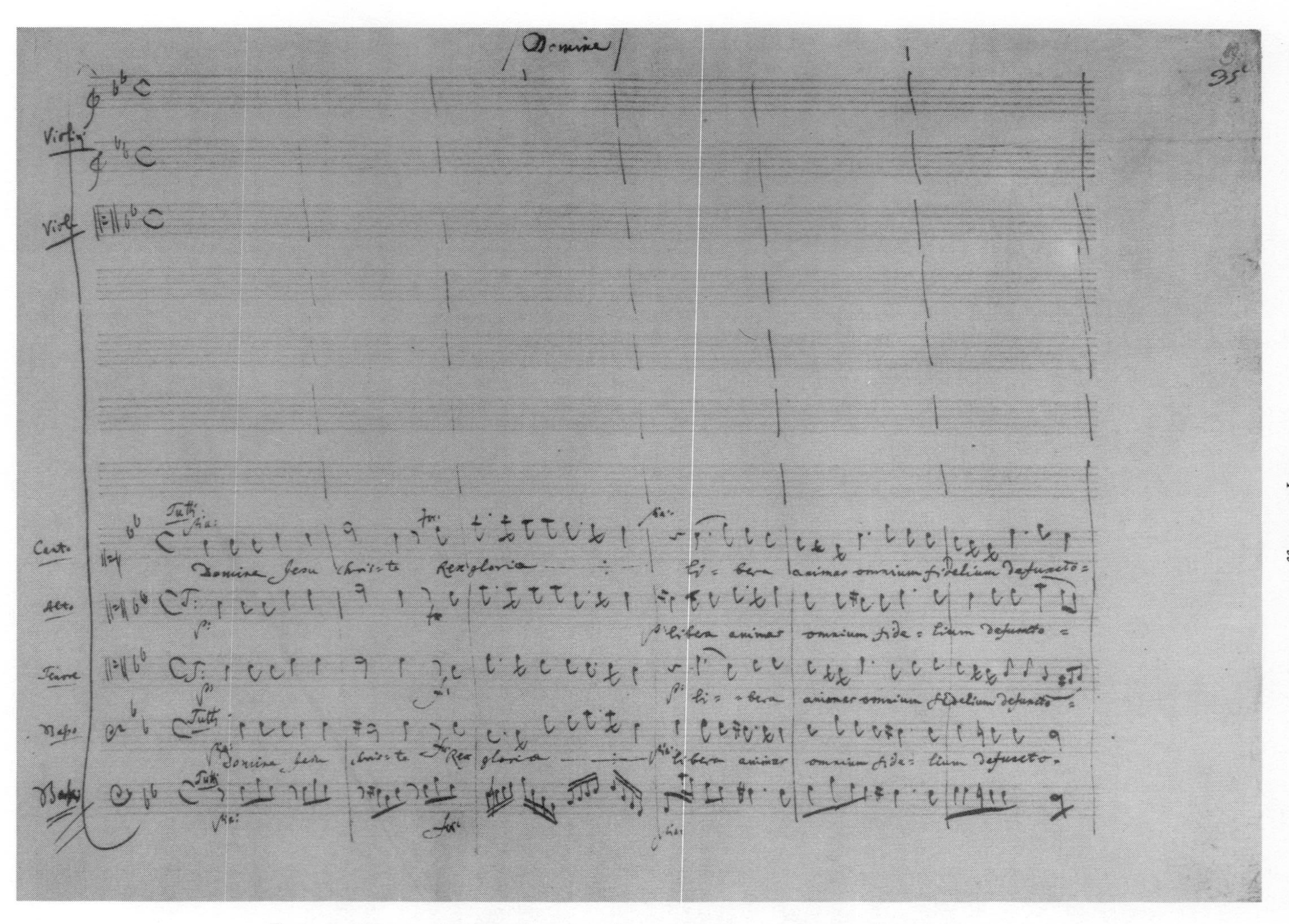

FIG. 2. Mozart, Autograph score of Requiem, fo. 35^{r}: Domine Jesu Christe.

Fos. 11–32 present a markedly different picture: here Joseph Eybler completed the instrumentation without regard for a uniform appearance (see Fig. 1). Nowak already described Süssmayr's instrumentation of the 'Dies irae' section as dependent on Eybler's. More unequivocally: Süssmayr copied Eybler's completed instrumentation from the autograph; his minor revisions of Eybler's competent work (not always for the better) are rarely more than editorial in nature. The same may also be true of the treatment of the Offertory, 'Domine Jesu' (see Table 1, col. 3). Walter Senn, in an article on the Abbé Stadler's role in assisting Constanze in the handling of Mozart's estate,[20] was the first to suggest that Stadler may also have had a hand in the completion of the Requiem. An examination of an early copy of the Offertory in Stadler's hand (Österreichische Nationalbibliothek, Mus. Hs. 4375 A) clearly shows that the Abbé worked on the instrumentation of the 'Domine Jesu' and 'Hostias' movements. However, he did not write directly into Mozart's draft score, but copied it first into a separate score. Süssmayr then, again, seems to have copied and edited Stadler's work. The priority of Stadler's occasionally sketchy instrumentation is suggested by a number of textual readings (see Figs. 3–4; trombone parts marked), but it cannot be established beyond any doubt. Therefore, Stadler's role in completing the Requiem must remain open.

The obviously well-co-ordinated and rather co-operative if hurried completion of the Requiem score was apparently dictated by three factors: (1) musical qualifications to meet the demands of the job; (2) pressure of time to fulfil the requirements of the commission; and (3) preparation of a uniform and 'original'-looking score for Count Walsegg.

Points (1) and (2) call for some additional comments. To (1): Constanze may not have been able to judge the individual compositional qualifications of Mozart's students, but she was looking for a master (Süssmayr's letter to Breitkopf specifically mentions the involvement of several 'masters'). Hence she proceeded according to seniority, apparently first asking Franz Jacob Freystädtler—at age 30 the most experienced of the small Viennese group of Mozart students and one with a strikingly Mozartian music hand. He started at the beginning with the easiest job, the colla-parte instrumentation of the Kyrie fugue, but gave up very soon, for unknown reasons (too busy or too much of a challenge?). The 26-year-old Joseph Eybler came next; we even have the receipt, dated 21 December 1791,[21] for the Requiem materials Constanze gave him. It seems unlikely that she waited more than two weeks after Mozart's death to make the necessary arrangements, so it is reasonable to assume (also in view of Freystädtler's minimal contribution) that Eybler was already the second choice. He too eventually gave up, though not so soon, and again for unspecified reasons. If the 43-year-old Stadler was the one to follow next, he was not a Mozart student but an old friend of the family. Stadler may have been the one who wisely changed the method of completing the score by not

[20] 'Abbé Maximilian Stadler: Mozarts Nachlaß und das Unterrichtsheft KV 453b,' *Mozart-Jahrbuch 1978*, 287–98.

[21] Otto Erich Deutsch (ed.), *Mozart: Die Dokumente seines Lebens* (Kassel, 1961), 375.

FIG. 3. Maximilian Stadler's score of Requiem (Österreichische Nationalbibliothek, Vienna; Mus. Hs. 4375), fo. 1r: Domine Jesu Christe.

FIG. 4. Franz Xaver Süssmayr's score of Requiem (Österreichische Nationalbibliothek, Vienna; Mus. Hs. 17561b), fo. 24^{r}: Domine Jesu Christe.

writing directly into the autograph but, rather, first making a facsimile-like copy, then entering the additions. His method may have been prompted by the visually disturbing results of Eybler's work, and it is conceivable, even likely, that Süssmayr started his task of copying and editing at this juncture, working in part concurrently with Stadler. Why and when Stadler ceased to participate is also unknown, but Süssmayr surely completed the bulk of the remaining work, especially the movements for which no completed vocal score existed and—to point (3) above—compiled a genuinely Mozartian-looking fair copy for Walsegg.

Briefly to point (2): The problem of the timing of the project must have played a decisive role from the beginning. The Requiem was under contract and Constanze needed the money; she gave Eybler as a deadline the middle of Lent, 1792. We do not in fact have any positive evidence when the score for Walsegg was finally completed. On 4 March 1792, however, Constanze signed a contract with the Prussian envoy in Vienna on the acquisition of scores by King Frederick William II, including a copy of the Requiem for 450 florins.[22] Since at least one copy had to be made from the score destined for Count Walsegg, the latter must have been finished at around this time, i.e. by early March 1792. Furthermore, Süssmayr dated the finished Rondo movement of Mozart's Horn Concerto in D major (K. 412) 6 April 1792, suggesting that he had ended his work on the Requiem by then. He also needed to get ready for the première of his own opera, *Moses oder der Auszug aus Aegypten*, scheduled by Schikaneder's troupe for 4 May 1792.[23]

III

Determining the course of events after Mozart's death is important with respect to the completion of the Requiem score. Investigating the course of events prior to 5 December 1791, however, opens up some perspectives regarding more specifically compositional issues.

The results of Alan Tyson's paper studies[24] indicate that Mozart, in all likelihood, began working on the Requiem only after his return from Prague, in mid-September 1791, leaving hardly more than two months before the beginning of his illness (20 November) for working on the Requiem, in addition to, among other things, putting the finishing touches on *The Magic Flute* (premiered on 30 September) and composing new larger works such as the Clarinet Concerto K. 622 or the Freemason Cantata K. 623 (dated 15 November—incidentally, the last entry in his *Verzeichnüß*). The Requiem autograph is made up of two paper types: Type I for fos. 1–8 and 11–22 and Type II for

[22] Wilhelm Bauer, Otto Erich Deutsch, and Joseph Heinz Eibl (eds.), *Wolfgang Amadeus Mozart = Briefe und Aufzeichnungen. Gesamtausgabe*, 7 vols. (Kassel, 1962–75), iv. 178.

[23] *W. A. Mozart, Requiem KV 626*, ed. Franz Beyer (Zurich, 1971), preface, 7.

[24] I wish to thank Alan Tyson for communicating his findings to me before publishing them in the *NMA* supplement.

fos. 9–10 and 23–45. Type II is traceable in Mozart autographs from spring 1791 on. Type I, however, does not occur in Mozart manuscripts before the middle of September 1791, and is found also in the Overture and other late additions to *The Magic Flute*, in the Freemason Cantata, and in the single sketch-leaf for the Requiem, which also contains a sketch for *The Magic Flute* Overture.

It seems plausible that Mozart in fact did not start working consistently on the Requiem until October, i.e. until after the first performances of *The Magic Flute*. Considering Mozart's working habits, it is also reasonable to assume that he did not begin preparing the final score (and the draft score is nothing but the initial layer of what was to become the final score) until he had at least a clear concept of the work as a whole, and that he would basically proceed according to the actual sequence of movements. A few observations are in order at this point.

The 'Lacrimosa' is generally considered to be the last piece composed because, unlike the later 'Domine Deus' and 'Hostias' movements, the autograph draft breaks off after eight measures. The documentation cited in support of this view is Eybler's inscription on fo. 33^r, at the beginning of the 'Lacrimosa': 'Mozart's last manuscript, bequeathed to the Imperial Library after my death.' The manuscript bequeathed to the Library consisted, however, of fos. 33–45, so the inscription refers to the entire fascicle. Hence there is no reason to assume that mm. 1–8 of the 'Lacrimosa' were written after the 'Hostias'. But why, then, did Mozart break off after only eight measures (not six, as misrepresented by Süssmayr in his letter to Breitkopf)? Two reasons come to mind. First, the 'Lacrimosa' verse of the Requiem Sequence ends with the same phrase as does the Agnus Dei of the Requiem, namely 'dona eis requiem'. It would make sense for the composer to make these identical phrases of text correspond musically as well, but this would mean that the Agnus Dei had to reach a certain degree of completion before the composer could finalize the 'Lacrimosa' ending. Second, the 'Amen' fugue to follow the 'Lacrimosa' had only been sketched in its exposition, and it is by no means clear that Mozart had decided to conclude the 'Dies irae' with an elaborate fugue. The original foliation of the autograph score, leaving only four pages for 'Lacrimosa' plus 'Amen', might be held against it, or else—and quite possible too—Mozart had an extremely concise movement in mind. Whatever the case, as Robert Levin noted, the main subject of the 'Amen' fugue is an inversion of the theme of the opening Requiem.[25] Taken together with the fact that the opening measures of the 'Lacrimosa' also refer to the very beginning of the Requiem, the breaking-off after eight measures has probably much less to do with Mozart's terminal illness than with his reaching a significant strategic point in the composition, causing the composer to reflect on the connection between two distant but related passages, the Requiem opening and the Agnus Dei ending.

Another important point pertaining specifically to the sketch-leaf (see Fig. 5) can be made. It is curious that the 'Amen' sketch precedes the 'Rex tremendae' sketch because it belongs to a later movement. There is no question that the 'Amen' sketch (beginning on

[25] 'The Unfinished Works of Mozart' (Senior thesis, Harvard University, 1969), 64.

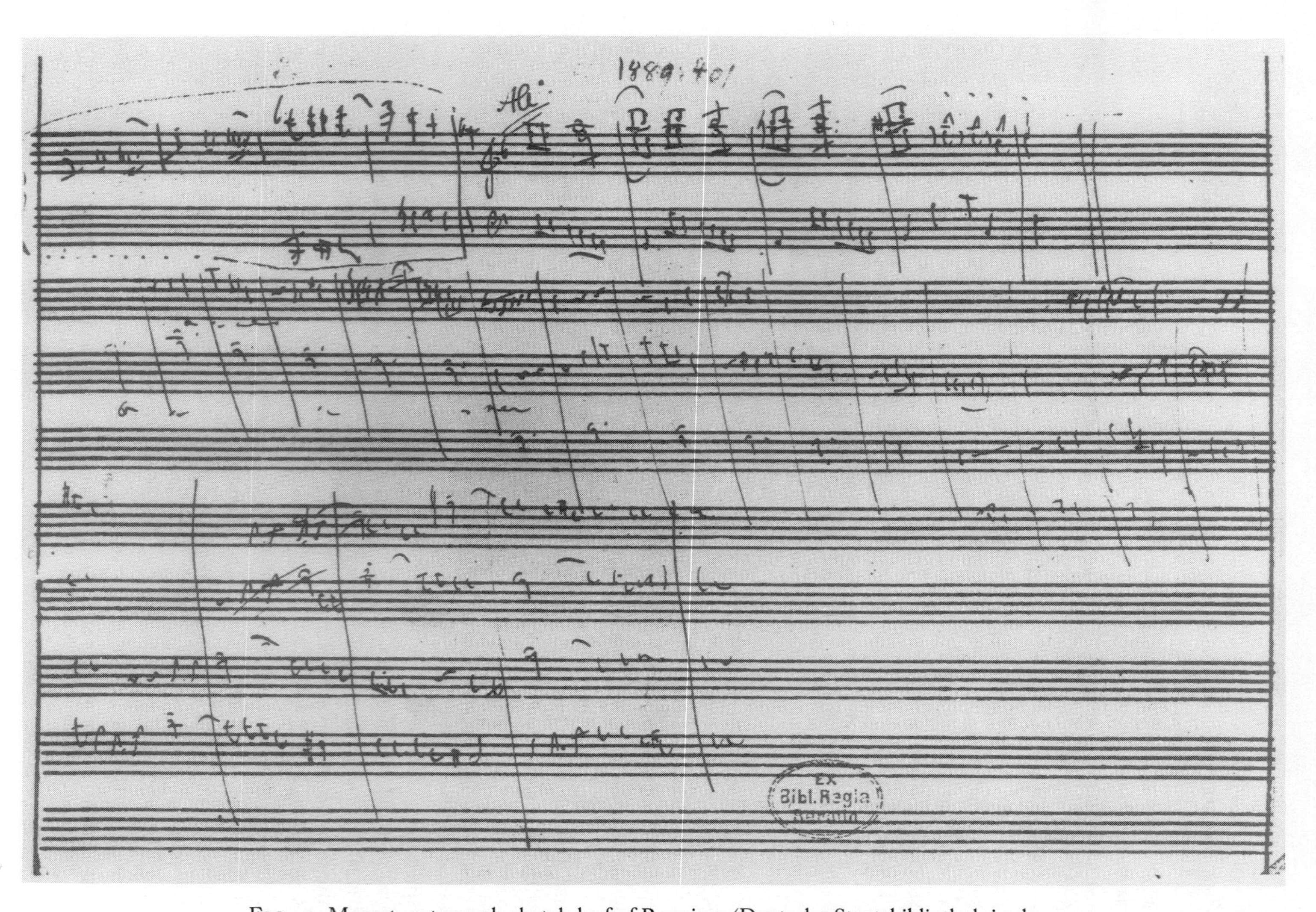

Fig. 5. Mozart, autograph sketch leaf of Requiem (Deutsche Staatsbibliothek in der Stiftung Preussischer Kulturbesitz, Berlin; Mus. ms. autogr. W. A. Mozart zu: KV 620), fo. 2r.

staves 3–5) was written down first. Furthermore, the 'Rex tremendae' sketch (staves 6–9) can only have been written in conjunction with the working-out of the canonic passage, mm. 7 ff., in the autograph score because the point of departure for the sketch, the two eighth-note D major chords at the beginning of m. 7, had already been notated. This can only mean that Mozart did the sketching concurrently with the preparation of the draft score (as in the 'Rex tremendae'), and he was sketching well ahead of actual work on the score (as in the case of the 'Amen'). The implications of this observation for the movements from Sanctus to 'Lux aeterna' are obvious and we shall return to them later.

The only surviving sketch-leaf reveals yet a third important point closely related to the overall stylistic orientation of the Requiem: Mozart focused virtually exclusively on the four-part vocal setting; the instrumental component is reduced to a minimum. An examination of the entire autograph score suggests that Mozart's composition of the Requiem resembled very closely his practice in string-quartet writing from the 'Haydn' quartets onward. He deals with the four-part setting as a whole, he lets it unfold in phrases and sections, he never singles out one voice over a longer period. In this respect the Requiem differs fundamentally from Mozart's Salzburg church music and also from the mature style of the C minor Mass K. 427 of 1783.

The absolute primacy of a transparent and coherent four-part vocal setting can first be found in the motet 'Ave verum Corpus' K. 618, dated 17 June 1791. The Requiem, though considerably different in gestures, textures, and integration of both retrospective and—in the Gluckian sense—decidedly 'classic' elements, takes the 'Ave verum' and its novel stylistic orientation as a point of departure. It seems as though Mozart wanted to give the genre of sacred music, in which he had been rather inactive for so long, a completely new direction—as he did with quite a number of other genres from the late 1780s on. For a closer context it might be relevant that, in early May 1791, he had received an appointment as honorary, non-salaried Kapellmeister of St Stephen's;[26] he must have welcomed the unexpected Requiem commission as an opportunity to turn his attention to a new genre and, at the same time, elevate it to a new level. Twenty years later, E. T. A. Hoffmann, in his influential essay 'Old and New Church Music' (1814), praised Mozart's Requiem as the ideal of a new kind of sacred music precisely because of the primacy of the vocal texture; he contrasts it with the more playful and considerably less solemn outlook of Haydn's late masses.[27]

The primacy of the vocal structure has consequences for the instrumentation of the Requiem, and Blume clearly misunderstood Mozart's intentions when he stated that the lack of oboes and flutes in the Requiem was inconsistent with the composer's late style. The degree of colla-parte accompaniment, for instance in the passages finished by Mozart himself, must not be underestimated. The contributions of Eybler, Stadler (?), and Süssmayr tend towards a continuous obbligato accompaniment, and it is interesting that Stadler later specifically refers to Süssmayr's work as Haydn-oriented.[28] This is not

[26] Deutsch, *Dokumente*, 346.
[27] 'Alte und neue Kirchenmusik', in *Schriften zur Musik*, ed. F. Schnapp (Darmstadt, 1963), 227.
[28] See Plath, 'Requiem-Briefe', 188.

the place to take issue with the details of Süssmayr's (and his collaborators') instrumentation,[29] but a major problem with the more recent attempts at correcting Süssmayr[30] or completely rewriting the orchestration[31] lies in the fact that they take Mozart's instrumentation from *The Magic Flute* and *La clemenza di Tito* as a stylistic and technical model. These works, however, with their prominent and sophisticated instrumental writing, are largely inappropriate models, which can only lead to an operatic 'Verfremdung' of Mozart's new style of church music.

The question arises, of course, in what way the movements newly composed by Süssmayr represent Mozart's ideals, if not his compositional concepts or even specific elements. The Sanctus and Benedictus movements, as has long been recognized, are particularly problematic. If one isolates the vocal substance in these movements, however, one discovers not only a strong resemblance in overall quality to that of the earlier movements, but also considerably fewer compositional flaws. The opening five measures of the Sanctus, for instance, represent a perfect vocal setting and one, furthermore, that includes a strong musical cross-reference to the opening measures of the 'Dies irae'; the problems begin only with m. 5 in the vocal setting, but already in m. 4 of the orchestral accompaniment, with a series of open parallel fifths.[32]

The Benedictus is comparable: the opening section of the vocal setting in both duo and quartet texture (quite apart from the often quoted thematic reference to Mozart's 1784 exercise book for Barbara von Ployer) has no counterpart, in terms of quality, in the orchestral writing. On the contrary, the instrumental opening of the Benedictus is particularly clumsy and inappropriate within the context of the style of Mozart's draft score, and is a mere anticipation of the vocal material. The Agnus Dei, on the other hand, juxtaposes a highly balanced and, in terms of rhetorical intensity, extremely effective four-part vocal setting and a complementary instrumental motif, exactly according to the manner of, for instance, the 'Domine Jesu'.

The Agnus Dei has always invited speculation that Süssmayr picked up material left by Mozart, the nature of which is hard to determine but consisted of at least a short vocal continuity draft with an instrumental 'motivum' (to use Süssmayr's term). It seems, primarily on the basis of the evaluation of the vocal substance, that Mozartian material—and certainly rather limited material—may have formed not only the point of departure for the Agnus Dei but for the Sanctus and Benedictus as well. Süssmayr's statement to Breitkopf that he had newly composed ('verfertigt') these movements would not be contradictory at all, because the materials presumably left by Mozart would have been

[29] Ernst Hess, in particular, has pointed out the major flaws and outright mistakes; see his 'Zur Ergänzung des Requiem'.

[30] Franz Beyer's edition (Zurich, 1971).

[31] Richard Maunder's edition (London, 1988); cf. also the review by Stanley Sadie, *Notes*, 46 (1990), 1052–5.

[32] The idea of differentiating between the parts of the Süssmayr score that are flawless and those that show errors in voice-leading and other mistakes has been developed by Robert Levin, who was kind enough to share some of his findings with me. See also his forthcoming edition of the Requiem (Hänssler Musik-Verlag).

very different from what we have: the completely finished vocal score with draft indications of the instrumental accompaniment; consequently, the burden of composition, rather than of invention, would indeed have rested solely on Süssmayr's shoulders. The result of his work, then, appears to be a curious mixture of good ideas, inadequate realization, and quite possibly misunderstanding of directions (as in the impossible presentation of the Hosanna, first in D major and later repeated in B flat); in short, anything but a homogeneous score.

The likelihood of Mozart's advance sketching is demonstrated not only by the sole surviving sketch-leaf, but also by a reference in a letter of 1827 from Constanze to Stadler regarding slips of paper, so-called 'Zettelchen', containing autograph material for the Requiem.[33] As early as 1800, at the collation session with Stadler, the existence of drafts ('Entwürfe') was mentioned (recorded by the Swedish diplomat Siverstolpe, an eyewitness to the scene).[34] There is, moreover, the reference in Süssmayr's letter to Breitkopf regarding intensive 'shoptalk' that took place between Mozart and his factotum (who is known to have assisted him with *La clemenza di Tito* and *The Magic Flute*), which might—among other things—have influenced Süssmayr's decision to use the Kyrie fugue for the 'Lux aeterna'. But there is also concrete evidence that Süssmayr used what he found on Mozart's desk, be it merely sheets of pre-ruled paper (paper type I of Mozart's autograph shows up, for instance, in fos. 17–20 of Codex a[2], i.e. at the very end of Süssmayr's score) or, more importantly, slips of paper with musical substance. A case in point is provided by the completion, or more precisely new composition, using genuine Mozart material, of the Rondo of the horn concerto K. 412.

The year 1791 as the date for Mozart's unfinished horn concerto K. 412 has only recently been established by Alan Tyson.[35] For the Rondo of the piece we possess two sources, a draft score by Mozart and a completed composition by Süssmayr (formerly considered to be by Mozart and, therefore, assigned the K. number 514). Both Mozart's draft score and Süssmayr's composition use exactly the same thematic substance, but it is clear that Süssmayr did not work from Mozart's draft score, as can be seen from his primitive harmonization and his mechanical treatment of the second violin, viola, and bass parts (see Exx. 1 and 2). I have to disagree with Tyson, however, who suggests that Süssmayr actually completed Mozart's draft score and chose to deviate from it. Franz Giegling suggests that Süssmayr saw the draft score briefly and then worked from memory.[36] The fact, however, that the exact correspondences between Mozart and Süssmayr's versions are limited strictly to the horn-part, and that Süssmayr uses a section clearly cancelled in Mozart's draft score, makes another procedure much more likely: in conjunction with his preparation of the concerto score, Mozart wrote a continuity draft for the horn-part (perhaps for a try-out with Leutgeb, for whom the work was intended

[33] See Stadler, *Vertheidigung*, 28.

[34] G.-C. Stellan Mörner, 'F. S. Siverstolpes im Jahr 1800 (oder 1801) in Wien niedergeschriebene Bemerkungen zu Mozarts Requiem, in Hellmut Federhofer (ed.), *Festschrift Alfred Orel zum 70. Geburtstag* (Vienna, 1960), 113–19.

[35] *Mozart: Studies of the Autograph Scores* (Cambridge, Mass. and London, 1987), 246–61.

[36] *NMA* V/14/5, preface, p. xvii f.

EXAMPLE 1. W. A. Mozart, Rondo for horn and orchestra, K. 514, autograph draft score

Example 2. W. A. Mozart, Rondo for horn and orchestra, K. 514, completion by Süssmayr

TABLE 2. *Sources for the Horn Rondo K. 412*

Hypothetical reconstruction of Mozart's continuity sketch of the horn-part and other notations	Süssmayr's version (K. 514; dated 6 April 1792)	Mozart's draft score (March–December 1791)
(1) mm. 9–16 = rondo theme, D major	9–16	9–16
(2) mm. 21–6, A major	25–30	21–6
(3) mm. 28–40, D major; m. 29 including V. 1	32–44	28–40
(4) mm. 48a–51a, A minor	59–62	cancelled
(5) lamentation (psalm tone), D minor/F major[a]	70–9	not included
(6) mm. 67–79, A minor	84–96	67–79
(7) mm 88–91, A major	109–12	88–91

[a] Actual location of lamentation melody uncertain (possibly notated on manuscript before Mozart wrote down the horn-part).

EXAMPLE 3. Modified version of the first psalm tone

and with whom he attended a performance of *The Magic Flute* on 8 October 1791).[37] It was this sketch-leaf that Süssmayr, without access to Mozart's score, turned into a fully developed score of his own. He followed the lines of the continuity draft faithfully (see Table 2, centre col.). This would explain why he pedantically included everything he saw, including two A minor passages, one of which Mozart had crossed out (passage 4) in his draft score. The piece of paper may also have contained, jotted down somewhere in between, the cantus firmus (a modified version of the first psalm tone generally used for the *lamentatio*; see Ex. 3), which Michael Haydn had used for the 'Te decet hymnus' section in the first movement of his Requiem of 1771; Mozart, who was familiar with Haydn's work, may have considered using the melody for the same passage in his own Requiem before deciding on the *tonus peregrinus*. If my hypothesis is correct, the surprising liturgical touch of Süssmayr's version of the rondo (K. 514), wherein mm. 70–9 the solo horn intones the *lamentatio* chant, may not be interpreted as a humorous insert[38] but rather a misguided faithfulness that forced him into the Requiem key area D minor/F major within an already disproportionate A minor episode.

[37] Briefe, iv. 158.

[38] As suggested by Engelbert Grau, 'Ein bislang übersehener Instrumentalwitz von W. A. Mozart', *Acta Mozartiana*, 8 (1961), 47.

This discussion of Süssmayr's work on the horn Rondo K. 412 presents, to be sure, at best inconclusive and indirect evidence for the one-time existence of further sketch and draft materials for the Requiem. It does, however, present concrete evidence for Süssmayr's handling of a situation where he was forced to compose—not just complete—a score on the basis of sketchy, loosely connected, perhaps slightly confusing musical information, from which he then more or less mechanically and routinely, rarely imaginatively, manufactured a product that exhibits Mozartian vocabulary without the proper language. Assuming that the Requiem materials were less extensive than what was available to Süssmayr for his composition of the horn Rondo, the analogy appears, nevertheless, to be striking. The problems of the Requiem's Sanctus, Benedictus, and Agnus Dei, with their obvious imbalance of impressive musical substance on the one hand and inadequate compositional treatment on the other, are fundamentally the same as those to be found in the horn Rondo, except that we are unable exactly to identify Mozart's contribution. We can only look for possible traces of his input. The nature of the extant Requiem sketches and draft score clearly suggests that the starting-point for all movements consisted of vocal lines. Our analytical attention must, therefore, focus on the only available document that is likely to provide clues, of whatever quality: the Süssmayr score. Rejecting this score—as is most drastically done in Maunder's edition—means nothing less than sacrificing the possibility of tracing original Mozart.

For this reason alone, the Süssmayr score deserves to be protected as the only contemporary historical, philological, and musical document of those Requiem portions which Mozart was unable to include in his draft score. To the listener, the Süssmayr score reveals an aesthetic dimension as well, because it is the only document that represents the genuine musical truth of the unfinished work. In fact, its rough juxtaposition and open intermingling of perfection and imperfection draws us directly into the realm and atmosphere of the inner Mozart circle trying to cope with an overwhelming legacy.

Leopold Mozart's *Violinschule* Annotated by the Author

ALBI ROSENTHAL

THE Preface, dated 26 July 1756, of Leopold Mozart's *Versuch einer gründlichen Violinschule* begins as follows, in English translation:

It is many years since I wrote the present rules for those who came to me for instruction in violin-playing. I was often greatly surprised that no textbook was forthcoming for the study of so popular and almost indispensable an instrument for most kinds of music-making as the violin: all the more so, as sound principles, and particularly some rules for particular bowings to serve good taste, had long been needed. I was often very sad to see how badly students had been taught so that one had not only to teach them from the beginning all over again, but also to take great pains to eradicate the faults they had been taught, or which had been allowed to develop. I felt great sympathy when I heard already fully developed violinists, who were sometimes not a little proud of their expertise, play very easy passages contrary to the intention of the composer, through using faulty bowing. Indeed, I was astonished when I had to observe that even verbal explanation and demonstration of how a piece should be played was often not enough for them to attain the true and pure way of performing.

I therefore contemplated having this *Violinschule* published. Indeed, I discussed this with a printer. However, great as my zeal always was to serve the musical world to the utmost of my power, I hesitated for more than a whole year: I was too ignorant in these enlightened times to venture into daylight with my modest efforts.

At last, I happened to receive a copy of Herr Marpurg's *Historisch-kritische Beyträge zur Aufnahme der Musik*. I read its Preface. He writes at the beginning that one cannot complain about the number of available writings about music. He demonstrates this, but regrets, among others, that there is still no method on violin-playing. This observation suddenly revived my previous resolution, and became the strongest stimulus to send these pages to the printer in my native city without delay.

Thus the first three paragraphs.

For the purpose of the present paper, it may be relevant to quote also from the sixth paragraph of this Preface. After stressing that the book could easily have been further enlarged in various directions, Leopold writes:

I have omitted everything that could have enlarged the book, and for the sake of the desired brevity, I decided that the beginnings of the music examples for two violins in the fourth chapter should not be extended further, and in general that the other examples should be somewhat shorter.

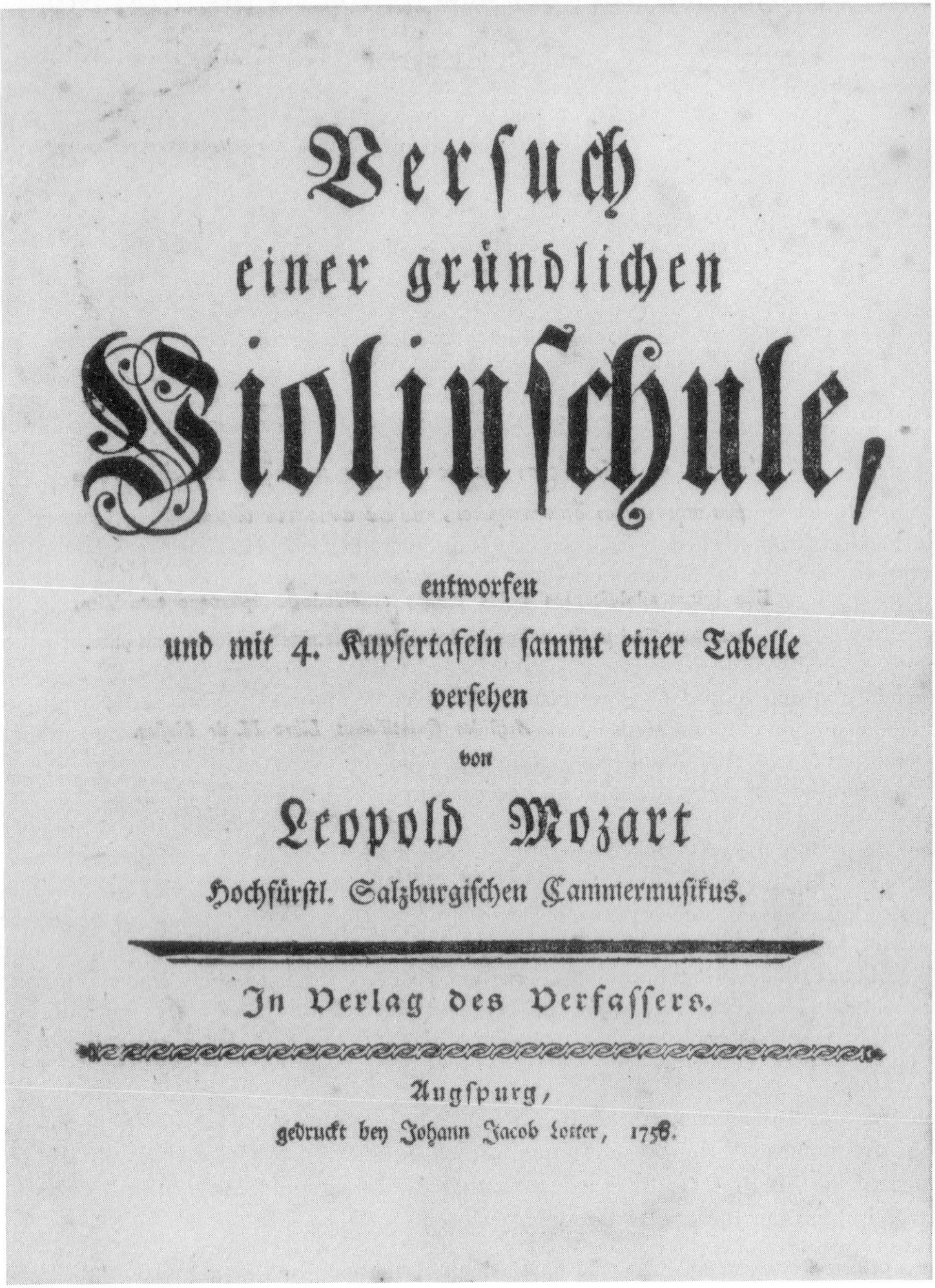

Versuch
einer gründlichen
Violinschule,
entworfen
und mit 4. Kupfertafeln sammt einer Tabelle
versehen
von
Leopold Mozart
Hochfürstl. Salzburgischen Cammermusikus.

In Verlag des Verfassers.

Augspurg,
gedruckt bey Johann Jacob Lotter, 1758.

FIG. 1. Title-page of Leopold Mozart, *Versuch einer gründlichen Violinschule* (1756), with altered date.

The fear that the volume might become unwieldy, and thereby also too expensive, unless the text were kept as concise as possible, and, particularly, the music examples shortened, is expressed clearly and repeatedly throughout Leopold's fascinating correspondence with his friend and publisher Johann Jakob Lotter in Augsburg, comprising no fewer than thirty elaborate letters written from Salzburg between 10 April 1755 and 1 April 1756.[1] These letters reveal Leopold Mozart not only as a consummate master of the theory and practice of violin-playing in all their aspects, but also as an author supremely well informed concerning every detail of book production, typography, layout, paper manufacture, illustration, etc. Moreover, his scholarly approach and methodical analysis of problems arising in the course of printing are admirable and illuminating. The discussions with the printer, beginning with the first sheet of the author's manuscript and continuing down to the setting of the publication date (often too optimistically by Leopold), are also a singular bibliographical record of German eighteenth-century book production.

The purpose of this paper is to present a hitherto unknown and undescribed copy of the first edition of the *Violinschule* with copious autograph annotations by Leopold, made in preparation for a new edition (private collection, England). Practically all the additions were incorporated in the second edition of 1769/1770. A fact not noticed before is the restoration to their original length of many music examples: the success of the book evidently allowed them to be given in full again, at least in parts, in the second and subsequent editions.[2] A full account of all Leopold Mozart's manuscript entries in this volume is given in the Appendix.

The following extracts from Leopold's letters to his printer give a vivid picture of the tribulations and troubles as the book was taking shape. Most of these passages have not been available in English translation before. Although other matters are included, too—among them the announcement on 9 February 1756 that his wife had, on 27 January, given birth to a son called Joannes Chrisostomus Wolfgang Gottlieb—the subject of shortening the music examples comes up again and again: it is this subject which forms the background to the alterations made by Leopold in the copy discussed here.

It is likely that Leopold made this revision not later than two years after the publication of the first edition of 1756: the printed date on the title-page is altered, in Leopold's hand, from 1756 to 1758 (see Fig. 1). According to Leopold's Preface to the second edition of 1769/1770, the first edition had become difficult to obtain soon after publication. Stocks of it were exhausted by 1766. His principal excuse for the long delay in presenting the second edition to the public was his occupation with other matters,

[1] Wilhelm A. Bauer, Otto Erich Deutsch, and Joseph Heinz Eibl (eds.), *Wolfgang Amadeus Mozart: Briefe und Aufzeichnungen. Gesamtausgabe* (henceforth *Briefe*), 7 vols. (Kassel, 1962–75), i. 3–48. To date, only seven of these letters are available in English translation, some in extracts only, in *A Treatise on the Fundamental Principles of Violin Playing by Leopold Mozart*, tr. Editha Knocker (London, 1948), pp. xix–xxiv.

[2] The 1948 English edition mentions a number, but not all, of the textual additions, and refers to their appearance only in the third edition of 1787, not in the second edition. The restoration of the music examples is not mentioned at all.

particularly the journeys to France, England, the Netherlands, and Italy with his son and daughter.

A full translation into English of Leopold's letters to Johann Jakob Lotter would be a most desirable task. For the purpose of this article, however, only such passages have been selected as have a bearing on the background of Leopold's entries in this annotated volume.

Salzburg, [10 April 1755] (Briefe, *i. 4*). Now, regarding my scribblings: I had, indeed, been eagerly looking forward to your letter, and in the next days I shall put into fair copy as much as will fill at least one sheet, and I will continue writing immediately. Meanwhile, I request you to inform me by the next mail, *how much would be the difference between 500 and 1,000 copies, how much the paper will cost, namely in medium quarto, in short, what would be the additional cost of an edition of 1,000 copies* . . . I contemplate that printing should start with the first main chapter, for the title-page, dedication, and preface can be printed at any time. I hope, because I have the honour of being the first to have this kind of work printed at your esteemed printing press since you were married and became the sole proprietor, that you will do something good for me, too.

Salzburg, 9 June [1755] (Briefe, *i. 4*). Meanwhile, I am sending you some more, up to § 15 of the third section, which section will comprise three more of my sheets. It begins with the beat (*Tact*).

Salzburg, 7 July 1755 (Briefe, *i. 7–8*). I would only ask you, particularly as regards the music examples, not to accept things when in doubt, but rather to send such passages back to me for correction first. I am pleased with the proof-sheet. Both format and type are good, and I am completely satisfied with them . . . You need not worry that the first sheet took fourteen pages . . . *First*, my remaining sheets are written much smaller, and more compressed; in spite of this there are a few more sheets to this manuscript than in the old one . . . *Secondly*, further on, where the *bowing*, *triplets*, and *changes of bow-stroke* are discussed, there are examples which one cannot compress tightly. You should, therefore, not use large note-type.

Salzburg, 28 August 1755 (Briefe, *i. 13*). I can well believe that you are surprised about my *music examples*. However, it just cannot be done differently; they have to look like this if one wishes to do them correctly and make them clear to one's fellow men. I have been extremely careful not to insert anything superfluous respecting the examples, in order not to lengthen the book unduly . . . Every connoisseur will find that each example has its particular use and that most of them are only there where they are needed. It is true, there are still examples enough in the main sections I still have in hand, but they are not as fearsome . . . As you now write that you do not know what the length of the *manuscript* will be because of the notes, I have now terminated with the *eleventh main chapter* . . . My *manuscript* therefore consists of 226 or 227 pages, and thus it can remain.

Salzburg, 24 November 1755 (Briefe, *i. 22*). . . . the music examples take most of the time.

Salzburg, 9 February 1756 (Briefe, *i. 33–4*). Here is sheet (J), duly returned. Please see to it that I receive each time a cleanly corrected and printed sheet of the previous proof, together with the quire that has new corrections, which I can then join to the quire I already have. *For concerning the example* on this proof, § 8 on p. 68 is linked with § 4 of this main section. On p. 69, § 9, the 9th § of the previous main section is quoted. If I had received sheet (H), too, I could have checked whether I had quoted correctly . . . I can tell you firmly that everything you will still receive from me in manuscript will consist of a maximum of six sheets of mine, of which, on five sheets, there are barely six very short examples, indeed, often only a few notes. By the way, I can inform you that on 27 January at 8 p.m., my wife was happily delivered of a son, but the *afterbirth* had to be taken from her, which left her astonishingly weak. Now, however, thank God, child and mother are well . . . The boy's name is *Joannes Chrisostomus, Wolfgang, Gottlieb*.

Salzburg, 23 February 1756 (Briefe, *i.* *37–8*). [Leopold corrects mistakes in the music examples on pp. 76, 78, and 79, then writes:] I notice that the examples enlarge the book considerably, and if I had the manuscript still in my hands, I would perhaps try to shorten them as much as possible. I could, for instance, on pages 73, 74, and 75, where there are two lines of examples, have left out the second line each time, although it would really be preferable to have them there. (See Fig. 2.)

Salzburg, 27 February 1756 (Briefe, *i.* *38–41*). [Leopold corrects two examples on p. 82, and gives instructions concerning examples on pp. 81, 85, 86, and 88; he then writes:] Now I must tell you of my fright when I saw that the first long example on p. 88, occupying one and a half lines in my manuscript, here fills an entire page. Continued like this, I could swear that the book would run to three good alphabets [of quire letters]. I therefore have to adopt a different method, and shorten the examples. If you have already set two or three, now stop sharp, and then carry on [with the text]. I mean that, of these two-part examples, leave out only the last ones, *namely* those in 12/8, 3/2, and also 3/1 time. I will be more precise: [Leopold writes out the first and fourth examples, and gives further instructions concerning the shortening of examples 2, 3, and 4, etc.]. Now comes the fifth main section. It has no examples. There are enough examples in the sixth main section. First, the second voice is to be omitted throughout, and I reduce the first long example thus:

As I now wish to shorten all examples in this manner, please send me by the next post the *manuscript* of the sixth main section: *On Triplets* etc. I will shorten it and will return it at once . . . Send me the *manuscript* beginning with the eighth main section and all subsequent matter. In a few hours I will shorten all examples where this can be done . . . Do it thus, and all will be well . . .

It occurs to me that you might have difficulty with typesetting, for example, where the sixth main section follows on the fifth in such a manner that you cannot separate the leaves. I am therefore writing out the examples as follows: [here follow the examples in § 4 to § 9]. In paragraphs 10, 11, 12, 13, 14, 15, and 16, set only as much of the upper voice as occupies one line in print; the rest, including the second violin part, is to be omitted. If, for example, you can print two measures on one line, it is all right. Where you cannot, set one and a half, or indeed only one measure. In other words: no example must exceed one line, and it can end wherever it has to, no matter. [Here follow corrections in examples 17, 18, and 19, and other instructions.]

Salzburg, 14 March 1756 (Briefe, *i.* *43–4*). [Leopold corrects examples on pp. 83 and 86, then writes:] Here are three main sections. The many examples on pages 137 to 140 I have abbreviated as much as possible. Do continue to set these examples: the beginning and end of each and its alterations may begin at the start, the middle, or the end of a line; it comes to the same thing. For these examples are identified sufficiently by numbers and letters . . . I have abbreviated whatever I could. You need not think, however, that I left out anything which might be detrimental to the book. No! . . . try to bring the smaller examples *into one line*, the longer ones,

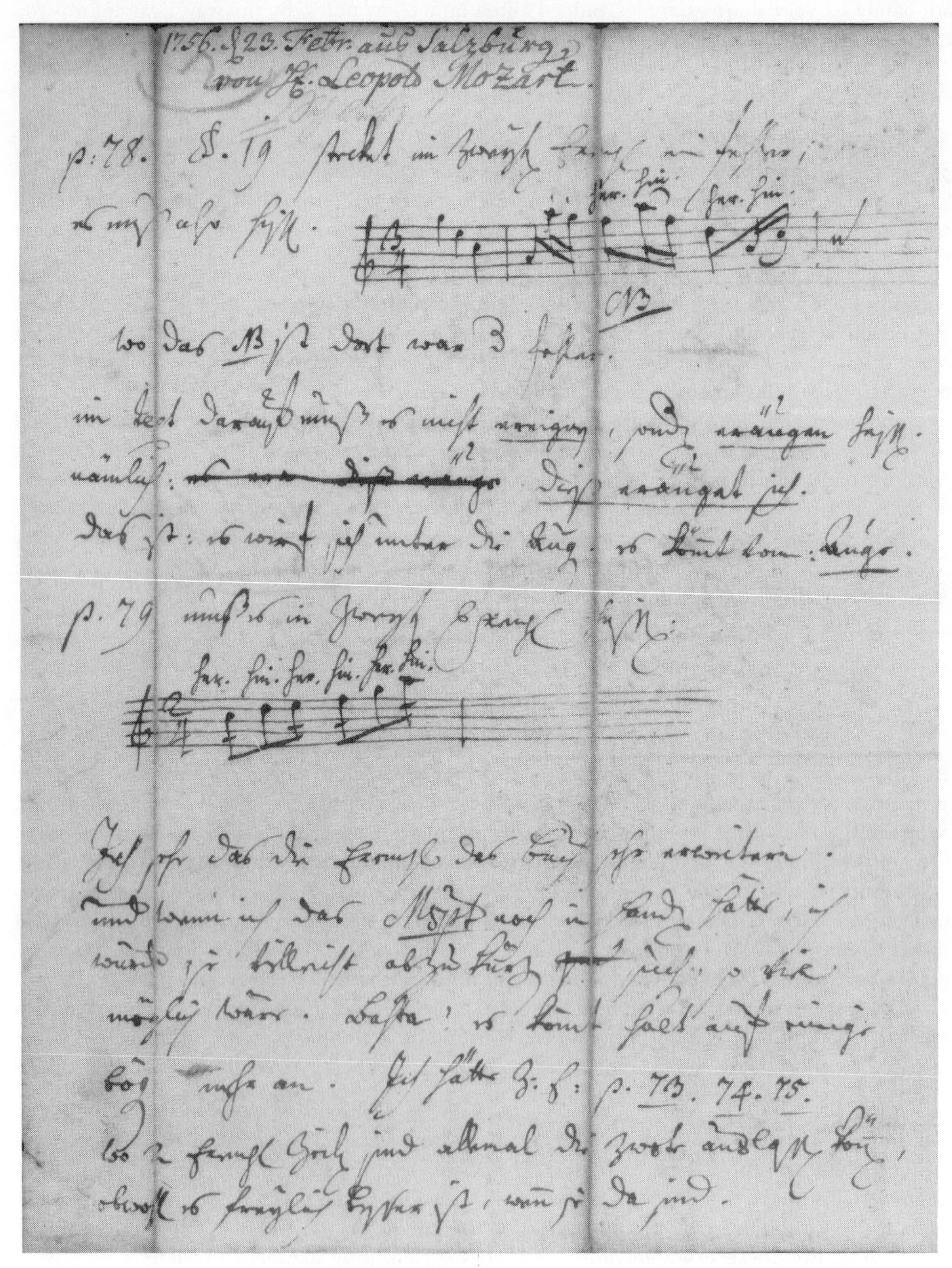

1756. d 23. Febr. aus Salzburg, von H. Leopold Mozart.

p:78.

NB

p. 79

FIG. 2. Leopold Mozart, letter of 23 February 1756 to Johann Jakob Lotter (private collection, England).

however, *into two lines*. Sometimes you will see a line drawn with *red crayon*, for example, in the *second example* on p. 158. The same at the end of both examples, *page 161* and page 162. *This signifies* that you can stop there, if need be, *if otherwise there would have to be a new line*. But you must add a *custos musicus* (~), signifying what the next note would be: for thus you may terminate with good conscience, and save a line.

The last extant letter was written on 1 April 1756 (*Briefe*, i. 47–8). Leopold still pleads, without hope, for publication of the book on 1 May, the name-day of the Archbishop: 'This is, by year and day, the only day still remaining until February next year.' In fact, the book appears to have finally seen the light of day shortly after Leopold dated his Preface 26 July 1756.

APPENDIX

Annotations by Leopold Mozart to the First Edition of his Violinschule

Text additions by Leopold Mozart are given in italics.

Title-page: 1756 altered in ink to 1758

p. 17: In the lower blank margin, Leopold supplied, in brown ink, the footnote (mm) called for in the print five lines from the end of the page:

(mm) Wer sich die Geschichte u[nd] Lehrsätze der alten u[nd] neuen Musik mehr bekannt machen will, der lese Marburgs [sic] *Einleitung in die Geschichte u[nd] Lehrsätze der alten u[nd] neuen Musik; und in Mizlers Bibliothek wird er vieles finden.*

Whoever would like to become more familiar with the history and precepts of old and new music should read Marpurg's Introduction to the *History and Precepts of Old and New Music*; and he will find much in Mizler's *Musical Library*.

p. 37: In the lower blank margin, Leopold added in brown ink:

Die Zertheilung dieser Noten durch den Bogenstrich findet nur Anfangs Platz, bis der Schüler die Gleicheit [sic] *des Tactes genau verstehet. Dann muss man aber die Abtheilung n[ich]t mehr hören. Man lese nur den gleich folgenden § 18.*

The division of these notes by the bow-stroke occurs only at the beginning, until the pupil understands the right division of time exactly. Then, however, the division must no longer be audible. See the immediately following § 18.

p. 41 (§ 13): Leopold added in the right margin (with a sign after the printed word 'His'):

oder Bis — or B sharp

6 lines lower, after printed 'B':

oder Bes — or B flat

p. 43 (§ 16): The three printed measures are altered by Leopold. After the first two beats of measure 1 there is a ⊖ sign and a slur extending over the remaining two and a half measures. Two measures are written on the blank staves:

p. 46 (§ 24): The three-line printed example is altered by Leopold. In the first line, the second half of measure 2 and the whole of measure 3 are crossed out, and the line ends, in Leopold's hand: . In the second line, the first six printed notes remain, the following five and the rest are crossed out and replaced by: . The whole of the third line is cancelled and replaced in the lower margin by:

p. 54 (§ 4), line 8, after 'Seyte den Klang': A manuscript sign with a similar one five lines below, before 'Wir sehen'. Line 11: 'dadurch' replaced in manuscript with '*folgl* [ich]'.

(§ 5), line 1, after 'Theile': A sign, and above it the manuscript addition:

nicht zu weit von der unten angebrachten Nusse	not too far from the nut fixed below

line 3, after 'Zeigefingers':

doch nicht steif sondern leicht ungezwungen	yet not stiffly, but lightly, freely

line 3, after 'Fig. IV':

und obgleich der erste finger bey der Verstärkung u[nd] Verminderung des Tones das meiste thun muss, so soll doch auch	and although the first finger must contribute the most towards increasing and diminishing the tone, yet

line 4: 'soll' deleted

p. 55 (§ 6), third line of 'Drittens', after 'ungezwungen': Manuscript footnote '(a)':

Will der Schüler den Ellenbogen nicht biegen, und geigt folglich mit einem steifen Arm u[nd] starker Bewegung der Achsel; so stelle man ihn mit dem rechten Arm nahe an eine Wand: er wird, wenn er beym Herabstriche den Ellenbogen gegen die Wand stösst, solchen ganz gewiss biegen lernen.	If the pupil will not bend his elbow, and consequently plays with a stiff arm and with strong movement of the shoulder; then make him stand near a wall with his right arm: he will, when he knocks his elbow against the wall during a down-bow, surely learn to bend it.

Also in 'Drittens', after 'die Hand', manuscript addition in the right margin:

ja vielmehr der Zeigefinger	even more the index finger

p. 56 ('Viertens'), first line, after 'einen langen': Manuscript insertion in the upper margin:

ohn abgesetzten, sanften u[nd] fliessenden Bogenstrich gewöhnen.	[accustom oneself to an] uninterrupted soft and flowing bow-stroke.

line 3: 'und etwa kaum die Seyten berühren' altered in the margin to:

die kaum die Seyte berühren	which scarcely touch the string

line 11, end of 'Sechstens': Manuscript footnote after 'nicht rein' in lower margin:

Man erinnere sich immer des am Ende des § 4 vorgeschriebenen Hilfsmittel: man sey nicht zu weichlich u[nd] lasse sich durch die kleine Empfindlichkeit, die diese Uebung anfangs wegen der Ausspannung der Nerven verursachet, nicht abschrecken.	One should always remember the remedy prescribed at the end of § 4: one should not be too soft-hearted and allow oneself to be deterred by the slight discomfort caused at first by this exercise due to the stretching of the nerves.

p. 57, § 8, line 6, after 'die Hand': Manuscript footnote written in the lower margin:

nach der Vorschrift des § 4 und § 6, und in dieser Stellung lasse man ihn unter Beobachtung aller oben angeführten Regeln die Musikleiter abgeigen.	according to the instructions of § 4 and § 6, and in this position let him, while observing all the rules given above, play the scale.

p. 64, line 1, after '(b) im': Manuscript addition above:
im natürl (B) oder in natural B, or

p. 70 (§ 2): At the end of this paragraph is a manuscript '(*a*)', without corresponding insertion.

p. 72, line 1: Two measures added in manuscript on printed blank staves:

line 2: One measure added in manuscript on printed blank staves:

(§ 6): One measure added in manuscript on printed blank staves:

(§ 7), last line: One measure added in manuscript on printed blank staves:

p. 73 (§ 8), second line of example: Three measures added in manuscript on printed blank staves:

(§ 9), last line of example: Three measures added in manuscript on printed blank staves:

her hin her hin

(§ 13): Two measures added at end of music example, to be inserted before the last two printed quavers:

p. 76 (§ 16): One measure added to the last line of music examples:

p. 77: One measure added to the first line of the music example:

One measure added to the third line:

p. 78 (§ 19), first line of the music example: One measure at end added in manuscript:

second line of the music example: One measure at end added in manuscript:

third line of the music example: One measure at end added in manuscript:

p. 79 (§ 21): Three measures added to the first line of the music example:

One measure added to the second line of the music example: 

p. 80 (§ 4): The last three notes of the first line replaced by two measures: 

Three measures added to the second line: 

p. 81 (§ 25): Two measures added at end of first line: 

p. 82 (§ 27), at the beginning of line three of the music example '(a)': Footnote in the lower margin:

Diess ist der einzige Fall, wo man die Vertheilung der Noten durch einen kleinen Nachdruck des Bogens vornehmlich vorzutragen pfleget: nämlich wenn mehr solche zu zertheilende Noten im geschwinden Zeitmasse hintereinander vorzukommen.

This is the only case where it is customary to mark the division of the notes by a little pressure of the bow, i.e. when more such notes occur in quick tempo, one after another.

p. 83 (§ 28): Four measures added to the second line of the music example (see Fig. 3):

(§ 29): Measures added to each of the 4 music examples:

p. 84 (§ 30): Two measures added to the first music example: 

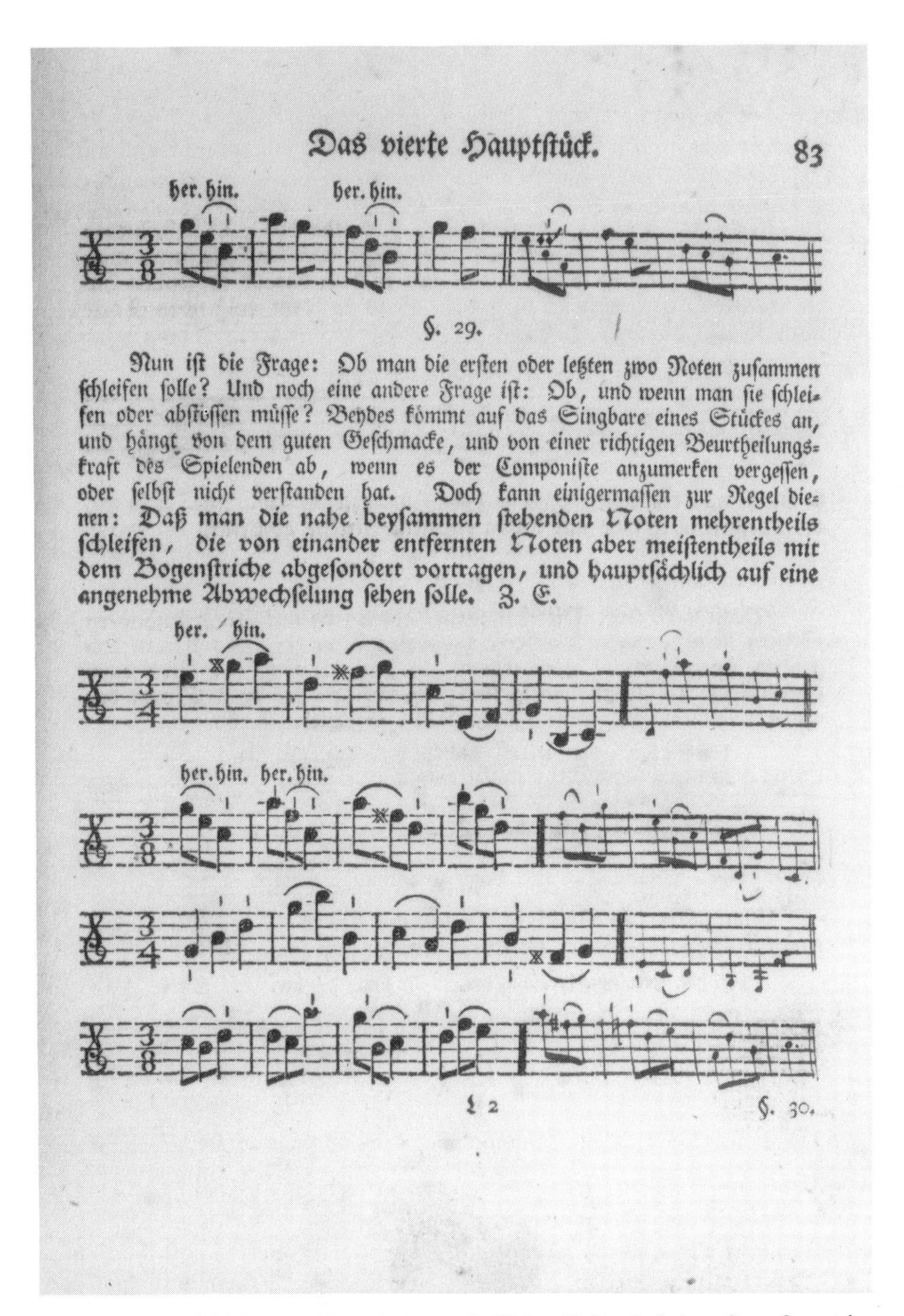

Das vierte Hauptstück. 83

her. hin. her. hin.

§. 29.

Nun ist die Frage: Ob man die ersten oder letzten zwo Noten zusammen schleifen solle? Und noch eine andere Frage ist: Ob, und wenn man sie schleifen oder abstossen müsse? Beydes kömmt auf das Singbare eines Stückes an, und hängt von dem guten Geschmacke, und von einer richtigen Beurtheilungskraft des Spielenden ab, wenn es der Componiste anzumerken vergessen, oder selbst nicht verstanden hat. Doch kann einigermassen zur Regel dienen: **Daß man die nahe beysammen stehenden Noten mehrentheils schleifen, die von einander entfernten Noten aber meistentheils mit dem Bogenstriche abgesondert vortragen, und hauptsächlich auf eine angenehme Abwechselung sehen solle.** Z. E.

her. hin.

her. hin. her. hin.

L 2 §. 30.

Fig. 3. Leopold Mozart, *Versuch einer gründlichen Violinschule* (1756), p. 83, with author's MS additions.

(§ 31): Two measures added to the music example: 

p. 85 (§ 32), end of the first paragraph, between 'stark an' and 'Z. E.':

nicht in der Absicht, dass alle dergleichen Passagen auf diese Art müssen gespielt werden: sondern um die Fertigkeit zu erlangen, aller Orten, wo es nöthig ist, die Stärke anbringen zu können.	not with the intention that all similar passages have to be played in this manner, but in order to attain the facility of emphasizing wherever necessary.

Two measures added to next line of the music example: 

p. 86 (§ 35): One measure added at the end of the example: 

(§ 36): One measure added at the end of the example: 

p. 105 (§ 10), line 10: 'mit socher Art' changed in manuscript in the margin:

ohne Erhebung des Bogens mit einer so anhaltenden Verbindung	without lifting the bow with so smooth a connection

p. 107 (§ 13), line 15: Manuscript (*b*) (indication of footnote 'b') written at end of previous sentence.

p. 125 (§ 9): One measure added to the music example: 

p. 129 (§ 18): One measure added to the music example: 

p. 147 (§ 1), line 2: The printed '(h)' is crossed out and (*B*) written above it. On line 8, after 'Applicatur', is the manuscript insertion:

oder Application.	or fingering.

p. 150 (§ 6): One measure is added to the top line of the music example: 

(§ 7), line 3: Footnote (*a*) is added after 'abgeigt':

Man nehme nur gleich die im vierten Hauptstücke nach § 39 kommenden Stücke; und spiele sie in der Applicatur.	Now take the pieces in the fourth main section of § 39, and play them in the positions.

(§ 8): One measure is added to the second line of the example: 

p. 155: In the first line of the example, measure 2 is crossed out, and one measure added:

(§ 18): Two measures are added to the last line of the music example:

p. 176 (§ 7): An alternative version of the eight notes in the penultimate line of the music example is written in the last line:

oder

p. 185 (§ 17), measure 1 of the last music example: The first four lower notes are crossed out and replaced by:

g f e d

p. 187 (§ 18): Added at the end of line 4 of the music example:

p. 201 (§ 10), 4 lines before the end: The lines following 'Vorschlags, und' are replaced, in the right margin, by:

die zwo kleinen Nötchen sammt der darauf folgenden Hauptnote werden gelind daran geschliefet, wie es schon § 8 ist gelehret worden.

the two little notes together with the following principal note are slurred smoothly thereon, as already taught in § 8.

Below, in the lower margin, a manuscript footnote:

(d) Wenn der Bass oder die Grundstimme immer in einem Tone ruht, darf man freylich nicht so vorsichtig handeln, und man kann alle aufsteigenden Vorschläge an bringen.

(d) When the bass or the fundamental voice always remains on one tone, one need not be so cautious, and one can add all ascending appoggiaturas.

p. 202 (§ 11): Manuscript corrections in the sentence 'Man pflegt auch oft [word deleted by underlining] den aufsteigenden Vorschlag *mit zwo Noten* von der Terze zu machen *und and die Hauptnote anzuschleifen*, wenn er [word deleted] *auch* gleich dem Ansehen nach *der Vorschlag* aus dem Nebentone herfliessen sollte (see Fig. 4).

Diesen Vorschlag mit zwo Noten heisst man den Schleifer. Added in place of 'Man macht ihn in solchem Falle aber meistentheils mit zwoen Noten. Z. E.'.

This appoggiatura with two notes is called the glide. In such a case one usually plays it with two notes. For example

First line of the music example, measure 3 in manuscript: measure 5 (end of same line: Before 'Wenn er' (next line, sentence deleted by underlining), footnote (*a*) in lower margin:

Der Schleifer wird aber meistens zwischen zwo entfernten Noten angebracht.

But the glide is used mostly between two distant notes.

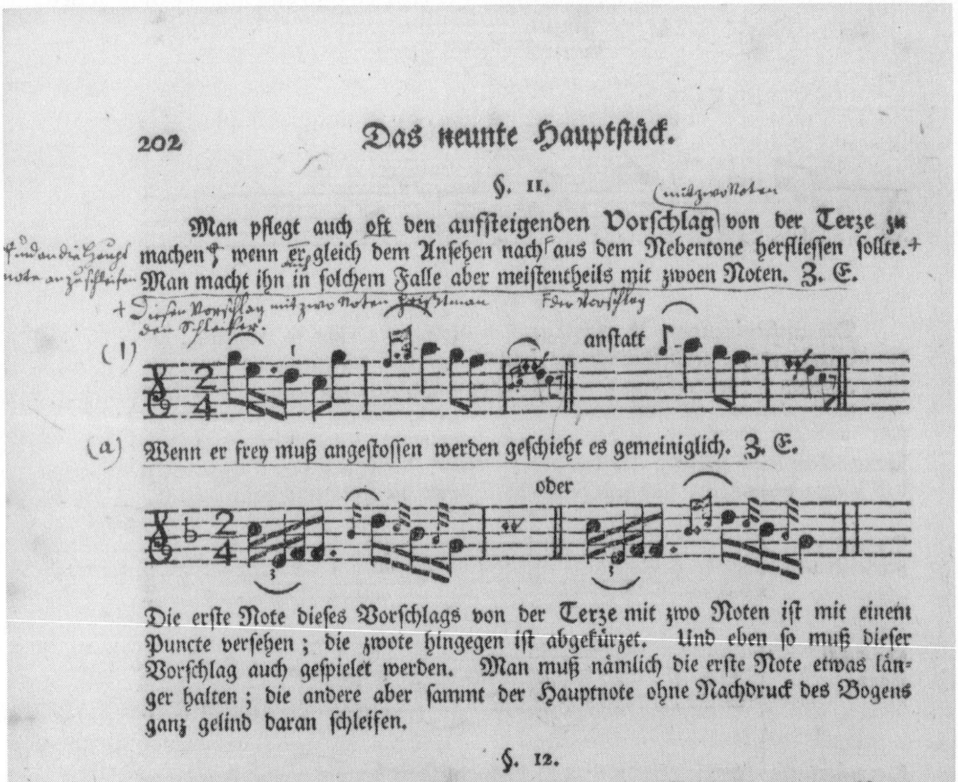

202 **Das neunte Hauptstück.**

§. 11.

Man pflegt auch oft den aufsteigenden Vorschlag von der Terze zu machen, wenn er gleich dem Ansehen nach aus dem Nebentone herfliessen sollte. Man macht ihn in solchem Falle aber meistentheils mit zwoen Noten. Z. E.

anstatt

Wenn er frey muß angestossen werden geschieht es gemeiniglich. Z. E.

oder

Die erste Note dieses Vorschlags von der Terze mit zwo Noten ist mit einem Puncte versehen; die zwote hingegen ist abgekürzet. Und eben so muß dieser Vorschlag auch gespielet werden. Man muß nämlich die erste Note etwas länger halten; die andere aber sammt der Hauptnote ohne Nachdruck des Bogens ganz gelind daran schleifen.

§. 12.

Man kann auch aus dem nächsten Tone einen Vorschlag mit zwo Noten machen, wenn man den über der Hauptnote stehenden Ton darzu nimmt. Z. E. (*)

§. 13.

Wenn man den aufsteigenden Vorschlag nur mit einer Note und aus dem nächsten Tone nehmen will; so klingt es gut, wenn er gegen der Hauptnote einen halben Ton beträgt. Z. E.

Deß-

FIG. 4. Leopold Mozart, *Versuch einer gründlichen Violinschule* (1756), p. 202, with author's MS corrections.

Further, in the lower blank margin:

Die erste unpunctierte Note wird stärker angegriffen u[nd] lange ausgehalten, die zwote abgekürzte aber in der möglichsten Kürze mit der Hauptnote stille daran geschleift. Man machet den Schleifer aber auch mit gleichen Noten, wie wir im Beyspiele (3) sehen. Doch fällt auch hier die Stärke auf die erste zwo Vorschlagnoten.

The first undotted note is attacked more strongly and sustained longer, the second abbreviated note, however, is quietly slurred onto the principal note. The glide is also made with notes of equal length, as is seen in example 3. Yet here, too, the stress falls on the first of the two appoggiatura notes.

p. 204 (§ 14), line 3, after 'weggespielet': 'selten' is deleted and replaced in the margin by:
nicht allezeit — not always

p. 205 (§ 18): 'So spielt man' below the last line of the example is replaced in manuscript:
So muss man es spielen, u[nd] auch schreiben. — Thus it must be played, and written.

p. 210 (§ 22), last line, between 'eine Note dadurch' and 'lebhafter': Inserted in manuscript:
singbarer, theils — singable, partly

p. 211 (§ 22): The page has a manuscript bracket from the top down to 'Mann kann', next to which is written in manuscript: *§ 23*.

pp. 212–14: '§ 23' is altered to *§ 24* and, below, '§ 24' is altered to *§ 25*. On p. 213, '§ 25' is altered to *§ 26*; on p. 214, '§ 26' is altered to *§ 27*.

p. 215: '§ 27' is altered to *§ 28* with a ⊑ sign. Before the next line ('Schier eben'), in manuscript: *§ 29*.

p. 216: '§ 28' is altered to *30*, after which there is a sign that the final paragraph below ('Diese Nachschläge') should be at the beginning of this paragraph 30. The whole of this printed § 28 has a manuscript cancellation bracket down to and including 'Und so wird es gespielet'.

p. 220 (§ 6), in front of the second line of the music example, below 'oder':
mit den Nachschlage — with the turn

p. 224 (§ 13), in the margin, next to line 2:
Nachschlag — turn

One measure is added to the music example: 

p. 225 (§ 16): The second half of the second sentence is corrected to read '. . . ausgestossen seyn *kann* [can] allemal bey der ersten von zween der Triller *ohne Nachschlag* [without a turn] angebracht werden'. In measure 2 of the music example, the slurs are corrected:

(other two lower slurs deleted). Added to the last line, after 'Stücken':

und es sind alle diese Triller ohne Nachschlag.	and all these trills are without turns.

p. 226 (§ 17), line 2: Added after 'Triller':

ohne Nachschlag	without a turn

(§ 18), line 1: Added after 'Triller':

ohne Vorschlag	without a turn

(§ 19): Added to the end of the first line of text:

in einem langsamen Zeitmaasse	in a slow tempo

and, in the next line, after 'Triller':

mit einem geschwinden Nachschlage	with a rapid turn

Above the last line of the example: *Adagio*

p. 227 (§ 20), line 2: Added after 'Triller':

ohne Nachschlag	without a turn

and, after the last line of the example, before § 21, an insertion sign, but without follow-up.

p. 228 (§ 22), second line of text, after 'zweyten Finger':

doch allzeit ohne Nachschlag	yet always without a turn

p. 230 (§ 26), first line of text, after 'jede Note':

anstatt des Nachschlages	instead of the turn

p. 232 (§ 29), after the end of the text paragraph:

Man schliesst aber sehr selten mit dem Nachschlage von zwo Noten.	However, one very rarely ends with a two-note turn.

In the four lines of examples, double-trill grace notes are inserted in manuscript between the penultimate and the final chord:

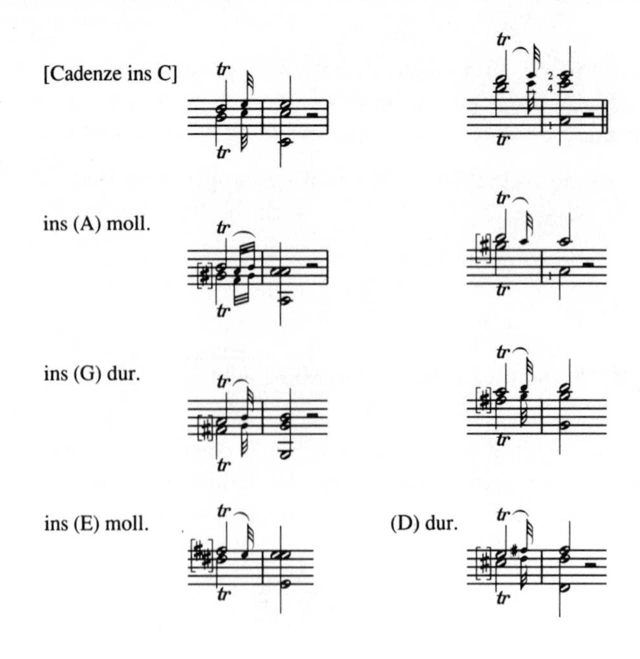

pp. 233–4: Similar resolutions are added on all six systems on this page, from 'H moll' to '(D) moll', and on p. 234 on the three systems from '(B dur)' to 'As dur'.

p. 234 (§ 30), line 1: After 'Doppeltriller' in manuscript:

ohne Nachschlag	without a turn

p. 238 (§ 1), last line: 'auch den Tremulanten' corrected in *Tremolato*.

p. 239 (§ 3), last line: 'Tremulo' corrected to *Tremolato*.

p. 242 (§ 9): The whole section below the music example, from 'Es wollen zwar' to 'Mordante nimmer', is deleted by a manuscript bracket.

p. 243 (§ 11), line 1: Manuscript insertion before the word 'Mordenten':

dieser Gattung	of this kind

The Analysis of Mozart's Arias

JAMES WEBSTER

I. THE IMPORTANCE OF ARIAS IN MOZART'S OPERAS

The vast literature on Mozart's operas includes relatively little detailed musical analysis. This neglect would be baffling indeed, if it did not reflect traditional uncertainties about the status of opera as 'absolute music', and a lack of consensus about how to understand it in technical terms.[1] The fact that Mozart, alone among the canonic opera composers, is equally celebrated for his instrumental music has tended on the one hand to inhibit close analysis of his operas, while on the other hand most of those who have attempted it have uncritically transferred 'instrumental' methods to the very different context of staged dramatic music. For example, with respect to individual numbers, the literature has privileged 'sonata form', which in fact plays a relatively minor role. On a larger scale, many critics have divined 'forms' and 'tonal progressions' governing successions of

[1] James Webster, 'To Understand Verdi and Wagner we must Understand Mozart', *19th-Century Music*, 11 (1987–8), 175–93 (on the Mozart analytical literature, 179–80, 191–2); Carolyn Abbate and Roger Parker, 'On Analyzing Opera', in Abbate and Parker (eds.), *Analyzing Opera: Verdi and Wagner* (Berkeley, 1989), 1–24.

In writing this study I have profited immensely from readings generously undertaken by Cliff Eisen, Mary Hunter, Roger Parker, John Platoff, and Linda Tyler.

discrete numbers, and have argued for the 'unity' of entire acts, indeed entire operas, in a manner that flies in the face of common sense and experience in the theatre. And the literature has focused excessively on Mozart's ensembles and finales—ostensibly his most 'dramatically flowing', most nearly through-composed music—at the expense of his arias.

All this reflects an essentially Wagnerian aesthetic—one which now seems increasingly inappropriate when applied to the very different context of Mozart.[2] The time seems ripe for a concerted attempt to develop 'Mozartian' critical paradigms and analytical methods. Two essential prerequisites will be (1) to abandon the habit of treating his operas as 'absolute music', divorced from the conventions of genre and the social circumstances in which they originated, and (2) to focus on arias—unquestionably the most important sort of number throughout eighteenth-century opera and, even in late Mozart, arguably as important as the ensembles and finales.

Regarding the first of these points: during the later nineteenth century and much of the twentieth, the prestige of 'absolute music', seen as opposed to the 'impure' genres of programme music and texted vocal music, fostered operatic analyses based on the procedures of instrumental music and, especially in Germany, nationalistic and idealistic interpretations of Mozart's operas as 'transcending' the Italianate 'models' which 'prepared' them.[3] But in the eighteenth century there was no such thing as 'absolute' music, instrumental or otherwise: all music was understood as rhetorical in nature. A great many instrumental compositions entailed explicit extra-musical associations.[4] Beyond that, every instrumental work was composed and understood within a context of genre, *Affekt*, and 'topoi' (or 'topics'), which in principle enabled its ideas and gestures to be located within a network of traditional associations, including dance-types and distinctions of social status.[5] Finally, the eighteenth-century sense of musical form itself was 'rhetorical'.[6] This was not limited (as musicologists have tended to assume) to

[2] See, for example, the post-post-modernist aesthetics of disjunction adumbrated in Carolyn Abbate and Roger Parker, 'Dismembering Mozart', *Cambridge Opera Journal*, 2 (1990), 187–95, or the somewhat troubled conclusion of my 'Mozart's Operas and the Myth of Musical Unity' (ibid. 197–218): 'How shall we understand a single Mozart number?'

[3] Especially in comprehensive studies of Mozart by experts on eighteenth-century opera, such as Hermann Abert, *W. A. Mozart*, 2 vols. (Leipzig, 1919–21; repr. 1956), and Stefan Kunze, *Mozarts Opern* (Stuttgart, 1984); see, for example, the latter, pp. 229, 297. Although Kunze rightly criticizes the tenor of most traditional attempts to relate Mozart to his contemporaries, which depend overmuch on superficial melodic resemblances and vague similarities of style, this does not justify his denial of Mozart's dependence on operatic conventions.

[4] See, for example, Eugene Helm, 'The "Hamlet" Fantasy and the Literary Element in C. P. E. Bach's Music', *Musical Quarterly*, 58 (1972), 277–96; Webster, *Haydn's 'Farewell' Symphony and the Idea of Classical Style: Through-Composition and Cyclic Integration in his Instrumental Music* (Cambridge, 1991), ch. 7.

[5] Leonard G. Ratner, *Classic Music: Expression, Form, and Style* (New York, 1980), parts I–II; Hartmut Krones, 'Rhetorik und rhetorische Symbolik in der Musik um 1800: Vom Weiterleben eines Prinzips', *Musiktheorie*, 3 (1988), 117–40.

[6] George Robert Barth, 'The Fortepianist as Orator: Beethoven and the Transformation of the Declamatory Style' (D.M.A. thesis, Cornell University, 1988); Mark Evan Bonds, 'Haydn's False Recapitulations and the Perception of Sonata Form in the Eighteenth Century' (Ph.D. diss., Harvard University, 1988), ch. 2, 'The Rhetorical Perception of Form'; David P. Schroeder, *Haydn and the Enlightenment: The Late Symphonies and their Audience* (Oxford, 1990).

musical 'figures' analogous to those of verbal rhetoric, or to schematic correspondences between the parts of a composition and the parts of an oration. On the contrary, it took for granted a general analogy between the events in a musical work and Aristotle's traditional understanding of rhetoric: 'the possible means of persuasion with respect to any subject'.

Notwithstanding Mozart's breath-taking compositional virtuosity, insight into character, richness and independence of orchestral writing, and the rest—which indubitably had had no equal on the stage since Handel—his operas reflected generic conventions (and audience expectations) as surely as Paisiello's, Cimarosa's, Dittersdorf's, or Haydn's. Like them, he depended on 'types' (of plot, character, aria, and ensemble), exploited the particular strengths of his singers, employed conventional topics, set Italian verses in standard rhythmic patterns, took advantage of traditional 'semantic' associations of particular keys and instruments, and so forth.[7] His oft-quoted assertion, 'In all the operas which could be performed from today until the time when mine is complete, there will not be a single idea [*Gedanke*] that resembles one of mine: I guarantee it!', is simply false.[8] (Among other things, it was a boast to his father—among all his correspondents the one to whom he wrote most misleadingly—in the context of their difference of opinion as to whether it would be harmful to postpone completion of *L'oca del Cairo*.) Even his finales are by no means as unique as has been assumed; many of his contemporaries' finales are just as long and (outwardly) complex, and most of his are more nearly sectional than 'integrated'.[9] (The finale to Act II of *Le nozze di Figaro*, of which so much has been made, is in fact highly unusual: it is his only finale whose tonal successions mimic those of a sonata form.) All this helps to explain the apparent paradox that, despite Mozart's prestige, the most important recent advances in our analytical understanding of the opera of his time have been made with respect to the music of other composers.

Finally, only by weaning ourselves from the ideal of absolute music, with its bias towards 'unity', can we appreciate Mozart's operas as 'multivalent'. This concept holds that the various 'domains' in an opera (plot, stage-action, characterization, text, vocal music, orchestral accompaniment, etc.) often function more or less independently, that their temporal patternings are not necessarily congruent and may even be incompatible,

[7] Reinhard Strohm, *Die italienische Oper im 18. Jahrhundert* (Wilhelmshaven, 1979), esp. 9–28, 354–77 (the latter on *Il rè pastore*); Andrew Steptoe, *The Mozart–Da Ponte Operas* (Oxford, 1988), chs. 1–6; Daniel Heartz, *Mozart's Operas*, ed. with contributing essays on Thomas Bauman (Berkeley, 1990), chs. 1–2, 7–8, 11, 13, 15, 17. The same point is made with respect to a single aria-type in John Platoff, 'The buffa aria in Mozart's Vienna', *Cambridge Opera Journal*, 2 (1990), 99–120.

[8] Letter of 10 Feb. 1784; Wilhelm A. Bauer, Otto Erich Deutsch, and Joseph Heinz Eibl (eds.), *Mozart: Briefe und Aufzeichnungen. Gesamtausgabe* (hereafter *Briefe*), 7 vols. (Kassel, 1962–75), iii. 300. (Translations from Mozart's letters are my own.)

[9] John Platoff, 'Music and Drama in the *Opera Buffa* Finale: Mozart and his Contemporaries in Vienna, 1781–1790' (Ph.D. diss., University of Pennsylvania, 1984), and id., 'Musical and Dramatic Structure in the Opera Buffa Finale', *Journal of Musicology*, 7 (1989), 191–230; Paul Horsley, 'Dittersdorf and the Finale in Late-Eighteenth-Century German Comic Opera' (Ph.D. diss., Cornell University 1988), Part II; Webster, 'Mozart's Operas and the Myth of Unity', 205–8, 215–16; Caryl Leslie Clark, 'The Opera Buffa Finales of Joseph Haydn' (Ph.D. diss., Cornell University, 1991).

and that the resulting complexity and lack of unity is often a primary source of their effect. Although the term was coined (by Harold S. Powers) in the first instance for the analysis of large, formally complex spans in more or less continuous nineteenth-century operas,[10] the concept is equally (if somewhat differently) relevant to eighteenth-century 'number' operas, whose generally rigid distinction between recitative (or dialogue) and concerted music is inherently multivalent. Many individual numbers as well are based on the interaction of more or less independent domains. The two most important post-war formal studies of eighteenth-century arias, by Reinhard Strohm and Mary Hunter, emphasize the relative independence of text, vocal music, and instrumental accompaniment, and the effect of this multivalence on the aria as a whole.[11] Not coincidentally, both also give ample attention to genre and convention.

Regarding the second point: it is high time we abandoned the Wagnerian prejudice of valuing Mozart's ensembles and finales more highly than his arias. After all, in the eighteenth century the aria was supreme: in historical tradition, strength of conventions, prestige among theorists and aestheticians, identification with 'star' performers, and interest on the part of audiences. An aria was the primary means of presenting a character's personality, crystallizing a 'moment' of emotion or inner conflict; it was comparable to a speech or soliloquy in Shakespeare or Racine, both in degree of passion and in depending on the arts of rhetoric.[12] Only accompanied recitatives were on average more intense, and they too were primarily devoted to utterances of single characters; that is, they were dramaturgically equivalent to arias.[13] And, again contrary to Wagnerian aesthetics, a succession of such moments can be highly dramatic (if not 'realistic'): the several arias for a given character can cumulatively develop a rounded portrait, as the contrasts and continuities among arias for different characters articulate the social and moral world of the drama.[14] The fact that Mozart's late operas include fewer arias and more ensembles than any earlier eighteenth-century operas (including his own) qualifies, but does not abrogate, this 'characterological' primacy. Moreover, I will argue that Mozart's arias are dramatic not merely in the senses just mentioned, but psychologically, in that many of them articulate a process of change or recognition. This suggests the possibility of a rapprochement between eighteenth-century and Wagnerian aesthetics, appropriate to the special character of Mozart's operas and their importance for later musical culture.

[10] In an unpublished study of Verdi's *Otello*, presented at a conference on Verdi and Wagner at Cornell University in 1984 (for the published papers, see Abbate and Parker, *Analyzing Opera*).

[11] Strohm, *Italienische Opernarien des frühen Settecento (1720–1730)*, 2 vols. (Cologne, 1976; = *Analecta musicologica*, 16); Hunter, 'Haydn's Aria Forms: A Study of the Arias in the Italian Operas Written at Esterháza, 1766–1783' (Ph.D. diss., Cornell University, 1982).

[12] James Parakilas, 'Mozart's *Tito* and the Music of Rhetorical Strategy' (Ph.D. diss., Cornell University, 1979).

[13] I distinguish 'drama' from 'dramaturgy', using the latter to designate aspects of construction and stagecraft, e.g., the employment of entrances and exits, the distinction between soliloquies and speeches made to other characters, etc.

[14] Winton Dean, *Handel and the Opera Seria* (Berkeley, 1969), 18–23, 156–77; Strohm, *Italianische Opernarien*, 15–22; Hunter, 'Text, Music, and Drama in Haydn's Italian Opera Arias: Four Case Studies', *Journal of Musicology*, 7 (1989), 30.

In what follows, I shall describe various 'types' governing Mozart's later arias (Sect. II); outline the 'multivalent' nature of his aria forms (Sect. III); analyse the Countess's 'Porgi amor' (*Figaro*, No. 10) in detail (Sect. IV); refine and qualify that analysis by comparing 'Porgi amor' to related arias (Sect. V); and conclude (Sect. VI) by returning to the issue of drama. (Many of these topics would be equally relevant in a study of ensembles.) Throughout, the reader must remember that no aria stands alone as an absolute-musical object of contemplation; each one represents one or more types, dramatizes the character's feelings or motivation, and relates multifariously to other numbers in the same opera. Even analytically, to ignore these aspects is to risk falsifying its meaning.

This study represents work in progress. Its most obvious lacks are of discussion of Mozart's earlier operas and those of his contemporaries—essential aspects of the topic, especially given the importance of types and conventions. But even within the circumscribed repertory of Mozart's later arias, and notwithstanding my attempt to survey every topic that is relevant for analysis, the results are provisional at best. Indeed, as we shall see, any notion of 'the' analysis of a Mozart aria is a chimera. I hope for nothing more than to stimulate discussion, and to encourage additional work in this field.

II. TYPES

Aria types

Types in eighteenth-century opera. All eighteenth-century arias were composed and understood in the context of long-standing dramatic, poetic, and musical conventions, which largely determined their significance. Each one functioned as the representative of a 'type'; these types were a special case (or subclass) of genre, analogous to 'minuet-types' or 'finale-types' in Classical-period instrumental music, except that they were far more pervasive and more constitutive of meaning.[15] No matter how unusual a given aria may be, this general dependence on types remains crucial for interpretation—even in the case of Mozart.

The various genres of eighteenth-century opera—*seria*, *buffa*, and 'mixed' genres such as *dramma giocoso* and *dramma eroicomico*[16]—developed distinct plot-types as subcategories.

[15] Among the more important recent discussions of musical genre are Wulf Arlt, 'Aspekte des Gattungsbegriffs in der Musikgeschichtsschreibung', in Arlt *et al.* (eds.), *Gattungen der Musik in Einzeldarstellungen: Gedenkschrift Leo Schrade* (Berne, 1973), 11–93; Carl Dahlhaus, 'Zur Problematik der musikalischen Gattungen im 19. Jahrhundert', ibid. 840–95; Jeffrey Kallberg, 'The Rhetoric of Genre: Chopin's Nocturne in G Minor', *19th-Century Music*, 11 (1987–8), 238–61; James A. Hepokoski, 'Genre and Content in Mid-Century Verdi', *Cambridge Opera Journal*, 1 (1989), 249–76.

[16] Abert, *Mozart*, *passim*; Georg Feder, 'Opera seria, Opera buffa und Opera semiseria bei Haydn', in Klaus Hortschansky (ed.), *Opernstudien: Anna Amalie Abert zum 65. Geburtstag* (Tutzing, 1975), 37–55; Martin Ruhnke, 'Opera semiseria und dramma eroicomico', in Friedrich Lippmann (ed.), *Colloquium: Die stilistische Entwicklung der italienischen Musik zwischen 1770 und 1830 und ihre Beziehungen zum Norden* (Cologne, 1982; = *Analecta musicologica*, 21), 263–74; Sabine Henze-Döhring, *Opera seria, opera buffa und Mozarts 'Don Giovanni': Zur Gattungskonvergenz in der italienischen Oper des 18. Jahrhunderts* (Laaber, 1986; = *Analecta musicologica*, 26); Helen Geyer-Kiefl, *Die heroisch-komische Oper ca. 1770–1820* (Tutzing, 1987); Heartz, *Mozart's Operas*, chs. 1, 3, 11, 17.

For example, *opere buffe* included the love-intrigue (Petrosellini's and Paisiello's *Il barbiere di Siviglia*), the Turkish comedy (Dancourt's/Friebert's and Haydn's *L'incontro improvviso*; compare Bretzner's/Stephanie's and Mozart's *Entführung*), the Goldonian farce (Haydn's *Il mondo della luna*), the 'tender' comedy (the various 'Pamela' plots; Puttini's and Haydn's *La vera costanza*), the pastoral (Lorenzi's and Haydn's *La fedeltà premiata*); the imbroglio (Da Ponte's and Mozart's *Figaro*), the 'demonstration' comedy (Da Ponte's and Mozart's *Così fan tutte*), and so forth.[17] Characters and vocal ranges also represented types: the noble personage wracked by the conflict between love and duty (performed by the *prima donna* or *primo uomo*), the *mezzo carattere*, often a minor noble or professional, or a person of uncertain background (when male, often a low voice), the upright suitor (tenor), the crafty male servant (bass), the cynical female servant, the buffoonish guardian (bass), the pastoral maid, and so forth.

The importance of all this to Mozart is implied by his almost schematic demands regarding the number of roles in a *buffa* plot, and the relations among the female characters; demands that reflected the singing personnel of the new Italian troupe in Vienna:

> I suppose that *Varesco* . . . could write a new libretto for me, with seven characters . . . The most necessary thing is that it be truly *comic* as a whole, and if possible include *two equally good female roles*: the one must be seria, the other mezzo carattere; but *in quality* both roles must be entirely the same. The third female can be entirely buffa.[18]

Although the secondary female roles in *Figaro* do not conform to this scheme, the Countess and Susanna come close to Mozart's specifications regarding the leading roles. And the three females in *Così* (Fiordiligi, Dorabella, Despina) and especially *Don Giovanni* (Anna, Elvira, Zerlina) exemplify it very well indeed.

Given this pervasive generic and characterological typology, it is hardly surprising that most arias conformed to well-established conventions as well. The latter were signified in part by the 'rhythmic topoi' (combinations of tempos, metres, and phrasing characteristic of functional music, especially dance-types, and hence often connoting a particular social standing),[19] in part by specialized operatic traditions that associated particular keys, melodic styles, and instrumentations with particular dramatic contexts. The differentiated employment of the winds was important. Except in overtures and the concluding sections of finales, clarinets played most often in E flat and A, less often in B flat, and rarely in other keys; flutes were more comfortable on the sharp side than the flat side; oboes were uncomfortable in keys 'sharper' than D, and were often omitted in A and especially E (as well as in E flat, as if in reaction to the presence of the clarinets);

[17] Hunter, 'Text, Music, and Drama', 56–7. On 'Pamela' operas, see Hunter, '"Pamela": The Offspring of Richardson's Heroine in Eighteenth-Century Opera', *Mosaic*, 18 (1985), 61–76. Wye Jamison Allanbrook's attractive interpretation of *Figaro* as (in part) a celebration of pastoral virtues (*Rhythmic Gesture in Mozart: 'Le nozze di Figaro' and 'Don Giovanni'* (Chicago, 1983), 1–2, 87–97, 127–31, 145–9, 172–7) does not establish it as a representative of 'the pastoral' as a type.

[18] Letter to Leopold Mozart, 7 May 1783 (*Briefe*, iii. 268; emphases original). Varesco had been the librettist for *Idomeneo*, and was to write the ill-fated fragment *L'oca del Cairo*.

[19] Allanbrook, *Rhythmic Gesture*, introduction and part I.

Mozart used trumpets only in C, D, and E flat; and so forth. (Of course, there are exceptions: Ilia's 'Se il padre perdei' (*Idomeneo*, No. 11) and Elvira's 'Mi tradì' (*Don Giovanni*, No. 21b), both in E flat, include a flute; the climactic duet in *Così* between Fiordiligi and Ferrando (No. 29), in A, uses oboes rather than clarinets.) Such preferences had long since created associations between certain winds and certain keys and, by extension, between those associations and particular dramatic contexts.[20]

The following descriptions indicate how these factors combine to create types among Mozart's arias:[21]

The *aria d'affetto* is a relatively brief, heartfelt aria sung by a noble or *mezzo* character, usually apostrophizing an absent or faithless lover (one strand of the tradition originated as *ombra* music; that is, as one type of 'cavatina').[22] It tends to be moderately slow, in 2/4 metre (occasionally 3/8) and E flat, and to feature clarinets, horns, and bassoons, but not flutes or oboes (this instrumentation is common in all Mozart's operatic music in E flat). The singer apparently eschewed elaborate vocal display. These arias lack major internal contrasts, favouring binary or unitary forms, as opposed either to elaborately formal ones like the da capo or the sonata, or 'simple' ones like strophic songs. Classic Mozartian examples include 'Porgi amor' and Tamino's 'Dies Bildnis' (*Die Zauberflöte*, No. 3). Less often, they are on the sharp side, frequently in A (again: clarinets were common), for example, Belmonte's 'O wie ängstlich' (*Die Entführung aus dem Serail*, No. 4) and Ferrando's 'Un'aura amorosa' (*Così fan tutte*, No. 17).[23]

The *noble or heroic aria* is usually sung by a *seria* character, and is usually in C or D and in 2/2 or 4/4. The vocal part is firm, steady, featuring relatively long phrases, wide leaps, 'measured' rhythms dominated by half- and quarter-notes and by dotted figures, and (even in Mozart) prominent coloratura passages. Trumpets and drums are often included, as are extensive concertante wind solos. The style is often conservative. Examples in late Mozart include Idomeneo's 'Fuor del mar' (No. 12), Konstanze's 'Martern aller Arten' (*Die Entführung*, No. 11), and Donna Anna's 'Or sai chi l'onore' (*Don Giovanni*, No. 10).[24]

The *female buffa aria* stands in the 'simple' keys C, F, or G (hence: no clarinets) and in 2/4 or 6/8 metre; it includes two main subtypes. (*a*) Comic, cynical, or 'saucy' servants' arias are based

[20] A useful account of these usages in Mozart is found in Frits Noske, *The Signifier and the Signified: Studies in the Operas of Mozart and Verdi* (The Hague, 1977; repr. Oxford, 1990), ch. 6, 'Semantics of Orchestration', although Noske ignores the role of tonality and performing technique in creating these associations. I owe the observations on technical limitations of eighteenth-century wind instruments to Neal Zaslaw.

[21] These descriptions are modern generalizations, and refer specifically to Mozart's practice in the 1780s. They must not be taken as necessarily applying to other repertories, still less as reflecting eighteenth-century terminology or classifications. The issue of the relations between Mozart's typologies and general ones cannot be addressed here, except to reiterate the fundamental methodological point that, in so far as types were ubiquitous, they were as relevant to Mozart as to any other composer, if not always to the same degree.

[22] On the cavatina, see Wolfgang Osthoff, 'Mozarts Cavatinen und ihre Tradition', in Wilhelm Stauder *et al.* (eds.), *Festschrift Helmuth Osthoff zum 70. Geburtstag* (Tutzing, 1969), 139–77; Helga Lühning, 'Die Cavatina in der italienischen Oper um 1800', in Lippmann (ed.), *Colloquium* (see n. 16), 333–68.

[23] Heartz, *Mozart's Operas*, 240–1, notes the similarities of these two arias. Noske, *Signifier and Signified*, 125, attributes the use of clarinets in 'Porgi amor' and 'Dies Bildnis' to the dramaturgical condition of being 'not (yet) involved in the plot'; this is already problematical for 'Dies Bildnis', and does not apply at all to 'Un'aura amorosa' and many other numbers.

[24] The latter aria serves as Allanbrook's paradigmatic example (*Rhythmic Gesture*, pp. 13–23) of an 'exalted march', incorporating the 'ecclesiastical' or 'white-note' style characteristic of the 'higher', 'old-fashioned' rhythmic topoi.

on detached short phrases with continual orchestral interjections on independent motives, and often much stage action. Despina is typical; the 'upper' limits are suggested by Susanna's 'Venite, inginocchiatevi' (*Figaro*, No. 12). (*b*) Sentimental arias often apotheosize the genuine emotions of simple folk; that is, they are a species of pastoral. Musically, they are distinguished from those in (*a*) primarily by longer, cantabile vocal phrases and less independent orchestral material. Zerlina is typical; she even seduced Adorno, in his only published essay on Mozart, into confessing his hope that her knowing innocence, on the historical cusp between feudalism and modernism, might have brought about that which he knew to be unattainable: individual and social 'reconciliation' (*Versöhnung*) through art.[25] Susanna's 'Deh vieni' (*Figaro*, No. 27) again raises the subtype to its highest level of sophistication and irony.

The *male buffa aria* is usually in 4/4; it exhibits greater variety of key than the female type. Usually based on a long, multipartite text, it often has two contrasting sections: the first based on detached two-bar phrases; the second, including patter, leading to a climax of comic action towards the end.[26] Among the many subtypes are 'catalogue' arias, as in Leporello's 'Madamina' (*Don Giovanni*, No. 4), and diatribes against women, as in Figaro's 'Aprite un po' quegl'occhi' (No. 26).

The *rondò* is an aria in two (or even three) tempi, usually for a female *seria* character. It is usually her last aria (the Countess, Donna Anna, Fiordiligi, Vitellia), and usually a soliloquy (all the above save Anna). The text is dominated by conflicting emotions, often moving from the character's individual plight to a more 'distanced' apotheosis or plea for pity. The usual tempo sequence is slow–fast(–faster); the first section exhibits great variety in metre and style, while the final section is almost always in 4/4 and often dominated by gavotte rhythms. Very often one or more obbligato instruments are prominent, 'commenting' on the singer and deepening her expression.[27]

Similar constellations of characteristics define many other aria-types which need not be described in detail here: rage and revenge, grief, panic, moralizing sentiments, servants' complaints, and so forth. An important category comprises 'realistic' arias; that is, representing music that ideally would be sung even in a spoken drama: serenades, Papageno's bird-catcher songs, Cherubino performing 'Voi che sapete' (*Figaro*, No. 11) for the Countess while Susanna 'accompanies' him on the guitar, and so forth. Despite their outward simplicity these arias are often dramaturgically complex, because they collapse the customary distinction between the characters' dramatic functioning and their unawareness, *as characters*, of the fact that they are singing.[28]

[25] Theodor W. Adorno, 'Huldigung an Zerlina', in *Moments musicaux* (Frankfurt, 1964), 37–9; repr. in *Musikalische Schriften*, iv (*Gesammelte Werke*, xvii; Frankfurt, 1982), 34–5; compare Allanbrook, *Rhythmic Gesture*, ch. 11. The special admiration for Zerlina's pastoral virtues reaches back at least as far as Alexandre Oulibicheff, *Nouvelle Biographie de Mozart*, iii (Moscow, 1842), 134–6, 159–62. For a lightly ironic modern variant, see Massimo Mila, *Lettura del Don Giovanni di Mozart* (Turin, 1988), 142–3.

[26] Platoff, 'The buffa aria'; compare Hunter, 'Text, Music, and Drama in Haydn', 46–52.

[27] On the *rondò*, see Heartz, 'Mozart and his Italian Contemporaries: *La clemenza di Tito*', *Mozart-Jahrbuch 1973/74*, 281–3 *et passim* (repr. in Heartz, *Mozart's Operas*, ch. 11, 305–7 *et passim*); Lühning, 'Die Rondo-Arie im späten 18. Jahrhundert: Dramatischer Gehalt und musikalischer Bau', *Hamburger Jahrbuch für Musikwissenschaft*, 5 (1981), 219–46; John A. Rice, 'Sense, Sensibility, and Opera Seria: An Epistolary Debate', *Studi musicali*, 15 (1986), 120–4, 134–8. Of course, the *rondò* (an aria-type) must be distinguished from 'rondo form'; I do so by using italics and the accent on *-ò* for the former.

[28] Edward T. Cone, *The Composer's Voice* (Berkeley, Calif., 1974), ch. 2. (For Cone's more recent, and to my mind problematical, view that operatic characters *are* always aware that they are singing—that they are

The same multilayering effect obtains in representations of other realistic music, such as dances, marches, and dinner music. Mozart's most astonishing stroke of this kind is the ballroom scene in the Act I finale of *Don Giovanni*—not merely because of his *tour de force* of orchestrating (in both senses) its fearsome complexities, but for a more fundamental dramatic reason: although each dance is performed by persons of the 'proper' class, the confusion on stage and rhythmic dissonance dramatize the licence and social disruption that are the Don's *raison d'être*. (He himself commanded this in the 'Champagne' aria (No. 11): 'Senza alcun ordine/la danza sia'.[29]) And when Figaro, in 'Se vuol ballare' (No. 3), vows to foil the Count's designs on Susanna, he uses a somewhat debased form of the minuet, an upper-class dance, to choreograph his plans: 'If you want to dance, my little Count, I'll play the guitar for you . . . I'll teach you the *capriola*.' (The capriola was a distinctly un-noble 'leaping' (goatish?) dance.) The implication is: 'I'll bring you down to my level, where your noble status won't save you.' Indeed, Figaro's violent description of how he'll do this is a contredanse, that is, a specifically middle-class dance. The aria thus dramatizes both the social and the dramatic relations between servant and master.[30]

Extensions. This dependence of aria-types on conventional combinations of attributes—actually the signifiers in an informal semiotic system—also enabled composers to extend their range, and to individualize them, by altering some but not all of the relevant attributes. I will briefly discuss five types of such alteration here.

1. With respect to the *aria d'affetto* as represented by 'Porgi amor' and 'Dies Bildnis', a sizeable group of Mozart arias retains the key of E flat, the clarinet/bassoon/horn wind-scoring, and the dramatic motive of an absent or troubled lover, but speeds up the tempo and alters the meter to 2/2 or 4/4. Cherubino's 'Non so più' (*Figaro*, No. 6) portrays the adolescent who is polymorphously 'in love with love' (with all women, and hence with no particular woman, not even the Countess); the 'unreality' of his emotion is analogous to the state of absence in 'Porgi amor'. As Heartz points out (p. 145), Figaro's comic yet tortured 'Aprite un po' quegl'occhi' shows a different face of the absence of love: its dark *alter ego*, jealousy. Dorabella's 'Smanie implacabili' (*Così*, No. 11) and Elvira's 'Ah chi mi dice mai' (*Don Giovanni*, No. 3) illustrate other ways in which the type can be varied: the former believes that her fiancé has just gone off to

'composers'—see 'The World of Opera and its Inhabitants', in Cone, *Music: A View from Delft* (Chicago, 1989), 125–38.)

[29] Allanbrook, *Rhythmic Gesture*, 220–2, 277, 283–4, 287; Kunze, *Mozart's Opern* 347–55 (compare his 'Mozart's Don Giovanni und die Tanzszene im ersten Finale: Grenzen des klassischen Komponierens', in Friedrich Lippmann (ed.), *Colloquium 'Mozart und Italien' (Rom 1974)* [Cologne, 1978; = *Analecta musicologica*, 18], 166–97).

[30] Allanbrook, *Rhythmic Gesture*, 79–82; on dances in *Figaro* generally, see ibid., Part II, *passim*; Kunze, *Mozarts Opern*, 240–5. Siegmund Levarie, *Mozart's 'Le Nozze di Figaro'* (Chicago, 1952), 29–35, makes essentially the same point about 'Se vuol ballare', without naming the contredanse; he suggests that the English and popular associations of Figaro's faster dance are a covert pun, referring to the Count's plans (mentioned in the preceding recitative) to take Susanna and Figaro with him to London.

war the latter raves against Giovanni, who has jilted her. All four arias thus exhibit a similar profile of relations to and differences from the *aria d'affetto* proper: agitated, confused, tortured, but still consumed by absent love, and still in E flat and with the same wind-instrumentation.

A different kind of variant is illustrated by Ilia's 'Se il padre perdei' (*Idomeneo*, No. 11), which resembles 'Porgi amor' in key, tempo, metre, density of motivic elaboration, the dramatic motive of absence, and a certain *Innigkeit*. But that motif is mixed with joy in a new-found homeland and incipient love: she addresses a king (rather than singing to herself); the winds are single rather than double, include flute and oboe and lack clarinet, and are overtly concertante; there is much variety of topic and phrasing; and the sonata-without-development form is long, varied, and elaborate. This is no cavatina, but a full-fledged aria.[31] Ottavio's 'Il mio tesoro' (*Don Giovanni*, No. 21) is also a true aria, notwithstanding his invocation of the absent Anna (she has exited following the sextet), the closely related key (B flat) and tempo ('andante grazioso'), and the requisite instrumentation. It is not a soliloquy (he is addressing three people), his request that they go to console his beloved is admixed with the promise of vengeance on Giovanni, and it includes considerable coloratura.

2. A central aspect of many eighteenth-century operatic plots is disguise.[32] Because the audience knew how a given character ought to sing in a given context and could therefore tell at once if the music was 'out of countenance' (Ratner), it was easy to achieve that double articulation necessary for the musical projection of a character in disguise. Mozart's musical disguises include Despina as doctor and notary in *Così* (the two men are a different case), Susanna and the Countess in Act IV of *Figaro*, and Giovanni and Leporello towards the beginning of Act II of *Don Giovanni*. The disguise entails a change not only of costume but of musical style, indeed often of voice—an operatic character's most intimate attribute. In *Così* Despina's changes of voice are merely comic, but in *Figaro* they become deeply poetic as well. In the finale of Act IV, Figaro initially does not realize that the person whom he addresses as 'the Countess' is really Susanna—despite having already heard her sing 'Deh vieni' in disguise!—because she alters her voice (m. 122: 'cangiando la voce'). His recognition comes only a little later, when she temporarily forgets to alter it (mm. 139–46), upon which he reacts 'Susanna!' (in an aside); compare the sequel, 'La volpe vuol sorprendermi', etc. (mm. 157–69). And at the beginning of 'Pace, pace mio dolce tesoro', when he finally confesses his knowledge, he explicitly says 'io connobi la voce che adoro' (mm. 278–9); the poetry is deepened in Susanna's laughing 'La mia voce?' and his reiteration, 'La voce che adoro'. Hence in the sequel, the comic exaggeration of his pretended love-making to 'the Countess' has a new meaning: instead of wanting to fool Susanna into believing that he thinks she really is the Countess (as in mm. 171–96, 215–32), now they both play-act for the benefit of the eavesdropping Count (mm. 314–22).

[31] Excellent descriptions are found in Abert, i. 700–3, and Kunze, *Mozarts Opern*, 138–47.

[32] See Michael F. Robinson, *Naples and Neapolitan Opera* (Oxford, 1927), 192–3.

The common plot-themes of the noble person disguised as a servant or raised in poverty offered rich possibilities for double meanings. Mozart's most prominent character of this sort is Sandrina, his 'finta giardiniera' (compare Cecchina in Goldoni's and Piccini's *La buona figliuola*). A comic analogue is Figaro himself, a servant who turns out to be Bartolo's and Marcellina's son ('comic', because they are only middle-class, and he is illegitimate to boot). Such devices, typical of late eighteenth-century opera, imply the rise in society of a new and uneasy interest in the complexity—and fragility?—of class relations.

3. Musical signifiers also tell us when a vain or foolish character unknowingly sings in a manner inappropriate to his class.[33] In 'Vedrò mentre io sospiro' (*Figaro*, No. 17), the Count gives vent to his outrage that Susanna was merely leading him on, and vows to prevent his servants' happiness as long as his own pleasure is denied. But its musical type is the heroic/noble aria in D with trumpets and drums. This is not only inappropriate—his only problem is wounded vanity—but he cannot carry it off: his lack of self-control, bordering on hysteria, prevents him from maintaining the measured, 'exalted' rhythms of the type. Further down the social ladder in *Figaro*, Bartolo's 'La vendetta' (No. 4), also a revenge aria in D, is a hilarious send-up of a middle-class professional ineffectually aping his betters. The trumpets and drums are mere bombast: notwithstanding his professional status as 'medico', Bartolo cannot even put together a coherent modulation. No wonder that, when listing the (more lawyerlike than surgical) devices he will employ on Marcellina's behalf, he descends to vulgar patter.

4. As this example illustrates, these techniques could also be placed in the service of irony and parody. In late eighteenth-century *opere buffe*—not merely 'mixed' genres like *drammi giocosi*—parodies of *seria* style were common.[34] Perhaps this reflects the latter's increasingly marginal status. Susanna's 'Deh vieni' is Mozart's most famous example of irony in an aria. Among his many parodistic arias are 'La vendetta', Dorabella's 'Smanie implacabili' and, less monolithically, Fiordiligi's 'Come scoglio' (*Così*, No. 14). Mozart's treatment of Elvira, as is well known, mixes sympathy and ridicule; this is obvious in her initial aria 'Ah chi mi dice mai', not least, as Noske points out (p. 88), owing to her entrance—inappropriately for a potentially *seria* character—in travelling-clothes ('in abito di viaggio'). In Figaro's pretended love-making to 'the Countess' (just described), it seems likely that we are supposed to take him as conscious of his buffoonery: see the pretentious irrelevance of the phrase 'Esaminate il loco' (mm. 186 ff.) and the exaggerated range of his triadic singing of it, and in the latter passage, the inappropriate syncopations in mm. 315–16, the foolishly 'expressive' arpeggiation of a minor ninth in

[33] This paragraph is based on Allanbrook, *Rhythmic Gesture*, 140–5.

[34] Mary Hunter, 'Some Representations of *opera seria* in *opera buffa*, *Cambridge Opera Journal*, 3 (1991), 89–108. On the complex and often disputed role of parody in *Così*, see, recently, Steptoe, *Mozart–Da Ponte Operas*, 221–30; Rodney Farnsworth, '*Così fan tutte* as Parody and Burlesque', *Opera Quarterly*, 6 (1988–9), 50–68; Mary Hunter, 'Così fan tutte et les conventions musicales de son temps', *L'avant-scène opéra*, No. 131–2 (May–June 1990), 158–65.

320–1, and so forth. And if he is conscious of this, he is an ironist, fooling first Susanna and then (together with her) the Count.

As these examples suggest, an essential aspect of musical parody is that our recognition of it often depends not so much on 'purely musical' excess or inappropriateness as on an incongruity between the music and dramatic or textual factors. (Analogous incongruities are characteristic of parody in general.) Musical signs are malleable, and can be used both 'authentically' and parodistically. The parody in 'Smanie implacabili' is signalled not only by Dorabella's over-reaction to her lover's departure (in the preceding *accompagnato*), in what we know to be a comic context, but also by her absurdly 'high' diction, such as the invocation of the furies: 'Esempio misero / d'amor funesto, / darò all'Eumenidi / se viva resto / Col suono orribile / de' miei sospir'. The point emerges clearly from a comparison with Cherubino's 'Non so più', which is outwardly similar (especially in the first part): see the rushing tempo, 2/2 metre, hasty 'vamping' beginning, ostinato accompaniment (only at first in 'Non so più'), 'breathless' vocal line, and mood of self-absorption. It would take very little alteration to Cherubino's music—or to the preceding recitative—to make his adolescent swooning seem as ridiculous as Dorabella's outrage.

5. Finally, one can extend the notion of types to ensembles and individual finale sections. Many ensembles belong to types, for example the 'farewell' (the sequence Nos. 6–10 in *Così*, or the trio No. 19 between Pamino, Tamino, and Sarastro in *Die Zauberflöte*; compare the end of the quintet No. 5, in the same key), or the seduction duet. Most of Mozart's seductions are in the key of A, and they share many aspects of construction and instrumentation as well.[35] (Since the oboes are often omitted in this key, the registrally distinct flutes and bassoons become especially prominent; Mozart often uses them to symbolize the male and female characters—though not always in obvious ways.) The signs of love-invocations are also found in ensembles and finale sections. Figaro's and Susanna's reconciliation scene in the Act IV finale is introduced by Figaro's 'larghetto' solo, in which he explicitly invokes the theme of unrequited love, comically transformed into cuckoldry, by comparing himself to Vulcan (whom Venus betrayed with Mars). However obscure Da Ponte's motivation for placing this Classical allusion in his hero's mouth (Beaumarchais has nothing comparable), and however uncertain the tone (the gorgeous music seems incompatible with Figaro's bitter irony), the key, tempo, instrumentation, and mood recall 'Porgi amor' (though they are here allied with the rhythmic topic of the minuet). Pamina's and Papageno's duet 'Bei Männern' in *Die Zauberflöte* (No. 7) not only resembles 'Porgi amor' and especially 'Dies Bildnis' in being in E flat with clarinets/horns/bassoons, moderately slow ('andantino'),[36] and outwardly simple in

[35] Richard Stiefel, 'Mozart's Seductions', *Current Musicology*, 36 (1983), 151–66 (adumbrated in Noske, *Signifier and Signified*, 125–7).

[36] For Mozart, 'andantino' was almost certainly slower than 'andante', not far from 'larghetto'; see Neal Zaslaw, 'Mozart's Tempo Conventions', in Henrik Glahn *et al.* (eds.), *International Musicological Society: Report of the Eleventh Congress, Copenhagen 1972*, 2 vols. (Copenhagen, 1974), ii. 720–33; Jean-Pierre Marty, *The Tempo Indications of Mozart* (New Haven, Conn., 1988), ch. 4.

form, but in its dramatic theme: the joy of conjugal love—a joy which in all three cases is absent. Similarly, as Heartz notes (*Mozart's Operas*, 240–2), the third section ('larghetto' 3/4) in the great duet (No. 29) between Fiordiligi and Ferrando in *Così* closely resembles 'Un'aura amorosa'.

Networks. All this suggests that we can construct a 'network' of operatic numbers related to any given number. Every aria resembles various others in various ways; these relations provide the typological context within which any analysis or interpretation should proceed. The resemblances are both dramatic (character-type, aria-type, dramaturgical context, motivation) and musical (vocal range and tessitura, topics, metre and tempo, key, instrumentation, formal type). A special case, overriding all other differences, comprises the other arias sung by the same character, as well as, to a lesser extent, arias in other operas written for the same singer. The totality of these relations constitutes the network, at whose centre lies the aria in question; thus each aria implies its own individual network. Of course, the relations are infinite, and the network represents our own selection and arrangement of them. Nor can we quantify closeness of relation in this sense; the network cannot be 'graphed'.[37]

Again, I shall illustrate the concept with respect to 'Porgi amor'. In Mozart's *œuvre*, the network I would construct for it includes the Countess's other aria, 'Dove sono' (No. 19); among other things, despite the differences in form, key, instrumentation, and style, it too is a soliloquy, still focused on her unrequited love for the Count. Cherubino not only has a crush on the Countess but is her godson; he sings 'Non so più' about her (in a sense), and 'Voi che sapete' directly to her, immediately following 'Porgi amor'. Susanna's relations with the Countess are central to *Figaro*; when singing 'Deh vieni' she is disguised as her mistress, and her inner nobility has long since become clear. In *Don Giovanni*, Donna Elvira is related to the Countess as a vocal type, though of course not as a personality; 'Ah chi mi dice mai' is an entrance aria like 'Porgi amor', and 'Mi tradì' a soliloquy. In addition, three arias for men come into question: Ottavio's 'Dalla sua pace' (*Don Giovanni*, No. 10*a*), Ferrando's 'Un'aura amorosa', and Tamino's 'Dies Bildnis': all are relatively slow, outwardly simple yet inwardly complex arias, sung by tenors about absent lovers; 'Dies Bildnis' in particular is closely related to 'Porgi amor' in both style and form.

Within this group, numerous differentiations can be made. Key and instrumentation play an important role. 'Non so più', 'Ah chi mi dice mai', and 'Dies Bildnis' all resemble 'Porgi amor' in being in E flat and scored for a wind complement of two clarinets, two horns, and two bassoons; 'Ah chi mi dice mai' is not only an 'entrance' aria, but is the only other aria in Mozart's Da Ponte operas that begins with a long, formal orchestral introduction. 'Mi tradì' is more distantly related, being longer and more bravura, and having only one clarinet and bassoon each, plus one flute (in part, this reflects its different status

[37] For an early version of this notion (lacking the term 'network') applied to Pamina's aria 'Ach, ich fühl's' from *Die Zauberflöte*, see Webster, 'Cone's "Personae" and the Analysis of Opera', *College Music Symposium*, 29 (1989), 44–65.

as an addition for the 1788 Vienna production). 'Un'aura amorosa', in the other 'clarinet' key of A, has the same scoring. 'Voi che sapete' is not in E flat, but in the closely related key of B flat, perhaps in part because it is unusual for a major character to sing more than one aria in the same key, or for two successive numbers to be in the same key. And as we have seen, keys were strongly correlated with character-type; thus Susanna, notwithstanding her inner nobility, sings arias only in the 'simple' keys G and F—even the complexly ironic 'Deh vieni' (see Sect. V). We have already noted that 'Dove sono' and 'Mi tradì' are soliloquies; so, essentially, is 'Ah chi mi dice mai' (Elvira believes she is alone, and the men's interjections are mere asides). 'Non so più', 'Un'aura amorosa', and especially 'Dies Bildnis' are equally self-absorbed, and would sound more or less the same even if no characters were listening on stage. Even 'Deh vieni' seems to express Susanna's true feelings, as much to the night air as for Figaro's benefit, and to this extent resembles a soliloquy. The dramatic motive of absent or unrequited love plays a role in 'Non so più', 'Dove sono', both of Elvira's arias, 'Un'aura amorosa', and 'Dies Bildnis'. Other things equal, an analysis of 'Porgi amor' made in awareness of this network of relationships will be more insightful than one that ignores them.

Formal types

Mozart's late operatic forms are more fluid and flexible, more through-composed, than those in either his earlier operas or his instrumental music.[38] The earlier operas included many arias in full and abridged da-capo, sonata, and concerto-like forms; many had long ritornellos and large-scale repetitions.[39] These characteristics became less common around 1780 (in *Zaide*, *Idomeneo*, and *Entführung*),[40] and from *Figaro* on they were downright rare (even in the late *seria* opera *La clemenza di Tito*).[41] In addition, the correlations between particular formal types and particular characters or dramatic contexts became less rigid. To be sure, elaborate introductions, accompanied recitatives, and two-tempo arias continued to be associated primarily with high-born or pretentious characters, the

[38] Three earlier German typologies of Mozart's aria forms are Karl August Rosenthal, 'Über Vokalformen bei Mozart', *Studien für Musikwissenschaft*, 14 (1927), 5–32; Hans Zingerle, 'Musik- und Textform in Opernarien Mozarts', *Mozart-Jahrbuch 1953*, 112–16; Sieghart Döhring, 'Die Arienformen in Mozarts Opern', *Mozart-Jahrbuch 1968/70*, 66–76. Of these, Rosenthal's is the most detailed and comprehensive, but is nearly unreadable, owing to its verbal density and its method of citing individual numbers merely by 'encoded' series/volume references to the 19th-c. complete edn., *W. A. Mozarts Werke* (Leipzig, 1876–1905; hereafter cited as 'AMA'); Zingerle's is painfully brief, but useful in insisting on the formal independence of text and music (remarkably, he uses the former as the basis for his typology); Döhring's is methodologically more sophisticated, but compromised by an over-readiness to equate 'difference' with 'drama'. None offers any detailed analyses. Furthermore, all unduly privilege letter-based formal schemes (*aba*, *abab*, etc.) at the expense of all other musical parameters.

[39] Martha Feldman, 'The Evolution of Mozart's Ritornello Form from Aria to Concerto', in Neal Zaslaw (ed.), *Mozart's Piano Concertos: Text, Context, Interpretation* (University of Michigan Press, forthcoming).

[40] Linda L. Tyler, '*Zaide* in the Development of Mozart's Operatic Language', *Music and Letters*, 72 (1991), 214–35.

[41] The remainder of this paragraph summarizes Webster, 'Are Mozart's Concertos "Dramatic"?: Concerto Ritornellos vs. Aria Introductions in the 1780s', in Zaslaw (ed.), *Mozart's Piano Concertos* (see above, n. 39), sect. III, first subsection.

'simple' keys (C, F, G) and metres (2/4, 3/8, 6/8) primarily with *buffa* ones. But Figaro sings *accompagnati* before both 'Se vuol ballare' and 'Aprite un po' quegl'occhi', as does Susanna before 'Deh vieni'; the orchestral introduction to the latter is a true ritornello, a very rare feature after 1782. (Nancy Storace, Mozart's original Susanna, was the *prima donna* of the Viennese company, and often received *rondòs* even when singing *buffa* roles[42]) Although Zerlina's two arias in *Don Giovanni* are similar dramatically (both console Masetto, with nobody else on stage), they differ markedly in form: 'Batti batti' (No. 12) has no orchestral introduction, while 'Vedrai, carino' (No. 18) has a substantial introduction which not only returns but is expanded at the end. The former, though a pastoral aria in key, metre, and style, even exhibits two tempi and a pervasive (if discreet) obbligato instrument (the cello).

An outline of the most common formal types in Mozart's Viennese arias is given in Table 1. They must be understood not as representations of 'the' form of any given aria,

TABLE 1. *Principal formal types in Mozart's arias of the 1780s*[a]

Formal type				Selected examples
I. Key-area forms[b,c]				
A. Binary				
1. Recapitulation	a b	a(c)	b	*Die Zauberflöte*, No. 10, 'O Isis und Osiris'
2. Tonal return section	a b	Free		*Figaro*, No. 26, 'Aprite un po' quegl'occhi' (part 1)
	I V	V	I	
B. Quatrain				
1. Simple	a a	b	a	*Die Zauberflöte*, No. 13, 'Alles fühlt der liebe Freude'[d]
	I V	V^7–I		
2. Complex				
a. Recapitulation	a b	x	a(+ b)	*Die Zauberflöte*, No. 3, 'Dies Bildnis'[e]
b. Tonal return section	a b	x	Free	*Die Zauberflöte*, No. 15, 'In diesen heil'gen Hallen'[d]
	I V	V^7–I		
C. Sonata without development				
1. Recapitulation	a b	a	b	*Die Entführung*, No. 10, 'Traurigkeit'
2. Tonal return section	a b	Free		*Tito*, No. 8, 'Ah, se fosse intorno al torno'
	I V	I	I	
D. Sonata				
1. Recapitulation	a b	c/dev.	a b	*Idomeneo*, No. 12, 'Fuor del mar'
2. Tonal return section	a b	c/dev.	Free	*Figaro*, No. 12, 'Venite, inginocchiatevi'
	I V	x–V^7—I		
E. Four-part	a b	a	c	*Tito*, No. 17, 'Tu fosti tradito'
	I V	I	I	

[42] John Platoff, personal communication.

TABLE 1. (*cont.*)

<table>
<tr><th>Formal type</th><th></th><th>Selected examples</th></tr>
<tr><td>II. Forms based on a tonally closed first part</td><td></td><td></td></tr>
<tr><td>A. ABA</td><td></td><td></td></tr>
<tr><td>1. Ternary</td><td>A | B | A
I | V | I</td><td>Tito, No. 6, ‘Del più sublime soglio’</td></tr>
<tr><td>2. Run-on</td><td>A | B ——— A
I | x —V⁷— I</td><td>Don Giovanni, No. 10a, ‘Dalla sua pace’</td></tr>
<tr><td>3. With conflated final section</td><td>A | B | A+B
I | V | I</td><td>Così, No. 17, ‘Un’aura amorosa’
(but see pp. 121–2)</td></tr>
<tr><td>B. Two-part (complex)[f]</td><td></td><td></td></tr>
<tr><td>1. Part 1: binary</td><td>A | B | A B (C)
I–V | V–I | I —— (V)–I</td><td>Figaro, No. 26, ‘Aprite un po’ quegl’occhi’</td></tr>
<tr><td>2. Part 1: ternary</td><td>A | B A | C (D)
I | V I | I</td><td>Don Giovanni, No. 18, ‘Vedrai carino’</td></tr>
<tr><td>C. Rondo (in modern formal sense)</td><td></td><td>Così, No. 26, ‘Donne mie’</td></tr>
<tr><td>D. One-part (undivided) forms</td><td></td><td>Die Entführung, No. 18, ‘Im Mohrenland’[d]</td></tr>
<tr><td>III. Two-tempo forms[g]</td><td></td><td></td></tr>
<tr><td>A. Rondò[h]</td><td>Slow | Fast
A|B|A | C
I |V|I (–V⁷) | I</td><td>Figaro, No. 19, ‘Dove sono’</td></tr>
<tr><td>B. Exposition-based</td><td>Tempo 1 | Tempo 2
A |B | C
I |V | I</td><td>Figaro, No. 17, ‘Vedrò mentre io sospiro’
(moderate–fast)
Don Giovanni, No. 4, ‘Madamina’
(fast–slow)</td></tr>
</table>

Notes:

[a] Based only on musical parameters, and applying to the vocal sections only.

[b] Forms whose first main part is an exposition, cadencing in the dominant (see text). I do not show differences in tonal plans based on the minor mode.

[c] The distinction between recapitulations and tonal return sections is discussed in the text.

[d] Each stanza of a strophic aria.

[e] Actually:

A1 A2 | B | C | D A2
I | V | V7 | I (see Sect. V).

[f] Occasionally called ‘four-part’ forms (compare I.E). Some forms of type II.B.2 exhibit an elaborate subdivision of C, e.g., c d c. Simple two-part forms, a a′ (both closing in the tonic), are found in late Mozart only in strophic numbers.

[g] Some forms of this type exhibit an elaborate subdivision of C, e.g., c d c. The rare arias in three or more tempi can be understood as elaborated variants of these forms.

[h] Only the most common subtype is shown here.

but as 'ideal types' in Max Weber's sense.[43] In Mozart's late arias, they provide no more than the conceptual or procedural framework within which events unfold. Notwithstanding the fact that the orchestral music and the text are also essential constituents of any aria form taken as a whole, the types as listed in Table 1 and discussed in this section are based on the vocal sections alone. (The reasons for this have to do with the multivalent nature of aria form; both orchestral and textual factors are discussed at length in Sect. III.)

Formal types in music must be distinguished on the basis of the interaction of three primary parameters: sectional structure, material, and tonality. I follow Tovey in distinguishing in the first instance between (1) the binary and sonata forms, based on an exposition, that is, a first main part that is formally and rhetorically complete, but closes outside the tonic and hence requires resolution later on (Table 1, part I); and (2) forms whose first part cadences in the tonic, and hence (except perhaps for a coda) usually ends the movement as well: A|B|A, A|B–A, rondo, and so forth (part II). With respect to the former group, in the context of eighteenth-century operatic studies there is good reason to adopt Ratner's general concept of 'key-area' form, based in part on eighteenth-century theory:[44]

Reprise I		Reprise II	
Paragraph 1	Paragraph 2	X-section	Return
I	V	–V^7	I

The very flexibility of this concept, especially with respect to the second half of the form, is appropriate to Mozart's free operatic forms, compared to his instrumental ones.

In late eighteenth-century arias, an exposition (Ratner's 'Reprise I') usually comprises two (and only two) paragraphs, which usually set different stanzas of the text (or are otherwise differentiated on non-musical as well as musical grounds); the first cadences in the tonic (with either a half or a full cadence), the second in the dominant.[45] But it does not necessarily behave like the exposition of an instrumental sonata form. In particular, the first paragraph often ends with an authentic cadence in the tonic and caesura (for example, Idomeneo's 'Fuor del mar', mm. 31–2, or Ottavio's 'Il mio tesoro', m. 29); frequently there is neither an organized transition nor a clear contrast in the dominant. Hence the sonata-like terms 'first group' and 'second group' (to say nothing of 'second theme') are usually best avoided, in favour of the neutral 'first' and 'second paragraph' or

[43] On musical form as a variety of 'ideal type', see Carl Dahlhaus, *Analysis and Value Judgment*, tr. Siegmund Levarie (New York, 1983), 45 ff.; compare Philip Gossett, 'Carl Dahlhaus and the "Ideal Type"', *19th-Century Music*, 13 (1989–90), 49–58. (Although Dahlhaus's application of the concept sometimes involved special pleading—see Gossett, sects. 3–4—its value as a general approach to problems of form is not thereby compromised.) Indeed, aria-types and even genres can profitably be considered as ideal types; the implications of this hypothesis cannot be pursued here.

[44] Ratner, *Classic Music*, ch. 13; also used by Allanbrook, *Rhythmic Gesture*. (I have slightly altered Ratner's scheme to conform more closely to specifically operatic procedures.)

[45] The importance of such expositions in late 18th-c. arias was first described in Hunter, 'Haydn's Aria Forms', ch. 5.

'tonic' and 'dominant paragraph'—especially since often either or both will not be recapitulated. What is essential is that the second paragraph end with a structural cadence in the dominant, strong enough to organize the entire form up to that point ('Fuor del mar', mm. 76 (voice) and 80–1 (orchestra); 'Il mio tesoro', m. 43); if this is lacking, the two paragraphs may not combine into an exposition at all.[46]

Following the exposition, however, anything can happen.[47] The material may be clearly recapitulated in whole or in part, or it may not. Even when the overall form seems clear and the moment of recapitulation is signalled unambiguously, what happens may be (or sound) completely new, for example, in Susanna's 'Venite, inginocchiatevi'. Furthermore, the return may be drastically 'underarticulated', compared to that in an instrumental sonata form: the opening theme may sneak in unawares, as in Elvira's 'Ah fuggi il traditor' (*Don Giovanni*, No. 8), mm. 26–8 vs. 5–7 (and not 25–6 vs. 3–5), or the return of the tonic itself may be casual, especially in male *buffa* arias (for example, Figaro's 'Aprite un po' quegl'occhi', m. 57). Even when much of the material of the exposition (or ritornello) does return, it may be fragmented, reordered, altered in rhetoric, and combined with new ideas (as in 'Porgi amor'). On the other hand, many arias have multiple reprises of a main theme: for example, the second part of Leporello's 'Catalogue' aria, mm. 124, 143, or Anna's 'Or sai chi l'onore', mm. 101, 110, 119. Such multiple reprises usually seem to be neither a special effect nor an indication of rondo form but, more simply, a rhetorical phenomenon: the character's need to reiterate or intensify the argument of the moment.

With the provisò that the boundaries between them are flexible, it seems useful to distinguish three types of final tonic section in key-area forms: regular recapitulations, free recapitulations, and tonal return sections.[48] Many late Mozart arias, particularly sonatas without development and ABA forms, have regular recapitulations (for example, Elvira's 'Ah chi mi dice mai' and Ferrando's 'Un'aura amorosa'). In a free recapitulation, important material from the exposition returns in such a way as to resolve earlier sections tonally and formally, but it is altered, reordered, abridged, supplemented, in whatever way is appropriate to the context. A clever example is Leporello's 'Ah pietà, signori miei' (*Don Giovanni*, No. 20), following the big sextet in Act II; much of the motivic material in the retransition (mm. 54 ff.) and recapitulation (64 ff.) is familiar, but everything is recomposed and reordered; the form—after a very clear exposition and development—is as hard to pin down as the wily servant who escapes while singing it. In a tonal

[46] A 'structural cadence' is a very strong, form-defining cadence at the end of a section (occasionally elided to the beginning of the next). In a sonata-form movement, for example, there may be as few as four: at the end of the transition on V/V, the end of the exposition, the beginning of the recapitulation, and the end of the movement.

[47] On this paragraph see Hunter, 'Haydn's Aria Forms', pts. III–IV; Webster, 'To Understand . . . Mozart', 181–2, 184–5; Platoff, 'The buffa aria'; Michael F. Robinson, 'Mozart and the *opera buffa* Tradition', in Tim Carter, *W. A. Mozart: 'Le nozze di Figaro'* (Cambridge, 1987), 11–32 at 24.

[48] I emphasized the role of free recapitulations in 'To Understand Mozart'; Hunter coined the term 'tonal return section' ('Haydn's Aria Forms', ch. 9), and it has been adopted by Platoff. This summary attempts for the first time to distinguish between them.

return section, by contrast, there is little or no thematic recapitulation; the singer returns to the tonic and effects closure without significant reprise, usually with new ideas, rhetoric, or *Affekt*. Still more radical are two-tempo arias, in which the second section presents a new state of being altogether, ordinarily without thematic recapitulation; these are almost by definition tonal return sections. Free recapitulations and tonal return sections both give precedence to rhetorical, dramatic, or psychological development over formal symmetry; the difference between them (which cannot be quantified) is simply the degree of change or novelty entailed. In Mozart's operas from *Figaro* on, both methods of ending an aria are as common, as 'normal', as regular recapitulations. For this reason, most of the formal types listed in Part I of Table 1 entail two subtypes: with a recapitulation, and with a tonal return section. For simplicity's sake, however, and to avoid neologisms, I use the formal designations 'binary', 'sonata', and so forth for arias having tonal return sections as well as those with regular recapitulations—notwithstanding the apparent anomaly of calling an aria whose final section is as free as that in Susanna's 'Venite, inginocchiatevi' (see Sect. V) a 'sonata form'. The fact remains that its proportions, sectional structure, and tonal organization are those of sonata form, and its tonal return section, which would indeed be incomprehensible in a Mozart instrumental movement, is *normal* in the operatic context. In all these cases, the distinction affects the final section in the tonic more than the formal type as such.[49]

Of the individual forms listed in the first part of Table 1, only the 'quatrain' needs further comment here. The term was coined by Dénes Bartha to denote a common, but little noticed, formal type in Classical-period themes, based on four phrases of more or less equal length:

a	a′	b	a
I–V	V–I	x–V^7	I–I
I–V	I–V		

Though derived in the first instance from folk- and dance-music, it was employed in art music not only for the main themes of slow and variation movements and rondos, but entire sections and small movements.[50] Familiar examples in instrumental music include the minuet of *Eine kleine Nachtmusik* and Beethoven's 'Ode to Joy' theme (without the repetition of mm. 9–16). Bartha emphasized the distinction between the parallelism of the first two phrases (except for their different tonal goals), and the intensification in the third; he also saw the active, run-on character of the 'enjambement' (elision) between the third and fourth phrases as crucial.

[49] For the view that this and comparable arias should not be described as sonata forms, see Platoff, 'The buffa aria', 105, 107–11, 117–20.

[50] Bartha, 'Song Form and the Concept of "Quatrain"', in Jens Peter Larsen, Howard Serwer, and James Webster (eds.), *Haydn Studies: Proceedings of the International Haydn Conference, Washington, D.C., 1975* (New York, 1981), 353–5 (with further references). A variety of quatrains on various structural levels (not all conforming to Bartha's model) are described in Malcolm S. Cole, *The Magic Flute* and the Quatrain, *Journal of Musicology*, 3 (1984), 157–76.

As implied by the diagram in the preceding paragraph, in Bartha's model the first half of a quatrain is either a normal antecedent–consequent period closing in the tonic, or an 'antiperiod', that is, a period whose *consequent* cadences off the tonic, most often in the forms —I| —V|, or —V| —V/V|. (Of course, the entire antiperiod functions as a higher-level antecedent to something that follows it.[51]) However in Mozart's late operatic forms in two parts of which the first part is a period—including single stanzas of strophic arias—the first part is always an antiperiod, never an antecedent–consequent structure. The importance of the quatrain is that it is the only formal type in which a sonata-form-like double return (to the opening theme and to the tonic simultaneously) occurs within a second part that is more or less the same length as the first. (In sonata form, the second part is much longer; in binary forms, there is no double return; in the sonata without development, the double return immediately follows the end of the exposition.) No other symmetrical two-part form is as complex or highly integrated.

Furthermore, as in all key-area forms, this variant of the quatrain often incorporates a contrast between the two phrases of the first half (instead of mere statement and variation). In this case, the fourth phrase often recapitulates *both* components of the first half (in elided or abbreviated form). An example on the smallest scale is the Trio of Haydn's String Quartet in C, Op. 33 No. 3 (see Ex. 1); the reprise, mm. 47–50, encompasses the

EXAMPLE 1. Quatrain form: Haydn, String Quartet in C, Op. 33 No. 3: Trio

[51] The coinage 'antiperiod' is my own; though common in the Classical period, this construction has been little studied. A few comments are found in Wilhelm Fischer, 'Zur Entwicklungsgeschichte des Wiener klassischen Stils', *Studien für Musikwissenschaft*, 3 (1915), 25–9, types 4 and 5; 'Zwei neapolitanische Melodietypen bei Mozart und Haydn', *Mozart-Jahrbuch 1960–1*, 7–22 ('umgekehrte Periode'); Eugene K. Wolf, *The Symphonies of Johann Stamitz: A Study in the Formation of the Classic Style* (Utrecht and Antwerp; The Hague and Boston, 1981), 195, 220 n. 58, 347; Hunter, 'Haydn's Aria Forms', *passim*.

essence of both phrases from the first half: mm. 47–8 recapitulate 35–6, while the cadence in 49–50 rhymes with and resolves the dominant cadence of 41–2. (Although Haydn's motivic relations are far more complex than this account would suggest, the 4×4 harmonic structure is not thereby compromised.) This principle of free development within the symmetry and intelligibility of a binary structure is highly characteristic of Mozart's later aria forms. Used straightforwardly in the individual strophes of songs for simple characters like Papageno ('Ein Vogelfänger bin ich ja', *Die Zauberflöte*, No. 2) and Monostatos ('Alles fühlt', No. 13), it also underlies numbers as rich and sophisticated as Tamino's 'Dies Bildnis'.

A related pair of entries in Table 1 that may be unfamiliar to some readers is II.A.2–3 (run-on A|B–A; ABA with conflated final section). The run-on A|B–A differs from the ternary A|B|A in that it exhibits a quatrain-like intensification during B–A. The B section (which still begins like a plain contrast) gradually becomes developmental and leads, not to a cadence, but to dominant preparation and the reprise of A; it is no longer independent, but elided to the reprise, as part of a single larger unit. For example, the B section of Don Ottavio's 'Dalla sua pace' moves from G minor (m. 17) to B flat (21), to V/V (26)—and then, by an astonishing enharmonic modulation, to B minor (29), and on to the home dominant (35–6). It is unstable both tonally (none of these keys leads to a strong cadence) and rhetorically (the topics change constantly); hence it is consequential that the final dominant is not a key, but the home dominant seventh: a preparation for the reprise which must follow.

In ABA with conflated final section, the reprise of A adverts to B material near the end, either by way of intensification and expansion within its latter stages, or following its completion (more or less as a coda). (This is common in instrumental music; familiar examples are the Adagio of Haydn's Symphony No. 92 ('Oxford'), mm. 99 ff. (compare 45 ff.), and the Largo of Beethoven's Piano Sonata in E flat, Op. 7, mm. 74 ff. (compare 25 ff.).) Now if in this context the initial A and B are connected by a transition (however brief), they may begin to lose their status as independent sections, and sound instead like the first two paragraphs of an exposition. In arias, the fact that even key-area forms often end the tonic paragraph with a full cadence and caesura—like the A|B of an ABA—further complicates the distinction. And if the second half of such an aria is freely recomposed, with a hint of B at the end, the difference between (say) a 'sonata without development' and an 'ABA with conflated final section' may evaporate:

A		B	|	A	B	(Sonata without development)
A	|	B	|	A (+B)		(ABA)
I		V		I		

In such cases, only the style, the rhythmic disposition (stable or progressive), and perhaps the proportions can distinguish the formal types.

For example, Ferrando's outwardly simple 'Un'aura amorosa' is analysed by Döhring as an ABA, by Hunter as a sonata without development[52]—and both are correct. 'ABA' emphasizes the text-form, the contrast between A and B, the stable character of the primary B theme (m. 30), the clear cadences at the end of each section (mm. 23, 41), and the overall division into three vocal sections. 'Sonata without development' emphasizes the separate modulating transition in mm. 23-9 (strongly cadencing on V of V), the greater length of the third vocal section (32 measures, as against 22 + 18), and especially the extension (mm. 63-73), which includes free reprises of various motives from the B section (see Ex. 2): the evaded V^2–I^6 cadence from mm. 36–7 and the melodic figures from 38–41 return in 62–7; the suddenly 'pure' eighth-note rhythm from m. 34 and steep vocal plunge from 35 return in 68–9 (the latter augmented). Rhetorically, too, the final vocal cadence seems to round off not just the final section, but the entire aria.

Similar ambiguities often attach to 'four-part', 'complex two-part', and other compound forms. Although many of these have the same sequence of four sections, ABAC, they exhibit different groupings among them, and hence represent different formal types:

Two-part (ternary)	A	B	A	|		C
	I	V	I	|		C
Two-part (binary)	A	B		|	A	C
	I–V	V–I		|	I	——
Four-part	A	B		|	A	C
	I	V		|	I	I

In addition, the majority of two-tempo *rondò*s are constructed like the first of these forms, except that 'C' differs much more strongly from the preceding section(s) (and is often elaborated as cdc or the like). They too often seem formally ambiguous; an example is 'Come scoglio', described briefly near the end of Sect. III. In many Mozart arias, 'the' form does not exist.

III. ANALYTICAL DOMAINS: TEXT, VOICE, ORCHESTRA

In this section I attempt a systematic exposition of the multivalent nature of arias. Methodologically, I distinguish between 'domains' and 'parameters': the former are the global, often independent 'systems' that govern an aria (text, music, stage-action, and so forth); the latter are the usually interdependent constituents within a given domain (for example, the domain 'music' includes tonality, rhythm, vocal tessitura, formal type, and so forth). Since stage-action, characterization, and plot-development cannot be 'analysed' in any conventional sense, for our purposes here the multivalent nature of arias can be understood in terms of three primary domains: text, voice, and orchestra.

[52] Sieghart Döhring, *Formgeschichte der Opernarien vom Ausgang des 18. bis zur Mitte des 19. Jahrhunderts* (Marburg an der Lahn, 1975), 97–8; Hunter, 'Haydn's Aria Forms', 44–5.

EXAMPLE 2. *Così fan tutte*, No. 17, 'Un'aura amorosa': (*a*) mm. 34–41; (*b*) mm. 60–73

The role of the orchestra

It will be convenient to begin with the orchestra. Hunter's study of Haydn—so far, the only comprehensive formal study of a large repertory of late eighteenth-century arias—separates the music into 'vocal' and 'instrumental' components, and thus obtains the three domains cited above (a vast improvement on the usual gross division between 'text' and 'music'). The distinction was due in the first instance to her focus on large-scale form in a repertory that resembles instrumental music more closely than do Mozart's later arias, and in which the introductory tutti is often form-defining. Indeed, she defines 'orchestral' music as comprising only those sections during which the singer is silent (introduction, interior punctuating passages, postlude), while 'vocal' music comprises *all* the music heard while the singer is singing, including the orchestral accompaniment.[53] This method, appropriate for the study of large-scale form, has two concomitant disadvantages: it underplays other, equally important distinctions between singer and orchestra (for example, contrasting simultaneous material), and it leads to an ambiguity in the orchestra's overall status: is it independent, as in the opening and closing tuttis, or at most 'co-dependent', as when accompanying the singer?

For these reasons, I prefer to define 'vocal' and 'orchestral music' simply as all the music performed, respectively, by the singer(s) and the orchestra. That is, they are two complementary 'strands' of the texture, proceeding simultaneously in time. Neither is self-sufficient; each requires the other. The advantages of this division go beyond analytical flexibility and clarity as to the orchestra's domain. It encourages dramatistic analysis of the complex and often shifting relations between the two complementary personae of an aria ('vocal' and 'instrumental', or 'protagonist' and 'agent'), which combine to unify the aria as an utterance of a 'complete persona'—the 'composer's voice' itself.[54] A focus on the singer's music emphasizes that a character is involved, whose feelings and motivation are the very reason for the aria's existence. Conversely, as an agent the orchestra comes into its own right; indeed it often includes several more or less independent agents. To be sure, the concept of the persona is subjective; from this point of view, Hunter's methodologically explicit approach remains an attractive alternative.

Furthermore, very few of Mozart's arias of the 1780s employ independent orchestral sections as constituents of form. (In this they differ from his earlier arias, as well as most of Haydn's.) About half the arias in the three Da Ponte operas include no independent introductory material; in most of the others the opening tutti is brief. The few exceptions seem to have as much of a dramaturgical function as a formal one: that of 'introducing' one or more new characters in the first concerted number of a new scene, as in 'Porgi

[53] 'Haydn's Aria Forms', 69.

[54] Cone, *The Composer's Voice*, especially chs. 1–2. For a variant of this theory specifically oriented towards Mozart arias, see Webster, 'Cone's "Personae"'. On 'agency' in this context, see Cone, ch. 5; Fred Everett Maus, 'Agency in Instrumental Music and Song', *College Music Symposium*, 29 (1989), 31–42; Webster, ibid., 50–1, 57, 64–5; and Cone's responses, ibid. 77–9. Kunze, *Mozarts Opern*, offers many relevant observations on Mozart's instrumental usage, without adumbrating a theory of musical agency.

amor' and 'Ah chi mi dice mai', as well as the Queen of the Night's 'O zittre nicht' (*Die Zauberflöte*, No. 4), where the scenic requirement of her 'entrance' from on high may also have played a role. (The principle applies to ensembles as well: see the opening duettino in *Figaro*, as opposed to No. 2; and, in *Così*, both the opening trio for the three men, as opposed to Nos. 2–3, and the duet No. 4 for the two sisters.) Even these introductions play no independent formal role in the aria as a whole, comparable to those in earlier arias.[55] By the same principle, Mozart's long orchestral postludes (which are uncommon from *Figaro* on) are in the first instance 'exit' music, as in Pamina's 'Ach, ich fühl's' (*Die Zauberflöte*, No. 17), or mark the end of a scene or act, as in Figaro's 'Non più andrai' (No. 9); in this respect they are the mirror image or long opening tuttis. Admittedly, they also have dramatic significance: they represent a new state of being that has developed during the aria (see Sect. VI). These factors support the view that in this repertory the operative musical domains are the vocal and orchestral strands, rather than the sections defined by the singer's participation as against silence.

Apart from its role in creating sectional structure, the orchestral accompaniment can influence the form and character of an aria by means of independent musical material, rhythmic profile, and semantic associations.[56] In Mozart (as opposed to many of his contemporaries), the orchestra almost always has independent material. An aria (or section) is usually characterized by a single basic accompanimental pattern; this is often even more important rhythmically than motivically, in that it forms part of the aria's overall 'topic'. But accompanimental motifs often have substantive, indeed illustrative value: in Donna Anna's 'Or sai chi l'onore', the off-beat thrusts in the bass; in Belmonte's 'O wie ängstlich' (*Entführung*, No. 4), the 'beating' sixteenths in violin octaves that illustrate the line 'Klopft mein liebevolles Herz' (one of several illustrative accompanimental motifs that Mozart himself pointed out in this aria);[57] in Pamina's 'Ach, ich fühl's', the inarticulate trudging in the strings; and so forth. In the latter case, the figure is virtually an ostinato, maintained throughout Pamina's song, and complexly opposed to it: it is an independent persona.[58] Pervasive ostinatos of this sort are common; see, for example, the bustling sixteenths in Guglielmo's 'Donne mie' (*Così*, No. 26), or the agitated off-beat swirls in Dorabella's 'Smanie implacabili'.

Another common orchestral feature comprises interjections (most often in the winds) that punctuate the rests at the ends of vocal phrases; for example, again in 'Or sai chi l'onore', the descending dotted figures in mm. 2 and 4. Often these motifs link the last note in one vocal phrase to the first of the next, creating a kind of operatic *Klangfarbenmelodie* (voice plus instrument), or a persona-like interaction with the singer; for example, the oboe/bassoon phrases in 'Dove sono' (mm. 2–3, 4–5, 8–9, etc.).[59] Especially

55 Webster, 'Are Mozart's Concertos "Dramatic"?', Sect. III.

56 A wealth of observations on these matters can be found in Viktor Zuckerkandl, 'Prinzipien und Methoden der Instrumentation in Mozarts dramatischen Werken' (Ph.D. diss., University of Vienna, 1927).

57 In the oft-quoted letter to his father, 26 September 1781 (*Briefe*, iii. 162).

58 Webster, 'Cone's "Personae"', 45–9.

59 Cone, *The Composer's Voice*, 26–9 (adumbrated by Noske, *Signifier and Signified*, 124).

in certain types of comic aria, the orchestra may deploy an entire battery of more or less independent motifs and short phrases, often in conjunction with gestures or stage-action and alternating with the voice; typical here is Susanna's 'Venite, inginocchiatevi'.

Occasionally, the orchestra plays an actual melody that is never given to the singer. A common location for such melodies is the beginning of the dominant paragraph of a slow aria: the winds play a heartfelt tune, often with fast notes over slowly moving harmonies, which the singer answers in more measured rhythms: see 'Porgi amor', mm. 26–34, and Donna Anna's 'Non mi dir', mm. 36–44. (In the former the wind theme to some extent anticipates the vocal theme; in Tamino's 'Dies Bildnis', mm. 16–19, his answer is more or less identical to the orchestral statement. Note Mozart's variety of procedure: the same formal and affective context—a new plea, at the beginning of the dominant paragraph, with structurally parallel orchestral and vocal phrases—is correlated with widely varying degrees of similarity or dissimilarity between the two phrases.) Finally, one or more instruments may assume a true concertante role, accompanying the singer, echoing and anticipating, indeed playing independent melodies. This is most common in two-tempo arias: see not only the horn in Fiordiligi's 'Per pietà' (*Così*, No. 25), the basset-clarinet in Sesto's 'Parto' (*Tito*, No. 9), the basset-horn in Vitellia's 'Non più di fiori' (No. 23) but also, in the different context of a *buffa* aria, the cello in Zerlina's 'Batti, batti'.

These solo instruments are no mere ornaments; by enriching the aria's sonic and material world, they comment on the singer's plight, deepen her expression, and provide an aura that would otherwise be lacking. Indeed they become independent agents, whether as reflections of the singer's psyche (producing that conversation with one's *alter ego* so characteristic of soliloquies) or as interlocutors. Mozart's operas exhibit a continuum of instrumental usage, from plain interjections to full-fledged agents, all of which are potential components of the form and dramatic expression. Perhaps this observation helps make sense of Konstanze's 'Martern aller Arten', whose elaborate 'concerto' for several instrumental soloists has proved such a stumbling-block. To be sure, it lies at one extreme of this continuum—but it remains on it. No other Mozart aria would be more appropriately granted this aura of enrichment: a unique gesture of defiance by an inwardly noble heroine. (Not even Pamina is called on to do anything comparable; indeed, to judge by her submissive response to Sarastro in the Act I finale, she would probably not be capable of it.)

With respect to rhythm, the orchestra naturally exhibits a greater range and variety of rhythmic values than the singer. More important, indeed pervasive, is a certain complementary relation between the orchestral and vocal phrase-structure.[60] As we shall see, the majority of vocal phrases lead from an up-beat (or 'weak' measure) to a down-beat

[60] This paragraph reflects Thrasybulos Georgiades, 'Aus der Musiksprache des Mozart-Theaters', *Mozart-Jahrbuch 1950*, 76–98; repr. in Georgiades, *Kleine Schriften* (Tutzing, 1977), 9–32; Stefan Kunze, 'Über das Verhältnis von musikalisch autonomer Struktur und Textbau in Mozarts Opern: Das Terzettino "Soave sia il vento" (Nr. 10) aus "Così fan tutte"', *Mozart-Jahrbuch 1973/74*, 217–32; Reinhard Strohm, 'Zur Metrik in Haydns und Anfossis "La vera costanza"', in Eva Badura-Skoda (ed.), *Joseph Haydn: Proceedings of the International Congress Wien 1982* (Munich, 1986), 279–94.

(or 'strong' measure), most often on a change of harmony; the arrival-point is confirmed by a rest directly following. By contrast, the strings tend to be more or less continuous in texture and activity, and (except at cadences) their phrasing is usually organized around initial down-beats (or 'strong' opening measures). The result is a complex interlocking of two rhythmic patterns; see, for example, the beginning of Cherubino's 'Non so più', shown in Ex. 3. The continuous orchestral fabric in the strings is organized in two-bar harmonic units which begin on the down-beat of every other measure (1, 3, etc.; see the brackets below the systems), while Cherubino's phrases begin at the end of a given bar and move *across* the change of harmony to the same down-beat on which the strings change harmony (see the phrasing indications above the vocal line). The independent orchestral motives that punctuate the rests following vocal phrases (noted on the stave above) usually fall in the middle of the measure, between the singer's end-accent on or just after one down-beat, and his resumption on or just before the next. That is, they are implicitly or explicitly syncopated, further increasing the rhythmic complexity (see the 'breathless' wind interjections in mm. 3 and 5). In this respect as well, the cadences move in the direction of uniformity: from m. 9 on, the winds double Cherubino in outline, in a kind of structural heterophony.

These complementary vocal/orchestral rhythms have large-scale consequences. At certain later points, the orchestra usually changes to a faster harmonic rhythm (here: in mm. 5–6a one harmony per bar, in mm. 6b–15a two per bar) and support of the singer's drive to the cadence. The resulting congruence, by contrast with the out-of-phase rhythmic profile that precedes it, creates strong cadential arrivals in mm. 12 (deceptive) and especially 15. To generalize: the phraseology and internal rhythms of voice and orchestra are highly variable, both within each domain and between different ones. Much of the life of Mozart's arias derives from this complex rhythmic play. Indeed it is this interaction, more than the mere existence of independent orchestral motifs, that seems most to distinguish his operatic music from that of his contemporaries.

Another important class of orchestral phenomena comprises what may be called the semantics of instrumentation, that is, conventional associations between particular instruments and particular dramatic contexts or implications (compare the descriptions of aria-types in Sect. II). Many of these associations originated with imitations of music heard in daily life: wind-instruments in marches and *Tafelmusik* (the Act II finale of *Don Giovanni*), pizzicato strings to imitate a guitar in serenades ('Voi che sapete'; Don Giovanni's 'Deh vieni alla finestra'), and so forth. (This principle is thus the same as that which led to the development of the rhythmic topoi.) Other associations were dependent on convention, and again affect mainly the winds: the ubiquitous horn-fanfares to signify cuckoldry, based on the punning double significance of *corno* (see the end of Figaro's 'Aprite un po' quegl'occhi'); the curious double meaning of the flute, signifying both chastity (due to purity of tone?) and licentiousness, as in the piccolo for both Osmin and Monostatos (the association derives ultimately from Pan); and so forth. In *Die Zauberflöte*, the flute's purity takes on additional layers of meaning: the magic

EXAMPLE 3. *Le nozze di Figaro*, No. 6, 'Non so più': mm. 1–36

13
etc.
Ch.
(3)
don - na mi fa pal - pi - tar. So - - lo ai
p
cresc.
p
I vii⁷/V V 7 I
17
Ch.
(3)
no - mi d'amor, di di - let - to. mi si tur - ba, mi s'al - te - ra il
21
Ch.
(4) (2+2)
pet - to e a par - la - re mi sfor - za d'a -
25
Ch.
(2)
(4)
- mo - re un de - si - o, un de -

power of music and a talisman of enlightenment; this is not merely semantic, but symbolic.

Textual parameters

The importance of the text. The first part of Table 2 lists the principal aspects of aria-texts that affect the form and style of musical settings. (In principle, one must distinguish between the libretto as a *text*—written by a poet, usually published in advance of the première, and available for reading during the performance—and the libretto in the sense of the words actually set to music.[61] Composers always introduce minor divergences in punctuation, orthography, and wording, most of which have little or no effect on the form or expression. In addition, owing to dramatic or practical exigencies, entire numbers from the original libretto may never be set to music at all, or may be trans-

[61] Among Mozart's operas, only *Die Zauberflöte* has been extensively studied from this point of view; see Peter Branscombe, '"Die Zauberflöte": Some Textual and Interpretative Problems', *Proceedings of the Royal Musical Association*, 92 (1965–6), 45–63; Gernot Gruber, 'Das Autograph der "Zauberflöte": Eine stilkritische Interpretation des philologischen Befundes', *Mozart-Jahrbuch 1967*, 127–49; *1968/70*, 99–110.

Evidence for multiple stages of libretti, of which the later may already reflect changes made on the composer's initiative, survives in the existence of different versions of those to *Idomeneo*, *Don Giovanni*, and *Così*; see Heartz, *Mozart's Operas*, 18, 28–32, 162–74, 233–4, 251–3.

TABLE 2. *Analytical parameters in an eighteenth-century aria*

- Text
  - Line construction
    - Length
    - Accentual pattern
  - Form
    - Rhyme-scheme
    - Stanza-pattern
    - Unitary? Contrasting sections?
  - Linguistic patterns (vowels/consonants, assonance, etc.)
  - Grammatical structure; esp.
    - Changes in subject of the discourse?
    - Changes in verb-tense?
  - Semantic content
    - Type? (E.g., 'simile' aria)
    - Voice (declarative? self-dramatizing? ruminative? moralizing? narrative? etc.)
  - *Affekt*
  - Dramatic context
    - Type? (e.g., serenade, male *buffa* aria, love/absence aria)
    - Dramaturgical function (sung alone? to another person or persons? to audience?)
    - Motivation (expression of feeling? rationalization? persuasion?)

- Music [voice and orchestra to be considered independently]
  - Formal organization
    - Clear formal type? 'Through-composed'?
    - Tempo changes? Major changes of *Affekt*?
    - Sections within a single tempo (how many? how created? how related to each other?)
    - Breaking of patterns? Interjection of recitative?
    - Regular recapitulation? Free recapitulation? Tonal return section?
  - Rhythm and 'topics'
    - Topic(s) prominent?
    - Declamation-patterns ('rhythmic profile')
      - Phrase-lengths
      - Up-beat vs. down-beat phrase-beginnings
      - On-beat ('strong') vs. after-beat ('weak') phrase-endings
    - Continuity vs. diversity
  - Material
    - Conventional associations? Types?
    - Unified? Diverse?
    - Developing variation?
  - Tonality
    - 'Semantic' (associational)?
    - Tonal structure
    - Significant pitches in vocal part
  - Use of instruments
    - Function (especially winds): independent material? independent rhythmic profile? concertante?
    - Semantic
    - Symbolic

formed into recitative, or even cut after having been composed[62]—not to mention the drastic changes usually entailed by later revivals.) The list of parameters in Table 2 begins with local and technical matters (prosody, rhyme, stanza structure) and then moves to broader aspects of character and motivation.

Contrary to a widespread opinion, Mozart insisted that appropriate poetry was essential for operatic composition. At least, this seems to me the larger sense of his often quoted remarks to his father defending Stephanie's libretto for *Die Entführung*:

In an opera the poetry must absolutely be the obedient daughter of the music. After all, why are Italian operas popular everywhere—even with everything in the libretti that is so hopeless?! . . . Because the music entirely dominates, and because of it one forgets everything else. Of course, an opera must please all the more when the plan of the drama [*Stück*] is well worked out, *and the words are written solely for the music*—but not when [one] fashions the words for the sake of a miserable rhyme here and there . . . or [writes] whole stanzas that ruin the composer's entire idea. *Verses are doubtless the most indispensable thing* [das unentbehrlichste] *for music*, but rhymes—for the sake of rhyming—the most harmful.[63]

Notwithstanding 'obedient daughter . . . the music dominates' and the rest, Mozart acknowledges that 'verses' are 'indispensable' for vocal music. He was presumably referring to poetic lines that imply tangible rhythmic profiles (see directly below). This also illuminates his occasional remark to the effect that he invented musical ideas before knowing the words—for example, earlier in the same letter: 'The poetry is entirely appropriate for the character of the stupid, gross, evil Osmin . . . it fits my musical ideas so well (which were already running around in my head)'; or, a fortnight earlier (also regarding Osmin), 'I have given Stephani complete specifications for the aria—and the main idea for the music was already complete, before Stephani knew anything about it.'[64] First of all, when (as in Mozart's operas from *Idomeneo* on) a libretto was newly written or arranged, it seems virtually certain that composer and poet would have discussed such matters as the metrical scheme and poetic diction appropriate for a given type of aria in a given context in the abstract, before either artist proceeded to a detailed working-out. (Indeed, such collaboration was doubtless one of the primary benefits of the sort of 'plan' to which Mozart alluded in the letter just quoted, and which we may presume he and Da Ponte executed in practice.) Even if this should not have been the case, Mozart's invention of appropriate ideas for a given aria without knowing the text testifies not so much to the 'primacy' of music over poetry (as the votaries of absolute music would have it), as to the strength of the conventions which largely determined the 'fit' between dramatic contexts, aria- and verse-types, and musical dispositions. Indeed, we know from his

[62] Notably in *Idomeneo*; see Heartz in *NMA*, II/5/11, pp. xi–xvi.

[63] 13 October 1781; *Briefe*, iii. 167 (emphasis added). In this case I see no sign of special pleading on Mozart's part, of the sort he admittedly often employed when writing to his father. Abert (i. 770–4) and Heartz (*Mozart's Operas*, 17, 28, 139–40, 154–5, 164–74) emphasize the importance of such a 'plan' for Mozart and his librettists.

[64] 26 September 1781 (iii. 162). An interpretation of this passage similar to mine is offered by Thomas Bauman, 'Coming of Age in Vienna: *Die Entführung aus dem Serail*', in Heartz, *Mozart's Operas*, 79–80 n. 20.

description of 'O wie ängstlich' (cited above) and from other contexts that he was grateful for appropriate verbal imagery as well. All this implies that his expressed contempt for rhymes was a kind of polemical synecdoche, standing for a general antipathy to purely poetic conceits introduced 'for their own sake'—not to mention that every closed operatic number he ever composed sets a rhymed text.[65]

Prosody and the rhythmic profile. A brief discussion of Italian prosody is necessary here, because many writers on Mozart appear to be ignorant of its principles. (German prosody causes fewer difficulties, in part because of the dominance of Germanic scholars in Mozart studies, in part because its principles are closer to those of English.) For example, every modern printed edition of a Da Ponte libretto that I have seen, whether in books or accompanying recordings, fails to observe many of his original line-divisions; those accompanying translations into other languages are often useless for this purpose. This is no pedantry: in Italian verse, the line-lengths and their accentual patterns are constituents of a text that is to be set to music. Each pattern not only fosters certain possibilities of declamation (and inhibits others), but also determines a good deal about what I call the 'rhythmic profile' of the music to which it would most naturally be set.[66]

An example of the sort of error that can arise is provided by a modern interpretation of the text to Cherubino's 'Voi che sapete'. It comprises thirty-two lines of *quinario* (five syllables) arranged in eight quatrains, not twenty-eight lines in seven quatrains, as it is usually printed: in the printed libretto, Cherubino's repetition of the first stanza at the end is written out, as an integral part of the poem. (It would be so even if Da Ponte's original had been different, with the final stanza as printed reflecting Mozart's intervention in setting it to music. By contrast, most aria-texts were not provided with corresponding repetitions in the printed librettos, notwithstanding the wholesale verbal repetitions entailed by their musical settings.) Each quatrain alternates *piano* and *tronco*

[65] Strohm, 'Merkmale italienischer Versvertonung in Mozarts Klavierkonzerten', in Lippmann (ed.), *Colloquium 'Mozart und Italien'* (see above, n. 18), 219, quotes Mozart's half-sentence 'Verses are doubtless the most indispensable thing for music' out of context, arguing that he was referring to an inherently 'versifying' character of *all* music, instrumental as well as vocal; this ignores Mozart's strong and unambiguous focus on opera libretti thoughout the passage.

The conflict between Mozart's polemic against rhymes and his compositional practice has been noted by Daniela Goldin, 'Mozart, Da Ponte e il linguaggio dell'Opera buffa', in Maria Teresa Muraro (ed.), *Venezia e il melodramma nel settecento*, ii (Florence, 1981), 270–1; Sheila Hodges, *Lorenzo Da Ponte: The Life and Times of Mozart's Librettist* (London, 1985), 64–5.

[66] The verse-types are exhaustively, if somewhat Teutonically, described in Friedrich Lippmann, 'Der italienische Vers und der musikalische Rhythmus: Zum Verhältnis von Vers und Musik in der italienischen Oper des 19. Jahrhunderts, mit einem Rückblick auf die 2. Hälfte des 18. Jahrhunderts', *Analecta musicologica*, 12 (1973), 253–369 (for 18th-c. examples: 293–6, 317–21, 356–69); 14 (1974), 324–410 (370–86, 404–6, 410); 15 (1975), 298–333 (300–3, 307, 316–23); summarized with respect to Mozart, and supplemented with examples from German texts, in Lippmann, 'Mozart und der Vers', in Lippmann (ed.), *Colloquium 'Mozart und Italien'*, 107–37. See also Strohm, 'Merkmale italienischer Versvertonung'; id., *Italienische Opernarien*, i. 117–25; id., 'Zur Metrik'; Carter, *Figaro*, ch. 5. A useful account based directly on Italian poetics is Robert Anthony Moreen, 'Integration of Text Forms and Musical Forms in Verdi's Early Operas' (Ph.D. diss., Princeton University, 1975), 9–26. Among general works on Mozart, Kunze, *Mozarts Opern*, offers the most helpful discussions of prosody.

endings (that is, 'plain' or normal endings, with one unaccented syllable following the final accent, as against those in which that unaccented syllable is 'cut', so that the accent falls on the end) in an *abab* rhyme-scheme.[67]

Voi che sapete	a
Che cosa è amor,	b
Donne vedete	a
Si l'ho nel cor.	b

Levarie interprets the poem as a 'sonnet': he conflates each quatrain into a couplet, so that the entire text (minus the repetition at the end) comprises fourteen lines. Notwithstanding Da Ponte's apparent reference to a famous line from Dante's sonnet-cycle *La vita nuova* ('Donne ch'avete intelletto d'amore'), this would still be no sonnet. The macro-lines would be in *quinario doppio* (not found in Da Ponte, and hardly characteristic of sonnets in general), and would include constant internal rhymes (more or less unheard-of in sonnets). The stanzas themselves would be couplets, rather than quatrains and tercets. In contrast to most true sonnets, there would be no reflection of the putative form in the poetic content, which is more or less unitary. Given all this, Levarie makes a virtue of necessity, arguing that Cherubino's poetry is 'somewhat childish' and 'naïve', in that he is unable to sustain long lines without the crutch of internal rhymes! (He may be excused, in so far as no less a figure than Schoenberg had previously suggested that Cherubino, who 'composed his own music', exhibited 'professional imperfections'.[68]) And (it must be repeated) a glance at Da Ponte's libretto would have revealed that the poem cannot be construed as a sonnet. This example is by no means isolated.

The majority of eighteenth-century Italian aria texts have relatively short lines of five to eight syllables, usually with two main accents per line, of which the last is usually the strongest. Not surprisingly, the corresponding musical phrases most often comprise two 'actual' measures, with a change of harmony on the second down-beat. Thus Cherubino sings:[69]

[67] Da Ponte, *Le nozze di Figaro* (Vienna, 1786), 30. I quote the original printed libretti throughout, except for modernizations of spelling and the correction of obvious errors: significant differences in Mozart's autograph wording are signalled in notes or the main text.

In rhyme-schemes, *piano* lines are shown in normal type (in this example: 'a'), *tronco* with underlining ('b'), and *sdrucciolo* (two unaccented syllables following the final accent) in italics.

[68] Levarie, *Mozart's 'Le nozze di Figaro'*, 81–2; Arnold Schoenberg, *Structural Functions of Harmony* (rev. edn., New York, 1969), 69 n. 2. Carter, 155 n., accepts Levarie's notion of 'fourteen' lines and certain aspects of his interpretation of the poem, as does Carl Schachter in 'Analysis by Key: Another Look at Modulation', *Music Analysis*, 6 (1987), 289–318 at 309, 312, although Schachter is properly sceptical as to the poem's status as a 'sonnet'.

[69] In musical/prosodic diagrams of the type given here, the metrical designations ('1 & 2 &') and chord-labels are aligned with the vowels, not the initial consonants. The musical metre is indicated to the left of the 'counting' numbers, and the verse-type by a number in parentheses: (5) = *quinario*, (6) = *senario*, etc. It goes without saying that these examples illustrate but a few of the hundreds of relevant variants.

2/4	1 & 2 &	1 & 2 &	1 & 2 &	1 & 2 &
(5)	Voi che sa-	pe—te	Che co-sa è a-	mor
	I	V^6_5	I vi ii^6	V

The qualification 'actual' takes account of variations in metrical notation: for example, depending on the tempo and speed of declamation, 6/8 or 4/4 can represent either one 'actual' measure or two (in the latter case, 2 × 3/8 or 2 × 2/4); conversely, 3/8 or 2/4 one 'actual' measure or only half of one; and so forth.[70]

Given this two-accent prosodic structure with the stronger accent towards the end, musical phrases tend to point towards the final textual accent on the second down-beat as a rhythmic goal (see again 'Voi che sapete').[71] (The tendency is observable even in *secco* recitative, where chord-changes invariably coincide with or directly follow the final accent of a line of text.) A longer phrase can be created only by deliberate compositional choice: for example, by adding melismas or internal word-repetitions, or by lengthening and stressing an ordinarily unaccented initial syllable. Even though *decasillabi* (ten-syllable lines) entail three textual accents, they are also most often set as two-measure phrases. *Ottonario* is more likely to engender phrases of three or four bars, whether by the admixture of longer rhythmic values or the insertion of a rest between the two 'halves' of the line (creating two half-phrases which together are longer than a single whole one): see the beginnings of 'Porgi amor' (shown in Sect. IV, Ex. 8) and 'Dove sono' (Sect. V, Ex. 12). Here too, however, the last accent is usually the strongest, and hence the musical phrases tend to be end-oriented. On the other hand, the longer the phrase and the greater the number of accents, the more likely it is that the initial down-beat will be nearly as strong, producing a strong–weak–strong organization (see below).

Thus a basic feature of the rhythmic profile is that, in general, phrases are variable at the beginning, predictable at the end. Within this framework, an equally important distinction stylistically (if not structurally) is the one between phrases that begin with an up-beat as against those that begin on a down-beat. Here, however, Italian versification shapes the musical result only in certain cases; especially in *quinario* and *settenario* (five- and seven-syllable metre), the initial accent is variable in placement (and in *quinario* in strength as well), and this variability is reflected in musical settings. By contrast, the strongly anapaestic *decasillabo* (ten-syllable metre) is usually set with a two-note up-beat, as in the beginning of Cherubino's 'Non so più' (see Ex. 3 above). As is common, the three accents are compressed into two measures, the strong end-accent coinciding with the change of harmony on the two-bar level. (Compare Figaro's 'Non più andrai', Antonio's music in the Act II finale, and so forth.) At the cadence, however, the line 'Ogni donna mi fa palpitar'—which at first (mm. 8–9) maintains the original two-bar profile—is expanded into a three-bar phrase with one accent per bar (mm. 10–12, 13–15; still in

[70] On this point see Allanbrook, *Rhythmic Gesture*, 23–5, 152–3, 187–90 *et passim*; Strohm, 'Zur Metrik'.

[71] Correctly emphasized by Strohm, 'Zur Metrik' (albeit too schematically; compare Lippmann's comment in the discussion, p. 294).

Ex. 3). In the beginning of the next paragraph in the dominant (mm. 16–18, 19–21), the 'opposite' expansion takes place: the first syllable is lengthened, becoming a down-beat in its own right. (The rhythmic organization of these three-bar phrases is thus strong–weak–strong.)[72] The resulting emphasis on the line-initiating words 'solo ... mi' composes Cherubino's narcissism directly into the music. In the last two lines of this stanza, finally, both methods of phrase-extension are combined, producing four-measure phrases in mm. 22–5, 28–31, 33–6(–7). And whereas the strong/weak organization of mm. 22–5 is ambiguous (owing to a conflict between phrase-beginnings in mm. 22 and 24 vs. end-accents in mm. 23 and 25), mm. 28–31 and 33–6 clearly exhibit Cone's paradigmatic strong–weak–weak–strong pattern—again: at the cadence. Through development of the rhythmic profile, Mozart thus shows Cherubino undergoing a psychological progression, from uncontrolled haste to expansive self-regard.

Quinario and *senario* (five- and six-syllable metre), and again *settenario* and *ottonario* (seven and eight), are essentially similar, except that the initial accent in the 'odd' member of each pair is variable, whereas in the 'even' member it is fixed: syllables 'x' and 4 in *quinario*, but 2 and 5 in *senario*; 'x' and 6 in *settenario*, but 3 and 7 in *ottonario*. Hence musical settings of each pair of verse-types are often equivalent, except that whereas the initial accent in *ottonario* and (especially) *senario* tends to be fixed (following one up-beat syllable in *senario*, two in *ottonario*), the initial accent in *quinario* and *senario* is variable. For example, the respective opening lines of the Count's aria in *Figaro* and Elvira's Act II aria in *Don Giovanni* are set as rhythmically similar two-bar phrases:

2/2	2 &	1 &	2 &	1 &
(7)	Ve-	drò men-	tre io so-	spi-ro
(8)	Mi tra-	dì que—	st'al—ma in—	gra-ta

On the other hand, like Cherubino's *decasillabi* in 'Non so più', these verses can be extended to three-bar phrases, as in the Count's

2/2	1 & 2 &	1 & 2 &	1 & 2	
(7)	Tu non na-	sce— sti, au—	da-ce	(mm. 52–4)[73]

or to four bars, as in Elvira's

2/2	1 & 2 &	1 & 2 &	1 & 2 &	1	
(8)	Pro——vo an-	cor per	lui pie-	tà	(mm. 64–7)

Thus by varying the rhythmic profile, a composer could articulate many different dramatic or psychological effects.

[72] This observation provides additional evidence for Cone's theory of the rhythmic structure of phrases in Classical-period music, whereby a primary model (in addition to the more common interpretations of weak–strong and strong–weak) is strong–weak–strong. See *Musical Form and Musical Performance* (New York, 1968), 26–31.

[73] Allanbrook (*Rhythmic Gesture*, 142–5) offers a subtle and provocative interpretation of this rhythm as representing the Count's raging frustration, albeit with a moment of uncertainty as to whether the cadential phrase, 'Di mia infelicità', would 'normally' be one or two bars long.

Especially in *quinario* and *settenario*, many texts exhibit great variability with respect to the initial accent:

(7) Aprite un po' quegl'occhi [initial accent on '2']
Uomini incauti e sciocchi [initial accent on '1']

These distinctions are usually observed in Mozart's settings:

4/4	1 2 3 4	1 2 3 4	1 2 3 4	1 2 3 4
(7) A-	pri—te un po' quegl'	occhi	Uomini incauti e	sciocchi

On the other hand, a weak initial syllable is often set as an initial down-beat. In the *ottonario* verses of 'Dove sono',

Dove sono i bei momenti
Di dolcezza e di piacer?

the phrases begin squarely on the down-beat, notwithstanding the weakness of the poetic syllable (especially in the second line); see Ex. 12. A frequently cited example occurs at the beginning of Don Ottavio's 'Dalla sua pace', where the unaccented initial syllables 'Dal-' and 'La' receive long, strong, initial musical accents, the latter on the highest note of the phrase:

2/4	1 &2 &	1 & 2 &	1 &2 &	1 & 2 &
(5)	Dal-la sua	pa—ce	La mia de-	pen-de

An example with unmistakable dramatic significance is found in the fast contredanse section of 'Se vuol ballare': Figaro first sings 'rovescierò' normally, with the initial accent on *ro*-, then artificially, with the accent on *ve*- (mm. 88–95; compare the slightly different version in 72–7, 96–103):

2/4	1 2	1 2	1 2	1 2	1 2	1 2	1 2	1
(5)	Tut-te le	mac-chi-ne	ro-ve-scie-	rò,	Tut-te le	mac-chi-ne ro-	ve-scie-	rò

This device is a subtle bit of word-painting (the reversal of accent illustrates the actual meaning of 'rovescierò'). But in a dramatic sense it signals that Figaro will indeed 'overturn' the Count's plans. (It is no accident that this word is the culminating *tronco* line of Figaro's entire concluding sestet.) Meaning is here created by a combination of rhythmic topics and poetic/musical details.

More 'artificial' (and rarer) are settings of an initial accented syllable off the beat. An example is Donna Anna's syncopated beginning of her duet with Don Ottavio early in Act I of *Don Giovanni*:

2/2 2	1 2	1
(7) Fug	— gi, cru-de-le,	fug-gi

To summarize: the beginnings of phrases are relatively variable, their endings relatively stable.

Text-form and musical form. Certain aspects of the overall construction of texts also influence musical form. Except for male *buffa* arias, the majority of eighteenth-century texts are divided into stanzas of four to six lines, articulated by rhyme and metre. Often, only the last line of each stanza is *tronco*; this produces a strong accent at the end, in contrast to the weak endings in the preceding *piano* lines:

Non più andrai farfallone amoroso	a
Notte, e giorno d'intorno girando:	b
Delle belle turbando il riposo,	a
Narcisetto, Adoncino d'amor.	c

This stanza-form was a godsend to composers. The several *piano* endings are most naturally set as weak melodic cadences, with a vocal after-beat; the orchestra is usually either off-beat as well, or rhythmically counterpointed as shown at the beginning of Ex. 3. By contrast, the single *tronco* line at the end becomes a strong cadance—the only one in the musical paragraph. The implications for large-scale structure are obvious. If both second and fourth lines were *tronco*, one could still distinguish them as half- and full cadences, the former perhaps with an appoggiatura (which rarely appears on stanza-ending cadences). See the Countess's 'Porgi amor' (Ex. 8); her first *tronco* line, '. . . a' miei sospir', is set as a half-cadence decorated with an appoggiatura (m. 25), while the second, '. . . almen morir', is a full cadence (m. 34). It is owing both to the greater variability of line-beginnings (described above) and this greater formal importance of line-endings that the ends of phrases, and especially the ends of paragraphs, are more important structurally than their beginnings.

On a larger scale, there is almost always a correlation between the first two textual units (the first two stanzas, or the two couplets of the first stanza) and the first two musical paragraphs (the tonic and dominant passages in an exposition, or the A|B of an ABA). And when the text as a whole incorporates changes—of line-length, rhyme-scheme, grammar, or diction—these often correlate with the overall musical form. A change in the *tronco* rhyme alone often suggests an overall poetic form. Even though many *buffa* arias have much longer texts than most others and are loose in structure, they usually exhibit a clear two-part form, which is usually reflected in the music.[74] Similarly, in some female two-tempo arias the formal division is prefigured in the construction of the text. These include both high-flown *rondò*s like Vitellia's 'Non più di fiori', which comprises two stanzas of *quinario* with *tronco* rhyme *-ar* and one stanza of *ottonario* with *tronco* rhyme *-à*;[75] and servants' cynical moralizings like Despina's 'Una donna a quindici anni' (*Così*, No. 19), which moves from *ottonario* with *tronco* rhyme *-è* to *quinario* with *tronco* rhyme *-ir*. Similarly, the complex form of Konstanze's 'Martern aller Arten' is, if not 'prefigured' in the text, compatible with the latter's three-part construction.[76]

[74] Platoff, 'The buffa aria', 102–5.

[75] As Lippmann points out ('Mozart und der Vers', 114 n. 24), Mozart multivalently reinserts the first two stanzas into the second (fast) section, without disrupting its musical continuity.

[76] Thomas Bauman, *W. A. Mozart*: Die Entführung aus dem Serail (Cambridge, 1987), 78–82.

Although Mozart occasionally declined these invitations to write two-tempo arias, he rarely ignored text-forms entirely.[77] In Figaro's 'Non più andrai', the end-oriented form culminating in the triumphant marching postlude corresponds to the text, which progresses from Cherubino as 'amorous butterfly' in half-scurrilous, half-admiring *decasillabo* (the verse-type the page himself had sung in 'Non so più') to Cherubino the soldier in *ottonario* (a more appropriate metre for the grown-up godson of a Countess).[78] 'Non so più' itself subtly composes out a textual distinction; see Sect. V.

In some cases the musical division is retained, but displaced to some location other than that suggested by the text. An example is Leporello's 'Catalogue' aria, whose textual form suggests a typical two-part *buffa* aria. (It is unusual that the two tempi form the progression fast–slow rather than slow–fast, although this feature is also found in an earlier 'catalogue' aria well known to Mozart, Figaro's 'Scorsi già molti paesi' from Paisiello's *Il barbiere di Siviglia*.[79]) The text comprises (1) eight lines of *decasillabo* (4 + 4, with *tronco* rhyme *-è*), in which he shows Elvira the catalogue and counts off his master's conquests country by country, closing with 'Ma in Ispagna son già mille e tre'; and (2) twenty-two lines of *ottonario* with *tronco* rhyme *-à*, in which he retails a typology of the Don's conquests, from 'V'han fra queste contadine' to the *envoi* 'Purché porti la gonnella, / Voi sapete quel che fa'. But the musical division comes later, following the first complete stanza of the second text section, in the middle of the typology; that is, the textual and musical forms are multivalent. (Here Mozart may have been responding to a formal and semantic division within the second textual section: 6 + 16 [= 4 × 4].) The fast section, an elaborate two-paragraph exposition, exhibits multifarious non-congruencies among vocal, orchestral, and text-forms in its own right.[80]

Conversely, formal divisions may appear in the music where none are implied by the text. The texts for the majority of Mozart's *rondò*s are restricted to a single line-length and stanza-structure; apparently the dramatic and dramaturgical context alone could suggest this form. On the other hand, most of these texts incorporate a rhetorical progression, typically from self-absorption to a plea for pity or the hope of resolution (see the discussion of 'Dove sono' in Sect. V); perhaps this reinforced the dramatic convention. Again, lower-class characters are sometimes granted this mark of distinction. The text of Zerlina's 'Batti batti' is uniform, comprising three stanzas of *ottonario* with *tronco*-rhyme *-ar*; nevertheless, Mozart sets it in two tempi, corresponding to the rhetorical change from 'batti' (etc.) in the first two stanzas to 'pace' (etc.) in the third—the *second*

[77] An example where Mozart may seem to ignore formal implications of the text is the much-discussed opening duettino in *Figaro*, which moves from two stanzas of *ottonario* to one of *decasillabo*, with no change of tempo, metre, themes, or topics. Nevertheless, he articulates the point of change as a musical culmination (Webster, 'To Understand . . . Mozart', 183–4).

[78] Paolo Gallarati, 'Music and Masks in Lorenzo Da Ponte's Mozartian Librettos', *Cambridge Opera Journal*, 1 (1989), 233–4; on the musical form, see Webster, 'To Understand . . . Mozart', 181.

[79] Abert, i. 363 n. 2; ii. 405 n. 3.

[80] Gallarati, 'Music and Masks', 235–6, discusses the large-scale multivalence (though the semantic distinction at line 15 is no more compelling than that at line 9, which does coincide with the metric change); Kunze, *Mozarts Opern*, 410–11, that within the 'allegro' section.

line of the stanza, be it noted, not the first. These examples suggest that, in principle, the rhetoric of a text could be as important as its construction in influencing musical form.

On another level, the disparity between the brevity of most aria-texts and their elaborate musical working-out requires a great deal of text-repetition, not only of individual phrases within a line and individual lines within a section, but of entire stanzas, indeed very often the entire text. The textual and musical forms are especially likely to diverge in later sections of an aria, creating a multivalent relation on the level of the aria as a whole.[81] In some cases, a single word or phrase may be so emphasized, by multiple repetitions or a recall in an unexpected place, that it becomes a formal element in its own right. For example, in Annio's 'Torna di Tito a lato' (*Tito*, No. 13), the key word 'torna' is not only repeated again and again in the first paragraph, but in the recapitulation is omitted from its first significant location—mm. 36–7 (= 2–3) move via a sequential repetition directly to the second paragraph of the first group (mm. 40 ff. = 14 ff.)—only to recur at the very end (50–1 = 20–1). The single word 'torna' becomes a motto governing the entire aria, almost independently of the overall ABA form. Even more astonishing is Despina's 'In uomini, in soldati' (No. 12): Mozart sets the first section of the aria to the last three lines of recitative (*versi sciolti*: freely arranged seven- and eleven-syllable lines):

In Uomini, in Soldati,	(7)
Sperare fedeltà?	(7, *tronco*)
Non vi fate sentir per carità!	(11, *tronco*)
Di pasta simile	(5, *sdrucciolo*)
Son tutti quanti:	(5)

That is, the aria-text begins with 'Di pasta simile', from where it proceeds in regular *quinarii*, in four sestets of identical construction—but this does not occur in the music until the change of tempo to 'allegretto' 6/8. The customarily rigid distinction between recitative and set-piece temporarily collapses.[82]

Musical parameters and multifunctional form

In practice, five musical parameters seem to be most important for aria forms (see the second part of Table 2): sectional organization, tonality, musical material, rhythm, and instrumentation. The analysis must be multivalent; that is, each parameter is at first considered separately; in addition, the vocal and the orchestral music must be examined separately as well. Although this method requires that the aria temporarily be treated not as a unity but as a congeries of discrete procedures, one's initial sense of artificiality soon yields to pleasure at the results. Later, these partial analyses must be recombined, together with consideration of the text, type, and dramatic context, into an overall view.[83]

81 These topics are discussed in detail in Hunter, 'Haydris Aria Forms', ch. 3.

82 I owe this observation to Ronald Rabin. (Goldin, 'Mozart, Da Ponte', 273, assumes that the first lines do constitute 'part of' the aria text.)

83 I have discussed this methodology in *Haydn's 'Farewell' Symphony*, 4–5, 112–13, 181, 196–7, 203, 298, 307; and 'Die Form des Finales von Beethovens 9. Sinfonie', in Siegfried Kross and Marie Luise Maintz (eds.), *Probleme der Symphonischen Tradition im 19. Jahrhundert: Internationales Musikwissenschaftliches Colloquium Bonn 1989: Kongreßbericht* (Tutzing, 1990), 157–86. (English translation foreseen for *Beethoven Forum*, 1 (1992)).

I have organized the following discussion around the issue of musical form, dealing with tonality, musical ideas, rhetoric, and rhythm as constituents of it, and concentrating on multifunctional form in two-tempo arias other than *rondò*s. (By 'multifunctionality' I designate forms that cannot be parsed according to a single type, or in which one or more sections are functionally multivalent. Multifunctionality is thus analogous to multivalence, except that the non-congruence in question applies not to the global domains (text, music, etc.), but specifically to the various musical parameters. I have discussed the functions of the orchestra above. I also discuss rhythm and tonality in Sects. IV–V below; on motivic organization see especially pp. 163–6 on 'Porgi amor'. See also the end of Sect. II (pp. 121–2), regarding ambiguities among ABA and four-part forms, especially in Ferrando's 'Un'aura amorosa'.)

It is usually not difficult to determine the gross sectional organization of an aria (that is, the number of major units, and their beginning- and ending-points). But Mozart's flexibility and fluidity of musical procedure often make it difficult or impossible to specify the function of a given section, and hence to determine the overall form.

As noted in Sect. II, Figaro's 'Se vuol ballare' is a two-tempo form based on the alternation of a relatively crude minuet and an aggressive contredanse. The text is in *quinario* with tronco rhyme *-ò* throughout; it comprises three quatrains followed by a sestet ('L'arte schermendo' . . . 'Tutte le macchine / Rovescierò'), followed by a repetition of the first stanza at the end (so in the original printed libretto). Even though there is no change of metre or rhyme, the distinction between three quatrains and one sestet, as well as the explicit textual reprise, prefigure Mozart's two-dance realization of Figaro's threats.

Nevertheless, the formal layout is difficult to parse (see Table 3). To be sure, the first three paragraphs (mm. 1–42) seem to constitute an exposition, and the next two (42–64) are developmental, in so far as they fragment the material and move to the dominant of D minor. Hence some critics have interpreted the first contredanse paragraph (m. 64), which is a variation of the minuet-theme back in the tonic, as a 'recapitulation', and the whole aria as an expression of the 'sonata principle'.[84] Nevertheless, something which is not only new, but whose very *raison d'être* is violent contrast, hardly qualifies as a recapitulation in any ordinary sense; even if this were granted, the aria could not be in sonata form, because the putative 'second group' (the minuet in the dominant, to the text 'Se vuol venire' etc.) never returns. On the other hand, the aria is not a simple ABA; the contredanse is too close to the minuet in structure, and too much a tonal return (if not a thematic or gestural one) to count as a 'B' section. The multifunctionality of the contredanse is only enhanced by its return as the orchestral postlude.

Its multifunctionality in the large is mirrored in the small. The contredanse naturally

[84] Levarie, *Mozart's 'Le Nozze di Figaro'*, 29, 32–3, noted that the contredanse is a variation of the minuet; Charles Rosen added the overall interpretation as a sonata form in *The Classical Style: Haydn, Mozart, Beethoven* (New York, 1971), 308–9. Carter, 76–8, makes excellent observations on the text of 'Se vuol ballare' and its relation to Mozart's music.

TABLE 3. *Formal diagram of 'Se vuol ballare'* (Le nozze di Figaro, *No. 3*)

	Minuet (Allegretto)					Contredanse (Presto)				Minuet	Contredanse
	1	21	31	42	55	64	80	88	96	104	123–31
Text lines	1–4	5–8	5–8	9	10–12	13–18	13–16	17–18	17–18	1–4	—
Figaro	A	A^1	A^2	C	A^3	A^4/D1	D2	D3	D3	A	—
Orch.	A	B	A	B	B	A^4/D1	D2	D3	D3	A	D3
Key	I	I	V	V	V/vi	I					
Cadence[a]	I	I^V	V		V/vi	I^V		I	I^V	I	I

[a] Here and elsewhere in diagrams and examples, 'I^V' stands for a half-cadence on the dominant.

proceeds as a double period with regular phrasing (32 = 8 + 8 + 8 + 8); the first half cadences on the dominant (mm. 75–9), the second on the tonic (m. 95). This periodic structure is reinforced by the text: Figaro sings the entire sestet in each half, emphasizing both cadences with his pointed *tronco* line 'rovescierò' (see p. 137). Hence the cadential phrase (mm. 88–95) sounds like the conclusion of the entire contredanse—but is instead repeated and, astonishingly, altered so as to land on the dominant (m. 103), with a fermata. The apparent conclusion in m. 95 is reinterpreted as the antecedent of a sixteen-bar antiperiod, 88–95 + 96–103. Because of the antiperiod structure, and especially the large-scale elision created by the double function of mm. 88–95, the concluding phrase 96–103 is no mere appendix; the entire contredanse unexpectedly turns into an 'open' section, cadencing on the dominant. This is another reason it is no mere middle section in an ABA: it prepares the true return, that of the original minuet. A nice tonal/formal expression of this difference is that the varied reprise (the contredanse) is prepared by the 'wrong' dominant, V/vi (mm. 55–63), the literal reprise (the minuet), by the 'right' dominant (100–3). The half-cadence ending of the contredanse's last phrase also strengthens the cogency of its return as the postlude (which could otherwise be understood only theatrically, as a rousing accompaniment to Figaro's exit): the contredanse too needs to be resolved with a full cadence, but since Figaro is unable (or unwilling) to do this, the orchestra does so for him.

Although the Queen of the Night's Act I aria 'O zittre nicht' has a clear sectional division, it cannot be reduced to any formal type. Schikaneder's text comprises five quatrains, grouped 1 + 3 + 1, and headed respectively 'Recitativ', 'Arie', and 'Allegro'.[85] In the first

[85] So in the original libretto printed by his and Mozart's fellow-mason, Ignaz Alberti (Vienna, 1791; facs. repr. ed. Michael Maria Rabenlechner, Vienna, 1942), 16–17.

and last stanzas, she addresses Tamino directly as 'Du'; in the middle, without referring to him, she relates the story of Pamina's abduction by Sarastro. This central narrative is itself tripartite: its middle stanza (the third overall) differs prosodically, substituting two-foot amphibrachs for the prevailing iambic tetrameter. Cutting across this apparently symmetrical text-form, however, the Queen's rhetoric progresses from flattery of Tamino and enlisting of his sympathy (stanza 1) towards her climactic vow (stanza 5) that if he rescues Pamina he shall win her as bride.

The headings in the libretto also imply a large-scale musical form: an accompanied recitative and a two-tempo aria, 'Arie ... Allegro'. (They might reflect Mozart's prior verbal instructions; see the comments regarding Osmin, above, p. 132.) But even though this form corresponds to the finished aria (see Table 4), it is not easy to define the relationships among these sections. Mozart wrote no titles or designations of parts in the autograph, merely the tempo-designations 'Allegro maestoso' and 'Allegro moderato' for the first and last sections; neither the term 'Arie' nor a tempo-marking appears for the middle section.[86] Nevertheless, Mozart must have understood the G minor section as the beginning of the 'aria': not only do key, metre, and tempo change, but the style: from accompanied recitative (short vocal phrases punctuated by orchestral motifs, in this

TABLE 4. *Formal diagram of 'O zittre nicht'* (Die Zauberflöte, *No. 4*)

A. Text						
Stanza	—	1	2	3	4	5
		'Recitativ'	'Arie'			'Allegro'
Metre	—	4 iambs	4 iambs	2 amphibrachs	4 iambs	4 iambs
Content	—	'Du schöner'	Narrative of Pamina's abduction			'Du Retter'
B. Music						
Bar	1	11	22	36	45	61
Tempo	Allegro maestoso		[none]			Allegro moderato
Style	—	Acc. recit.	Arioso			Bravura
Tone	—	Persuasion	Lament	*Unheimlich*	Lament	Peroration
Key	B♭	B♭ - G m	G m			B♭
Metre	4/4		3/4			4/4
Orch.	Majesty		Colla parte	Bn. + Va.	Colla parte	Majesty

[86] See the published facsimile, ed. Karl-Heinz Köhler (Berlin, 1979), and compare *NMA*, II/5/19, p. xvii. (The heading 'Recitvo' at m. 11 is not in Mozart's hand.) Marty, *Tempo Indications*, 205, argues that the *AMA*'s tempo-marking 'Larghetto' is more appropriate than the *NMA*'s 'Andante' (though the latter surely construes 'Andante' in the modern sense of 'slow', rather than in the 18th-c.'s of 'moderate', and hence resembles Marty's 'Larghetto').

case derived from the introduction) to continuous and coherent (albeit freely developing) concerted music.

Alas: if the 'aria' begins in m. 22, it consists of a tonally open progression, G minor–B flat! This (we still believe) cannot be the basis of a Classical-period form; among other things, no other Mozart number exhibits such a form. On the other hand, we can obtain a closed B flat tonality for the whole only by including the introduction and recitative—entities that, no matter how closely connected psychologically or musically with a concerted number, are not ordinarily construed as part of it.[87] What then is the function of the long orchestral introduction? Its music relates only to the recitative. Is it purely scenic/dramaturgical, providing the Queen's chariot sufficient time to descend from on high? If not, what is the entity to which it is the introduction: the recitative alone, or the number as a whole? Is it part of the number, or not? (Ordinarily, long introductions present central thematic material, which returns during the orchestral accompaniment of the singer and/or as a postlude; see 'Porgi amor' and 'Ah chi mi dice mai'.) Nor are the topics, overall rhythmic profiles, or motifs of the introduction and closing Allegro closely related. For example, the rising triads $\hat{1}$–$\hat{3}$–$\hat{5}$ at the beginning of introduction and recitative (mm. 1–3, 11) and the final Allegro (64), and the occasional dotted rhythms and the (less focused) aura of majesty in the latter, hardly justify calling it a 'reprise' of or 'return' to the former.[88]

The crucial point is that the G minor music itself is more or less through-composed. Except for a fleeting recall of mm. 28–31 in 45–6—admittedly at the beginning of the tonal return section—it is more *arioso* than aria, with the motifs and rhythms constantly changing (mm. 22, 28, 32, 37, 45, 47, 49, 51, 53), and very few text-repetitions. Its most continuous paragraph is the amazing *unheimlich* viola/bassoon narrative-music that sets the textually unique middle stanza (mm. 36–44).[89] In this sense, only the rhetorically and tonally stable (if technically spectacular) final section is aria-like; but it alone cannot constitute a 'form'. The Queen *progresses*, from introduction through narrative to peroration. Her dazzling rhetoric seduces not only Tamino, but ourselves; it is as if we dared not enquire too closely into the mechanisms of her through-compositional sorcery. By contrast, the Queen's other aria ('Der Hölle Rache')—a hysterical harangue directed at someone (Pamina) who knows her all too well—employs a schematically clear binary form. The disjunction between her 'extreme' coloratura and her formal stiffness recalls Donna Elvira's in 'Ah chi mi dice mai', discussed in Sect. V below.

[87] In his autographs Mozart ordinarily titled an *accompagnato* separately, and ended it as a separate entity as well, in so far as he did not further write on the leaf in question, but rather began the following concerted number on a separate page. Admittedly, the use of dialogue rather than recitative in *Die Zauberflöte* compelled him to write down the Queen's entire musical number as a single entity.

[88] Certain motivic resemblances do exist between this number, sung to Tamino, and *his* music in other numbers: m. 11 to his crucial realization 'O ew'ge Nacht' in the Act I finale (m. 141), noted by the sharp-eyed Abert (ii. 656 n. 2); m. 74 (first violins) to his recognition 'Die Liebe', in 'Dies Bildnis' (mm. 30–1, derived by inversion from mm. 7–8). None of this is relevant to the question of its internal organization.

[89] On the dramatic implications of this passage, see Webster, 'Cone's "Personae"', 57–8, 64–5.

In many Mozart arias, a section whose function seems clear with respect to one musical parameter—tonal structure, thematic content, orchestral participation—takes on a different cast when examined from another perspective. The most common location for this multifunctionality is the beginning of a recapitulation. Konstanze's Act I aria in *Die Entführung*, 'Ach ich liebte', sets a brief text of two stanzas, twice through; it expresses the contrast between former happiness in love and present anguish at separation. Its first statement assumes two-tempo form: the first stanza 'adagio', a kind of introduction in *arioso* texture; the second 'allegro', a very broad exposition with much coloratura (vocal cadence m. 49, orchestral m. 53). In the beginning of the second half, however, Mozart does not revert to 'adagio'; he recasts the first stanza *in tempo* as a ruminating passage, which combines the formal functions of retransition on the dominant (mm. 53–64) and a free reprise of the original 'adagio' music (64–75 ≈ 1–8). Thereafter the music reverts to the second stanza and its music (mm. 76 ff. = 10 ff.) and continues with a more or less complete recapitulation. A comparable conflation of form and tempo is found in Konstanze's bravura aria 'Martern aller Arten'. The vocal exposition ('allegro') includes a second group in the dominant (mm. 93–146), closing with a structural cadence, but this is recapitulated as an insertion within the 'allegro assai' passages that precede and follow it (mm. 197–241 enclosed by 160–96 and 242 ff.). What is more, in conformity with the prevailing concertante style, its latter stage is transformed into a cadenza (mm. 217–41), a function not present in the exposition.

Mozart seems to have associated multifunctionality in a recapitulation with heroines in distress or high dudgeon; see Fiordiligi's 'Come scoglio', mm. 58–65 vs. 1–15 and, to a lesser extent, Dorabella's 'Smanie implacabili': mm. 42–9 modulate V/ii–ii–V–I, rather than simply stating the tonic as at the beginning. Even in Elettra's wild 'Tutte nel cor vi sento' (*Idomeneo*, No. 4) in D minor, the reprise beginning in C minor (vii$^{\flat}$), which has been much puzzled over, is constructed in much the same way (see Ex. 4*a* and *b*). In all other respects, the recapitulation is regular (with two added bars, 88–9), and it moves back towards the tonic well within the first group: mm. 87–8 = 25–6 (V^{0}/V–V^{6}), from which the tonic enters in sequence (88–9 = 29–30); the remainder of the first group, up to the dominant arrival (97 = 37), is a literal repetition. This textual and thematic reprise beginning a step down from the tonic is in principle no different from Dorabella's reprise beginning a step up; its shocking foreignness correlates with the extremity of her passion. And in a larger tonal sense, it is 'consequential'.[90] It arises as a mixture of the dominant (C) of the F major second paragraph; indeed, the move to C minor where C major is expected recalls Elettra's earlier obsessive mixtures of F minor within F (mm. 40–7, 53–4, 67–8). The voice-leading into and out of C minor is also straightforward (see Ex. 4*c*): the B/d^{3} of the preparatory diminished seventh (m. 76)—the same chord as her first diminished seventh (m. 25)—leads by simple neighbour motion (C/e$\flat^{3}$) back to B/d^{3} (84) and thence to a recapture of the same diminished seventh a third higher (D/f^{3}) (m. 87); this leads directly to the home V^{6} and D minor. Interestingly,

[90] The concept of 'consequentiality' (as opposed to the problematical 'necessity') I take from Edward T. Cone, 'Twelfth Night', *Journal of Musicological Research*, 7 (1986–8), 136–41, 147–9.

EXAMPLE 4. *Idomeneo*, No. 4, 'Tutte nel cor vi sento'

(*a*) mm. 19–41 (*b*) mm. 71–101 (*c*) Voice-leading analysis

a)

1 Gr.

19 (a)

Chi?

Tut - te nel cor vi sen - to vi sen - to, vi

p *cresc.*

i

22 (b)

sen - to fu - rie del cru - do a - ver - - -

f *sfp*

V°/ V

26

- no, fu - rie del cru - do a - ver - - -

p *sfp*

V⁶

30 (c)

- no, lunge a si gran tor - men - to a -

fp *fp*

i

33

- mor, mer - cè, pie - tà, a - mor, mer -

fp *fp*

36
-cè, pie - tà.
V
39
2 Gr.
Chi mi ru - bò quel co - re,
V/ iii
etc.
b)
72
End exposition
cru - - - - del - tà.
III
74
a 1 Gr.
Tut - te nel cor vi
III: V°/ V
VII: V° —— i ♭
78
b
sen - to, vi sen - to, vi sen - to, fu - rie del
cresc.

cru - do a - ver - - - no, fu - rie del
VII: V6
= i: VI6
cru - do a - ver - - - no, del cru - do a - ver - - -
V°/ V
V6
(7)
c
no, lunge a si gran tor - men - to a - mor, mer - cè, pie -
– i
- tà, a - mor mer - cè, pie - tà.
V
2 Gr.
Chi mi ru - bò quel co - re,
V

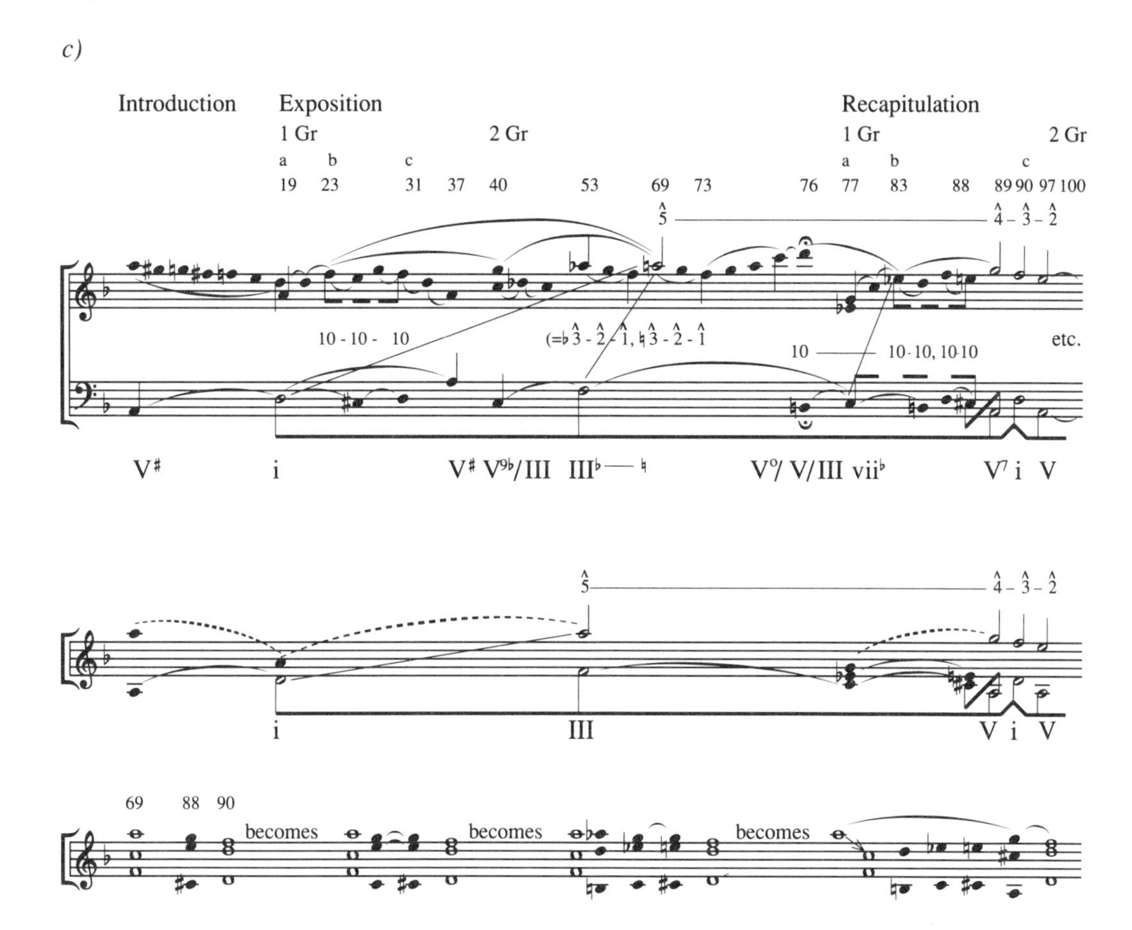

Mozart resorted to the same key-relation, vii♭–i, in the same key and formal context, in the tumultuous 'Dies irae' from the Requiem (m. 31, at 'Quantus tremor est futurus'). Moreover, there is neither a comparable use of C minor within any D minor number in *Don Giovanni* nor, as far as I am aware, a use of vii♭ at a thematic reprise in any other Mozart minor-mode movement in any key. Should this be taken as implying that Mozart's characterization of Elettra is related to the Last Judgement more closely than to mere tormented jealousy—or the reverse—or neither?

A somewhat different kind of sectional multifunctionality occurs in the later stages of many recapitulations, where reorderings or additions often change the formal function of 'the same' passage (compare 'Martern aller Arten', just described). An affecting example is found in the Larghetto section of Donna Anna's *rondò* 'Non mi dir'; see Table 5. The tonic paragraph (mm. 20–35) is a double period (antiperiod + period). The latter, unusually, changes topic from the heartfelt melody A to a thirty-second note figure B in the strings (derived, some will feel, by free diminution from the melody's head-motif).

Table 5. *Formal diagram of 'Non mi dir'* (Don Giovanni, *No. 23*)

	Larghetto								Allegretto moderato
	16	20	28	36	44	48	55	61	65
t-lines	–	1–2	3–4	5–6	6	1–2	5–6	6	7–8
al paras.		Tonic		Dominant	+ Retr.	Recap.		+ Prep.	
hestra	A (tune)	A	B (32nds)	D (winds 3rds/6ths)		A	B[E]	Recit.	A′ → accomp.
ia	–	A	C (mixed)	E (mixed)	C′	A	C[E]	C″	A′ → F etc.
iality	I	I— IV	I	V— v	V7	I	I— i—	iv— IV	I

Hence although the half-cadence in mm. 26–7 is tonally resolved in 34–5, Anna's theme remains 'up in the air'. Instead, the new music in mm. 28 ff. is rhythmically active, like a transition; it therefore sounds a little odd when it remains firmly in the tonic and cadences there. Nevertheless, the dominant paragraph (mm. 36–44, plus a retransition in 44–7) is a far greater contrast, both in its independent wind-melody D in thirds and sixths preceding the vocal phrases (compare the analogous passages in 'Porgi amor' and 'Dies Bildnis') and in Anna's new long-note melodic entries (E). Relevant here is her affective change to the minor mode on the second phrase, setting line 6, 'Se di duol non vuoi ch'io mora' (mm. 42–3).

The recapitulation (mm. 48 ff.) comprises a repetition of the two ideas from the tonic paragraph, A and B/C (that is, the form yet again marries a key-area tonal plan to a ternary sectional organization). The tune A now supplies the full cadence that was missing from the tonic paragraph of the exposition; that is, mm. 54–5 are multifunctional, in that they relate thematically and procedurally to 26–7, but provide tonal closure in the same way as 34–5. (To put it another way, in one sense they actually resolve mm. 26–7.) But this change alters the function of the ensuing period B/C. In the exposition it was a large-scale consequent, tonally resolving the antiperiod A, that is, part of the first group. Now, however, it *follows* such closure, and hence has become the second group! Indeed, B/C and its extension include a change to the minor (mm. 57 ff.), which subliminally recapitulates the most prominent affective event from the vocal paragraph D/E in the dominant. Strong confirmation of this reorientation is provided by the text: rather than setting lines 3–4 as before, this theme now 'recapitulates' lines 5–6—from the same dominant paragraph.

Elettra, Konstanze, Donna Anna, Fiordiligi, Dorabella—all these high-flown Mozartian heroines associate extremes of conflicting passion with multifunctional form. Surely this is not the only such conjunction between a particular multivalence and a particular dramatic context in Mozart's arias.

IV. 'PORGI AMOR'

In this section I shall attempt to show what can (and cannot) be achieved in a detailed analysis of a single aria. My choice of 'Porgi amor' is based on a number of factors. By common consent, it is one of Mozart's greatest arias, as revelatory of the Countess's character as it is beautiful. It has been widely studied; in the present methodological context, the existence of a considerable previous literature is a positive advantage. (An objection that 'Porgi amor' is atypical—that few late Mozart arias present a new character in a new scene without preceding recitative, or have a long opening tutti—would be misguided. Notwithstanding the importance of types, no late Mozart aria is 'typical' in this sense; each one is tailored to a particular character and dramatic situation.) Finally, 'Porgi amor' has relatively few notes—no mean advantage in the struggle to comprehend Mozart's infinitely flexible operatic composition.

'Porgi amor' is a soliloquy, of a special sort: it has the dramaturgical function of introducing a new character. At this point, we know of the Countess only that she is a noblewoman of middle-class origins and her husband a jealous philanderer, and that Cherubino has a crush on her. As such the aria is predestined to be an intimate portrait. The text is a single stanza of *ottonario*:

1	Porgi amor[a] qualche ristoro	a	Grant, O Love, some respite
2	Al mio duolo, a[b] miei sospir:	b	To my grief, to my sighs:
3	O mi rendi il mio tesoro,	a	Either restore my treasure to me,
4	O mi lascia almen morir.	b	Or else[c] let me die.

[a] Presumably the god of love, i.e., Cupid.
[b] Correctly, this would be 'ai miei sospir[i]'; Mozart writes 'a' miei'.
[c] Literally: 'at least'.

The poem can be interpreted as end-oriented. The first couplet is a single sentence, in which the Countess prays in general terms for relief from the burden of her grief. The second makes her desire explicit—that her husband be restored to her—but transforms it into the first member of a binary opposition expressed in syntactically parallel clauses: 'Give me love or give me death'. The second couplet is more specific, more complex, and more urgent. The relatively strong internal caesuras in lines 1–2 (commas are implied before and after 'amor') become far weaker in the run-on lines 3–4, and the climactic (if scarcely unexpected) word 'morir' is reserved for the last end-rhyme.[91]

The orchestral introduction combines two primary topics *di mezzo carattere*: the yearning amoroso of the melody and chromatic accompanying motifs, and the 'slow march' of the forte opening fanfare and dotted rhythms (mm. 7, 9, 13–14).[92] (See Ex. 5, which gives the aria in full, and the outline of the form in Table 6. In this and all subsequent analyses, bold-face numerals in the text and formal diagrams are equivalent to encircled numerals in the examples; both indicate primary musical ideas.) The tutti actually has six distinct ideas: **1** introductory fanfare; **2** heartfelt melody; **3** a combination of 'slow march' and 'amoroso' winds; **4** syncopated, stepwise-descending melody; **5** forte cadence (slow march); **6** codetta (amoroso). (The final two phrases thus separate out the complex **3** into its constituent topics.) The dynamics and instrumentation change constantly: **2** through **6** alternate soft and loud; **2** through **5**, strings alone vs. full orchestra; **1** through **5**, détaché vs. legato. The first three ideas include internal contrasts as well: ***1a***, forte fanfare on the tonic triad, followed by ***1b***, detached unisons, piano, in the strings; in **2**, the long-note melody ***2a*** simultaneously with the after-beat chromatic neighbours ***2b***; in **3**, forte vs. piano, a richer variation of mm. 7–8 in 9–10, and full orchestra vs. concertante winds (the latter recur in **6**). This profusion of ideas marks the Countess as a complex personality capable of deep feelings, under the sway of conflicting emotions.

[91] For this reason, Osthoff (see n. 22) and, following him, Kunze, *Mozarts Opern*, associate 'Porgi amor' with the tradition of *ombra* scenes in E flat (one of the primary origins of the cavatina).

[92] Allanbrook, *Rhythmic Gesture*, 101–4 (with discussion of the implications for the Countess's persona and her relations to other characters).

TABLE 6. *Formal diagram of 'Porgi amor'* (Le nozze di Figaro, *No. 10*)

	Ritornello						Exposition									Tonal return section							Postlude			
	1	3	7	11	13*b*	15	18	20	22	24	26	28	30	32	34*b*	36*b*	37*b*	38	39	41	42	43*b*	45*b*	47*b*	49*b*	51
Vocal paragraphs							I				II (26–34*a*				+ 34*b*–36*a*)	III							IV			
Text-lines							1*a*	1*b*	2*a*	2*b*		3		4	4	1	2		3	4		4*b*	3	4		
Ideas (voice)							**2**		**4′**			**3″/4′**		**3″/4′**	**4″**	**7**	**7**		**8**	**4‴**	**4**		**8(2)**	**8(2)**		
Ideas (orch.)[a]	**1**	**2**	**3**	**4**	**5**	**6**					**3′**		**3′**			?		**(4′)**				**5*b***			**6**	**1*b***
Phrasing[b]	2	2+2	2×(1+1)	$2\frac{1}{2}$	2	3	2+2		+ 2+2		2 × (2+2)				+2	$2\frac{1}{2}(1+1\frac{1}{2})$			2	3(1+2)		2	2 +	2	(1+1) + 1	
Structure	Complex paragraph						Antiperiod				Weak period			+	Ext.	Complex							Weak period			
Harmony[c]				vi	ii^6_5-cad.				vi-cad.					cad.				V^{9b}/V –vi			–vi	ii^6_5-cad.	2 cadences			
Tonality	I						I ————			———— IV	V				V^7	I							I			

[a] Significant independent motifs that differ from the voice, or are heard when the voice is silent.

[b] The phrasing is more complex than can be shown here, especially with respect to elisions and double functions of half-bars in the ritornello and paras. II and III. See text.

[c] Significant harmonic events (unusual or striking chords, structural cadences, etc.)

EXAMPLE 5. *Le nozze di Figaro*, No. 10, 'Porgi amor'

Note: regarding the motive designations **a**, **b**, etc., see p. 164.

10
cl.
bn.
hn.
I
vn.
II
va.
b.
à 2
tr
vi
ii 6 5
V
15
La C.
Por - - gi a -
I
4
5
5a
5b
5c
6
6a
6b
6c
6d
6e
2

19
I
vn.
II
va.
4′
La C.
- mor_ qual - che ri - sto - ro al mio duo - lo, a’
b.
3′
24
cl.
p
hn.
p
I
vn.
II
va.
3′/4′
La C.
miei _______ so - spir _ .
O mi
b.
I V

29
3′
cl.
bn.
hn.
I
vn.
II
va.
3′/4′
La C.
ren- di il mio te - so - ro,
o mi la - scia al- men mo -
b.
V
34
cresc.
4″
7
- rir, o mi la - scia al - men mo - rir. Por- gi a- mor qual- che ri -
V
V7

37
bn.
I
vn.
II
va.
La C.
b.
p
8
sto-ro al mio duo-lo a'miei so - spir. O mi ren - di il mio te - so - ro, o mi
vi
41
5b
cl.
bn.
hn.
4'''
4
8(2)
la - - scia al-men mo-rir, al - men mo - rir. O mi ren - di il mio te -
vi ii 6 5 V 8—7 5— 4—3 I

The phrasing and harmonic contents vary as well, in such a way as to bind the succession of complexly related phrases into a single, coherent, end-oriented paragraph, comparable to a Mozart concerto ritornello.[93] The 'annunciatory' **1** is on the tonic, with no explicit harmonic progression. **2** and **3** are both 2 + 2 (maintaining two bars as the phrase-module), but whereas **2** is a small-scale antecedent–consequent period (I–V; V–I), **3** repeats its 'open' I–V^7 progression. By contrast, **4** and **5** are undivided phrases that differ in length; while **6**, though reverting to parallel subphrases, 'diminutes' these as 1 + 1. **1–3** and **6** employ only tonic and dominant, effectively only in root position, while **4** and **5** include numerous harmonies in various inversions; the most important chords for later events are C minor (vi) and ii$^6_5$ in m. 13. In addition, phrases **2** and **3** are cadentially frustrated: the small-scale antecedent–consequent period **2** 'ought' to be followed by a stronger period or a cadential sentence, 1 + 1 + 2, but **3** is merely another non-cadential

93 Webster, 'Are Mozart's Concertos "Dramatic"?', sects. III–IV. Levarie, *Mozart's 'Le Nozze di Figaro'*, 75–7, offers an excellent analysis of the ritornello phrasing, and of the exposition as a recomposition of phrases **2** and **3**. But I do not agree with his calling mm. 11–17 a 'coda' (the structural cadence does not arrive until m. 15).

2 + 2 which, though complex and resolute, leads only to the piano, syncopated **4**. Thus **4** and **5** go beyond **2** and **3** not only in their rhythmic variety and harmonic range, but in their twofold drive to the cadence through the deceptive resolution in m. 13 to the tonic in m. 15. The latter arrival is even stronger than it would be on the basis of its harmonic progression alone; it is a true structural cadence, the goal of the entire introduction. Hence the piano **6** has the character of a codetta. This ritornello construction is unique in Mozart's late arias.[94]

The aria as a whole both is, and is not, constructed analogously to a concerto movement. The vocal sections create a 'key-area' form in four paragraphs (see Table 6). Its first half is a regular exposition in two equal paragraphs (8 + 8): the first in the tonic, setting the first text-couplet, the second in the dominant, on the second couplet. The two final paragraphs in the tonic are largely new and hence constitute not a recapitulation, but a tonal return section. Paragraph III is longer than the others, includes the entire text, reaches the greatest level of musical complexity, and leads to a structural cadence. Paragraph IV has a double function: on the one hand, it is like a vocal codetta, in so far as it is much shorter than the others, follows a structural cadence, and merely repeats the final text-couplet; on the other, it brings a pair of strong cadences that grant tonal and thematic resolutions not achieved in para. III. Notwithstanding its intensification (reminiscent of the third member of a quatrain), para. III returns to the tonic immediately following the end of para. II and remains there throughout; hence the aria comprises an exposition and a tonal return section, analogous to a sonata without development (Table 1, I.C.2).

But this form is complicated by its relationships to the opening ritornello. (I deal here only with the large-scale thematic units labelled **2 3 4**, etc., reserving discussion of motivic relations for later.) First, the formally articulated themes **2–3** from the ritornello recur as the principal themes of the two exposition paragraphs, presented with equal formality in two periods of eight measures each. Even details match: in the winds, the succession in theme **3** from sixteenths (m. 8) to thirty-seconds (9–10) recurs in their two separate statements of **3**′ in the exposition (26–7, 30–1). Secondly, the structural cadence of the otherwise freely composed para. III rhymes with that of the ritornello (mm. 42–5*a* ≈ 11–15*a*): first, the Countess reverts to theme **4**, descending from *g*″ in syncopated rhythm to *g*′, complete with deceptive cadence on vi; then the winds enter on a ii^6_5 chord (5*b*), introducing the same cadential progression as in mm. 13*b*–15.[95] Finally, the intro-

[94] The closest approach to a ritornello-like introduction on this scale in his other Viennese arias is Tito's 'Se all'impero' (No. 20); there are no others in the Da Ponte operas, and none in *Die Zauberflöte*. On Donna Elvira's 'Ah chi mi dice mai', see sect. V.

[95] It has been objected that m. 43*b* differs from 13*b* in that it is *piano* and omits the 'slow march' topic. But they appear in the same context (following the deceptive cadence at the end of theme **4**, and introducing the structural cadence); both have the harmony ii^6_5 (which is heard nowhere else); the exposed winds in mm. 43*b*–4 (the only place in the tonal return section where they all play) stand for the full-orchestra attack of m. 13*b*, but (as is common) alter it so as not to discompose the singer. The connection, though subtle, is powerful—not least due to its multivalence: it is a reprise with respect to tonality, instrumentation, and formal context, but varied in rhetoric.

duction's codetta **6** returns more or less literally as the orchestral postlude. This is the most ritornello-like event of all: just as in a concerto movement, the opening tutti turns out to be a microcosm of the whole:

Ritornello:	**2–3** (formal)	**4–5** (cadence)	**6** (codetta)
Aria:	**2–3** (exposition) . . .	**4–5** (cadences) . . .	**6** (postlude)

Ritornello and aria share the same overall form, culminating in the succession of two cadences, the structural **5** and the codetta **6**.[96]

In other respects, however, the Countess's music cannot be reduced to a working-out of the ritornello. The exposition alters the character of the themes, making them less martial and more sentimental. In para. I, although mm. 18–21 repeat theme **2** with only minor changes, the ensuing 'long-note' phrase (22–5), descending in measured steps from the high tonic all the way to f', recalls the descending octave of the legato theme **4** (owing to the altered rhythm, I call it **4**′). An additional link is provided by the rhyme between the appoggiatura-resolution figure $a^{\flat}{}'$–g' (m. 13) and the Countess's cadence on $g'f'$ (m. 25), one step lower. In addition, the ascending-fifth sequence emphasizing the minor degrees vi and iii strikes a grave new harmonic note (related to the deceptive cadence in m. 13, the only minor triad in the ritornello). Similarly, para. II transforms theme **3** from an alternation of 'march' and 'amoroso' into a dialogue between winds and voice, which nevertheless maintains its original 2 + 2 phrasing and the 'formal' unity of topic and tone. The disappearance of the *forte* and the Countess's legato and stepwise version of **3** transform it, again, into something more like **4**. The retransition confirms this orientation by inverting **4** (hence **4**″) into an upward rise from $b^{\flat}{}'$ all the way to $a^{\flat}{}''$; the interval of a seventh is the same as that covered by the initial vocal descent from $e^{\flat}{}''$ to f' (mm. 22–5).

In contrast, the tonal return para. III is irregular in phrasing and, at first, thematically. There is, to be sure, a complex rhythmic symmetry, 5(3 + 2) + 5(3 + 2); but all four of these phrases are different. The paragraph begins with a pair of short phrases (**7**) in fast syllabic declamation, which race through the entire first couplet in two bars (compared to eight in the exposition), before halting on the dissonant and chromatic A♮. This leads to an important new phrase **8**, in dotted rhythm, which cadences deceptively on vi (an anticipation of the 'structural' deceptive cadence in m. 43). Now follows the first climax: the Countess gathers her strength for a stepwise rise of a ninth, no less, from f' to g''; the wide span induces her to accelerate to sixteenths (hence **4**‴; compare mm. 36–7). The high g'' is elided to the syncopated descent on the original form of **4** (described above), and to the more or less themeless structural cadence over the harmonic progression of **5**. In para. IV, by contrast, the Countess sings **8** twice in a row in a balanced 2 + 2 period,

[96] This ritornello function has gone more or less unnoticed. Abert (ii. 263–4) asserts that the orchestral prelude is merely introductory, with no relationship to the second half of the aria. Levarie, *Mozart's 'Le Nozze di Figaro'*, 75–8, calls it the first strophe (A) of a bar-form (AA′B). Allanbrook, *Rhythmic Gesture*, 101–2, focuses on its topical content rather than its construction (or that of the aria as a whole). Kunze, *Mozart's Opern*, 299, mentions the wind-postlude, but only to speculate on its role as a sign of 'the hereafter'.

ending both times with a full cadence—a combination of material, tonal, and rhythmic stability heard nowhere else.

There is also a progression in the relations between the two personae, Countess and orchestra (represented mainly by the winds). At first they appear as formally distinct entities, each in turn dominating one of the two opening units (ritornello and para. I). In para. II, they become more closely related as alternating phrases; nevertheless, they remain temporally separate and bound within a formal double period: $2 \times (2 + 2)$. Towards the end, however, the bassoon entry on *g*♭′ over V⁹/V (m. 38) is not merely a madrigalism on 'sospir', but the first approach of the wind-persona to that of the Countess: the bassoon actually counterpoints her melody (the first such event in the aria). Finally, the wonderful chord in m. 43*b* introduces the structural cadence itself—and the winds accompany her in realizing it (this is the only moment in the tonal return section when the entire orchestra plays). The fact that this recall of **5*b*** is non-thematic only increases its poignancy: it is as if the winds finally acknowledge an empathy with her grief, but have no 'words' with which to express it. The vocal and instrumental personae merge into a 'complete' persona, as a dramatic event at the end of the aria.

A comparable progression takes place with respect to the Countess's rhythmic profile. In the vocal exposition, with only a single exception in each case, every phrase and subphrase begins on a down-beat and concludes with an after-beat ending, and many are subdivided. In the tonal return section, by contrast, every phrase begins with an up-beat and remains undivided, and strong down-beat endings become increasingly prominent. (Her *ottonario* lines are long and complex, and the first two have internal caesuras; this permits Mozart to repeat the entire text in the second half of the aria to fundamentally different musical rhythms.)

In the vocal exposition, the first two lines in the tonic (mm. 18–25) are divided into subphrases, all but the last of which begin on a down-beat: *Por*-gi amor; *Qual*-che ristoro; *Al* mio duolo. The tendency of Italian verses to be set as two-bar phrases is thus observed, but on the level of the subphrase. By contrast, the dominant paragraph (mm. 26–34), while maintaining down-beat attacks, changes to undivided phrases of three bars, which overlap to produce a large-scale rhythm in twos. The 'pure' *ottonario* profile of a two-note up-beat to a two-bar phrase, corresponding to accents on the third and seventh syllables, is heard only in her retransitional soaring up to high *a*♭″ (mm. 34*b*–6*a*).

In the tonal return section, however, in conformity with the greater rhythmic flexibility of para. III in general, this profile changes radically. In the hasty theme **7**, the first syllable '*Por*-gi', though still accented locally, is subordinate both to 'a-*mor*' (on the quarter) and to 'ri-*sto*-ro' (on the next down-beat). The entire phrase expresses an 'up-beat' quality not heard before: it begins without down-beat following a fermata, as it were without rhythmic foundation (just as it lacks bass), and rushes breathlessly through the entire bar towards the fall onto 'ristoro'. And in the answering phrase the ending on 'so-*spir*' is immeasurably stronger: no after-beat sixteenth as in m. 37, but that unexpected, long, dissonant A-natural. This rhythmic profile is then regularized in the following phrase **8** (mm. 39–40), which restores the two-bar *ottonario*—definitively: from here on, its characteristic two-sixteenth-note up-beat initiates every vocal phrase.

With respect to line-endings, the profile is equally clear, and has if anything greater structural import. In the vocal exposition, every phrase and subphrase except the last ends with a melodic after-beat (usually articulated as an appoggiatura-resolution pair), including not only the tonic cadence at the end of line 1 (ri-*sto*-ro, m. 21), but even the *tronco* ending of line 2 ('so-*spir*', m. 25). Only with the concluding 'mo-*rir*' (m. 34) does the Countess end on the beat (confirmed in her retransitional flight up to $a^{\flat}{}''$). In the tonal return section, however, there are three down-beat endings. We have already noted the affective dissonance on 'so-*spir*' (m. 38). The other two both set the final 'mo-*rir*'—precisely at the two structural cadences (mm. 45, 49). Overall, the rhythmic profile perfectly articulates the form. Down-beat beginnings in the exposition, up-beat in the return; after-beat endings everywhere except at the structural cadences (at the end of the exposition and of the two tonal return paragraphs) and for the sake of a particularly sensitive word-painting. The firm beginnings and regular phrasing of the exposition express the contemplative, formal aspect of the Countess's grief, while the ever-changing, goal-oriented phrases of the tonal return express her yearning for something absent—or for release from care.

If the paragraph structure and rhythmic profile of 'Porgi amor' are relatively clear, the motivic development is complex, indeed at times scarcely analysable. (This statement is not as radical as it may appear. Motivic relations in Haydn's and Mozart's music are often more or less undecidable, and analytical results are valuable only in so far as they foster a comprehensive view of a composition as a whole.)[97] Indeed the motivic saturation in Mozart's operatic numbers often far exceeds that in his instrumental music. There seem to be three primary aspects. (1) On the level of the phrase, the rhythmic profile remains central: it provides both continuity in the large and flexibility of detail (as suggested by the text, the musical rhetoric, the role of the orchestra, the situation on stage, and so forth). (2) On the local level, the motifs are governed by Schoenberg's concept of 'developing variation'; that is, ongoing development of contiguous or neighbouring foreground motifs (as opposed to distant or 'hidden' ones).[98] (3) Mozart's music also depends on 'tonal motifs', of the sort uncovered by Schenkerian analysis; for the sake of clarity in the presentation, I consider the latter separately below.

In the following discussion, the motivic designations **a**, **b**, etc. are applied *independently* with respect to each thematic unit **1**, **2**, etc.; that is, in each theme they begin over again with *a* (**1a** = motif ***a*** in theme **1**; **1*b***, motif ***b*** in theme **1**; **2*a***, motif ***a*** in theme **2**, etc.). There is no implication of relatedness between different motifs whose final terms (the

97 Webster, *Haydn's 'Farewell' Symphony*, 194–204.

98 On developing variation, see Walter Frisch, *Brahms and the Concept of Developing Variation* (Berkeley, Calif., 1984), ch. 1; Carl Dahlhaus, 'What is "Developing Variation"?', in *Schoenberg and the New Music*, tr. Derrick Puffett and Alfred Clayton (Cambridge, 1987), 128–33.

letter) happen to agree, nor of a lack of relatedness between those whose final terms happen not to agree. For example, in the codetta **6**, the descending horn arpeggio (m. 15) is **6*a***, but this implies no 'derivation' from **1*a***, **2*a***, etc. (If it were to be shown as derived, then as **3*b*′**, an inversion of **3*b***, the ascending arpeggio in the bass in the same metrical position.) By the same token, there is no implication of relatedness between the various motifs within a given theme: the melodic phrase **2*a*** is obviously distinct from the off-beat neighbour figure **2*b***. (The reason for this procedure will become clear in the sequel.)

The instrumental ritornello itself is motivically complex. For example, the innocent-looking piano phrase **1*b*** following the opening fanfare, comprising three 'hovering' after-beats/up-beats (Kunze), obviously relates to the final codetta motif (**6*e***)—though the latter is already a variation. But in the immediate context, consider the accompaniment figure **2*b***: like **1*b***, it is an after-beat motif of three notes lacking any attack on a strong pulse, and beginning with a half-step. (Of course, it is also different: twice as fast, legato, chromatic, a complete neighbour.) And several other after-beat motifs occur, always in different forms: repeated notes in m. 4; forte arpeggiation up through the tonic triad in m. 7, bass (and piano arpeggiation down through the tonic triad in m. 15, horns); the descending piano arpeggio in the violins **3*d*** underneath the warbling clarinets. Each of these motifs is both the same as **1*b*** and different from it (and in different ways): which shall we construe as 'derived', and which as 'new'? Or take the first important melodic interval, the upward fourth B♭–E♭ (m. 3) at the beginning of **2*a***, in its relation to the beginning of theme **3**. The latter begins with a two-note motif B♭–G (m. 7); is this a 'variant' of m. 3? Both begin on a down-beat that is the beginning of a new theme; both start on a long B♭ and skip to the nearest triad-pitch on or within the second beat; both are slurred. On the other hand, m. 3 is piano and for first violins alone, m. 7 forte and played in rhythmic heterophony by most of the orchestra; the one skips up, the other down; one is amoroso, the other march-like; one introduces a unitary thematic *Gestalt*, the other a complex mixture of topics. Shall we call **3*a*** a variant of **2*a***? Is the syncopated arpeggiation of a fifth B♭–F in m. 5 a variant of the plain fourth-leap B♭–E♭ in m. 3? or the *piano* third A♭–F on the down-beat of m. 8 a variant of B♭–G in m. 7? (A Schenkerian would certainly say so.) Although such questions are crucial, they are not decidable on systematic grounds, but only in a particular analytical and interpretative context. (This is the reason for choosing neutral motivic labels, as described in the preceding paragraph.)

As we saw above, the Countess's vocal exposition is straightforwardly related to the ritornello. But motivic sources for the first half of the main tonal return paragraph (mm. 36–40) are scarcely to be found. Her breathless beginning on **7** seems essentially new; motivic *Gestalt* dissolves into rhythmically undifferentiated sixteenth-notes. In instrumental music, the 'retrograde diminution' that one might spy in her two-note motifs D–E♭ (m. 36), compared to her original appoggiatura E♭–D (m. 19)—notwithstanding their common position at the beginning of each half of the aria, on the same word ('amor')—would be too abstract and temporally distant to be significant. In an aria, however, where the singer's timbre and vocal production often change noticeably on each pitch, the possibility of a subliminally grasped connection cannot be excluded. As implied above, the dotted-rhythmed theme **8** (mm. 39–40) is to be understood primarily as a variant of the *ottonario* profile, not as a motivic derivation. (The overall rhythmic differences are too strong to justify a derivation from the dotted 'slow-march' topic of the ritornello, or as a 'diminution' of the Countess's opening motif.) At m. 41, however, the rising sixteenth-note scale must surely be heard as a diminution of **4**″ in 34–6, especially since it leads directly to a return of the original **4**. Similarly, although the ensuing cadential phrase (mm. 44–5) covertly recapitulates theme **5** from the ritornello, there is no motivic resemblance; the Countess's unadorned skips are 'pure' cadence. The entire passage up to the high *g*″ in m. 42 is not only *Fortspinnung*-like in construction but uncategorizable in content. The impression is of freely developing song, such that even analytically derivable motifs are understood not primarily as based on, or as 'representatives' of, familiar ideas. The Countess is confused, grief-stricken, searching for an answer, in a song which streams forth incoherently as in despair.

By contrast, as we have seen, the end of the third paragraph subliminally recapitulates **4** and **5** from the ritornello, and her final paragraph comprises two balanced statements of theme **8**, both with strong full cadences (mm. 46–7, 48–9). (The interpretation '**8**(**2**)' in Ex. 5 and Table 6 depends on tonal voice-leading considerations to be described below.) It is at once something we've heard before, and intelligible in construction. It also repeats the entire second text-couplet (**8** enters both times on 'O mi rendi il mio tesoro'); this is the only time we hear this line neither interrupted by the orchestra (as in para. II) nor articulated by non-parallel, melismatic ideas (as in para. III). The ending may be understood as resolving her indecision or, at least, as articulating a commitment to try her best ('or die in the attempt'—a less fatalistic reading of the final text-line). By this interpretation, the aria *progresses*: from an initial stage in which the Countess knows that she is unhappy but has simple or fatalistic ideas about it (paras. I and II), through a stage of confused reflection and 'working through' (para. III), to a new state of being (para. IV). Though still on the horns of her dilemma, she now understands how she feels, in an appropriately complex way.

Admittedly, this technical account captures only a modest proportion of Mozart's 'developing variation' in this aria. His late operatic language is so free and fluid that any attempt to fix it motivically, especially in arias for high-born characters, soon leads to diminishing returns. It is not a question of lack of scholarly zeal, still less of a scepticism that would deny the very possibility of cogent analysis. On the contrary, this ongoing, unceasing, motivic development is a fundamental element of Mozart's chameleon-like dramatic genius. It enables him constantly to very nuances, tone, rhetorical implications, all within intelligible forms and types. No more than Shakespeare's poetic imagery in his plays can the inexhaustible motivic flux in Mozart's operas be pinned down to particular analytical meanings.

By contrast, the prospects for analysis of large-scale tonal structure in Mozart's operatic numbers seem promising. Somewhat surprisingly, the most fruitful method seems to be a combination of Schenkerian tonal/structural voice-leading analysis and a focus on the 'high-note' construction of the vocal line. ('Surprisingly', because one might have supposed that the ostensible strictness and hierarchical orientation of the former would be incompatible with the contingency and foreground orientation of the latter.) The penetrating, aurally tangible quality of vocal lines in performance, as well as singers' variations in timbre from one pitch to another, almost seem to rescue Schenkerian analysis from the reductive abstraction into which it often falls, while conversely Schenker's rigour and theoretical sophistication offer the best possible antidote to the impressionistic arbitrariness of so much operatic discussion.[99] (In such analyses it is usually essential, at least in the foreground and middleground, to notate the vocal line and the orchestral music other than the bass on separate staves. Even though one might be able to dispense with this procedure in 'Porgi amor', I do so anyhow, for the sake of the methodological point.)

In 'Porgi amor', the crucial structural issue is the pitch g'' (see Ex. 6).[100] Given the Countess's tessitura—she frequently rises over $e^{\flat}{}''$, but never as high as $b^{\flat}{}''$—her background head-note in a Schenkerian sense can only be $\hat{3}$. But g'' proves to be equally important for her psychology. Her opening idea 2 (mm. 18–21) establishes g'' as a musical 'problem'. Her first phrase skips up a fourth from $b^{\flat}{}'$ to $e^{\flat}{}''$; her second skips up a fifth to f'' (see the brackets in Ex. 6). Although each note turns into a dissonant appoggiatura over the barline and locally resolves downwards, the structural implication is that, since she must eventually attain the background head-note, her third phrase will continue the ascent and reach g'' over I. But it does not: mm. 22–5, perhaps in response to the text ('duolo . . . sospir'), change both topic and direction and descend from $e^{\flat}{}''$ all the way down to g'–f' ($\hat{3}$/I–$\hat{2}$/V) at the first structural half-cadence. The latter establishes the potential for a background only in the lower register; this is too easy to be meaningful. The remainder of the aria is 'about' the Countess's need for and eventual achievement of g''. In a highly poetic touch, she actually sings g'' in m. 21 (see '!' in Ex. 6), but only as a fleeting *échappée* within the appoggiatura-resolution figure f''–$e^{\flat}{}''$. (Compare the more elaborate and more dissonant ornament at the corresponding place in the ritornello, m. 6.) It is as if an understanding of her situation were within her grasp, but she had not yet learned how to articulate it. Poetic as well are her passing recalls of $e^{\flat}{}''$ on the way down (mm. 23, 24), the latter actually 'reflecting' her initial structural interval, $b^{\flat}{}'$–$e^{\flat}{}''$ (also indicated by brackets).

The dominant paragraph II is based (as usual) on $\hat{2}$/V. But the repeated high f'' (linking with the cadential f' in m. 25), notwithstanding its prominence, is unclear in back-

[99] There are very few Schenkerian analyses of Mozart arias; the most sophisticated is Carl Schachter's of 'Voi che sapete', in 'Analysis by Key'. On the importance of high-note organization in Mozart's vocal parts, see Levarie, *Mozart's 'Le Nozze di Figaro'*, 78–80, 155–61; Webster, 'To Understand . . . Mozart', 188–90.

[100] The importance of the Countess's g'' is well described by Levarie (*Mozart's 'Le Nozze di Figaro'* 78–80; cf. Carter, *Figaro*, 110–11), but without attention to the tonal structure.

EXAMPLE 6. *Le nozze di Figaro*, No. 10, 'Porgi amor', voice-leading analysis
(*a*) foreground (*b*) middleground

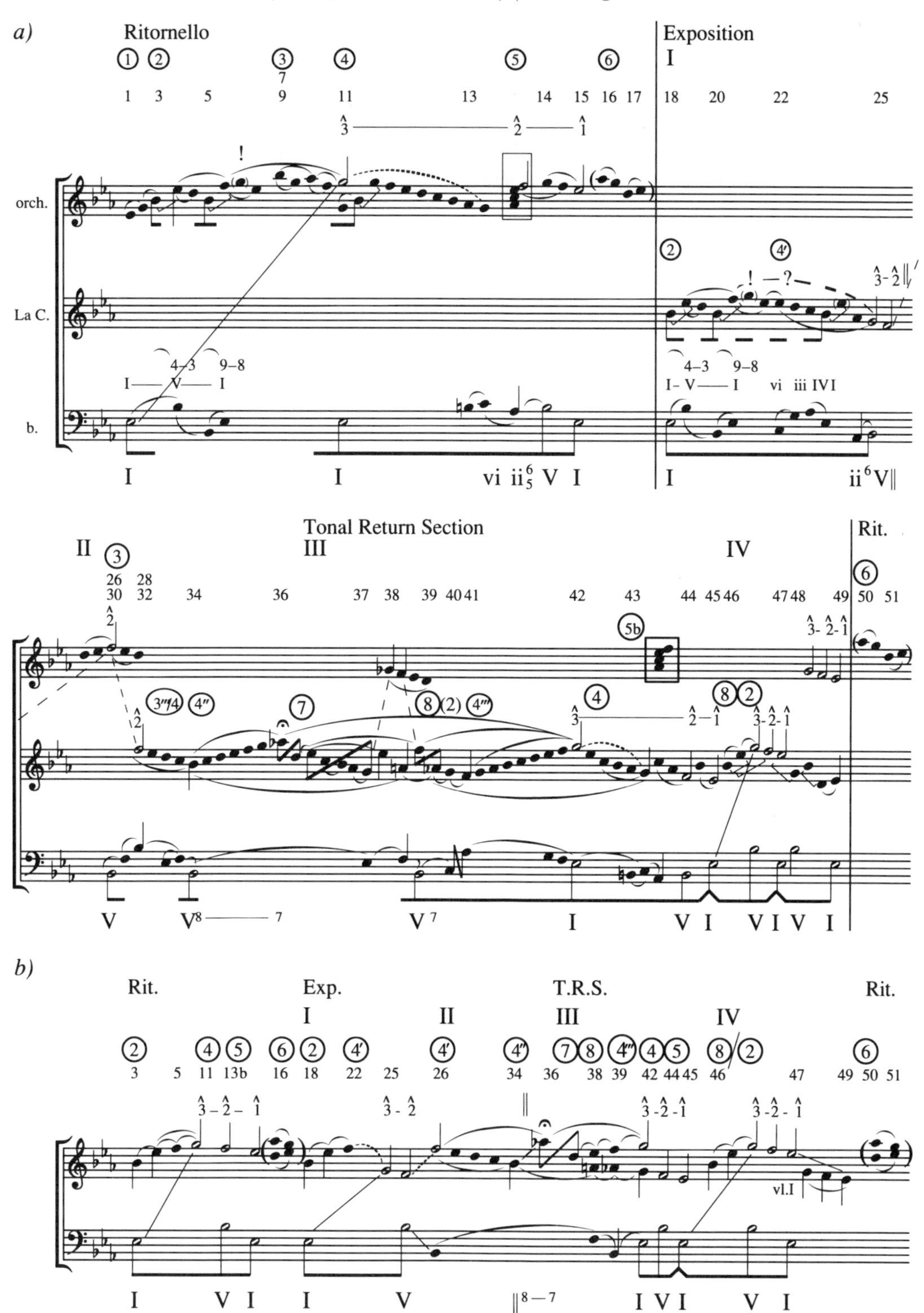

ground function, owing to the absence of any preceding background $\hat{3}$ in the same register. In any case, the Countess uses it only as a platform from which to descend; this formal, expository mode is incompatible with further striving towards her goal. Only after the structural cadence in V does she gather her forces for a renewed attempt—and overshoots *g″*, all the way to *a♭″*! She is (as it were) so taken aback that, in the sequel (mm. 36–41), she not only immediately abandons this register, but fails to resolve the long-held *a♭″* at all; it is 'left hanging'. This is especially important because, in the deep middleground and background, this dissonant $\hat{4}$ is the crucial upper neighbour that transforms the dominant as key into the 'home' dominant seventh. Hence when in m. 42 she finally achieves a high *g″*—on a down-beat and over a root-position tonic, and approached by a long rising scale similar to the one that previously led to *a♭″*—it is no abstract tonal goal, but a powerful, long-range melodic resolution. (As suggested by the light scoring and the Countess's disorientation, the resolution to the tonic in m. 37 seems to affect only the foreground; the repetition of the same phrase lands on V^9/V (m. 38), from where the dominant is prolonged until m. 42. A full analysis of Mozart's remarkable voice-leading in this passage must be left as an 'exercise for the reader'.) This very strong $\hat{3}$/I represents the Countess's first unambiguous attainment of the background head-note (nothing comparable happened in this register in para. I, and the tonics in mm. 34–5 are rhythmically weak and in the low register). Indeed, it comes just in time, immediately preceding the deceptive cadence on vi and the ensuing descent $\hat{3}$–$\hat{2}$–$\hat{1}$ at the structural cadence at the end of the paragraph.

But even this cadence is not sufficient. The Countess skips down from the high *g″* in m. 41 to *e♭″*, leaving it hanging like *a♭″* before it (note the difference from the stepwise descent in the ritornello, m. 11), and she again moves down to *g′* at the deceptive cadence; the authentic cadence (mm. 45–6) is relegated to the lower octave. A cadential descent in the high register is withheld until the final brief paragraph. The first of the Countess's two renditions of **8** re-ascends straight up the triad to *g″*; indeed, she recapitulates the pitch-content of her original **2a** (mm. 18–22), in such a way as to fulfil its hitherto unrealized potential: *b♭′*–*e♭″*–*g″* (see again the brackets in Ex. 6). From there, for the first and only time, she descends directly by step to the tonic, over a very strong I^6_4–V^7–I cadence. Her balancing final phrase connects the two registers one last time, but without the $\hat{3}$–$\hat{2}$–$\hat{1}$; the latter is, however, heard in the first violins, precisely at the cadence. But this phrase reveals another aspect of her quest. Her striving for high *g″* entails increasingly large leaps up from *b♭′*: a fourth to *e♭″*, a fifth to *f″*—and, vocally the most difficult of all consonant leaps, a major sixth to *g″* (see the brackets in Ex. 6*a*). As if reflecting this, her final phrase descends through the *e♭″*–*e♭′* octave by means of two interlocking sixths, *e♭″*–*g′* and *b♭′*–*d′*. (Her only other sixth is the join of themes **7** and **8** over the dissonant V^9/V in m. 38—should *a′* and *f″* be sung detached, or with a portamento?—and its goal is *f″*, not *g″*, just as one would expect at this stage of her 'working through'.) The background descent and double cadence in para. IV bring a psychological resolution as well as a musical one: the Countess achieves the notes and masters the skips towards which she has been striving, and makes sense of them, integrating them into the context of the whole aria. Indeed, as Abert implied (ii. 246 n.), her final phrase audibly projects this whole: while traversing her entire tessitura, it rises to *g″* on 'il mio tesoro', and falls back to *e♭′* on 'morir'.

At the end of 'Porgi amor', everything functions in concert (something we grasp only on the basis of close analysis of each). The text reaches a semantic climax on 'morir' at the end of a poetically significant form. (To be sure, this climax has been heard twice before, in contexts which musically have not attained closure.) The end of the third vocal paragraph and the orchestral codetta gather the entire aria into a ritornello-form that composes out the premise of the opening tutti. The Countess's vocal form is strongly articulated in four paragraphs, of which the last two both end with structural cadences. The rhythmic profile moves from formal, down-beat-initiated, off-beat-ending phrases to free, up-beat-initiated, down-beat-ending ones. The phrasing moves from periodic two- and four-bar phrases through a passage of complexity back to two-bar units; in parallel, the motivic structure moves from intelligibility through free association to a different kind of intelligibility. The tonality strives for cogent functioning of the structural high-notes, and achieves it—but only in the final phrases. The orchestral and vocal personae, at first formally separate, move through alternating dialogue and simultaneous counter-melody to a unified articulation of the structural cadence. This multilayered resolution at the end makes it seem as if the Countess has articulated her yearning for release, not merely felt it as before: an apotheosis. Although nothing 'happens' in 'Porgi amor', it is intensely dramatic.

V. COMPARATIVE ANALYSES

Even if this account of 'Porgi amor' should be judged adequate on its own terms, it cannot stand alone: as noted in Sect. I, any analysis that ignores an aria's relations to the larger context risks misunderstanding. But this relationship is dialectical: to an equal degree, our experience of 'Porgi amor' reflects back on the generalizing methodologies of types, domains, parameters, and the rest; the Countess's sorrow humanizes them, renders them for the first time tangible and concrete. The embedding of 'Porgi amor' in its context entails a series of briefer comparative analyses, drawn from the network of Mozart's arias related to it, as described in Sect. II. (In other contexts, of course, the sample would include arias by other composers, preferably belonging to a well-defined repertory or type; for example, entrance arias for a sentimental heroine,[101] or heartfelt love/absence arias in *opere buffe* premiered in Vienna in the 1780s.[102]) In this way I hope

[101] Mary Hunter informs me that she has located about seventeen arias in late eighteenth-century *opere buffe* that are dramaturgically similar to 'Porgi amor': each 'marks the first moments on stage of a woman who (typically) is the sentimental focus of the plot'. Most are in flat-side keys, and are either laments or pastoral in tone.

[102] In 'The buffa aria', Platoff does this for bass comic operas from this repertory, including comparisons to Figaro's 'Aprite un po' quegl'occhi'.

to survey a diverse but notionally coherent repertory (rather than arbitrarily chosen examples), to shed further light on 'Porgi amor' itself, and to indicate something of the nature and limits of similarity among Mozart's arias—and hence something of their inherent character as well.

'Dove sono' resembles 'Porgi amor' in being a soliloquy; the Countess is plagued by the same mixed emotions. The text is again in *ottonario*, but in three stanzas rather than just one, without large-scale formal divisions; each stanza has an *abab* rhyme-scheme and its own *tronco* ending.

1	Dove sono i bei momenti	a	Where are the beautiful moments
2	Di dolcezza e di piacer,	b	Of sweetness and pleasure?
3	Dove andaro i giuramenti	a	Where flee the vows
4	Di quel labbro menzogner?	b	Of those mendacious lips?
5	Perché mai, se in pianti e in pene	c	Why, since in tears and pain
6	Per me tutto si cangiò,	d	Everything has changed for me,
7	La memoria di quel bene	c	Has the memory of that happiness
8	Dal mio sen non trapassò?	d	Never disappeared from my breast?
9	Ah! se almen la mia costanza	e	Ah! if only my constancy
10	Nel languire amando ognor	f	In anguish still loving
11	Mi portasse una speranza	e	Could bring me hope
12	Di cangiar l'ingrato cor.	f	Of changing his ungrateful heart.

Nevertheless, it implies a rhetorical progression, which corresponds to Mozart's two-tempo form. Whereas the first two stanzas are lost in self-pity, the third, though remaining doubtful (conditional mood), evokes a measure of 'hope' that her fidelity will 'change' the Count's feelings. Unlike the internal progression on 'Porgi amor', this one is tangible, unmediatedly audible. This difference relates to the larger context: instead of grieving in isolation, the Countess is now a party to the plot against her husband, and increasingly intimate with and dependent on Susanna—her servant. But not without mixed feelings, expressed forcefully at the end of her preceding *accompagnato* ('A quale / Umil stato fatale io son ridotta / Da un consorte crudel, che . . . / Fammi or cercar da una mia serva aita!'); its last clause Mozart sets vigorously yet pathetically in A minor, ending on a half-cadence which unexpectedly yields without transition to the bittersweetly yearning aria in C (see Ex. 7).[103]

The conventional view according to which 'Dove sono' is more dramatic than 'Porgi amor' reflects the Wagnerian bias in favour of through-composed music, represented in this case by its 'progressive' two-tempo form. In other respects, however, these two arias have a great deal in common. 'Dove sono' also has *g″* as structural high-note, and the tessituras are virtually identical (*d′–a″* vs. *d′–a♭″*). In itself, this would not be unusual; what is remarkable is that the Countess undergoes the same process of 'working

[103] Abert (ii. 284 n. 2) points out the link between this ambivalence and the Count's frustration in his own aria, heard not much earlier: 'Vedrò mentre io sospiro / Felice un servo mio?'

EXAMPLE 7. *Le nozze di Figaro*, No. 19, 'Dove sono': end of accompanied recitative

through': at first unable to attain g'', she comes increasingly close, and in the Allegro finally makes it her own.[104] The vocal climax, soaring to a'' and chromatically descending to g'' (mm. 85 ff.), and the ensuing high-points in 97 and 101–2, go beyond mere contrast of tempo and *Affekt*; the Countess progresses towards and eventually achieves a goal. Even her initial 'overshooting' to the upper neighbour a'', m. 85, though very different in expression, structurally resembles her $a^{\flat}{}''$ in m. 36 of 'Porgi amor'. The relations between the two arias are themselves multivalent: their similarities in tessitura and musical procedure cut across the differences of key, instrumentation, and form: we hear the same character, troubled by the same problems. In their common end-orientation, they are equally dramatic—subliminally in the one case, overtly in the other.

Like many of Mozart's *rondòs*, 'Dove sono' exhibits the formal type

A	B	A	C
I	V	I	I

In these arias the *secondo tempo* avoids any hint of key-area form; it usually remains in the tonic, with at most passing modulations to the subdominant or the tonic minor. (Even Vitellia's 'Non più di fiori', whose *secondo tempo* is no mere 'c d c', but amazingly turns into a modulating rondo form, avoids the dominant key in favour of i, IV, and ♭III.) But in 'Dove sono', the link between the two sections is closer than usual, This is not primarily a matter of thematic relations, or the fact of the Andante's breaking off on a V^6_5 chord, but of through-composition: closure is denied at the end of the Andante, and eventually fulfilled in the Allegro. In the A section of the Andante, the Countess's gradual rise towards (but not to) g'' entails a sensitive emphasis on e'' and f'', which involves the entire texture (see Ex. 8). Her second phrase (mm. 3–4) makes e'' a dissonant suspension

[104] Compare the similar interpretation of this process in Levarie, *Mozart's 'Le Nozze di Figaro'*, 78–80, 155–61; seconded by Carter, *Figaro*, 110–12. (A *Schönheitsfehler* for us all is that the Countess twice sings g'' in the B section of the Andante, the second time (m. 28) with root-position support.)

EXAMPLE 8. *Le nozze di Figaro*, No. 19, 'Dove sono'

(*a*) mm. 1–18

(*b* mm. 49–63

a)

A1 A2

La C.

Do - ve so - no i bei mo - men - ti di dol - cez - za, e di piacer,

b.

(not IV) (not 7–6)

13

A2a A2b

La C.

di quel lab - bro men - zo - gner, di quel lab - bro men - zo - gner?

b.

b)

49

A2a

La C.

di quel lab - bro men - zo - gner? Ah! se al - men la mia co - stan - za nel lan - gui - re a - man - do o -

b.

56

A2b'

La C.

- gnor, mi por - tas - se u - na spe - ran - za di can - giar l'in - gra - to cor, di can - giar l'in - gra - to cor.

b.

over *f* in the bass; this *e″* resolves *up* to *f″*, violating its natural tendency to descend to *d″*. The significance of this progression emerges from a comparison with the virtually identical phrase in mm. 1–2, where *c″* remains consonant over *f* on the second beat of m. 1, and the step up to *d″* establishes the same ii^6 as the subdominant function. Mozart 'marks' this ii^6 as significant: it is slightly unexpected in m. 1, associated with the irregular resolution in m. 3, and appears three times in the first eight-bar period—a highly unusual concentration on a single chord of subdominant function to the exclusion of others. The relation between *e″* and *f″* is recomposed in the consequent, where the dissonant *f″*/V^6_5 in m. 6 resolves down to *e″*/I. But this *e″* remains consonant; the *e″*/ii^6 configuration is not regularized until the final phrase of the A section (mm. 15–16*a* ≈ 6–7*a*). Again, *f″*/V^6_5 resolves to *e″*/I, and *e″* is suspended over ii^6; now, however, it resolves *down* to *d″*, and on to the cadence. (The fleeting chordal decoration *f″* in m. 16 is a poetic reminder of the Countess's uncertainty in m. 3.)

However, in the reprise of A she breaks off precisely on that *f″*/V^6_5 sonority (m. 51 ≈ 15). Not only is the cadence subverted, but the melodic line cannot complete its background $\hat{3}$–$\hat{2}$–$\hat{1}$. Nor is this a stable half-cadence (as at the tempo-change in Donna Anna's 'Non mi dir'): both the Countess and the orchestra halt on the two tendency-tones *f″* and b—*sf*, fermata, pregnant pause, and all. Indeed, she begins the Allegro on the same *f″*, and prolongs the dominant (now in root position) all the way to m. 56; the unstable progression is still unresolved. Her first return to *e″* is the upbeat to m. 57 (coinciding with the first appearance of the climactic text-couplet), and it introduces a conflated recapitulation of both unresolved passages from the Andante. Over the barline, *e″* again becomes a 'reattacked' dissonant suspension over ii^6 (compare mm. 3*b*, 16*b*); it again descends to *d″* with a fleeting *échappée* to *f″* and, as in mm. 16–18, proceeds to a strong authentic cadence. (Mozart's part-writing is even more sophisticated in the repetition (upbeat to m. 59), where the second violins, $b^\flat$ turns the firsts' *e′* into an explicit dissonance—which nevertheless moves down, 'against' its tendency, to the crucial *d′*.) To round off the paragraph, mm. 61–3 recapture the likewise unrecapitulated progression *f″*/V^6_5–I and ground it in an even stronger cadence. The ii^6 chord maintains its primacy.

Thus the initial Allegro section freely recapitulates both unresolved progressions from the Andante: the '*e″*/ii^6 problem' and the interrupted cadence at the end. The form is multifunctional (see Table 7): the Andante is no mere ABA′, for A′ does not conclude until the first Allegro paragraph. The *secondo tempo* functions of culmination and apotheosis do not begin until the new material in mm. 63–4 and 66, leading eventually to the vocal climaxes described above. Two primary musical parameters, tempo-contrast and structural/tonal progression, have conflicting division-points; they are mediated by the third parameter, the material. The avoidance of closure enables the Countess to fulfill her progression towards her goal across the entire aria.

In 'Non so più', the adolescent Cherubino is polymorphously 'in love with love': with all women, and hence with no particular woman. (In his last recitative expostulation, he tells

TABLE 7. *Formal diagram of 'Dove sono'* (Le nozze di Figaro, *No. 19*)

	1	5	9	13	15*b*	16	17	18	19	37	49	51	53	57/59	60	61	62	63
Tempi	Andante												Allegro					
Sections	A1	A2	A1	A2*a*	A2*b*				B	A1 A2 A1	A2*a*		A2*b*′					C
Harmony	I	V	I		V^6_5	I–ii^6	V	I	V	I		V^6_5	V^7	ii^6–V^7	I	V^6_5–I	ii^6–V^7	I

Susanna that she may read 'Voi che sapete'—his own song—'ad ogni donna del palazzo'.) To be sure, this week (at least) he suffers from a crush on the Countess. But in so far as such puppy-love is not 'real', it is analogous to the state of absence which motivates 'Porgi amor'. It is surely for this reason (among others) that 'Non so più' is in E flat and has a wind complement of clarinets, horns, and bassoons. Like 'Porgi amor', it is Cherubino's 'entrance' aria, and is equally revealing of his personality; like her, he sings in a *de facto* soliloquy, addressing not the bemused Susanna but himself (as he says in the last couplet, quoted below).

Cherubino's closeness to the Countess also lies 'in' his music. His tessitura is almost identical to hers: $e^{\flat\prime}$–g'', compared to d'–$a^{\flat\prime\prime}$, which is to say that he remains within the consonant tonal space of a tenth over the tonic, while she extends it a semitone on either side. (It would probably be irresponsible to interpret her implicitly dissonant tessitura as representing psychological complexity—suffering adulthood—compared to his unformed adolescent personality. But this difference is not merely a question of their overall ranges: 'Voi che sapete' goes down as far as c'.) And like the Countess, Cherubino begins in the middle of his tessitura and gradually works his way up towards g'' (see Ex. 3, in Sect. II). But what a difference! Moving up from $b^{\flat\prime}$ through c'' and d'', he twice attains $e^{\flat\prime\prime}$ (mm. 6, 8), from where he immediately and effortlessly moves straight up the scale to g'' (m. 10), on the strong initial down-beat of the concluding line of the stanza, and he repeats the gesture following the deceptive cadence. His last phrase in this paragraph, descending through the triad all the way to $e^{\flat\prime}$, encapsulates his entire tonal space. (Compare the beautiful word-painting at the two climaxes of the second part (mm. 67–9, 85–8, shown in Ex. 9 below), when he speaks of his foolish sentiments wafting away on the zephyrs—'Che il suon de' vani accenti / Portano via con se': the descending chromatic swirl 'catches' his falling words in the breeze, and the unbroken diatonic rise of a ninth carries them off into the sky, all the way to g''.)

Cherubino thus differs from his troubled godmother in that, with respect to the same basic tessitura, he repeatedly attains his structural high-point. Where they resemble each other is in postponing any structural melodic descent in the 'obligatory' (high) vocal register until the end. To appreciate Mozart's technique here, we must first briefly describe the form of 'Non so più'. It is in two parts, as suggested by the text:

1	Non so più cosa son, cosa faccio,	a	I don't know any longer what I am, what I do,
2	Or di fuoco, ora sono di ghiaccio	a	Now I'm on fire, now I'm of ice;
3	Ogni donna cangiar di colore,	b	Every lady makes me blush,
4	Ogni donna mi fa palpitar.	c̲	Every lady makes me tremble.
5	Solo ai nomi d'amor, di diletto,	d	At the mere words 'love', 'delight'
6	Mi si turba, mi s'altera il petto,	d	I get agitated, my heart pounds;
7	E a parlare mi sforza d'amore	b	And a desire which I cannot explain
8	Un desio ch'io non posso spiegar.	c̲	Compels me to talk of love.

9	Parlo d'amor vegliando,	e	I talk of love when awake,
10	Parlo d'amor sognando,	e	I talk of love when dreaming,
11	All'acque, all'ombre, ai monti,	f	To the waters, the shades, the mountains,
12	Ai fiori, all'erbe, ai fonti,	f	To the flowers, the grass, the fountains,
13	All'eco, all'aria, ai venti,	g	To the echo, the air, the winds—
14	Che il suon de' vani accenti	g	Which carry away the sound
15	Portano via con se.	h	Of my empty words with them.
16	E se non v'è[a] chi m'oda,	j	And if there is nobody to listen to me,
17	Parlo d'amor con me.	h	I talk of love to myself.

[a] Mozart writes: 'E se non ho chi m'oda'.

It comprises eight lines of *decasillabo*, 4 + 4, with *tronco* rhyme *-ar*, in which Cherubino describes his amorous confusion, and nine lines of *settenario*, with *tronco* rhyme *-è*. The latter section comprises two stanzas of unequal length (7 + 2 lines): the first (as Allanbrook notes) is pastoral in tone, while the concluding couplet makes explicit the narcissism which animates the entire text. Each stanza of this section is syntactically a single sentence governed by the phrase 'Parlo d'amor', which frames the entire passage by beginning both the first two lines and the final one.

This text-form is subtly reflected in the music (see Table 8). Notwithstanding the turn to A flat at the beginning of C1—nor even the rather more solid establishment of this key at the comparable place in an early draft of this aria[105]—this aria is not in rondo form (as has often been asserted). For this to be so, C1 and/or C2 would have to be a coherent episode with independent material and (initially) stable construction, and A would have to return later in the tonic. But A never returns, and even C1 includes only sequential passing modulations through A flat (mm. 52–5) and F minor (56–9) on the way to the dominant (60) and back to the tonic (as cadence, not as reprise), while C2 never leaves the tonic at all. Admittedly the beginning of C1, with Cherubino's first long rest and a slowing-down of the harmonic rhythm, initially sounds like an episode, but this impression is not confirmed. Rather, it is a two-part form of the type ABA|C, with the second half articulated as C1 C2 D. This not only conforms to the text-structure, but produces two parts of almost identical length (51 bars vs. 50, counting the elided m. 51 twice). What is more, it resembles the other arias in Mozart's network composed 'against' the *aria d'affetto* (see p. 109): Figaro's 'Aprite un po' quegl'occhi' is a two-part *buffa* aria, AB|A′B′; Elvira's 'Ah chi mi dice mai' and Dorabella's 'Smanie implacabili' are both sonatas without development (again, two parts of equal length).

Nor is the second part a 'coda' (as it has often been called, for no better reason than that it follows the reprise of A and essentially remains in the tonic). To construe the entire last half of a movement in this way is not only inherently implausible, but ignores the normality of long concluding tonic sections in operatic numbers. They are found not only in single-tempo arias ('Aprite un po' quegl'occhi'; Zerlina's 'Vedrai carino'), but also in *rondò*s (as noted above). These sections are essential components of the arias they

[105] *NMA*, *Figaro*, ii. 630, at mm. 51 ff.

TABLE 8. *Formal diagram of 'Non so più'* (Le nozze di Figaro, *No. 6*)

	1	16	38	51 (54)	73	92	96	99
Text	*Decasillabo*: confusion			*Settenario*: pastoral		narcissism		
Text lines	1–4	5–8	1–4	9–15	9–15	16	17	17
Material	A	B	A	C1	C2	D1	D2	D2
Tonality	I	V	I	(IV–ii–V⁷–)I	I	I⁶ ———		ii⁶–V–I

conclude, whether as a climax of manic activity in *buffa* arias, or as an apotheosis ('Vedrai carino'). To call them codas ignores this length and centrality; like many uses of 'sonata form', it is an uncritical borrowing from the lexicon of instrumental analysis.

Moreover, the second half of 'Non so più' not only establishes the important new topic of the pastoral but brings Cherubino's background descent to the tonic (see Ex. 9). In the first part, his confident repeated ascents to *g*″/I (mm. 10, 13; Ex. 3) are followed neither by direct stepwise descents to the tonic nor indeed any cadential tonic in the 'obligatory' high register; *g*″ is left hanging. At most, one could connect the high *g*″ (m. 10) to low *f*′ (11), and across the deceptive cadence to *e*♭′ (15). To be sure, the winds proceed $\hat{3}$–$\hat{2}$–$\hat{1}$ on both occasions. But we expect that in an aria the essential melodic events, structural as well as aesthetic, will take place in the vocal part. And even if we were to interpret the difference in terms of contrasting personae—the winds projecting that 'normal' behaviour of which Cherubino is incapable—his failure to descend by step to the tonic would still undermine the sense of closure. The B section in the dominant (as is normal) is based on $\hat{2}$ (*f*″; mm. 18, 21–2, 28, 33); the return of A is a literal repetition. Thus the first part never brings a vocal descent from *g*″ to *e*♭″ in register.

But the second part does not regain $\hat{3}$ at all until the first climax on 'Portano via con se' (m. 69; shown in Ex. 9*a*). The fermata and implied slur on 'se', emphasizing the skip *g*″–*e*♭″, audibly link it to the structural *g*″ in the A section, from which Cherubino skipped down to *e*♭″ no fewer than four times. To be sure, Cherubino now resolves this into a $\hat{3}$–$\hat{2}$–$\hat{1}$ descent over a very strong cadence (mm. 71–2)—but only in the lower register, and without the winds; true closure is not achieved. The second C section, even dreamier than the beginning of the first, repeats the rise to *g*″ (m. 88); but the ensuing cadence is subverted to a I⁶ chord (m. 91), where a pause leads to the Adagio setting of the penultimate line. But there is no root-position dominant; I⁶ is prolonged *through* the Adagio into the *primo tempo* (mm. 94, 96, 98). The only root-position V–I progression anywhere after m. 72 comes in the final two, almost formulaic measures, which, unlike 71–2, are forte and include the entire orchestra. And this progression, preceded by ii⁶, supports Cherubino's only succession *f*″–*e*♭″ in the tonic key in the entire aria. Hence it also resolves the *g*″/E♭ from m. 88 into a structural $\hat{3}$/I–$\hat{2}$/V–$\hat{1}$/I progression—again, the only one in the aria in the obligatory register. The link to m. 88 is unmistakable, not merely because of the evaded cadence in m. 91, but because by now Cherubino has left *g*″ hanging in register six times; our need to hear it resolve is correspondingly strong.

EXAMPLE 9. *Le nozze di Figaro*, No. 6, 'Non so più'
(*a*) mm. 64–74
(*b*) mm. 87–100

(*a*)

[m.49] [cf. Ex. 3, mm. 9–10]

Ch. all' e - co, all' a - ria, ai ven - ti, che il suon de' va - ni ac-cen - ti ___ por-ta-no via con se ___, por - ta - no via con se. Par - lo d'a-mor ve - glian - do,

b. *fp* *f* *p*

V⁷ I IV V I

(*b*)

[mm. 73–86]

Adagio Primo tempo

Ch. por-ta-no via con se _, por - ta - no via con se _. E se non ho chi m'o-da, e se non ho chi m'o-da, par-lo d'a-mor con me,_ con me _, par-lo d'a-mor con me.

b. *f* *p* *cresc.* *f* *p* *f*

I V (2) I⁶ I⁶ I⁶ I⁶ ii⁶ V⁷ I

Thus notwithstanding Cherubino's different mood, style, and degree of tonal confidence, 'Non so più' exhibits similarities with 'Porgi amor' that go beyond their common key, instrumentation, and motivation of unfulfilled love. Both problematize $g'' = \hat{3}$ in E flat (albeit in very different ways), and are on one level 'about' solving that problem. Both include two structural cadences in the tonic in the last two vocal sections, of which the first is relegated to the lower register, such that closure in the high register is reserved for the last vocal phrase or pair of phrases. And both climaxes bring the dramatic crux: only there does the Countess articulate her feelings; only there does Cherubino, in his most rhythmically vigorous, least self-conscious phrase, say what he is really doing: talking of love to himself. Both arias are end-oriented.

Donna Elvira's 'Ah chi mi dice mai' is similar to 'Porgi amor' in that it is an 'entrance' aria that begins with a very long orchestral introduction (this occurs nowhere else in Mozart's Da Ponte operas). But this introduction functions differently: after being repeated underneath Elvira's opening stanza and its later reprise (mm. 12–20 = 1–9 = 58–66), it disappears; that is, it plays no ritornello-like role in the overall vocal form. The latter (apart from the introduction and Elvira's bravura wind-up) is a straightforward sonata without development (see Table 9).

The exposition comprises the usual two paragraphs, one in the tonic and one in the dominant, setting the first and second stanzas of text. And the recapitulation is regular, except for a cut in the middle of the second paragraph (and the wind-up, not shown in Table 9). Notwithstanding the cut and the suppression of the first cadence (IIB2, mm. 35–7), Elvira repeats all her material from the exposition, in the same order. Although Giovanni's 'Udisti: qualche bella', etc. ('D.G.1') is thereby lost—which is only logical: he can hardly 'notice' Elvira twice—both his 'Poverina!' ('D.G.2') and his and Leporello's final couplet are retained, in the same functional positions.[106] Mozart's treatment of the men's comments is multivalent. In the libretto they are all given as *versi sciolti* (recitative), *following* the set-piece, whereas he integrates them into the concerted music. (Admittedly, their first one-and-one-half lines have seven syllables like Elvira's *settenario*, and the couplet is rhymed. Compare, on both points, the beginning of Despina's 'In uomini', described on p. 140.) All this supports what is clear on dramaturgical grounds alone, that this number is an aria, not a trio.[107]

Elvira commits solecisms which the Countess would never countenance. As noted earlier, her entrance in travelling-clothes immediately marks her as comic. Her language

[106] I construe the cut as coming *after* Elvira's first statement of the 'wide-leap' motive IIB1: the recapitulation of the rising tremolos in m. 76 (= 30, not 42) binds mm. 77–80 to 68–76, as in the exposition mm. 31–4 were bound to 22–30 (IIB1 follows IIA). Hence the deleted passage begins at the cadential IIB2: at m. 81 Giovanni interjects not 'Udiste' etc. (= 35) but 'Poverina' (80–1 = 45–6). Elvira's succession IIB1–[D.G.(2)]–IIB2 is thus maintained intact. But even if the alternative location for the cut (mm. 31–41) were preferred, the integrity of the recapitulation would be preserved.

[107] Gallarati, 'Music and Masks', 242, and Heartz, *Mozart's Operas*, 165–7, note the status of these lines as recitative. Kunze, *Mozart's Opern*, 405, states that numbers consisting of an aria plus occasional asides (of which the aria-singer was often unaware) were common in 18th-c. *opere buffe*, and had their own name: 'Aria con pertichini' (understudies)!

TABLE 9. *Formal diagram of 'Ah chi mi dice mai'* (Don Giovanni, *No. 3*)

Exposition										
	12 (13)	22 (24)	31	35	37 (38)	42	46	48	53	
Paragraph	I	IIA	IIB1	IIB2		IIB1		IIB2		
Text lines	1–4	5–6	7–8	8	[D.G.1]	7–8	[D.G.2]	8	[D.G. + Lep.]	
Tonality	I —— I^V	V		Cadence	V			Cadence	V	
Recapitulation										
	58 (59)	68 (70)	77				81	83	88	92
Paragraph	I	IIA	IIB1					IIB2		III
Text lines	1–4	5–6	7–8				[D.G.2]	7–8	[D.G. + Lep.]	8
Tonality	I —— I^V	I						Cadence	I	I

is raving: 'barbaro . . . l'empio . . . Vo' farne orrendo scempio, / Gli vo' cavar il cor'. Her music is at once obsessive (constant dotted rhythms and melodic skips) and excessive: her 'wide-leap' dotted-rhythmed style (mm. 31–4, etc.) and concluding coloratura (mm. 92–4, etc.) would be more appropriate in a true *seria* character than one whose background and class are uncertain at best—even if she knew how to employ such devices.[108] To listeners who know *Figaro*—as did a great many of those who witnessed the original Prague production—her status as a neurotic analogue to the Countess emerges from her very opening phrase, which has the identical contour and rhythmic structure as that of 'Porgi amor'. A comparable disjunction is heard on the largest scale as well: Elvira's ravings proceed in the context of a stiffly symmetrical sonata-without-development form. 'Ah chi mi dice mai' captures in music the neurotic's fixations: unable to control her behaviour and feelings, at the same time she is rigidly conventional, because only thus can she keep the insecure personality-structure underneath from breaking down. (Compare the Queen of the Night's 'Der Hölle Rache', mentioned in Sect. III.) In this notional context the Countess's sanity shines through almost as strongly as in *Figaro* itself. Mozart's remarkable characterization of Elvira thus depends on the generic subtext that the genuine emotion corresponding to her outbursts—an emotion she cannot articulate—is the *aria d'affetto* about an absent lover; is 'Porgi amor' itself.

Susanna is a *mezzo carattere* of another sort: a servant whose intelligence and good sense reveal her as possessing an inner nobility that is the equal of the Countess's. This trait permits development of the dramatic theme (emphasized by Allanbrook) of the humanity that underlies class distinctions, which becomes increasingly important towards the end of the opera; it culminates in a visible representation of this equality, when mistress and servant are disguised as each other, in a pastoral world that celebrates the possibility of human affection in society. (The fact that disguises were a stock-in-trade of eighteenth-century comic opera does not vitiate their deeper significance in this case.) Thus while Susanna's 'Venite, inginocchiatevi' in Act II, however inventive and fetching, is by type a pure *buffa* aria, 'Deh vieni' in Act IV is another matter.

Despite Susanna's disguise and her complex motivation of wanting to teach Figaro a lesson about trust—she knows that he is eavesdropping, and that he will fear that she is sincere in addressing the Count—'Deh vieni' seems to reveal her true self. To put this in pointed form: we believe that it is no different from what she would sing if she and Figaro were not ensnared in a misunderstanding—if she were entirely alone, awaiting him in the night for love. In fact, however, this belief is everything other than self-evident; it depends both on the aria's articulation of character and on its process of change. Outwardly, it is true to Susanna's *buffa* character: a pastoral serenade, F major, 6/8 metre, uniform rhythm, simple diatonic harmonies. Strong corroboration is provided by Mozart's decision to abandon an earlier draft (to a different text), of a very different type: a 'Rondò', no less (as he designated it), introduced by a longer and more dramatic version

[108] Abert (ii. 404 n. 1) cites earlier examples of the (parodistic?) transfer of 'wide-leap' style from its original heroic context to *buffa* operas. Every commentator emphasizes, with varying interpretative nuances, Elvira's 'false' usages of *seria* style.

of the *accompagnato*, in the key of E flat and alla breve, with less ambiguous lyrics in 'high' *ottonario* tone, and musical style and topics to match. These characteristics are proper to the Countess, not Susanna (not even when disguised as her mistress); they could never have created the effect of Susanna singing in her own voice.[109] To be sure, 'Deh vieni' exhibits two high-class traits: it begins with a ritornello,[110] and the winds are treated as a persona, much in the manner of 'Dove sono'. We can only speculate that Mozart intended this formal and textural complexity to reflect not merely Susanna's disguise as a higher-class person, but her inner nobility as well.

The text is a pastoral love-poem, whose prosody is highly unusual in Mozart: five rhyming couplets of *endecasillabo*, a metre characteristic of Venetian serenades, here without *tronco* line-endings.[111]

1	Deh vieni, non tardar, o gioja bella,	a	Come, do not delay, oh beautiful joy,
2	Vieni ove amore per goder t'appella;	a	Come where love calls you to pleasure
3	Finchè non splende in ciel notturna face,	b	While night's torch does not shine in the sky,
4	Finchè l'aria è ancor bruna, e il mondo tace.	b	While the air is still dark, and the world is silent.
5	Quì mormora il ruscel, quì scherza l'aura,	c	Here the stream murmurs, here plays the breeze
6	Che col dolce susurro il cor ristaura;	c	Which with sweet whispers restores the heart;
7	Quì ridono i fioretti, e l'erba è fresca	d	Here the little flowers laugh, and the grass is cool;
8	Ai piaceri d'amor quì tutto adesca.	d	Here everything lures to the pleasures of love.
9	Vieni, ben mio, tra queste piante ascose	e	Come, my darling; among these secluded plants
10	Ti vo' la fronte incoronar di rose.	e	I want to crown your brow with roses.

[109] On Mozart's draft, see Abert, ii. 295–6; *NMA*, II/5/16, i, pp. xx–xxi (as 'No. 28'), and ii, Anhang, III.10–11; Alan Tyson, '*Le nozze di Figaro*: Lessons from the Autograph Score', in *Mozart: Studies of the Autograph Scores* (Cambridge, Mass., and London, 1987), 122–4. Tyson interprets the key of this fragment (E flat) in terms of 'tonal planning': he hypothesizes that Mozart at one point projected Susanna's aria to *precede* Figaro's, and that (No. 26) was the proper position for this key. It seems to me more likely that his decision to change the aria so drastically in style and form (as well as key) would have been taken primarily on 'characterological' grounds, with any changes in tonal succession a consequence of this, rather than the other way round. Heartz, *Mozart's Operas*, 151–2, offers a more nuanced version of Tyson's hypothesis (he knows that the key of E flat in this context necessarily would represent the Countess's persona). He speculates that Mozart's motive was not so much 'characterological' (as I would have it) as to 'avoid excessive bathos' towards the end of the opera. (A further complication is that the tone and style of Mozart's 1789 replacement for 'Deh vieni', the elaborate *rondò* 'Al desio di chi t'adora', can only represent Susanna as adopting the Countess's voice. And yet it is in F! By this time, however, 'Aprite un po'quegl'occhi' in E flat had long since become a fixture, and therefore Susanna's aria could no longer stand in that key. Perhaps the very disjunction between the Countess's 'voice' and Susanna's key contributes to that falseness of tone which all modern commentators find in 'Al desio'.)

[110] Webster, 'Are Mozart's Concertos "Dramatic"?', end of Sect. 3 (including a formal analysis).

[111] Kunze, *Mozart Opern*, 300, drawing on Wolfgang Osthoff, 'Gli endecasillabi villotistici in *Don Giovanni* e *Nozze di Figaro*', in Maria Teresa Muraro (ed.), *Venezia e il melodramma nel settecento*, 2 vols. (Studi di musica veneta, 7; Florence, 1981), ii. 293–311.

Mozart sets it as three paragraphs (mm. 7–20, 21–32, and 33–48), of which the first two constitute a uniform antecedent–consequent period: the first sets text-lines 1–4 and moves from tonic to dominant (clinched by the wind-ritornello in mm. 18–20); the second sets lines 5–8 and moves back to the tonic. All the vocal phrases are three bars long (as are the two ritornello phrases at the beginning) and have no text-repetitions; the basic instrumental disposition (pizzicato strings and punctuating wind after-phrases) does not change. It is almost a conventional serenade.

Not, however, the final paragraph. It sets only the climactic final couplet, and includes numerous word-repetitions (the key words 'Vieni' and 'incoronar' three times each; the entire last line twice). The phrasing changes from uniform 3s to flexibly organized 2s and 4s; Susanna abandons the repetitive long–short motives of the serenade in favour of a varied rhythmic palette ranging from sixteenths to one-and-a-half measures, and enriched by fermatas. The harmony becomes richer too, introducing one new sonority after another: I^6 (m. 34), IV (m. 39—the subdominant seems critical),[112] V^2 (m. 39) and, in one of Mozart's most poetic deceptive cadences, vi (m. 42). Even more important, perhaps, is the fusion of personae: Susanna appropriates the rising sixteenth-note motive of the winds (mm. 39, 43)—and yet they still sound *over* her (36–8, 44–5), rather than merely punctuating as before. Most striking of all are the *arco* violins that enter unexpectedly (m. 32) at end of the second paragraph and link it to the final one. They add a new rhythmic dimension, their off-beats complementing Susanna's on-beat phrases no less surely, if more subtly, than the wind-scales complement her longest notes.

But they do more: they transform Susanna's yearning into outright desire. As she calls to her lover more urgently ('Vieni, ben mio'), the dry pizzicatos dissolve into liquid, undulating violin motifs rising into the night sky, surrounding the pleasing pain of her long B natural appoggiatura on 'mio': the first moist tinglings of sexual arousal. (Compare the use of the same motif in the passionate C-major portion of Don Giovanni's seduction of Elvira in the trio 'Ah toli, inguis to lore'.) It is this change, I believe, that accounts for our feeling that Susanna here reveals her true self. Not the mere fact of change, but its meaning: she drops the ironic mask of a serenade that, even given her upright character, could have been meant for the Count's ears, and speaks the naked truth: 'Come to me, my love'. Given eighteenth-century conventions, it is not surprising that, again in consonance with the text (and notwithstanding the climax of her wide-open arpeggio and the sustained wind-chord in mm. 40–1), the final passage reverts to the propriety of a poetic metaphor. Nevertheless, it remains free; Susanna sings in her own voice until the end.

Not that 'Venite, inginocchiatevi' is any less remarkable. Its construction as an 'action aria', contrasting the orchestra's ever-changing illustrations and suggestions of the action

[112] Mozart often holds the subdominant (or another structural chord) in reserve until late in an aria, as if to provide thereby a greater degree of solidity or depth (compare the crucial ii^6_5 in the winds in 'Porgi amor'). This happens as well in Zerlina's related aria 'Vedrai carino' (m. 62; I owe the latter observation to Berthold Höckner).

with Susanna's more or less declamatory *parlando*, is well understood. (To invoke an orchestral 'persona' here would be too clever by half; this concept seems better suited to instrumental reflections of a character's psychology than tangible representation of stage-action.) But the overall form has never been properly described. Although it includes considerable suggestion of stage-action, it is not 'realistic': for example, it includes both text-repetitions and formal reprises.

Ironically, 'Venite, inginocchiatevi' is the clearest example of sonata form in any aria from Mozart's Da Ponte operas—'ironically' because, although the literature has over-emphasized the importance of sonata form in Mozart's operas generally, this aria has never been interpreted in this way.[113] Admittedly, the recurring theme **3** adds an additional formal layer; it always enters at the end of a section, usually in conjunction with a structural cadence (see Table 10). This is not rondo-like, however; the main theme of a rondo begins the movement and is later associated with reprises; nor are mm. 1–10 'introductory'. Rather, it subtly suggests the ritornello principle, one of whose two distinguishing features is that the opening paragraph closes with a strong cadence in the tonic, which returns to round off the other main sections, especially the final one in the tonic. Here, all three formally decisive paragraphs—I (first group; mm. 1–14), II (second group; 23–52), and IV (recapitulation; 82–102)—end with **3**. By contrast, the development (III) cannot end with closure, and the final paragraph in the tonic (V) need not (it is a large-scale rounding-off in its own right). The last appearance of **3** (mm. 95–102) is the most important: only here does Susanna sing the entire four-bar phrase without omission, only here does it become a full eight-bar period; its 'end-rhyme' relationship to the end of the first group and the exposition pulls the entire form together.

Although the recapitulation of the putative sonata form is problematical in some respects, the exposition + development construction of mm. 1–81 is crystal clear. Among other things, it conforms to the text (whose form also clarifies certain ambiguities in the 'purely musical' functions of mm. 14–22, 32–7, and 52–61).

1	Venite, inginocchiatevi:	*a*	Come, kneel down,
2	Restate fermo lì,	b	Stay still there.
3	Pian piano or via giratevi:	*a*	Quiet; now turn around;
4	Bravo, va ben così.	b	Bravo! that's good.
5	La faccia ora volgetemi,	*c*	Now turn your face to me,
6	Olà quegli occhi a me.	d	Hey! eyes towards me!
7	Drittissimo: guardatemi,	*a*[a]	Straight ahead, look at me,
8	Madama qui non è.[b]	d	Madame is not here.

[113] Abert and Levarie, focusing on the repeated statements of theme 3 (see below), interpret the aria as a rondo form. Kunze correctly rejects this, but on the basis of a confusion between rondo form and the *rondò*; he merely parses the aria into three sections (mm. 1–36, 37–80, 80–118), whose functions in the overall form are not specified. Allanbrook's fetching interpretation of the aria's meaning ('to demonstrate the proper way to deal with the powers of Eros') is based primarily on a topical analysis, not a formal one. On the bias towards sonata form in the Mozart literature, see Webster, 'Mozart's Operas and the Myth of Unity', 200–1, 204, 205–6, 212–13; Platoff, 'The buffa aria', 105, 107–11, 117–20.

TABLE 10. *Formal diagram of 'Venite, inginocchiatevi'* (Le nozze di Figaro, *No. 12*)

	1	9	11	14	23	32	37	40	47	52	61	65	69	73	76	80	82	90	95	99	102	110	114
	Exposition									?	Development				Retr.	?	Tonal return section				+ Coda (?)		
Paragraph	I			?	II(*a*)			II(*b*)		III(?)	III						IV				V		
Text lines	1 2 2*a*		2	3 4	5–6	7	8	5–7	8	2, 3*b*, 7*b*, 4*a*(!)	9	10	11	12–13	12–13	—	14–17	14–17	18–19	18*a*, 19	19	19	19*b*
Sus. ideas	2 2 (2/3)		**3*a* *c***	2	2	2	**3 *bc***	2′	**3*bc*+2**	(2′)	2	2	2	2	2	—	2′	accel.	**3*abc***	**3 *bc***	7	8*a*	8*b*
Orch. ideas	1	1 (2/3)	**3*abc***	3′+4	4+5	6	**3*abc***	6	**3*abc***	3′+4	4+5	4+5	4+5	(2)	3′(6)	?!	3′	3″(6)	**3*abc***	**3*abc***	7		9
Cadences				(14)I		(32–6)V/V		(40)V		(52)V					(76)V7						(102)I	(110)I	
Caesuras						(36)		(46)								(80)			(94)			(110)	
Tonality	I				V						ii	I	IV	(ii^6)—	(V^7) ———		I						

9	Più alto quel colletto . . .	e	Your collar higher . . .
10	Quel ciglio un po' più basso . . .	f	Your eyebrows a little lower . . .
11	Le mani sotto il petto . . .	e	Hands beneath your chest . . .
12	Vedremo poscia il passo	f	Let's see how you walk
13	Quando sarete in piè.	d	When you're on your feet.
[*piano alla Contessa*]			
14	Mirate il bricconcello,	g	Look at the little rascal,
15	Mirate quanto è bello!	g	Look how pretty he is!
16	Che furba guardatura,	h	What a sly glance,
17	Che vezzo, che figura!	h	What charm, what a figure!
18	Se l'amano le femmine	*j*	If women love him,
19	Han certo il lor perchè.	d	They certainly have their reasons.

[a] Technically not an '*a*' rhyme (*-atemi* vs. *-atevi*), but in the context it seems preferable to construe it so.
[b] i.e.: 'Don't pay any attention to Madame' or 'Pretend Madame isn't here'.

As so often, the first two stanzas (four lines each, 2 + 2, with many *sdruccioli*, indicated here by italics) are set as the two paragraphs of the exposition. In the first (*tronco* rhyme *-ì*), Susanna bids Cherubino come to her, kneel down, and turn around while she combs his hair; it corresponds to para. I in the tonic (through m. 22). In the second (*tronco* rhyme *-è*), she struggles to keep him from gazing at the Countess as she completes his toilet and dresses him with the bonnet; this is para. II in the dominant, subdivided as II*a* (mm. 23–40) and II*b* (40–52), each subsection giving the stanza in full. Then the prosody changes to a stanza of five lines without *sdruccioli* and only one *tronco*: Susanna instructs Cherubino on his dress and deportment, and ends by telling him to try walking around; appropriately, this more nearly through-composed poetry is set as the modulating para. III, ending on the dominant. The fourth stanza, six lines (again only one *tronco*), is the most distinct of all. Susanna, her task completed, speaks directly to the Countess, while both women marvel at Cherubino's seductiveness. Tonally this is the recapitulation, which culminates in her pointed final couplet, 'Se l'amano le femmine / Han certo il lor perchè', set to the last return of the form-organizing theme **3**.

The opening period is not merely introductory, but establishes two fundamental aspects of the aria: the pattern of beginning a phrase in the orchestra, Susanna answering in the second or third bar (see the diagonal lines in Table 10); and her own two-bar 'rhythmic profile'. (Its two ideas are subliminally related, in that Susanna's phrase **2** composes-out a falling third, and in this sense is a free augmentation of the motifs of the orchestral **1**; see the brackets in Ex. 10, mm. 1–4.) Hence the first group (through m. 14) does not merely cadence with theme **3**, but establishes a basic model of musical procedure: an alternation of orchestral activity and vocal parlando eventually leads to the shared melody **3**, as a culmination. This pattern recurs in both subparagraphs of the second group, and the recapitulatory para. IV as well. (A different kind of reason for abandoning the thematic material of the opening is suggested below.)

No less cogent than the function of the first two paragraphs as an exposition—given the differences between arias and instrumental movements—is that of mm. 61–80 as the development (by some criteria, it would be 52–80). The modulatory sequence through the closely related keys ii, I, IV, the lingering on the 'gazing' theme 5 through three statements, the gorgeous piling-up of the winds into triple octaves—all this is different from the exposition, and thus counts as 'developmental'. The sequel is even clearer in formal function (see Ex. 11): the progression IV–ii^6–vii^7/V–V (mm. 72–6; note the increase in activity), and even more the equally long prolongation of this 'home' dominant (76–80), unmistakably constitute a retransition: it would not be out of place in a Mozart instrumental movement. Indeed the text (and let us hope the stage-action) signal that an 'event' is imminent: 'Get up; let's see how you walk!'

But now follows a Beethovenian stroke (in technique if not expression): the dominant is extended for two more bars (a long time in this context), without thematic content, utterly still (*pp*) except for the pulsation in the inner strings, moving from a unison D (m. 80) to D/C (m. 81) ... and *nothing happens*! The phrasing implies a resolution in m. 80; the two-bar extension, surely, one in m. 82. But the music ticks on; D/C moves only to D/B; there is no root, no attack on the down-beat. Only afterwards do the basses enter; only when the violins answer in pseudo-imitation do we grasp that theirs is a significant motif (from mm. 14–15 and the up-beat to theme 5, ultimately from 8–9; compare 76–9); only then does Susanna ('piano alla Contessa') breathe out in wonderment, 'Just look at the little rascal', etc., in a free diminution of her basic rhythmic module **2**, in this sense a recapitulation of the second-group passage mm. 41–4. Cherubino is transformed, comically but also erotically; Susanna's and the Countess's mutual marvelling at the result is the first step in their path towards understanding and trust. It would be difficult to imagine a more effective musical rendition of a change of being. Mozart accomplishes it by the sheer negativity of a reprise without content, all the more effective for following one of the strongest reprise-preparations anywhere in his late arias.

This section is a recapitulation only in a gestural and tonal sense, not a thematic one (especially given the ritornello-like aspects of **3**); that is, it is a tonal return section, and 'Venite, inginocchiatevi' exhibits sonata form only to this extent. Nevertheless, the sectional, tonal, and gestural aspects of this formal type remain relevant: Cherubino's achievement of comic/feminine grace, Susanna's and the Countess's epiphany of wonder, would scarcely be meaningful except against the background of a notional formal resolution. (Relevant here is the subtle concluding section, which is no mere 'coda'; its sixteen bars go together with the tonal return section to make up an overall tonal return section of thirty-six bars, an appropriate length following an exposition of fifty-two and a development of thirty.) This epiphany against an expectation of recapitulation is the other reason (hinted at above) why the opening period never returns: during these two short minutes, Susanna has moved beyond formalism.

To conclude, let us turn to Tamino's 'Dies Bildnis'. Notwithstanding its position in a German opera, it is an Italianate love/absence aria by type; notwithstanding Tamino's being a man falling in love with a woman whom he knows only through her portrait, whereas the Countess is consumed by an all too familiar grief, no other Mozart aria

Example 10. *Le nozze di Figaro*, No. 12, 'Venite, inginocchiatevi'
(*a*) mm. 1–4
(*b*) mm. 8–18
(*c*) mm. 23–7

14
fl.
ob.
bn.
hn.
I
vn.
II
va.
S.
b.
3′
4
2
p
li.
Pian pia - no or via gi - ra - te - vi:
c)
23 1mo
5
[CHERUBINO mentre SUSANNA lo sta acconciando guarda la CONTESSA teneramente.]
La fac - cia o - ra vol - ge - te - mi:

EXAMPLE 11. *Le nozze di Figaro*, No. 12, 'Venite, inginocchiatevi': mm. 73–85

resembles 'Porgi amor' as closely.[114] They share the key of E flat, the rare tempo/metre combination of Larghetto 2/4,[115] the instrumentation of clarinets/horns/bassoons, and the dramatic motif of the absent loved one (admittedly in different senses). They also share the dramaturgical function that each is the first extended solo for its character, the chief musical 'portrait', couched as a soliloquy. (The facts that Tamino has already sung

[114] This typological significance of 'Dies Bildnis' seems not to have been remarked on. Abert (ii. 644) notes that the device of a protagonist's falling in love with a portrait was common not only in fairy-tales, but in 18th-c. French and German comic operas, and (646) relates 'Dies Bildnis' typologically to the Italian-German 'Ariette' that was popular in Vienna at the time. Both the initial motif of a rising sixth followed by a descending scale, stated twice within a I–V, V–I framework, and the three-note off-beat chromatic motif of 'Ich fühl' es', were commonly associated with love's yearning; see Abert, i. 364, 762; ii. 479, 645. It also appears elsewhere in *Die Zauberflöte*; see Webster, 'Cone's "Personae"', 51–4.

[115] Used by Mozart in only five extant movements, all late and great arias, of which three are in E flat (the third is the bass concert aria 'Mentre ti lascio o figlia', K. 513), and the other two, interestingly, in the registrally neighbouring keys of E ('In diesen heil'gen Hallen') and F ('Non mi dir'); see Marty, *Tempo Indications*, 60–1 and cat. 17. (Although the heading 'Larghetto' in the autograph of 'Porgi amor' is not in Mozart's hand, it is entirely appropriate: Marty, 206, 232.)

in terror in the introduction, and that during 'Dies Bildnis' Papageno remains on stage, do not alter these points.) Finally, they share an outwardly straightforward one-tempo form in four paragraphs, with relatively few notes, as the basis for the richest imaginable musical and psychological content. (Abert's reference to the characterological similarity between Tamino and Cherubino, both of whom are young men 'falling in love', seems superficial by comparison.)

Schikaneder's text comprises fourteen lines, divided 4 + 4 + 3 + 3:

Dies Bildnis is bezaubernd schön,	a	This portrait is bewitchingly beautiful
Wie noch kein Auge je gesehn.	a	As no eye has ever seen before.
Ich fühl' es, wie dies Götterbild	b	I feel it: how this godly image
Mein Herz mit neuer Regung füllt.	b	Fills my heart with new emotion.
Dies Etwas kann ich zwar nicht nennen,	c	This something to be sure I cannot name,
Doch fühl' ich's hier wie Feuer brennen;	c	But I feel it burning here like fire;
Soll die Empfindung Liebe sein?	d	Is the sensation love?
Ja, ja, die Liebe ist's allein.	d	Yes, yes, it is love alone.
O, wenn ich sie nur finden könnte!	e	Oh, if only I could find her!
O, wenn sie doch schon vor mir stünde!	e	Oh, if she already stood before me!
Ich würde,—würde,—warm und rein	d	I would,—would,—warm and pure
Was würde ich! —Sie voll Entzücken	f	What would I do? —Full of rapture,
An diesen heißen Busen drücken,	f	Press her to my ardent breast,
Und ewig wäre sie dann mein.	d	And forever would she then be mine.

It has been called a sonnet, notwithstanding the metre (tetrameter, not pentameter) and identical concluding rhyme in the last three stanzas.[116] It is certainly well made; the four stanzas progress from Tamino's initial undifferentiated reaction to the portrait ('bezaubernd schön . . . ich fühl' es'), through the realization that he has fallen in love ('die Liebe ist's allein'), and the confusion engendered by awakened but unfulfilled passion, to conviction. Stanzas 3–4 are interestingly run on by Schikaneder: Tamino repeats 'würde', then breaks off inconsequentially for 'warm und rein', and resumes only in the next stanza ('Was würde ich!'); the decisive turn to 'sie [an mir] drücken' does not follow until the middle of the line.

All this Mozart wonderfully composes into the aria, so as to account for both these aspects of the poetic form. The third musical paragraph (mm. 34–43) concludes with the climactic utterance 'Was würde ich', and the fourth begins with 'sie voll Entzücken'; that is, the paragraph structure is—necessarily—multivalent with respect to the text (it conforms to the sense, but not to the stanza structure). On the other hand, the third paragraph, which is set entirely over a dominant pedal, abandons B♭ precisely at this climactic phrase, moving up by step and pausing on D, such that the final chord is V^6_5, and Tamino's question is left hanging in the air—not only tonally, but literally: there follows

[116] Kunze, *Mozarts Opern*, 598, appealing to Georgiades, but without citation; in Georgiades's discussion of this number to which Kunze (elsewhere) refers, *Schubert: Musik und Lyrik* (Göttingen, 1967), 122–5, there is no mention of the poetic form.

that magical bar of silence (44) during which his very soul seems to hang in the balance, until the decisive declarations of the final section. I write 'question' advisedly: Mozart changed Schikaneder's exclamation-point (which in the poetic context has a little the air of a rhetorical question) to a question-mark: for him, Tamino has not yet worked through his feelings, and the silence composes out the psychological gap between confusion and resolve.

The entire aria is equally sensitive to the text, synthesizing internal action and reflection by means of unusually supple phrasing and remarkably dense motivic development; on these levels it can almost be called through-composed.[117] But this progressive form proceeds within a clear quatrain structure; see Table 11. Notwithstanding complexities arising from the paragraph-subdivisions (see below), the quatrain form is clear, above all because of its correspondence to the four stanzas of text and the tonal/structural functions. The exposition (as so often) comprises two paragraphs, on the first two text-stanzas (note the parallelism with respect to the subparagraphs: lines 1–3 + 4; 5–7 + 8).[118] The third paragraph—this is the key to the quatrain interpretation—is an intensification on the dominant: no word-repetitions, new attack- and phrase-rhythms, off-beat wind chords, unstable dynamics (*cresc.*—*f p*), harmonic complexity and Tamino's 'broken' phrasing in mm. 40–3, the threefold surging up a seventh from *b*♭ to *a*♭′ (compare mm. 7–8). This gestural and rhythmic climax combines with the very long dominant pedal and the confused, self-questioning character of the text to create great tension, comparable (within Mozart's limits of style) to the retransition in a Beethoven symphony movement. Thus when the root-position tonic finally arrives at the beginning of the fourth paragraph, the resolution is far stronger than the mere concept 'entrance of the reprise' can convey, indeed sufficient to express Tamino's newly won determination. The four paragraphs—tonic; dominant; intensification; tonic resolution—perfectly incorporate the quatrain principle.

At the same time, the subdivisions within the first, second, and fourth paragraphs create a different form. Most important is the distinction between the first subparagraph A (mm. 3–9), which introduces Tamino's sixth-leap plus descent and 'die Liebe', and halts suddenly on the seventh *b*♭–*a*♭′ (Götterbild'); and the second subparagraph B (mm. 10–15), a twofold concluding phrase, at once more melodic and strongly cadential. As a whole, the entire paragraph thus incorporates the succession exposition–full cadence; that is, like the first paragraph in 'Venite, inginocchiatevi' (and most of the other arias cited in n. 118), it grafts a hint of ritornello form onto a key-area first group. Furthermore, the return to the tonic (beginning of the fourth paragraph, mm. 45 ff.) does

[117] Kunze, 598–606 (a detailed and penetrating analysis, which I need supplement here only on the tonal/formal level).

[118] Abert (ii. 644 and n. 4), who describes the form as 'in three parts, as given by the tonal relations' states erroneously that it is very rare (presumably he means: in Mozart) for the first paragraph to close with a full cadence in the tonic. Even if one gives him the benefit of the doubt and takes him to refer only to key-area forms, and not ABA, rondo, and two-tempo forms, the counter-examples in *Figaro* and *Don Giovanni* alone include 'Voi che sapete', 'Venite, inginocchiatevi', 'Aprite un po' quegl'occhi', the 'Catalogue' aria (first part), 'Batti, batti', 'Metà di voi quà vadono', and 'Il mio tesoro'. Perhaps he meant 'exposition'.

TABLE 11. *Formal diagram of 'Dies Bildnis'* (Die Zauberflöte, *No. 3*)

	1–2	3–9	10–15	16–25	26–34	34–43	44	45–51	52–61	61–3
Paragraph		I*a*	I*b*	II*a*	II*b*	III	!	IV*a*	IV*b*	
Text lines	—	1–3	4	5–7	8	9–12*a*	—	12*b*–14	14	—
Content		A123	B	C	D(A2)	E		E–A1'3'	B(+)	
Phrasing[a]	1+1	2+2+3	3+3	5×2	2+2+3+2	(2+2)+(4×1)	1	5×1+2	3+3+2+2	1+2
Harmony	I	I–V^7	I^6–V–I	V–V/V	V/V–V	V^7 $^6_5$	!	I—V^7	I^6–V–I	I–V–I
Tonality	(I)	I		V		V^7		I		

[a] Without indication of overlapping orchestral phrases in paras. III–IV (see the text), or of elisions, etc.

not lead to A; rather, it maintains the unstable, intensifying rhetoric of paragraph III: see the continued restless alternation between the strings and Tamino, the continued striving up to $a^{\flat}{}'$, the rhyme of the pulsing bass $E^{\flat}$ with the earlier pulsing bass $B^{\flat}$ (Kunze notes this), the continued thirty-second-note texture. This passage is thus multi-functional: though harmonically stable and a tonal resolution, it maintains the unstable motifs and gestures from before. A thematic return comes only in paragraph IV*b*, preceded with amazing subtlety by a sudden turn (mm. 50–1) to IV and ii^6, on a motif which is at once an inversion of Tamino's first motif (A1) and a reference to the contour of 'Götterbild' (A3). Now follows a literal repetition of the cadential phrase B (plus an ecstatic extension): a thematic reprise that is not a recapitulation, but a rounding-off, as at the end of a ritornello form. This arrival at a point of culmination, this self-realization, on a ritornello-like return to stable material in the tonic from early in the aria, resembles nothing so much as mm. 42–51 of 'Porgi amor'.

What is more, both arias share a preoccupation with the high-note G. Tamino, a prince in the first flush of manhood, has even less trouble with it than Cherubino, let alone the Countess: following the orchestra's lead in mm. 1–2, he leaps up to it effortlessly (or so we hope) from the B♭ a major sixth below, and he will reach it no fewer than thirteen times during the aria (the Countess only manages it twice). Similarly, he outdoes his initial leap as early as 'Götterbild' in m. 9, and A♭ also becomes very prominent (eight occurrences, against one for the Countess). Indeed the sixth (seventh) up from $b^{\flat}$ determines virtually his entire tessitura (he pays no attention whatever to low $e^{\flat}$); the $b^{\flat}/g'$ skip even recurs twice in the dominant (mm. 24, 28). Of course, g' ($\hat{3}$) also serves as his background head-note: established immediately in m. 3, he recaptures it in m. 13 (the second cadential phrase), via the neighbour $a^{\flat}{}'$ in m. 9, from where he leads it down by step to the tonic, over a very strong authentic cadence. The larger tonal structure is directly audible: $\hat{2}$/V in the second paragraph (m. 18, etc.), is transformed back into $\hat{4}/V^7$ in the intensifying third paragraph (mm. 35, 37, 39, and the last beat of 43). Here again, the true resolution seems to come not in paragraph IV*a*, but IV*b*: $a^{\flat}{}'$ is still far more prominent than g' in the melody of mm. 45–8 (not to mention the climax in 50, immediately preceding the reprise of B); notwithstanding the bass and the governing foreground tonic chord, one seems to hear V^7 still projected above it. The first untroubled $\hat{3}$/I arrives, just as the thematic events would suggest, in m. 55, at precisely the analogous place to that in the opening paragraph. But in the first flush of his fairy-tale love, Tamino twice evades the melodic E♭ at the cadences in mm. 57 and 59, so that he can twice return to his triumphant high g' and lead it down to that tonic, for the first and only time since m. 15, on the very last note of his song.

Tamino's tonal structure is as end-oriented as his text, his musical ideas, and his form. The entire final paragraph is an apotheosis: first tonally; then thematically, formally, and structurally; last of all gesturally, in his extravagant extra cadences. And this represents his most profound point of contact with the Countess. Notwithstanding the lack of audible action in either aria, or their differences in gender, language, and mood, or even Tamino's final ecstasy in contrast to the Countess's sad reflection—notwithstanding all this, both characters reach a strongly articulated apotheosis whose focus is high G. (As noted above, the Countess's orientation towards high G throughout her soloistic or 'leading' music in *Figaro* mirrors Tamino's throughout *Die Zauberflöte*, especially in his crucial colloquy with the Priest in the Act I finale.) 'Dies Bildnis' and 'Porgi amor' resemble each other not merely in belonging to the same type, but on deep levels of musical and psychological experience as well.

VI. ARIA AS DRAMA

The chief structural feature shared by the arias examined in the preceding two sections is that of developing towards a culmination or a changed state of being: the Countess's self-realization in 'Porgi amor' and resolve to take action in 'Dove sono'; Cherubino's move from distraction through dreaminess to the articulation of narcissism; Elvira's coloratura in 'Ah chi mi dice mai'; Susanna's turn from ironic serenade to genuine desire in 'Deh vieni'; her and the Countess's marvelling at the magic of Cherubino in disguise at the end of 'Venite, inginocchiatevi'; Tamino's ecstasy in 'Dies Bildnis'. Moreover, such end-orientation is not restricted to *Figaro* or to a few privileged arias; it is a fundamental principle of organization in late Mozart.

When (from *Figaro* on) he includes a substantial postlude, it almost always seems to have a primarily dramatic role, rather than a formal one. (Its immediate function, of course, is dramaturgical: to serve as exit-music.) His postludes almost always represent a new state of being or dramatic insight that has developed during the aria. Thus in 'Non più andrai' the postlude signifies Cherubino's implied growth from an adolescent 'butterfly' to a man, a soldier; in Pamina's 'Ach, ich fühl's' the orchestra cries out her grief at what she believes to be Tamino's rejection of her, more articulately than she can herself.[119] Other arias incorporate the same principle, albeit less obviously. Ferrando's 'Un'aura amorosa' (see the end of Sect. II), as if in reaction to his expansive final cadence, concludes with a new martial topic, while further developing various motifs and tonal relations from the aria. Even the proper and old-fashioned Don Ottavio, in 'Il mio tesoro', exits to a complex postlude involving three contrasting ideas (mm. 93, 96, 98, plus a chromatic link in 95), which derive from different parts of the aria; as a whole it is considerably more vigorous than the introduction. Presumably he has persuaded himself of his claim that he must now attempt to bring Giovanni to justice. The only exceptions to this developmental principle are the simplest or most realistic arias: true serenades, such as Giovanni's 'Deh vieni alla finestra' (note the contrast to Susanna's 'Deh vieni'); hymns, such as 'O Isis und Osiris'; and Papageno's bird-catcher songs. Among other things, most of these are strophic. And even Papageno's 'Ein Mädchen oder Weibchen' entails two tempi in each stanza, a cumulative buildup of the glockenspiel figuration, and the addition of winds for the last stanza.

In general, however, in late Mozart the concept 'aria' was coterminous with the concepts 'goal', 'change', 'culmination'—in a word, with *drama*. This result should negate

[119] Webster, 'To Understand . . . Mozart', 181; 'Cone's "Personae"', 45–50.

once and for all the traditional Wagnerian notion that Mozart's most dramatic arias (some have said his only dramatic ones) are those in two tempos, because only they are through-composed.[120] On the contrary, in principle all Mozart's late arias are dramatic. The difference between 'Porgi amor' and 'Dove sono' is not that the former lacks drama; it is that in 'Porgi amor' the Countess's self-realization is largely intuitive, pre-verbal (and our awareness of it more or less subliminal), while the resolution in 'Dove sono' is conscious, verbally articulated (and has been better understood). In terms of personae, we might say that in 'Dove sono' the Countess herself undergoes a dramatic process, while in 'Porgi amor' it is only Mozart, only the composer's persona, which does so. (This suggests yet another operatic twist on Cone's theory: it would appear that in this sense the composer's persona is less articulate than his heroine's.) Similarly, it would seem odd to argue that 'Deh vieni', with its transformation of ironic serenade into sexual arousal, is less dramatic than 'Venite, inginocchiatevi', merely because the latter includes much action on stage, exhibits 'busy' independent orchestral motifs, or is in sonata form.

This pervasively dramatic character of Mozart's late arias has technical and formal correlates. Although many begin with an exposition, their later course of events cannot be predicted. Sonata form and its allies are conspicuously rare. Although regular recapitulations occur, they are neither more common nor more characteristic than free recapitulations and tonal return sections. (Again: the latter are as characteristic of one-tempo arias as of those in two tempos.) Similarly, Mozart's inexhaustibly flexible motivic development (which has received short shrift in this study) brings ever-new variants and combinations of the musical ideas, whenever and however the context warrants. All this too is inherently dramatic, even if nothing seems to happen on stage.

But this interpretation is not as incompatible with the traditional one as might at first appear. Like a good Wagnerian, I seem to accept the paradigm of change, if not explicitly as a criterion of value, at least implicitly as a fundamental mode of Mozart's operatic forms. I strive to organize an elaborate analysis (with its apparatus of multivalence, domains, and the rest) in terms of a higher-level 'coherence'. Furthermore, I argue that this coherence is congruent with a character's psychology, and that it is through that congruence that we apprehend the drama of a Mozart aria.[121] Hence I must reiterate the importance of genre, types, text-forms, rhythmic profiles, and all the other factors that bind every Mozart aria to its context. Although it would be naïve to call for a 'synthesis' of Wagnerian aesthetics and a revisionist criticism based on eighteenth-century conventions and traditions, surely any satisfactory approach to Mozart's arias will, at the least, have to take account of both paradigms. It will also have to take account of the dichotomy between the necessity for 'close' analysis (without which few of the results obtained in this study, or Allanbrook's or Kunze's, would be possible) and that of abandoning a dependence on formal models and analytical paradigms drawn from instrumental music.

[120] For example, Joseph Kerman, *Opera as Drama* (2nd edn., Berkeley, Calif., 1988), 77–9.

[121] This notion of a correspondence between the music, and the text and/or the drama, is a central tenet of Wagnerian aesthetics. See Abbate and Parker, 'Dismembering Mozart', 192–4.

An equally important point is that any viable method of approaching Mozart's operatic numbers will entail a combination of analysis and interpretation. Of course, all analysis implicitly entails interpretation. One's choice of works and numbers for study, one's goals and methods, one's way of presenting the results, all reflect critical judgements.[122] But if all analysis is implicitly interpretative, so does every interpretation depend on analysis, our only source of understanding, even if it remains unconscious. Analysis and interpretation—historical interpretation as well as hermeneutic—are always joined in our understanding of past artworks. This is doubly true for opera. In operatic analysis, the interpretative act necessarily becomes explicit, an integral component of the critical discourse. From the infinite web of relations within an aria, and between an aria and other numbers (in the same opera and in others), one must inevitably select particular aspects for study; the choice makes sense only in terms of one's interpretation of that aria, and of the work of which it is a part. Moreover, as we have seen again and again, there is no such thing as the 'purely musical' significance of operatic events. Texts and dramatic situations are constituents of a musical number; keys, rhythms, and instrumentations have conventional associations, including topical and semantic ones; forms and motifs are multifunctional; characters' relations to 'high-note' tonal structure can be understood only in terms of their psychology; and so forth. Although these statements sound like truisms, their implications for analytical practice are by no means as widely observed as they should be.

The need for interpretation can embrace larger music-historical considerations as well, and I would like to suggest one here. The most important and underrated aspect (as I see it) of Mozart's later operatic forms is the freedom of his recapitulations (or whatever music follows the exposition or other closed initial part); this freedom includes rhythmic, gestural, and motivic developments as well as those on the scale of large sections. But this raises a double historical/stylistic puzzle. (1) Why does this unpredictability, this multifunctionality, apparently have no counterpart in his instrumental music, whose recapitulations are famous for their formal symmetry? There is one and only one sonata-form repertory whose recapitulations are as free as those in Mozart's later operas: the instrumental music of Haydn. Among his first works to exhibit this freedom in full flower are the string quartets Op. 33—of all Haydn's works, the ones that influenced Mozart most strongly (at least according to the predominant musicological tradition).[123] But (2) given that influence, why did Mozart's instrumental music maintain its symmetrical cast? The years in question, the first half of the 1780s, were precisely those during which his operatic forms moved from relatively conventional models to an inexhaustibly flexible freedom. Perhaps, consciously or unconsciously, he felt that the proper place to exploit Haydn's 'dramatic' forms was in his most literally dramatic music: in his operas.

[122] Joseph Kerman, 'How We Got into Analysis, and How to Get Out,' *Critical Inquiry*, 7 (1980–1), 311–31; Webster, *Haydn's 'Farewell' Symphony*, 5–7, 112–13, 115–16, 179–82, 248–9; Lawrence Kramer, 'Hermeneutics and Musical Analysis: Can They Mix?' (forthcoming).

[123] On the chronological development of Haydn's free recapitulations, see Donald Francis Tovey, 'Haydn's Chamber Music' (1929), in *Essays and Lectures on Music* (London, 1949), 54–6; Webster, *The 'Farewell' Symphony*, 165–6.

Be this as it may, I must close with a reiteration of my central thesis. Nothwithstanding the increased number and prominence of ensembles and finales in Mozart's late operas (and their privileged position in the critical tradition), his arias are of equal importance. This importance does not depend only on the aspects of convention, character-development, and social/moral world (however important these may be). His art of forming even an aria so outwardly uneventful as 'Porgi amor' into a psychological progression, of making the end articulate a different state of being from the beginning, is inherently dramatic. Indeed, his gift for articulating such developments *within* the context of type and genre goes a long way towards explaining his superiority to his contemporaries: a superiority which is grounded in compositional ability as much as psychological insight, and which, within the technical domain, depends as much on his motivic and formal flexibility as on the independence and complexity of his orchestral texture. In counterpoint to Wagner's famous title, appropriated in the previous 'Mozart year' (1956) by Kerman (who exhibited little more patience with arias than Wagner himself), we may indeed say that in Mozart, 'aria is drama'.[124]

[124] Coincidentally, Linda L. Tyler has recently made the identical reappropriation, in the different but related context of Mozart's compositional revisions: 'Aria as Drama: A Sketch from Mozart's *Der Schauspiel-direktor*', *Cambridge Opera Journal*, 2 (1990), 251–67.

Mozart's Orchestral Flutes and Oboes

NEAL ZASLAW

THE 'full high-Classical orchestra' is usually said to comprise, besides strings, pairs of flutes, oboes, clarinets, bassoons, horns, trumpets, and timpani.[1] These are, for instance, the forces called for in four of Haydn's 'London' symphonies, in the early symphonies of Beethoven and Schubert, and in plenty of other orchestral works from the end of the eighteenth and beginning of the nineteenth centuries. But as a way of understanding Mozart's (or, for that matter, Haydn's) orchestral textures, this notion may be more obfuscating than clarifying.

Of Mozart's numerous orchestral works, only the following relatively few include the complete complement of the 'full high-Classical orchestra':

Les petits riens, K. 299*b*	1778
Symphony in D major, K. 297 (300*a*), 'Paris'	1778
Idomeneo, K. 366	1780–1
Kyrie in D minor, K. 341 (368*a*) (plus 2 horns)	?1780–8
Die Entführung aus dem Serail, K. 384	1782
Symphony in D major, K. 385, 'Haffner' (2nd version)	1783
'Mandina amabile', K. 480 (without trumpets or drums)	1785
Der Schauspieldirektor, K. 486	1786
Le nozze di Figaro, K. 492	1786
Don Giovanni, K. 527 (plus trombones)	1787
Così fan tutte, K. 588	1790
Die Zauberflöte, K. 620 (plus trombones)	1791
La clemenza di Tito, K. 621	1791

Nearly all of these are works for the theatre. Striking by their absence are most of Mozart's symphonies and all of his piano concertos.

Like many orchestral composers, Mozart wrote for forces that differed according to genre, local traditions, and the availability or unavailability of players. (For instance, the first two works on the list above, having been written in and for Paris, should perhaps be distinguished from the rest, written for central European conditions.) The apparent flexibility of Mozart's orchestral requirements, however, need not disguise certain underlying norms, which can be perceived despite the variations that occur.

[1] J. A. Westrup *et al.*, 'Orchestra', in Stanley Sadie (ed.), *The New Grove Dictionary of Music and Musicians* (London, 1980), xiii. 679–91 at 683; Christopher Rouse, 'Orchestra', in Don M. Randel (ed.), *The New Harvard Dictionary of Music* (Cambridge, Mass., and London, 1986), 572–5 at 573.

In Mozart's orchestral works of the 1760s and 1770s the norm was pairs of oboes and horns, with bassoons for the most part apparently tacitly treated as non-obbligato instruments doubling the bass-line (even though in a few of these works the bassoons have independent parts in isolated movements).[2] The oboists were generally expected to be able to double on flutes. This situation is reflected in the wording of an attempt by Leopold Mozart to sell some of his son's symphonies to the Leipzig publisher Breitkopf, describing them generically as 'symphonies for two violins, viola, two horns, two oboes or transverse flutes, and *basso*'.[3] Some of Mozarts orchestral works—early and late, almost always in C, D, or E flat major—also added trumpets and timpani.

There are a few exceptions to the general rule that, in his early orchestral works, Mozart called for flutes *or* oboes rather than flutes *and* oboes. These works (which do not call for a 'full high-Classical orchestra') prove to be almost all autonomous symphonies fashioned by Mozart from overtures to his stage works:

La finta semplice, K. 51 (46*a*)	1768
Mitridate, rè di Ponto, K. 87 (74*a*)	1770
Ascanio in Alba, K. 111 [+ 120 (111*a*)]	1771
Il sogno di Scipione, K. 126 [+ 161/163 (141*a*)]	1771
La finta giardiniera, K. 196 [+ 121 (207*a*)]	1775
Il rè pastore, K. 208 [+ 102 (213*c*)]	1775

In addition, three symphonies, a symphonic minuet, and two stage works—incidental music for a spoken play and a fragmentary Singspiel—call for both flutes and oboes:

Symphony in E flat, K. 184 (161*a*)	?1773
Thamos, König in Ägypten, K. 345 (336*a*)	?1776–9
Zaide, K. 344 (336*b*)	1779–80
Symphony in G, K. 318	1779
Symphonic Minuet in G, K. 409 (383*f*)	1782
Symphony in D, K. 504	1786

After he moved to Vienna in 1781, Mozart continued to consider pairs of oboes and horns (with or without trumpets and timpani) a viable form of orchestration, at least until mid-1786,[4] but he conceived a new norm alongside the old one as an artistic alternative. This involved pairs of oboes, clarinets, (obbligato) bassoons, and horns, with a single flute. As in the earlier period, some works also added trumpets and timpani, but unlike the earlier period, the oboists were no longer expected to play flutes on request. These are the orchestral works calling for one flute and two oboes:

[2] For instance, in *Mitridate, rè di Ponto*, K. 87 (74*a*), the Symphony in G major, K. 110 (75*b*), and the Symphony in G minor, K. 183 (173*dB*).

[3] Letter of 7 Feb. 1772; Wilhelm A. Bauer, Otto Erich Deutsch, and Joseph Heinz Eibl (eds.), *Wolfgang Amadeus Mozart: Briefe und Aufzeichnungen, Gesamtausgabe* (hereafter *Briefe*), 7 vols. (Kassel, 1962–75), i. 456.

[4] Cf. K. 371, 373, 374, 119 (382*h*), 414 (385*p*), 386, 433 (416*c*), 417, 419, 462 (448*b*), 449, 470, and 495, and of course some individual numbers in the late operas.

Piano Concerto Rondo in D, K. 382	1782
Mass in C minor, K. 427 (417*a*)	1782–3
Piano Concerto in B flat, K. 450	1784
Piano Concerto in D, K. 451	1784
Piano Concerto in G, K. 453	1784
Piano Concerto in B flat, K. 456	1784
Piano Concerto in D minor, K. 466	1785
Piano Concerto in C, K. 467	1785
Dir, Seele des Weltalls, K. 429 (468*a*)	1785
Piano Concerto in E flat, K. 482	1785
Piano Concerto in A, K. 488	1786
Piano Concerto in C minor, K. 491	1786
Piano Concerto in C, K. 503	1786
'Alcandro, lo confesso . . . Non so d'onde viene', K. 512	1787
'Bella mia fiamma . . . Resta, o cara', K. 528	1787
Piano Concerto in D, K. 537	1788
'Dalla sua pace', K. 540*a*	1788
'Un bacio di mano', K. 541	1788
Symphony in G minor, K. 550	1788
Symphony in C, K. 551	1788
Piano Concerto in B flat, K. 595	1791
'Per questa bella mano', K. 612	1791
Laut verkünde unsre Freude, K. 623	1791

Hence, a pattern emerges: although Mozart's orchestral norm changed after his move to Vienna in 1781, neither his early nor his late norm called for pairs of flutes and oboes playing simultaneously. Non-Parisian works calling for pairs of flutes and oboes both before and after 1781 seem usually to have originated as theatre music, or to have been derived from theatre music. What explanation can be offered for this?

The sole passage in the Mozart family's extensive correspondence that might possibly be relevant offers little apparent help. Writing home from Milan during rehearsals for *Mitridate*, Leopold Mozart reported that the opera orchestra there consisted of 14 first violins, 14 second violins, 6 violas, 2 cellos, 6 double basses, 2 flutes, 2 oboes, 2 bassoons, 4 horns, 2 trumpets, 2 harpsichords, etc. And he added parenthetically that any time flutes were not called for, the flautists picked up oboes and played along on the parts of the full-time oboists.[5] This is an intriguing performing practice, which—as far as I know—has been neither discussed nor attempted. But it sheds no light on the question why Mozart's theatre works frequently required pairs of flutes *and* oboes, whereas other orchestral works generally did not. We shall return to this puzzle at the end of this essay.

The most promising explanations for the flute/oboe interchanges are based upon three related factors: timbre, range, and size of orchestra or density of orchestration.

[5] Letter of 15 Dec. 1770; *Briefe*, i. 408.

The matter of timbre is commonsensical. Altering the orchestral colour of a movement or an aria by substituting flutes for oboes, or vice versa, is a straightforward but effective way of varying character. The most common configuration involves an 'andante' movement in which all or some of the following may be combined to create a special sound: trumpets and drums (if present in the previous movement) cease playing, the key changes, usually to one that places the horns in a lower and therefore less brilliant register, the violins are muted, the cellos and basses are pizzicato, and flutes replace oboes.[6] Sometimes the flutes are programmatic, in the sense that a pastoral aria text may imply or refer to shepherds' pan-pipes;[7] often their appearance seems motivated by more generalized needs for suggesting a mood, painting a scene, or providing an aesthetic contrast.

The ranges of Mozart's flutes and oboes, not so very different on paper, are quite different in practice. Mozart's oboes have middle *c'* as their bottom note and *d'''* as the top. His flutes have *d'* as their lowest note and *g'''* or even *a'''* as their top note.[8] But the ranges of the flutes and oboes were not equally useful throughout their extents. The tone of the flutes' lowest octave was so gentle as to be of limited use in orchestral music, while the top fifth of their range was considered shrill by mid-eighteenth-century standards and therefore to be used with great caution. The oboes were powerful right down to their bottom *c'* (sometimes too much so) but thinned out above the treble stave. Notes above *c'''* or *d'''* were considered unreliable and given only to outstanding soloists, for instance, to the Mannheim virtuoso Friedrich Ramm in the Oboe Quartet, K. 370 (368*b*), where a virtue is made of their thinness.

There may be another factor adding to the inherent softness of the flutes in their lowest ranges and the thinness of the oboes in their highest range. Or at least my subjective impression from listening to many hours of rehearsals and performances of orchestras playing eighteenth-century instruments is that the relative softness of the flutes in their lowest range and of the oboes in their highest range is exaggerated by some thus-far-unidentified characteristic of their overtone structures, which cause their sound to be absorbed into the string tone in those registers proportionally more than in the rest of their ranges. For providing wind sonorities in orchestral tutti passages, then, the highest notes of the oboes and the lowest notes of the flutes are problematic.

In his earlier orchestral norm, Mozart tends to deal with these problems by keeping the flutes above the treble stave much more than he does the oboes, which he tends to

[6] Among symphonies, for example: K. 43, Anh. 221 (45*a*), 100 (62*a*), 75, 130, 183, 201 (186*a*), 203 (189*b*), and 200 (189*k*).

[7] For instance, the first number of *Il rè pastore*.

[8] The only exceptions are the middle Cs in the solo part in the Flute and Harp Concerto, K. 299 (297*c*), presumably written for an instrument with an extension, and at the beginning of the Finale of the Symphony in F, K. 130. In the latter case, Mozart wrote the flutes colla parte with the violins, apparently failing to notice that the violins twice exceeded the flutes' range. He wrote out the recapitulation in a revised version (mm. 107 f.), even though the first ten bars are identical in musical substance to the opening of the exposition, and contrary to his frequent practice of leaving a blank at recapitulations with instructions, which in this case would have read 'Da capo zehn Täkte'. In this written-out recapitulation, the flutes are placed an octave higher in the two offending passages.

keep further down in the stave. And the choice of instrument is often related to the key. Mozart is more likely to write for flutes in works or movements in F, G, or A than in C, D, or E flat. This choice is driven by the horns, which in the 'higher' keys (with shorter crooks inserted) will occupy a generally higher tessitura. Since the pairs of flutes or oboes often must function to form acoustically well-spaced four-note chords with the horns, the higher the horns are pitched, the less room remains above them for flexible placement of the chosen woodwind pair. The presence of a few more notes at the top of the flutes' range alleviates this technical problem.

In Mozart's earlier norm, with the winds just pairs of oboes and horns and the bassoons reinforcing the bass-line, modest-sized string sections would have allowed a satisfactory balance between strings and winds. When the bassoons became obbligato instruments and clarinets were added to the wind section, larger string sections were necessary for good balance.[9] Large string sections make it all the more urgent to keep the oboes and flutes in their optimum ranges if they are to function effectively in both solos and tuttis. (This changed somewhat in the nineteenth century, when steps were taken to make the flutes and oboes louder in general and more even over their entire ranges.) This practice leads to Mozart's later norm: two oboes in their best ranges and one flute in its most brilliant range cover the entire orchestral spectrum of treble pitches with a tone sufficiently powerful to write effective tuttis. In this configuration, a second flute would occupy roughly the same range as the first oboe, and thus may have been redundant, or at least dispensable.

And there may have been another factor: in the string choirs of many of the orchestras Mozart dealt with, the violins were more numerous, and the violas less numerous, in proportion to the rest of the strings than in modern orchestras, whether symphonic or chamber orchestras. In the tiniest orchestras of the 1760s, 1770s, and 1780s, with pairs of oboes and horns, this may not have affected the balance between strings and winds. In larger orchestras, however, a pair of oboes alone could not adequately balance the large number of violins in the tuttis. In the early part of the century the solution was to double or triple the oboe parts, as in orchestral suites of French overtures and dances, and as suggested by Leopold Mozart's 1770 letter from Milan quoted above. In the 1780s Wolfgang Mozart seemed to favour two oboes plus a flute, except for the still-to-be-explained preference in theatrical works for two oboes plus two flutes.

Anyone who has had to think about the acoustics of various more or less successful halls and theatres knows that, as a first-order generalization, halls which are excellent for speech are seldom truly first-rate for music, and that the converse holds as well: halls which are flattering for music rarely favour speech. All public performers, whether speakers and actors or singers and instrumentalists, dread 'dead' halls, lacking in presence or in resonance. But these two groups want different kinds of resonance, emphasizing the higher partials for speech, and the lower ones for music. Speech in a

[9] Neal Zaslaw, *Mozart's Symphonies: Context, Performance Practice, Reception* (Oxford, 1989), 450–62.

music-venue sounds mushy, consonants especially being hard to differentiate. Music in a speaking-venue lacks warmth and sounds scratchy, with undue emphasis on non-musical noises and insufficient reinforcement of those aspects of sound production which western classical musicians consider 'good tone'. Put another way: in a theatre designed to maximize the projection and comprehension of speech, instrumental music is in danger of being dominated by the sounds of turning pages, shuffling feet, rushing breath, clicking keys, and scratching rosin, in addition to an exaggerated shrillness of tone.

A possible link between these universally acknowledged acoustical verities and Mozart's orchestration is suggested by Michael Forsyth's important recent book entitled *Buildings for Music*.[10] To summarize drastically one aspect of a detailed study, which discusses many of the most famous music-venues in the history of Western music: theatres emulate an out-of-doors acoustic, in particular that of Greek and Roman amphitheatres, which early on had solved the problem of amplifying speech so that it could be comprehended by crowds. Renaissance and Baroque theatres are evolved forms of those ancient amphitheatres, with walls and roofs added. This is splendidly illustrated by the first such structure, the extraordinary Teatro Olimpico in Vicenza (1580), still standing and still used for plays and operas.[11]

Concert-rooms, on the other hand, emulate a cave-like acoustic in the guise of the salons, drawing-rooms, music-rooms, and great halls of palaces, which many of the earliest of them were. Instead of the semicircular or horseshoe shape of theatres, music-halls tend to be narrow, rectangular spaces. Forsyth dubs these 'shoebox' halls. The most famous eighteenth-century shoebox hall was that in the old Leipzig Gewandhaus (1780–1; see Fig. 1), where on 12 May 1789 Mozart led an orchestral concert of his own music.[12]

The 'link'—and the hypothesis I therefore wish to put forward—is this: for Mozart, having pairs of both flutes and oboes must have been a way of dealing with theatre acoustics, which may have been less favourable to orchestral sonorities than rectangular halls. True, many of the theatres in question, including the Burgtheater in Vienna, were used for opera, which does not thrive in a purely speech-orientated acoustic. But the Burgtheater (see Fig. 2), like most eighteenth-century theatres, served for spoken plays and opera. And an opera singer probably has reason to prefer a compromise acoustic: some musical resonance to enhance the beauty and carrying power of the voice along with some speech acoustics to make possible comprehension of the sung (and, in a Singspiel, spoken) texts.

Naturally, these orchestrational niceties were refinements that might be dispensed with if necessary. Surely Mozart did perform works designed for one acoustic in the other when the need arose. Yet if my hypothesis is correct, it may explain hitherto mystifying aspects of three of Mozart's symphonies.

[10] Michael Forsyth, *Buildings for Music: The Architect, the Musician, and the Listener from the Seventeenth Century to the Present Day* (Cambridge, Mass., 1985).

[11] Richard Leacroft, *The Development of the English Playhouse* (Ithaca, NY, 1973), 65–8.

[12] For fuller details, see Zaslaw, *Mozart's Symphonies*, 423–7.

FIG. 1. The Old Gewandhaus Concert Hall, Leipzig, built by Johann Friedrich Dauthe, 1780–1. Watercolour by Gottlob Theuerkauf, 1895, a year after the hall's demolition. (Museum für Geschichte der Stadt Leipzig.)

(i) When Mozart was in Vienna in 1768, he composed a D major symphony (K. 45); its instrumentation calls for 2 oboes, 2 horns, 2 trumpets, timpani, and strings. The autograph manuscript is dated 16 January. This work was presumably intended for private concerts in the drawing-rooms of Viennese palaces.

Three days after dating K. 45, the Mozarts had an audience with the Empress Maria Theresa and her son, the recently crowned Emperor Joseph II. Joseph suggested that the 12-year-old composer write an opera, which was to become *La finta semplice*. This work, kept from the stage in Vienna by a cabal, was nonetheless intended for the imperial opera company in the Burgtheater. Mozart revised his symphony K. 45 to turn it into the overture to *La finta semplice*. This involved a number of refinements and alterations, only one of which pertains to the present discussion: the addition of a pair of flutes to the pair of oboes.[13]

[13] Ibid., 114–18.

Fig. 2. Interior view of the Burgtheater, Vienna. Engraving by Johann Ernst Mansfeld from Joseph Richter, *Bildgalerie weltlicher Misbräuche* (Vienna, 1785).

(ii) Mozart's reason for writing the brilliant Symphony in E flat, K. 184, has never been determined. But, unlike Mozart's other symphonies of the period, K. 184 does call for pairs of both flutes and oboes. Given the norms of Mozart's orchestration, this must at least open the question of whether the work was intended for a theatrical function and a theatre acoustic. The fact that the movements run one into the next, linked by incomplete cadences, reinforces this notion, since many three-movement overtures are organized that way, for instance, Mozart's G minor overture to his oratorio *La Betulia liberata*, K. 118 (74*c*).

Taking note of the theatrical character of K. 184, commentators have guessed that it may have been intended as an overture for Mozart's incidental music to *Thamos, König in Ägypten*, K. 345,[14] which is a work one might expect to have been provided with an overture. Attempts to confirm or refute this suggestion would probably have been easier had not the dating of both works proved confused. The eight numbers of the *Thamos* music as they come down to us apparently date from Salzburg productions mounted in 1776–7 and 1779–80. But two choruses, Nos. 1 and 6, exist in earlier versions, which apparently originated in 1773. The playwright, Tobias Philipp Freiherr von Gebler (1726–86), was an Austrian civil servant. The choruses in his play, intended to be in the spirit of ancient Greek choruses, were originally composed by one Johann Tobias Sattler. Gebler was, however, dissatisfied with the Tobias's music, and, in a letter of 13 December 1773 to the Berlin writer Nicolai, he reported: 'I enclose . . . the music to *Thamos*, as it was recently composed by a certain Signor Mozzart [*sic*]. It is his original conception, and the first chorus is very beautiful.'[15]

So if Mozart wrote an overture for *Thamos*, he most probably would have done so either in 1773 (Mozart and his father were in Vienna from 16 July until sometime in September of that year on unknown business and could have met Gebler then) or in 1774 (Gebler's play was performed in the Kärtnerthortheater on 4 April 1774); or in Salzburg in 1776–7 or 1779–80. The date written on the autograph manuscript of K. 184 has been heavily defaced and can barely be deciphered, so the usual reading of it as '30 March 1773' may or may not be correct. Wolfgang Plath has accepted the traditional reading of the date on the basis of Mozart's handwriting, and Alan Tyson has revealed that the autograph of K. 184 is written on a type of paper used by Mozart in Salzburg between approximately March 1773 and May 1775.[16] So although the dating of both K. 184 and 345 is uncertain, the possibility of a connection between them cannot be ruled out.

In any case, it is known that, probably with Mozart's consent, the travelling theatrical troupe of Johann Böhm, active in Salzburg in 1775–6, used K. 184 as the overture to the spoken play *Lanassa* by Karl Martin Plumicke. Böhm's production of *Lanassa* also used Mozart's *Thamos* music, with new words, as incidental music. This fact may be juxtaposed with two others: (*a*) a Frankfurt manuscript, probably from the late 1780s, which contains the *Thamos* incidental music with the *Lanassa* texts, includes the first movement only of K. 184, without trumpets, as the overture;[17] (*b*) that movement is copied into Mozart's autograph manuscript of K. 184 in part by his father, in part in a third hand.[18]

[14] For fuller details, see Zaslaw, *Mozart's Symphonies*, 247–51.

[15] L. von Köchel, *Chronologisch-thematisches Verzeichnis sämtlicher Tonwerke Wolfgang Amadè Mozarts*, 6th edn. by Franz Giegling, Alexander Weinmann, and Gerd Sievers (Wiesbaden, 1964), 353.

[16] Wolfgang Plath, 'Beiträge zur Mozart-Autographie II: Schriftchronologie 1770–1780', *Mozart-Jahrbuch 1976/77*, 131–73 at 147; Alan Tyson, *Mozart: Studies of the Autograph Scores* (Cambridge, Mass., 1987), 164, 170.

[17] Wolfgang Plath, 'Mozartiana in Fulda und Frankfurt. (Neues zu Heinrich Henkel und seinem Nachlaß)', *Mozart-Jahrbuch 1968/70*, 333–86 at 366. According to information published by Walter Senn and Ernst Hintermaier and a private communication from Cliff Eisen, this copyist was the Mozarts' long-time friend and favoured copyist, Joseph Richard Estlinger.

[18] Plath, 'Beiträge zur Mozart-Autographie II'.

This last circumstance suggests that the first movement had been in existence before the other two, and that, when a new symphony was needed, Leopold Mozart and the copyist were employed to extract the earlier work from some other manuscript to speed the process of Wolfgang's adding the other movements to it. (There is an analogous case of a pre-existent Minuet copied by Leopold Mozart into Wolfgang's autograph manuscript of the Symphony in F, K. 112.[19])

Trumpets aside, the first movement of K. 184 as it appears in the Frankfurt (*Lanassa*) manuscript is more or less identical to the same movement as it appears in the 'autograph' (symphony) manuscript, at least as far as the number of bars, pitches, and rhythms are concerned. But the placement of slurs as well as of staccato and dynamic indications is sufficiently different in the two sources as to suggest that one cannot have been copied directly from the other. Perhaps Mozart's lost autograph manuscript of this movement (possibly originally attached to the early version of the *Thamos* music) was the model both for the copyist in charge of turning the *Thamos* music into the *Lanassa* music and for Leopold Mozart assisted by a Salzburg copyist to copy it into a symphony manuscript as the first movement of K. 184.

(iii) In 1782 Mozart's father, writing from Salzburg, asked him for a new symphony for celebrations for the ennoblement of Wolfgang's childhood friend Sigmund Haffner the younger.[20] This commission resulted in the creation of the 'Haffner' Symphony, K. 385, whose orchestration calls for 2 oboes, 2 bassoons, 2 horns, 2 trumpets, and timpani. It was performed in Salzburg at a palace or stately home sometime in August 1782. Later Mozart asked for the return of this work, so that he could perform it in Vienna during Lent. This he did, at a benefit concert for himself held in the Burgtheater on 23 March 1783. For that occasion he added pairs of flutes and clarinets to the orchestration. Mozart's expansion of the winds in K. 385 may have been an effort to take full advantage of the Viennese orchestral forces at his disposal, but it was quite probably also an attempt to alter a work calculated for a hall to make it ideal for a theatre.

If the hypothesis of this article is correct—that Mozart sometimes made fine adjustments to his orchestration in anticipation of the acoustic in which a piece was likely to be performed—then there are implications for modern attempts at understanding and recreating his performing practices.

I have argued elsewhere[21] that (outside of recording studios) it can be a serious error to recreate player for player Mozart's (or his contemporaries') orchestras for performances in spaces of vastly different size and acoustic from the ones for which those eighteenth-century groups were designed. What we must pay attention to is not only

[19] Zaslaw, *Mozart's Symphonies*, 190–1. Other overtures which Mozart turned into three-movement symphonies by adding movements are: *Ascanio in Alba*, K. 111, with K. 120 (111*a*); *Il sogno di Scipione*, K. 126, with K. 161/163 (141*a*); *La finta giardiniera*, K. 196, with K. 121 (207*a*); and *Il rè pastore*, K. 208, with K. 102 (213*c*). For fuller details, see Zaslaw, *Mozart's Symphonies*, 188, 245, 292, 296.

[20] For fuller details, see Zaslaw, *Mozart's Symphonies*, 376–82.

[21] 'Three Notes on the Early History of the Orchestra', *Historical Performance*, 1 (1988), 63–7.

what size forces Mozart and others assembled (when limited funding was not a factor) for given performance venues, but the principles they observed in doing so. If we can abstract those principles, we may hope to apply them to the venues given us by modern concert life.

There are many small or even not so small but finely resonant halls in which a tiny orchestra can sound wonderful, with clear textures, solid tuttis, and real presence even in the back rows of seats. There are other halls, larger or less resonant, in which small orchestras sound tinny, dead, distant, or quaint. The strength of orchestral forces will ideally be in proportion to the liveness or deadness of a venue, taking the style of the music and its proper balance into account as well. For example, in a small (by modern standards, at least), resonant opera-house of baroque design (or on a recording), the forces of Mozart's Prague orchestra, with only seven or eight violins, may have sounded splendid, and presumably could again; in most modern concert-halls and opera-houses, such forces may sound weak, even when modern rather than period instruments are employed.

Thus, when our large modern orchestras play eighteenth-century music in their large modern halls, they should not necessarily cut down their forces to half the strings and only one wind-player per part. Much more logical, and much more in keeping with eighteenth-century principles (as exemplified in some of the period's own large-scale concerts), would be to keep the strings at that full strength so painstakingly evolved to sound well in such large venues, using single winds only in solo and piano passages but doubled winds in forte and tutti passages. If Mozart's intentions in this regard may be surmised from the surviving evidence, this proposal may represent the best way of realizing his orchestral works under modern concert conditions, whether with modern or period instruments.

Proposed New Dates for Many Works and Fragments Written by Mozart from March 1781 to December 1791

ALAN TYSON

IT would be very helpful to know all the compositions that Mozart wrote from March 1781 to December 1791, and at what stage each was written. For that would be useful information for various features of his stylistic development, and of his biography.

The important catalogue of Mozart's works that Ludwig Köchel produced in 1862 (= K^1) is entitled 'a chronological thematic catalogue', and he entered all the finished works known to him in what he regarded as their chronological order, assigning them dates, and giving each of them a number in that sequence; the fragmentary works were not included in the main catalogue, but listed in an appendix (*Anhang*), without dates and without incipits. Yet he had to make conjectures as to the true dates of many of the finished works (and he frequently adopted dates that had been already suggested by Johann Anton André and by Otto Jahn), because the autograph scores of many works did not carry any date by Mozart on them.

Although Mozart dated many of the autographs that he wrote in Salzburg up to 1780, he seems to have done that less often in Vienna from 1781. But what he did from 9 February 1784 till 15 November 1791 was to enter his finished works, giving them dates, in his Thematic Catalogue. So a great many of the finished compositions of the last eight years of his life receive his reliable dates. This was very helpful for the last part of Ludwig Köchel's catalogue.

But when Alfred Einstein produced the third edition of Köchel's catalogue (= K^3) in 1937, he gave many of Köchel's entries new dates (and therefore new numbers), and he also inserted the fragmentary works into the main catalogue, giving them dates and numbers, so that he had to alter the numbers of a great many works. And in the next new edition, the sixth edition (= K^6) of 1964, quite a few more works were given new dates, and therefore new numbers.

Since K^6 is the catalogue that is most up to date, and most readily available to people today, I shall refer to Mozart's works in accordance with its dates and its new numbers for them. It seems to me that about a hundred of the K^6 entries for Mozart's late Vienna years are misdated. Each of my entries below begins with the K^6 number, a short description of the work, and K^6's proposed date in quotation marks; my own proposed date follows.

It will be seen that I believe many of Mozart's fragmentary works were misdated by Einstein in K³, and his misdatings are often repeated in K⁶. For Einstein probably had no way of investigating the true date for most of the fragments; he merely linked each of them with a finished and dated work that had the same instrumentation, and perhaps sometimes also the same key. Occasionally this gave a fragment a plausible date, but it appears that frequently he selected the wrong finished work for dating the fragment. And very often a fragment's true date does not correspond to that of any finished work.

Quite often it seems that many fragmentary works are given more or less the same date. For instance, several fragmentary fugues are dated early 1782: K. 375*d* (Anh. 45), K. 375*e* (401), K. 375*f* (153), K. 375*g* (Anh. 41), and K. 375*h*. (All these seem to me to be misdated.) And a great many canons are dated from March to April 1782: K. 382*a* (229), K. 382*b* (230), K. 382*c* (231), K. 382*d* (233), K. 382*e* (234), K. 382*f* (347), and K. 382*g* (348). (There are no autographs of the first five, so I cannot date them, but the last two seem to me to be misdated.)

Moreover, several violin sonata fragments are dated *c.* August–September 1782: K. 385*c* (403), K. 385*d* (404), K. 385E (Anh. 48), K. 385*e* (402), and K. 385*f* (396). (The first four of these five seem to me to be misdated.) And several string quintet fragments are dated to the first half of 1787: K. 514*a* (Anh. 80), K. 515*a* (Anh. 87), K. 515*c* (Anh. 79), K. 516*a* (Anh. 86), and K. 516*c* (Anh. 91). (Of these five I think that the first and fourth are correct, and that the other three are misdated.)

Most of the nine string quartet fragments seem to me to be obviously misdated. For K. 405*a* (Anh. 77), K. 417*d*, K. 458*a* (Anh. 75), and K. 458*b* (Anh. 71) have been dated by the 'Haydn' quartets, but I date them at the time of the 'Prussian' quartets. K. 417*c* (Anh. 76) is later than the 'Haydn' quartets, and K. 587*a* (Anh. 74), with the same watermark, has been assigned to the 'Prussian' quartets; these two fragments were probably written *between* these two times, i.e. *c.* 1786 or 1787. And although K. 589*a* (Anh. 68) has been assigned to the 'Prussian' quartets (especially to K. 589 in B flat?), it should be assigned to the 'Haydn' quartets (especially to K. 458 in B flat!).

Two string quartet fragments are, however, correctly dated in K⁶: K. 464*a* (Anh. 72), in A major, is quite correctly linked with Mozart's work on his A major quartet K. 464. And K. 589*b* (Anh. 73), in F major, is quite correctly linked with Mozart's work on the last two 'Prussian' quartets, K. 589 in B flat and K. 590 in F.

Mozart's Thematic Catalogue is described in the label on its cover as a 'Catalogue of all my works from the month of February 1784 until the month of 1 ' (= to the end of his life in December 1791). So if an undatable finished work is *not* entered in this catalogue at any point, it has been assumed that it was finished *before* February 1784, and it has accordingly been given a Köchel number below K. 449, the first work in the catalogue.

Yet it is clear that occasionally Mozart did not enter works written after February 1784; some of them were perhaps written for friends, or for his family, or for private performances, rather than for public use. Here are a few of these omissions, which have therefore been misdated.

K. 298, flute quartet in A, according to K^6 'composed in the spring or summer of 1778 in Paris'. Although Mozart wrote at least two flute quartets in December 1777 and early 1778 in Mannheim, just before he went to Paris, K. 298 was written much later, in Mozart's Vienna years. The Vienna paper types that were used for it, and the Paisiello opera theme in its last movement, suggest that it was probably finished late in 1786, or perhaps in 1787.

The five Notturni K. 436, 437, 438, 439, and 439*a* (346), 'Das Bandel' K. 441, and the E flat Horn Concerto K. 447 are not in Mozart's Thematic Catalogue, so they have been dated and given numbers before K. 449 of February 1784. Yet they are in my list of misdated works; they are all later than the start of the Thematic Catalogue.

I must now describe my evidence for my dates. This is based on the various paper types that Mozart used, often at very different dates. The paper types are distinguished by their different watermarks, and also by the number of staves on each page and the measurement of those staves (I record the distance in mm. from the top line of the first stave to the bottom line of the bottom stave). Very often I can find that a paper type was used by Mozart only in 1791; or in 1790 to 1791; or only in 1781; or in 1785–6, etc. But there are some paper types that he used very often, at different times—those are not helpful in dating a work.

Although most of the entries in my list are for misdated works, I have also referred to some compositions which were finished at an established date, but some of their parts were written earlier, at different times, for example for the production of some operas, or the earlier start of some piano concertos, etc.

Some clues as to the dates of many of Mozart's autographs are also provided by features of the handwriting; the evidence of the *Schriftchronologie*, as determined by Wolfgang Plath, is very convincing in the years up to 1780. But in his Vienna years Mozart's handwriting did not change very much; it is possible to find evidence that something was written in the Vienna years up to about 1785, or was written in the later Vienna years; but the precise year is hard to identify from the handwriting.

Quite often the chronology for a work published in the *Neue Mozart-Ausgabe* may represent a correction to its date in K^6.

My main list is of many works that K^6 places in Mozart's last years in Vienna, from March 1781 to the end of 1791, but which have probably been given wrong dates. But first I give a list of some works that K^6 puts quite a long time before March 1781, but which were probably written by Mozart in his last $10\frac{3}{4}$ Vienna years.[1]

Piano sonatas: K. 300*h* (330), K. 300*i* (331), and K. 300*k* (332). Piano sonatas in C, A, and F, all three 'supposedly composed in the summer of 1778 in Paris'. But this date is much

[1] For the sake of completeness I have included in both lists a number of works that I have dealt with in my HUP book, *Mozart: Studies of the Autograph Scores* (Cambridge, Mass., 1987).

too early; they were probably all written during Mozart's visit to Salzburg in the second half of 1783, for they are on papers that he used there then. K. 315*c* (333). Piano sonata in B flat, 'supposedly composed in the late summer of 1778 in Paris'. But this is not on a French paper but on a paper made at Steyr, and Mozart probably bought it on his way back to Vienna from Salzburg in November 1783.

Piano variations: K. 300*e* (265). Twelve variations on 'Ah, vous dirai-je, Maman', 'supposedly composed in the early summer of 1778 in Paris'. But this was written in Vienna not before the summer of 1781, or perhaps a bit later. K. 300*f* (353). Twelve variations on 'La belle Françoise', 'supposedly composed in the summer of 1778 in Paris'. But this was written in Vienna after Mozart's arrival there in March 1781, or perhaps a bit later.

Orchestral minuets: K. 363. Three minuets, 'supposedly composed in 1780 in Salzburg'. But I think they were written in Salzburg in the second half of 1783.

Flute quartets: K. 285*b* (Anh. 171). Flute quartet in C, 'presumably composed in January or February 1778 in Mannheim'. But this was partly drafted on a paper that Mozart first used in Vienna early in 1781, and then in the summer of that year. K. 298. Flute quartet in A, 'composed in the spring or summer of 1778 in Paris'. But see above for the evidence that it was probably finished in Vienna late in 1786, or perhaps in 1787.

Church music: K. 186*i* (91). Kyrie, 'supposedly composed in 1774'; K. 196*a* (Anh. 16), fragmentary Kyrie, 'supposedly composed in January 1775 in Munich'; K. 323 (Anh. 15), fragmentary Kyrie, 'supposedly composed in 1779 in Salzburg'; and K. 323*a* (Anh. 20), fragmentary Gloria, 'supposedly begun in 1779 in Salzburg'. But all these are on a paper that Mozart never used before the end of 1787, and often used in 1788 and later. (Incidentally, K. 186*i* was not composed by Mozart; he made a copy of a Kyrie by Carl Georg Reutter.) K. 258*a* (Anh. 13), fragmentary Kyrie, 'presumably composed in December 1776 in Salzburg', is on another paper of the later Vienna years, first used in early 1787 and after that until 1791. K. 368*a* (341). Kyrie, 'supposedly composed between November 1780 and March 1781 in Munich'. The autograph is lost, so we no longer have any physical evidence. But in the past Mozart was not thought to have written church works in his Vienna years (apart from a few, such as the C minor Mass K. 417*a* (427), and his final Requiem, etc.), and therefore many of his autographs with church works which we now know were written in his last four Vienna years were dated well before 1781. So perhaps this Kyrie was not written before Mozart's arrival in Vienna, but when he had been in Vienna for several years.

Here is my list of the works dated from 1781 to 1791 in K⁶, which seem to me to be placed at the wrong times.

K. 370a (361). The wind serenade in B flat for thirteen instruments, 'supposedly composed in the first half of 1781 in Munich and Vienna'. The *NMA*, VII/17/2, suggests a date of 1783–4. Although it is clear that it was written entirely in Vienna, over half of its leaves (fos. 1–26 and 48–9) are on a paper that Mozart seems to have used only in 1781—though the work may have been finished in 1782.

K. 372a (400). Fragmentary Allegro in B flat for piano, 'supposedly composed in 1781 in Vienna'. This is on a paper that I think Mozart did not use until 1782. (And Ludwig Köchel's date for it was 1782, based on a date written on the autograph in an unidentified hand.)

K. 374g (Anh. 46). Fragmentary Andantino in B flat for piano and violoncello, 'supposedly begun in the summer of 1781 in Vienna'. This too is on a paper that I think Mozart did not use until 1782.

K. 375d (Anh. 45). Fragmentary fugue in G major for two pianos, 'presumably composed in the spring of 1782 in Vienna'. This is on a paper that Mozart used only from the end of 1785 until the end of 1786—a time he used it often.

K. 375e (401). Fragmentary fugue in G minor for piano, 'supposedly begun in the spring of 1782 in Vienna'. The *NMA*, IX/27/2, describes it as a fragmentary fugue in G minor for organ, and offers the date of 'Salzburg, 1773'. It is not on a paper of Mozart's Vienna years after March 1781, but on one that he obviously used about a decade earlier.

K. 375f (153). Fragmentary fugue in E flat major for piano, 'supposedly composed in the spring of 1782 in Vienna'. This is on a 10-stave paper (*not* 12-stave, as K⁶ says) which Mozart used in Salzburg on his visit there in the second half of 1783. So I think this was written in Salzburg at that time (though there is also a sketch-leaf on another type of paper that is perhaps earlier).

K. 375g (Anh. 41). Fragmentary fugue in G major for piano, 'supposedly begun in the spring of 1782 in Vienna'. But this is on the last page of two leaves of a very early Salzburg paper, which was certainly not used by Mozart after his departure in 1777 on his trip to Paris. On the first three pages of these two leaves is K. 166*h* (Anh. 23), an early fragmentary psalm.

K. 375h. Fragmentary fugue in F major for piano, 'presumably begun in the spring of 1782 in Vienna'. This is on a 10-stave paper (also used for K. 375*f*/153) that Mozart used in Salzburg in the second half of 1783.

K. 382f (347). Canon for six singers, 'supposedly composed in 1782 in Vienna'. But this leaf, with its stave-rule, is on a paper that Mozart first used at the end of 1784, and mainly in 1785.

K. 382g (348). Canon for three choirs of four singers, 'supposedly composed in 1782 in Vienna'. It is on a paper that I think Mozart did not use until 1783.

K. 383b (Anh. 33 and Anh. 40). Fragmentary fugue in F major for piano, 'supposedly composed in the spring of 1782 in Vienna'. But this is on a leaf of a paper that Mozart never used before December 1787, but used very often in 1788, and also in 1789.

K. 383C (Anh. 32). Fragmentary fantasy in F minor for piano, listed in K⁶ as 1782. In

1964 Wolfgang Plath observed, in photographs of this lost autograph, sketches for *Così fan tutte* on the verso of the leaf. The rastrology depicted in the photographs suggests a type of paper not used before the beginning of 1790 (the *Così* sketches being late plans for a cut in the Act II finale).

K. 383*c* (Anh. 38) and **K. 383*d*** (Anh. 39). Fragmentary theme in C (for variations?) for organ, and fragmentary fugue in C minor for piano, 'supposedly composed in the spring of 1782 in Vienna'. These are both on a single leaf of a paper that I think Mozart did not use before 1783.

K. 383*e* (408/1). March for orchestra in C major, 'supposedly composed in 1782 in Vienna'. This date is probably justifiable, but it is worth mentioning that the three leaves are *Hochformat*, with 14 staves, a type of paper that he bought and used quite often in Paris in 1778. (K. 468, dated by Mozart in his Thematic Catalogue as '26 March 1785', is on the same paper; see below.)

K. 383*i*. A sketch for a symphonic movement or for an overture, 'presumably originated 1781/82 in Vienna'. I would date it 1782 only, for it is on a leaf of a paper that he apparently first used in 1782. And on the same leaf there is a sketch for the A major piano concerto K. 385*p* (414), this sketch being K. 385*o* in K[6], which is dated 'probably in the autumn of 1782 in Vienna'.

K. 385*b* (393). An entry of five *solfeggi* for a voice, 'supposedly composed in August 1782 in Vienna'. Nearly all could date from 1782, but No. 3 is on two leaves of a 10-stave paper that Mozart used in Salzburg in the second half of 1783.

K. 385*c* (403). Fragmentary sonata in C major for piano and violin, 'supposedly composed in August or September 1782 in Vienna'. But this is on four leaves of a paper that Mozart apparently first used early in 1784.

K. 385*d* (404). Fragmentary Andante and Allegretto in C major for piano and violin, 'supposedly composed in 1782 in Vienna'. But this is on a leaf of a paper that Mozart used only from the end of 1785 until the end of 1786.

K. 385*E* (Anh. 48). Fragmentary sonata movement in A major for piano and violin, 'supposedly composed in 1782 in Vienna'. But this is on a leaf of the same paper as K. 385*c* (403), one that Mozart apparently first used early in 1784.

K. 385*e* (402). Fragmentary sonata in A major for piano and violin, 'supposedly composed in August or September 1782 in Vienna'. Since the autograph has not survived, it would be useful to study the *c.*1821 facsimile of the first page, as it might give a clue to the paper. And the fact that it has at the top // Sonata II[da] //, deleted, may be evidence that it was formerly planned to be included as the second item in the Artaria edition of six sonatas published as Op. 2 in November 1781.

K. 385*h* (Anh. 34). Fragmentary Adagio in D minor for piano (or organ), evidently proposed for 1782. Yet on the same leaf is K. 576*a* (Anh. 34), which is assigned to 1789. This paper was first used by Mozart in late 1785, but the paper with the stave-rule of K. 385*h* was used from 1786 until 1790. So this fragment must be dated much later.

K. 386*b* (412 + 514). Horn Concerto in D major, 'supposedly composed at the end of 1782, the Rondo dated Vienna, 6 April 1787'. This is very inaccurate. The true autograph has just two movements, a finished first movement and a very unfinished rondo. What was accepted as another autograph, of the rondo in a finished version, was written by Süssmayr, and his date for it was 'Good Friday, 6 April 1792' (misread as 1797, and thought to be Mozart's joking way of expressing 1787).

Mozart might have started to write the first movement before 1791, the first four leaves being an earlier paper, but one he used also in his last year; he did not finish the first movement, and did not write the rondo fragment, until 1791. So this is not Mozart's first horn concerto, but his last (and unfinished) one.

K. 405*a* (Anh. 77). Fragmentary fugue in C major for a string quartet, 'supposedly begun in 1782 in Vienna'. But this is on a leaf of a much later paper, which Mozart first used near the end of 1789 and mainly in 1790 and 1791. Perhaps this fugue may be associated with the Prussian String Quartets, which he finished in 1790.

K. 416*f* (293). Fragmentary concerto in F major for oboe, 'supposedly composed in February or March of 1783 in Vienna'. But this is on a French paper with 10 staves, which Mozart must have bought in France, and presumably used in the autumn of 1778, or when he returned to Mannheim in November 1778.

K. 417*a* (427). The Mass in C minor, 'composed between the summer of 1782 and May 1783 in Vienna'. It seems certain that he wrote part of the work after that, when he moved to Salzburg in the second half of 1783; most of the extra wind-parts are on Salzburg paper, with 10 staves.

K. 417*c* (Anh. 76). Fragmentary string quartet movement in D minor, 'supposedly originated in June 1783 in Vienna'. But this is on a leaf of a paper that Mozart seems first to have used when he had more or less finished the first two acts of *Figaro*, that is at the end of 1785; he used it quite often after that, in 1786, and occasionally later. (Cf. K. 587*a*/Anh. 74.)

K. 417*d*. Fragmentary string quartet movement in E minor, 'supposedly composed in June 1783 in Vienna'. But this is on a leaf of the paper also used for K. 405*a*—a paper that Mozart first used near the end of 1789 and mainly in 1790 and 1791. So perhaps this too may be associated with the Prussian String Quartets, which he finished in 1790.

K. 422. Fragmentary *L'oca del Cairo*, comic opera, 'composed in the second half of 1783 in Salzburg and Vienna'. The Act I Finale, No. 7 (in *NMA*, No. '6') is on a paper that I think Mozart did not use in Vienna until early in 1784 (unless he used it first for this autograph in December 1783).

K. 422*a* (Anh. 14). Kyrie fragment, 'supposedly composed in the summer of 1783 in Salzburg'. But this is on a leaf of a paper that Mozart first used at the end of 1787, and mainly in 1788, and occasionally later. We know that he wrote quite a lot of fragmentary church works in his last few Vienna years.

K. 424*a* (430). *Lo sposo deluso*, fragmentary comic opera, 'presumably composed in the second half of 1783 in Salzburg and Vienna'. But parts of the autograph score, with arias 2 and 3, are on a paper with a stave-rule that I think Mozart did not use till 1784 and the next years.

K. 425*a* (444). The Introduction to a symphony in G by Michael Haydn, 'probably composed at the beginning of November 1783 at Linz'. Yet the autograph score of the Introduction, the symphony's first movement, and the start of the second movement (the rest of the score was written by a copyist) is on a paper that Mozart first used in Vienna, from early in 1784.

K⁶ Anhang A 52 is part of the Finale of another symphony (in D) by Michael Haydn, and it is written on a paper made at Steyr near Linz. So if a Michael Haydn symphony was performed at Linz at the same time as the Mozartian 'Linz' Symphony, in Mozart's concert there, it may perhaps have been this other Michael Haydn symphony.

K. 426*a* (Anh. 44). Fragmentary Allegro in C minor for two pianos, 'supposedly composed in December 1783 in Vienna'. But this is on a paper that Mozart only used from the end of 1785 until the end of 1786.

K. 436, 437, 438, 439, and 439a (346), five Notturni for two sopranos and a bass, 'supposedly composed in 1783 in Vienna'. But the surviving autographs of their accompanying wind-instruments (and the vocal parts also for K. 437) are on a paper that Mozart did not use before 1787.

K. 441. 'Das Bandel', for soprano, tenor, and bass, with a string quartet accompaniment, 'supposedly composed in 1783 in Vienna'. Although someone has written on the first leaf of the autograph 'Wien 1783', the first two leaves have 16 staves. This is a paper type that Mozart probably bought at the very beginning of 1786, and wrote on 37 leaves of it the autograph of K. 491, the C minor piano concerto that was finished by 24 March 1786. (K. 491*a*/Anh. 62, a leaf with his first idea for the slow movement, is also on the same paper.) It seems as though these 40 leaves are in fact from a batch of 10 sheets of this paper. It would appear very likely that this score of 'Das Bandel' was written therefore in 1786, or possibly in 1787.

K. 442. Three fragmentary movements for a piano trio, in D minor, G major, and D major, 'supposedly composed in 1783 in Vienna'. It seems a great mistake to consider these to be fragmentary movements for the same work, for they were written at rather different times. The first fragment is on a paper that Mozart first used at the very end of 1785 mainly for work on the last two movements of *Figaro*; he used it later in 1786 and 1787, and even in 1791. The second fragment is on a paper first used from July 1786 until the middle of 1787, and once in 1791. The third fragment is on a paper used first in 1787, and sometimes in each year till 1791. So none of these fragments can have been written in 1783. And the handwriting of the three fragments does not suggest that they were written at about the same time; they were written at different times, probably during the years 1786 to 1788.

K. 447. Horn Concerto in E flat, 'supposedly composed in 1783 in Vienna'. The structure of this autograph is unusual (and possibly intended to be comical): the 11 leaves are of 8 different paper types, and are mostly single leaves—a structural feature that is not to be found in any other autographs. One of these papers is one that he first used for *Don Giovanni*, not before the late spring of 1787. So 1787 is the earliest possible date for this horn concerto.

K. 449. Piano Concerto in E flat. This was clearly finished by 9 February 1784. Yet the first 10 leaves are on a paper that he used almost only in the second half of 1782, and it seems that was when he wrote bars 1–170 on the leaves up to the end of fo. 9ʳ (the next 3 pages being left blank). Then these 10 leaves became a fragment; he used fo. 10^v for sketching an aria. But at the very end of 1783 or the beginning of 1784 he decided to resume work on the concerto, continuing the fragment, deleting the sketch, and adding new papers. The fact that the concerto had been begun in 1782 might explain why it employs a smaller orchestra than the other 1784 concertos.

K. **452*a*** (Anh. 54). Fragmentary piano and wind quintet in B flat, 'presumably composed in the spring of 1784 in Vienna'. The single leaf of this work has just come to light, and it is on a paper that was used several times in Vienna in 1783.

K. **458*a*** (Anh. 75). Fragmentary minuet in B flat for string quartet, 'presumably composed at the beginning of November 1784 in Vienna'. But this is a leaf of the much later paper which Mozart first used near the end of 1789 and mainly in 1790 and 1791. So perhaps this was written in 1790 for a planned Prussian Quartet.

K. **458*b*** (Anh. 71). Fragmentary string quartet movement in B flat, 'presumably composed at the beginning of November 1784 in Vienna'. But this is also a leaf of the much later paper which Mozart first used near the end of 1789 and mainly in 1790 and 1791. So perhaps this too was written in 1790 for a planned Prussian Quartet.

K. **459*a*** (Anh. 59). Fragmentary piano concerto movement in C, 'presumably composed in December 1784 in Vienna'. But this is more likely to be an idea for the slow movement of K. 453, finished by 12 April 1784, rather than for the slow movement of K. 459, finished by 11 December 1784. K. 453's slow movement and finale are on the *same* paper as this fragment.

K. **468**. *Gesellenreise* for voice and piano, dated by Mozart in his Thematic Catalogue '26 March 1785'. This is no doubt accurate, but the autograph is a single leaf of *Hochformat* (vertical format) paper with 14 staves, a paper that he bought and used quite often in Paris in 1778. As is said above, he used three other leaves of it for the March, K. 383*e* (408/1), which he apparently wrote in Vienna in 1782. The present leaf is probably from the same sheet as these other three leaves.

K. **468*a*** (429). Fragmentary cantata, 'perhaps composed in 1785 in Vienna'. The first six leaves are on a paper that Mozart first used at the very end of 1785, and then in 1786; and the other six leaves are on a paper that he first used in July 1786. So 1786 is a better date.

K. **479*a*** (477). *Maurische Trauermusik*, 'probably composed about 10 November 1785 in Vienna'. This is very likely, for the two masons had died on 6 and 7 November, and the service was held on 17 November. Confusion has been caused by Mozart's date in his Thematic Catalogue, 'July 1785', that is before the two masons had died. This was probably a faulty reference to a vocal version of the same work, which was apparently written in July 1785 and performed at a masonic ceremony on 12 August 1785.

K. **480*b*** (434). Fragmentary terzetto for tenor and two basses, 'presumably composed at the end of 1785 in Vienna'. Although Mozart had started to use this paper by the end of 1785, he used it mainly in 1786, and I think that this trio was written in 1786, after *Figaro*.

K. **484*b*** (Anh. 95). Fragmentary Allegro assai for two clarinets and three basset-horns, 'perhaps composed at the end of 1785 in Vienna'. But the leaf is on a paper that Mozart apparently did not use before 1786.

K. 484*c* (Anh. 93). Fragmentary Adagio for clarinet and three basset-horns, 'perhaps produced at the end of 1785 in Vienna'. But this leaf is on a paper that Mozart did not use before the very end of 1787, and mainly in 1788, and occasionally later.

K. 484*d* (410). Adagio for two basset-horns and bassoon, 'perhaps composed at the end of 1785 in Vienna'. Yet this leaf, with its particular stave-rule, is on a paper that Mozart nearly always used earlier, mainly in the second half of 1782.

K. 488. Piano Concerto in A, dated by Mozart in his Thematic Catalogue '2 March 1786'. Although this is very obviously when the work was finished, the first eight leaves are on a paper that was mainly used in 1784 and early in 1785. When Mozart first started K. 488 on these leaves, it was at a time when his orchestration did not include clarinets.

K. 494*a*. Fragmentary movement for a horn concerto, 'perhaps begun in July 1786 in Vienna'. It might have been a little earlier, in the second half of 1785—though July 1786 cannot be excluded as possible.

K. 495*a* (Anh. 52). Fragmentary piano trio movement in G, 'composed in Vienna, probably in June/July 1786'. The paper of this leaf, with its particular stave-rule, was never used by Mozart before 1787.

K. 497*a* (357). Fragmentary Allegro for piano with four hands, 'presumably composed in the late summer of 1786 in Vienna'. But this is on two leaves of a paper that Mozart first used at the very end of 1787, and very often in 1788, and occasionally later.

K. 500*a* (357). Fragmentary Andante for piano with four hands, 'composed before 4 November 1786 in Vienna'. But this is on three leaves of a paper that Mozart did not use before March 1791.

K. 501*a* (Anh. 51). Fragmentary piano trio movement in B flat, 'probably composed in November 1786 in Vienna'. Yet this is on a leaf of a paper that was mainly used in 1784 and early in 1785.

K. 502*a* (Anh. 60). Fragmentary piano concerto movement in C, 'composed in Vienna, presumably in November 1786'. Yet this too is on a leaf of a paper that was mainly used in 1784 and early in 1785. So this is likely to have been an idea for the early 1785 C major piano concerto, K. 467, not for K. 503. (And K. 467 has quite a bit of this paper.)

K. 503. Piano Concerto in C, dated by Mozart in his Thematic Catalogue '4 December 1786'. Although it is clear that this was when it was finished, it seems likely that the text on fos. 1–5 and fo. 7 was partly written in 1784 or early in 1785, because this was another paper that was used at that time.

K. 515*a* (Anh. 87). Fragmentary string quintet movement in F, 'probably composed in April 1787 in Vienna'. But this is on a leaf of a paper that Mozart did not use before March 1791.

K. 515*c* (Anh. 79). Fragmentary string quintet movement in A minor, 'presumably composed in May 1787 in Vienna'. But this is on two leaves of a paper that Mozart did not use before March 1791.

K. 516*b* (406). The String Quintet in C minor that is an arrangement of the wind serenade which he had written in 1782, K. 384*a* (388), 'probably arranged in the spring of 1787 in Vienna'. But ten of the autograph's thirteen leaves (fos. 3–11, 13) are of a paper that Mozart first used at the very end of 1787, and very often in 1788, and occasionally later. It seems probable that this C minor string quintet was finished early in 1788.

K. 516*c* (Anh. 91). Fragmentary quintet in B flat for clarinet and strings, 'presumably composed in the spring of 1787 in Vienna'. But the two leaves are of a later paper, which Mozart first used near the end of 1789 and mainly in 1790 and 1791.

K. 522. *Ein musikalischer Spass*, entered by Mozart in his Thematic Catalogue with the date of '14 June 1787'. That is obviously when it was finished, but it is possible that he started it before the end of 1785, or perhaps in 1786.[2]

K. 527. *Don Giovanni*, dated by Mozart in his Thematic Catalogue '28 October 1787'; it received its first performance, at Prague, the day after.[3]

K. 532. Fragmentary terzetto for soprano, tenor, and bass, 'supposedly composed in 1787 in Vienna'. This paper, with a stave-rule of 188.5 to 189^{-} mm., was used by Mozart in 1784 and 1785; he used the same paper, with a stave-rule of 187.5 to 188^{-} mm., in 1787. But the stave-rule of K. 532 is that of the earlier paper.

K. 535*b* (Anh. 107). Fragmentary contredanse for two violins, bass, flute, oboe, bassoon, and horn, 'presumably composed at the beginning of 1788 in Vienna'. This single leaf seems to be a quadrant (that has no watermark) of a paper that Mozart probably first used in about August 1789, and in 1790 and 1791.

K. 537. 'Coronation' Piano Concerto in D, dated by Mozart in his Thematic Catalogue '24 February 1788'. This is obviously when it was finished, but much of the concerto was partially written early in 1787.[4]

K. 537*a* (Anh. 57). Fragmentary piano concerto movement in D, 'presumably begun in February 1788 in Vienna'. But these two leaves are of a paper that Mozart almost always used from the end of 1785 until the end of 1786.

K. 537*b* (Anh. 61). Fragmentary piano concerto movement in D minor, 'presumably begun in February 1788 in Vienna'. But this is a leaf of a paper that was otherwise used by Mozart only at the very end of 1786.

K. 538. Aria for soprano, 'Ah se in ciel, benigne stelle', dated by Mozart in his Thematic Catalogue '4 March 1788'. The autograph also has this date, and is on the principal paper of 1788. Yet there is also a *particella* of this aria on a very much earlier paper; although the aria of 4 March 1788 was written for his sister-in-law Aloysia Lange, née Weber, it seems probable that the *particella* was written for her, still Aloysia Weber, in Munich at the end of 1778. So most of this aria was written about nine and a half years before the final version was produced.[5]

K. 546*a* (Anh. 47). Fragmentary sonata movement for piano and violin, 'presumably

[2] For my evidence, see *Mozart: Studies of the Autograph Scores*, 234–45.

[3] For my discussion of the order in which the sections were written, see 'Some Features of the Autograph Score of *Don Giovanni*', *Israel Studies in Musicology*, 5 (1990), 7–26.

[4] For the evidence, see my introduction to the Dover facsimile edn. of the autograph (New York, 1991).

[5] For my evidence, see *Mozart: Studies of the Autograph Scores*, 28–9 or 232–3.

composed in June 1788 in Vienna'. But this leaf is on a paper that Mozart first used near the end of 1789 and mainly in 1790 and 1791.

K. **560**. Canon for four voices in F major, dated by Mozart in his Thematic Catalogue '2 September 1788'. Stefan Zweig's autograph, listed in K[6], does not have these words, but those listed in K. 559*a*. The autograph that does have K. 560 words is the one that was owned by the late Professor Otto Winkler, although it is not in F major but in G major; and its paper suggests that it was not written in 1788 but in 1783.

K. **562*a***. Canon for four voices in B flat, listed among the productions of 1788. But it is on a paper that was mainly used by Mozart with the same stave-rule in 1785 and perhaps very occasionally in 1786 and 1787.

K. **562*e*** (Anh. 66). Fragmentary trio for violin, viola, and violoncello, 'supposedly composed in September 1788 in Vienna'. But its two leaves are on two different later papers, both first used fairly near the end of 1789, and in 1790 and 1791.

K. **580*b*** (Anh. 90). Fragmentary quintet in F for clarinet, basset-horn, violin, viola, and violoncello, 'presumably composed in September 1789 in Vienna'. But it is on two papers which both have stave-rules that were used mainly in 1787.

K. **581*a*** (Anh. 88). Fragmentary quintet for clarinet, two violins, viola, and bass, 'perhaps composed in September 1789 or later, in Vienna'. The first theme is that of Ferrando's aria No. 24 in *Così fan tutte*. The autograph is on a paper that Mozart used from late 1789 until 1791, so it is likely that the quintet borrows from *Così*, rather than *vice versa*. This would suggest that 1790 is the earliest possible date.

K. **587*a*** (Anh. 74). Fragmentary string quartet movement in G minor, 'presumably composed at the end of 1789 in Vienna'. This leaf is on a paper that Mozart first used near the end of 1785 to continue his work on *Figaro* (after he had already written most of the first two acts). He used it afterwards in 1786 and 1787, and for four leaves of *Die Zauberflöte* in 1791. It may be that the present leaf had a fragment of a string quartet written perhaps in 1786 or 1787, which he kept for possible use in a Prussian Quartet, but then he decided to reject it, and wrote on the same leaf a sketch for the canonic passage in the Act II Finale of *Così fan tutte*. So he used this leaf at the *very* end of 1789 (or the first days of 1790), but the string quartet fragment may possibly have been written two or three years earlier.

K. **588*b*** (236). Andantino for piano, the theme (for variations?) of the aria 'Non vi turbate, no' from Gluck's opera *Alceste*, '1790 in Vienna' (date not in K[6], but in K[3]). This autograph is a small part of a leaf, with only 5 staves (not 6 staves, as is said in K[6]—a description of its appearance in a corrupt facsimile!), of a paper that Mozart first used in 1782, and also in 1783 and 1784. It seems very likely that Mozart wrote this theme by Gluck in order to play variations at a concert (with Gluck present) in the spring of 1783.

K. **589*a*** (Anh. 68). Fragmentary string quartet movement in B flat, 'presumably composed in May or June 1790 in Vienna'. This leaf is of a paper that Mozart first used in 1782, and then in 1783 and 1784; so perhaps it may be associated with work on the 'Haydn' Quartets.

K. **590*a*** (Anh. 29), K. **590*b*** (Anh. 30), and K. **590*c*** (Anh. 37). Three fragmentary piano sonata movements in F, 'presumably composed in June 1790 in Vienna'. As all the three are on single leaves of a paper that Mozart first used at the very end of 1787, and very often after that in 1788, and sometimes in 1789, it is just possible that these fragments were written about a year or two earlier.

K. 592*b* (Anh. 83). Fragmentary string quintet movement in D, 'composed in Vienna, probably at the end of 1790'. This is a leaf of a paper that Mozart first used at the very end of 1787, and very often after that in 1788, and sometimes in 1789. So it is possible that this fragment was written earlier.

K. 595. Piano Concerto in B flat, dated by Mozart in his Thematic Catalogue '5 January 1791'. Although the last 12 leaves are of a paper that Mozart first used in the second half of 1789, and then in 1790 and 1791, the first 38 leaves are on the paper that he first used at the very end of 1787, and very often after that in 1788, and sometimes in 1789. I wonder whether Mozart wrote some of this concerto's first movement, and perhaps a little of the slow movement, and the beginning of the finale, in 1788 or 1789, but completed it much later.

K. 609. Five contredanses for two violins, bass, flute, and trumpet, 'presumably composed in 1791 in Vienna'. These three leaves are of a paper with a stave-rule that was used by Mozart almost entirely in 1787. So this autograph must be a few years earlier.

K. 610. A contredanse for two violins, bass, two flutes, and two horns, called 'Les filles malicieuses', entered by Mozart (without details of its scoring) in his Thematic Catalogue with the date of '6 March 1791'. But perhaps this date was for his *final* version of this work. For it was included, with somewhat different scoring, as 'No. 5' in K. 609. Moreover, the autograph of K. 610, with the scoring listed here, is on a leaf with 10 staves, being a paper that he used during his visit to Salzburg in the second half of 1783. So the two autograph versions that we have of K. 610 should probably be dated 1783 and 1787; perhaps Mozart produced a third version in March 1791?

K. 613*a* (Anh. 81). Fragmentary string quintet movement in E flat, 'composed in Vienna, probably in April 1791'. These two leaves are on a paper that with this stave-rule was mainly used by Mozart at the end of 1784 and in 1785. So perhaps this fragment is really much earlier?

K. 613*b* (Anh. 82). Fragmentary string quintet movement in E flat, 'composed in Vienna, probably in April 1791'. This is on a paper with a stave-rule that Mozart used in 1786 and 1787, and once in 1790.

K. 620. *Die Zauberflöte*. This was entered by Mozart in his Thematic Catalogue in July 1791, with the later added statement that it was performed on 30 September 1791. On 28 September he put in another entry, for 'the priests' march' and for 'the overture', two numbers written almost two months after most of the rest. But there are also three second-act numbers (Nos. 16, 17, and 19) on the same late paper on which he wrote the overture, and also a draft for the priests' march. So these three second-act numbers were apparently also finished at the end of September, though perhaps they were just revised versions of what he had completed in July, and so not entered again in his catalogue.

K. 620*b* (Anh. 78). A contrapuntal study, 'probably made in September 1791 in

Vienna'. This leaf, with this stave-rule, is a paper that was used by Mozart in 1782, and once in 1785.

K. 621. *La clemenza di Tito*. This was entered by Mozart in his Thematic Catalogue on 5 September 1791, with the statement that it was performed at Prague on 6 September.[6]

K. 621*a* (Anh. 245). Aria for bass, 'supposedly composed in September 1791 in Prague'. The surviving leaf of the autograph is not of a Prague paper but of the paper that he first used on his arrival in Vienna from Prague (after *Don Giovanni*) in December 1787, and then frequently in 1788.

K. 621*b*. Fragmentary basset-horn concerto in G, 'probably composed in 1791 in Vienna'. The melody shows that this is an early version (in a different key) of the October 1791 clarinet concerto in A major, K. 622. But this basset-horn concerto's twelve leaves are on two rather earlier papers; so was this fragment perhaps written in about 1787?

[6] For the evidence for the chronology of all its numbers, see *Mozart: Studies of the Autograph Scores*, 48–60.

Mozart's Last and Beethoven's First: Echoes of K. 551 in the First Movement of Opus 21

CARL SCHACHTER

INTRODUCTION

BEETHOVEN's First Symphony might seem to have little in common with the 'Jupiter' except for features so general as to be meaningless: both are symphonies, both are in C, and both have slow movements in F marked 'Andante cantabile' (Beethoven adds 'con moto'). Yet a close study of their first movements reveals an intriguing similarity in the tonal plans of their development sections. The similar feature is a rather unusual modulatory progression, and Beethoven's realization of it resembles Mozart's in many details as well as in its larger structure. The modulation is unusual enough, and the resemblance close enough, to suggest that the Mozart work was a direct influence on Beethoven and to reduce the likelihood that the similarity is mere coincidence.[1] The movements also contain other points of resemblance, though none so significant. The most striking is the use of similar melodic figures as prominent motivic elements in the opening theme of the two expositions: both themes contain a reiterated rising fourth G–C in up-beat rhythm (Ex. 1). Unlike the modulatory plan, these up-beat flourishes are stock figures which might appear in a thousand other pieces as well, but taken together with the modulation they add to the family resemblance. (Even the shared C major has perhaps a significance as part of a complex of similarities that it would lack as an isolated feature.)

[1] We can safely assume that Beethoven knew the 'Jupiter'. Although the score was not published until *c.*1810, the Viennese music dealer Johann Traeg had advertised manuscript copies of the symphony as early as 1792 (describing the work as 'one of [Mozart's] last works and among his masterpieces'), while the Offenbach publisher Johann Anton André had issued the first edition of the parts in 1793; for Traeg, see Alexander Weinmann, *Die Anzeigen des Kopiaturbetriebes Johann Traeg in der Wiener Zeitung zwischen 1782 und 1805* (Vienna, 1981), 35. The symphony was frequently played in Vienna during the 1790s, and early reviews regularly described it as 'well known'. See, for example, *Allgemeine musikalische Zeitung*, 3 (1800), 27, where the 'Jupiter', G minor, and E flat symphonies are already regarded, at least implicitly, as an important trilogy; and *AmZ*, 10 (1808), 495, where K. 551 is described as a 'classic'. For other views of the work, see Stefan Kunze, *Wolfgang Amadeus Mozart. Sinfonie in C-Dur KV 551. Jupiter Sinfonie* (Munich, 1988), 129–33. In any case, it is inconceivable to me that Beethoven would not have familiarized himself with Mozart's last symphony, a work that in some ways anticipates his own direction as a symphonist—in the intensity and seriousness of the Andante, for example, and the climactic character of the Finale. Even if he had no access to a copy of the score, Beethoven would surely have been able to assimilate much of the music by ear; and he could have supplemented his listening by a perusal of the parts. That he dedicated his symphony to Baron van Swieten proves nothing, of course, but it is suggestive of Beethoven's artistic links with Mozart and, in particular, with Mozart the contrapuntist.

EXAMPLE 1*a*. Mozart, Symphony K. 551, I, m. 1

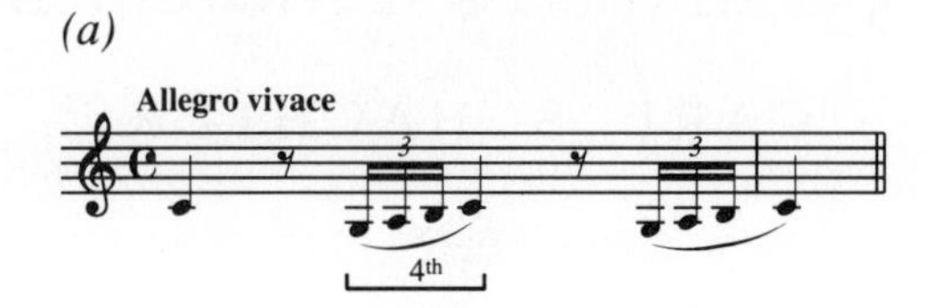

EXAMPLE 1*b*. Beethoven, Symphony No. 1, I, mm. 13–15

I shall begin this study by examining the two passages that I consider related. The larger contexts of the passages are not at all similar, and I shall therefore proceed to a discussion of the two development sections in their entirety. I shall then widen the focus to encompass the movements as wholes, concentrating on other similarities, especially the motivic resemblance shown in Ex. 1. Finally, I shall consider some of the broader implications of my ideas about the pieces, referring briefly to other works by Mozart, Haydn, and Schubert that use modulatory techniques related to those in the 'Jupiter' and the Beethoven First.

MOZART: THE MODULATORY PROGRESSION

Let us begin by looking at the similar passages in the two development sections, starting with the Mozart. Ex. 2 contains a middleground reduction of mm. 121–57, the development's opening phase; the reduction should be studied together with the score. The dotted barlines in the graph show the five main subdivisions of this passage; I have numbered the subdivisions to make discussion easier to follow. The G major close of the exposition quickly gives way to an E♭ transposition of the initial theme of the third or closing group, mm. 123–32 equalling mm. 101–10 of the exposition (see number 1 of the graph). A modulatory passage follows, based on a fragmentation of the theme's cadential tag (number 2). The theme itself could come out of a comic opera—which in fact it does, for it is drawn from the aria 'Un bacio di mano', composed by Mozart for insertion in Pasquale Anfossi's *Le gelosie fortunate*, which was performed in Vienna in June 1788, a few months before the 'Jupiter' was composed.[2] But its development quickly leaves the

[2] The symphony quotes part of the aria almost note for note; for purposes of easy identification, I shall refer to this tune as the *buffo* theme.

Example 2. Mozart, Symphony K. 551, I, development to m. 157

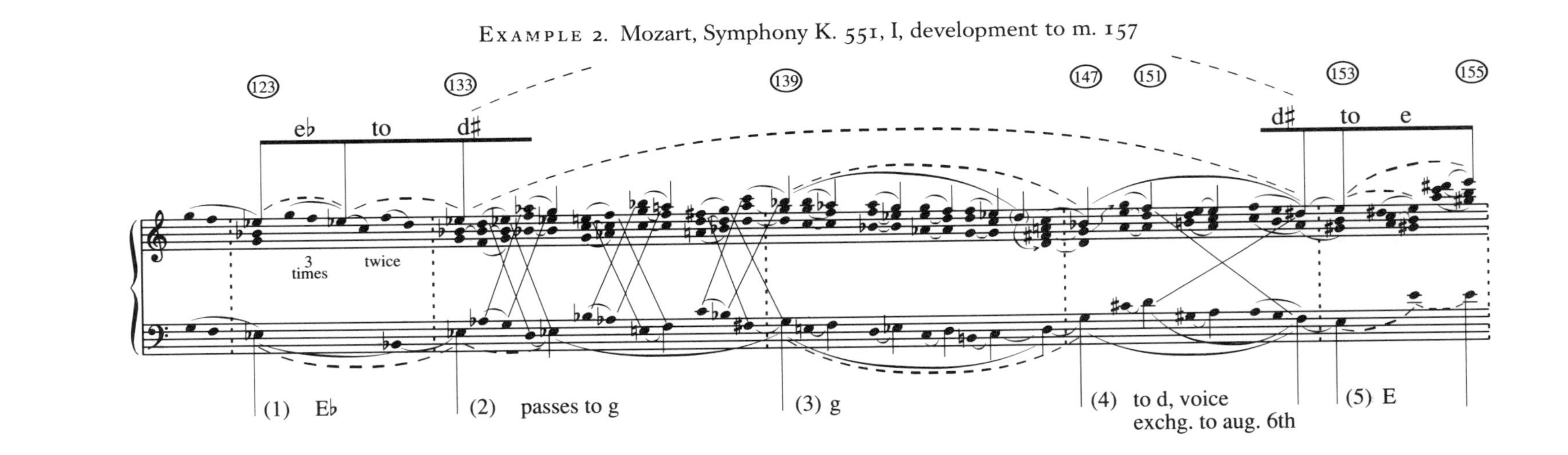

drawing-room to embark upon a strenuous tonal voyage, propelled by close imitative counterpoint that is filled with conflicting accents and coloured by rapid tonal fluctuations.

The ultimate goal of this passage, and the first point of arrival after the E♭ major, is an extended E major triad that begins at m. 153 and persists through m. 157 (number 5). This harmony, though clearly an important landmark, is not stated as a local tonic. Instead, it takes on the colour of a dominant, an impression that results in large measure from the augmented sixth F–D♯ that resolves into it (m. 152). As it happens, no A minor goal materializes, so the E chord turns out not to function as a dominant in any very meaningful way; it leads, rather, to an F major 'false recapitulation' that forms the focal point of the whole development section.

The engine of this motion from a tonicized E♭ major to a seemingly 'dominantized' E major is the augmented sixth on F, whose D♯ sustains the *sound* of the initial E♭, but with an altered tonal *function* that directs it into a resolution on E. Perhaps more than any earlier master, Mozart was drawn to such enharmonic transformations, and the unprecedented richness and scope of his large structures owe much to the connections between distant areas that enharmonicism effects. Immediate enharmonic transformations are easy to recognize, and Mozart's penchant for them was recognized (and criticized) at least once in his own time. I refer to Giuseppe Sarti's strictures on two of Mozart's quartets, specifically to the first movement development of K. 421 (417b), where a seventh F–E♭ is reinterpreted as an augmented sixth in order to resolve to the V of A minor.[3] Harder to spot, but even more interesting, are long-range enharmonics like this one, where the D♯ is separated from the E♭ by intervening material, but where the reinterpreted sound none the less forms the path between point of departure and goal. Music analysts have become aware of these big enharmonic adjustments (together with many other elements of large structure) only since Schenker pointed them out, but the ability to hear them certainly formed part of the technical equipment of the great Classical and Romantic masters.[4]

Occupying the space between the E♭ major and the augmented sixth on F is a complicated and intense passage that touches upon several key areas in its course, but that centres on only one of them: G minor. As upper third of E♭, and sharing two common tones with it, the G minor helps to keep its sound alive. At first (number 2) E♭ rises to G through a passing F, each step elaborated by applied chords and voice-exchanges. A descending passage (number 3) balances the preceding rise; despite fleeting toniciza-

[3] See 'Auszug aus dem Sarti'schen Manuscripte, worin Mozart bitter getadelt wird', *Allgemeine musikalische Zeitung*, 34 (6 June 1832), 373–8. The article cites Sarti's own title for the essay as 'Esame acustico fatto sopra due frammenti di Mozart'. If the essay is authentic (which is probable, though not entirely certain), it is contemporary with Mozart even though published long after his death, for Sarti had died in 1802. See the very interesting article by William J. Mitchell, 'Giuseppe Sarti and Mozart's Quartet, K. 421', *Current Musicology*, 9 (1969), 147–53.

[4] See Schenker's reading of the 3rd movement development of Beethoven's Op. 10 No. 2 in *Free Composition*, trans. and ed. Ernst Oster (New York, 1979), Figs. 62/11 and 100/4*a*. The enharmonic transformation that he shows is not without similarity to the one discussed here.

tions, it serves to prolong G minor. At the end of its prolongation, G minor becomes the IV of a fleeting D minor (mm. 149–51, number 4), whose function it is to give the augmented sixth local preparation through a chromaticized voice-exchange: D and F in m. 151 become F and D♯ at the end of 152, and the A minor in between is a passing chord within the voice-exchange. Thus the G minor, linked to E♭ through common tones and to the augmented sixth through the D minor that prepares it, eases the drastic move from a temporary E♭ tonic to an E major that would seem to be the V of a putative A minor. One could hardly imagine a tonal process whose outcome appears less predetermined and yet sounds so inevitable once it arrives. The goal thus reached turns out to be only a temporary halt within a much larger motion, but before we go on to its continuation, let us turn to the Beethoven passage.

BEETHOVEN: THE MODULATORY PROGRESSION

Example 3 shows a middleground reduction of mm. 144–60, where a tonicized E♭ major moves to an E major goal, just as in the Mozart: in both works, an augmented sixth on F (with D♯ as enharmonic transformation of E♭) ushers in the E. And—again as in the Mozart—the E major is extended (until m. 173) in the manner of a dominant preparation for an arrival on A minor. In contrast to the Mozart, however, the passage forms the culmination of the development rather than its initial phase, and the E major here is linked directly to the C major of the recapitulation by a connecting arpeggio on V/7 of C.

EXAMPLE 3. Beethoven, Symphony No. 1, I, mm. 144–60

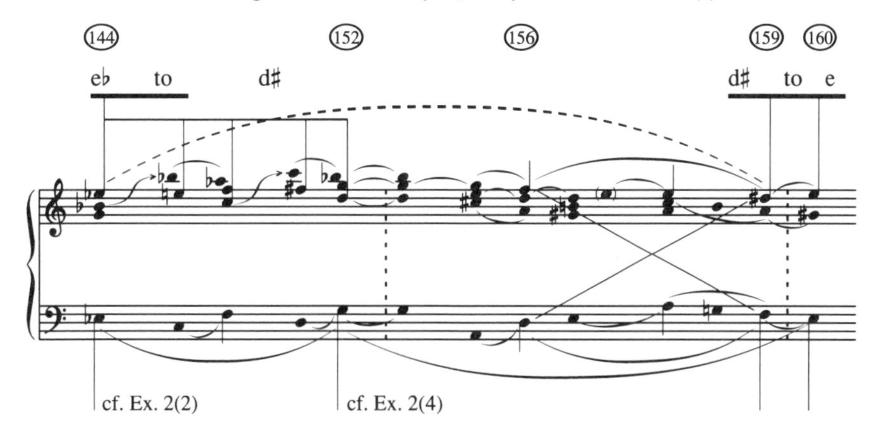

The similarity to the Mozart extends to the way the modulation is organized. Note that there is a rising motion to G minor, much like Mozart's, and a transition—also like Mozart's—from G minor to the E major chord by means of D minor and a chromaticized voice-exchange filled in by an A minor passing chord. Measures 144–52 correspond to 129–39 of the Mozart, and mm. 152–60 to 147–53; m. 159 of the Beethoven sounds almost like a quotation of Mozart's m. 152, with identical material in the bassoons and second oboe. Nothing in the Beethoven, however, resembles Mozart's complex prolongation of G minor, and indeed the entire passage is simpler and less emotionally fraught.

MOZART AND BEETHOVEN: VOICE-LEADING STRUCTURE

In both symphonies, the move to the E major chord arises out of similar contrapuntal procedures: V supporting $\hat{2}$ (at the end of the exposition) is the originating point of a chromatic rise in the upper voice counterpointed by a diatonic descent in the bass. The progression results in a passing augmented sixth, and it often occurs in unprolonged form, as in the opening of the development section of Haydn's great E♭ sonata, first movement. I have quoted this fragment in Ex. 4*a*, but transposed to C to facilitate comparison with the symphonies. This device can form the basis of the most varied passages of harmonic transition; two remarkable C major examples from Mozart—both quite different from the 'Jupiter'—are the first-movement developments of the 'Dissonance' Quartet (end of exposition to m. 121) and the Piano Trio, K. 548 (end of exposition to m. 87). The prolongation of E♭ major in the two symphony movements stabilizes the chromatic passing-note of the upper voice, but transformed enharmonically. This procedure relates to, and probably derives from, the very common technique of preparing a seventh as a diatonic consonance, usually an octave or tenth.[5] Example 4*b*

EXAMPLE 4. Examples of the passing augmented sixth
(*a*) after Haydn
(*b*) 8 prepares 7
(*c*) 8 prepares ♯6; cf. K. 551

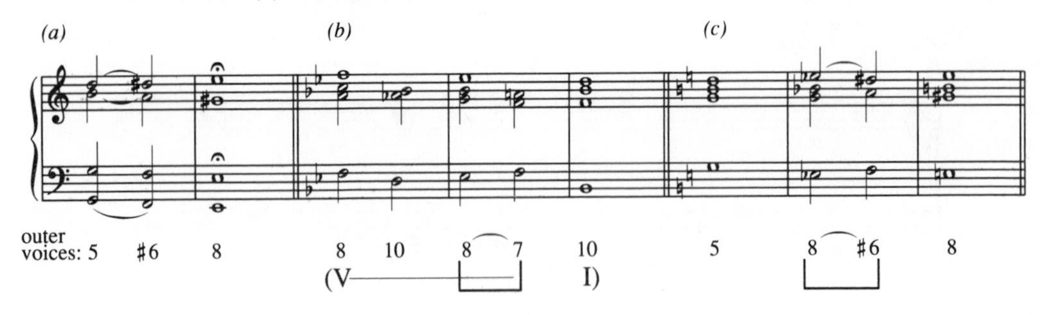

[5] Oswald Jonas gives a good account of this technique in his *Introduction to the Theory of Heinrich Schenker*, trans. and ed. John Rothgeb (New York, 1982), 100–3. Readers unfamiliar with Schenkerian theory might be puzzled by my giving so much weight to the augmented sixths—chords generally regarded as purely local chromatic embellishments—and correspondingly less weight to some key areas. One of the great strengths of Schenker's approach, in my opinion, is his tendency to regard music as shaped not only by stable elements (like key areas) but also by dynamic elements like dissonant and chromatic sonorities. The evaluation in each case depends upon context. Readers might wish to consult two of my articles that touch upon this issue: 'Analysis by Key: Another Look at Modulation', *Music Analysis*, 6 (1987), 289–318, esp. 292–304, and 'The

shows how an F seventh chord might be so introduced within a larger prolongation of V in B♭. The E♭ to F/7 (contrapuntally 8–7) corresponds to the E♭ to F/A6 of the symphony passages (shown in reduction as Ex. 4*c*), but the effect could not be more contrasting: on the one hand, simple diatonic relationships under the direct control of the B♭ tonic; and, on the other, a vastly expanded tonal domain in which two distant regions become conjoined through the enharmonic association.

MOZART: THE DEVELOPMENT AS A WHOLE

The salient difference in the contexts of these passages is that the Mozart continues on to new goals within the development, whereas Beethoven links his E major chord directly to the recapitulatory tonic. As mentioned earlier, Mozart leads the E major of m. 153 to an F major statement of the opening theme, and the F, based on a neighbour-note harmony, moves to the structural G (V of C) that forms at once the development's culmination and the retransition into the recapitulation. The large-scale upper-voice motion is sketched in Ex. 5; it is a rising fourth from D to G, made stepwise by the E and F of the E major and F major chords of mm. 153 and 161, and intensified chromatically by E♭/D♯ (mm. 123–52) and by F♯ in 178. Mozart composes this rising fourth-progression with an Olympian grandeur that by itself would justify the symphony's nickname;[6] the motion spans some sixty bars from the end of the exposition to the

EXAMPLE 5. Mozart, Symphony K. 551, I, development: large-scale upper voice motion

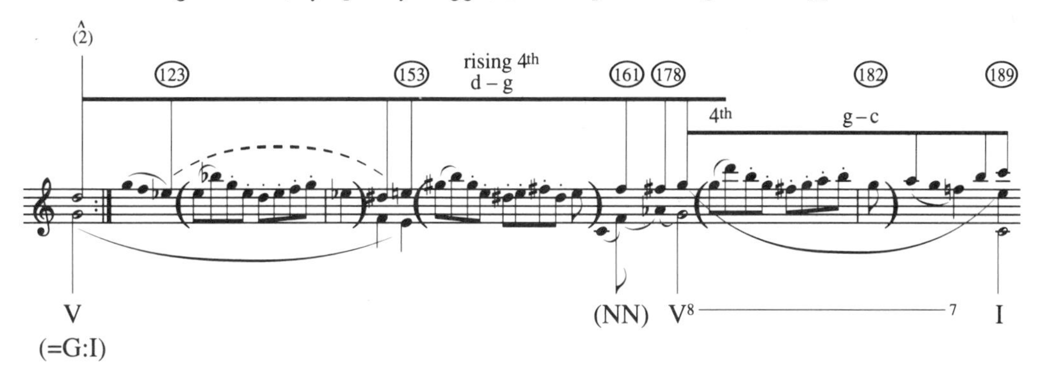

First Movement of Brahms's Second Symphony: The Opening Theme and its Consequences,' *Music Analysis*, 2 (1983), 62–7.

[6] Tovey devotes a fair amount of space in his rather skimpy essay on the 'Jupiter' to ridiculing the nickname, largely, it would seem, because he regards Mozart's artistic personality as Greek rather than Roman. See Donald Francis Tovey, *Essay in Musical Analysis*, i (London, 1935), 195–8. I do not set very much store by the name, but I imagine that most people understand it as referring to the undeniable scope, power, and majesty of the work rather than to any specifically Roman character. It is curious, however, that the overture to *La clemenza di Tito*—an opera with a Roman theme—should in fact resemble the first movement of the 'Jupiter' in more than one feature. It is in the same key; there is an almost identical triplet flourish spanning a

arrival on G in m. 181. At three crucial points, the upper voice quotes the 'buffo' theme's closing tag, and these citations, each one higher than the last, constitute a chain of associations that make the large-scale ascent perceptible to the listener despite the long, eventful, and complex intervening passages. The retransition adds a seventh to the dominant pedal and simultaneously leads into the C of the recapitulation with another rising fourth, G–A–B–C—a wheel within a wheel.

Example 6*a* shows a chordal reduction of the entire development, enabling us to view the section from the F major 'false recapitulation' to the goal dominant. In it we can see that the F major connects to the V chord through an augmented sixth A♭–F♯ that constitutes a chromaticized F chord, made active in the direction of G; thus the augmented sixth is the end-point of an F prolongation. Between the F and its chromatic alteration is a tonicized A minor that functions as upper third of F, much like the earlier G minor that was upper third of E♭. The reduction of the opening part of the development shows the parallelism between the G minor and A minor episodes, a parallelism that extends to the affective character of the two passages and even to the intervallic structure of the outer-voice counterpoint (see the brackets under the figures between the staves.) Functionally, the two upper thirds are analogous but not equivalent: the G minor occurs between a chromatic sound and its enharmonic transformation, the A minor between a diatonic sound and its chromatic alteration.

EXAMPLE 6*a*. Mozart, Symphony K. 551, I, development: chordal reduction

The motion from F to A is shown in 6*b*, at numbers 1 and 2. Like the E♭ to G earlier on, it forms a rising sequential progression through a third, but this through three 'dominant' seventh chords (on C as V of F, through a passing D, to E as V of A). Such a procedure entails the threat of parallel and unresolved sevenths, and of fifths as well.

G–C fourth (but in thirty-seconds, not sixteenths); there are similarities of sound and character in the opening theme; and, most significantly, there are related chromatic and enharmonic procedures in the development (see below, 'Three Related Works'). So perhaps Johann Peter Salomon was on to something, if it really was he who invented the nickname. For an interesting account of the origin of the sobriquet 'Jupiter', see Neal Zaslaw, *Mozart's Symphonies: Context, Performance Practice, Reception* (Oxford, 1989), 441–2.

EXAMPLE 6*b*. Mozart, Symphony K. 551, I, development: F major to goal V

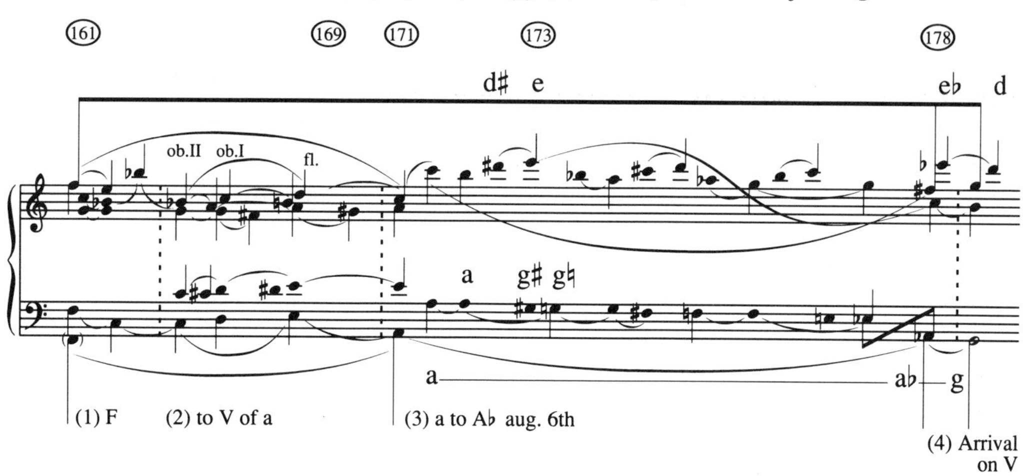

Mozart averts this danger through a most remarkable use of 'reaching over'; each seventh resolves to the fifth of the next chord, whose seventh enters in a new upper voice assigned to another instrument (the three sevenths are given to second oboe, first oboe, and flute respectively). Although the dissonances resolve contrapuntally, only the last seventh chord moves to an expected harmonic goal, and the effect is strangely disorienting. This passage, incidentally, derives from mm. 5–8, the 'answer' or consequent part of the opening phrase. At the beginning these measures provide the movement's first harmonic closure; at three later points, however, precisely this idea is used to open up the structure to wider horizons: mm. 28–37 (exposition bridge), 216–25 (recapitulation bridge), and this passage.

Number 3 of Ex. 6*b* presents the motion from A minor to the A♭ augmented sixth. With its syncopated rhythms and pervasive chromaticism, it is the most conflicted passage of the entire development: the path to the final V is a steep one. In the course of this development, two chromatic sounds have taken on special importance: E♭/D♯ and G♯ (as third of the E chord). Both of these sounds are now incorporated into the augmented sixth and resolved into the goal dominant: A♭ (enharmonic of G♯) moves to G in the bass, and E♭ moves to D in the flute and violins (the parallel fifths inherent in this progression are displaced by the free rhythms of Mozart's setting, but the E♭–D resolution is unmistakable—see especially the flute and first violin parts in mm. 178–80). Note the prominent D♯–E of mm. 172–3 (especially the flute and two violin parts), which recalls the big E♭/D♯–E motion of the development's initial phase. Even more remarkable is the bass-line, which descends by whole tone through the tritone A–E♭. The E♭ 'goal' becomes part of the augmented sixth, moves up three octaves, and ultimately resolves into the D of the V chord. It is perhaps not an accident that the first chromatic move in this bass—A-G♯-G (mm. 171–3) foreshadows the A-A♭-G of the inclusive structure.

BEETHOVEN: THE DEVELOPMENT AS A WHOLE

Example 7*a* contains a synoptic sketch of the Beethoven development, showing the larger context of the E♭-D♯ enharmonic. As a whole, the bass-line of the development moves down from the structural V before the double bar through III♯ (the E major chord) to the recapitulatory I.[7] The upper voice proceeds from D through E♭/D♯ to an E (over III♯) that anticipates the recapitulatory $\hat{3}$ (which, incidentally, does not appear at the beginning of the recapitulation, but only at the *ff* of m. 196). The arpeggiated V/7 of mm. 174–7 is not a harmonic goal, but rather a link connecting III♯ and I; in addition it fulfils an important motivic function, as we shall see presently.

EXAMPLE 7*a*. Beethoven, Symphony No. 1, I, development: general plan

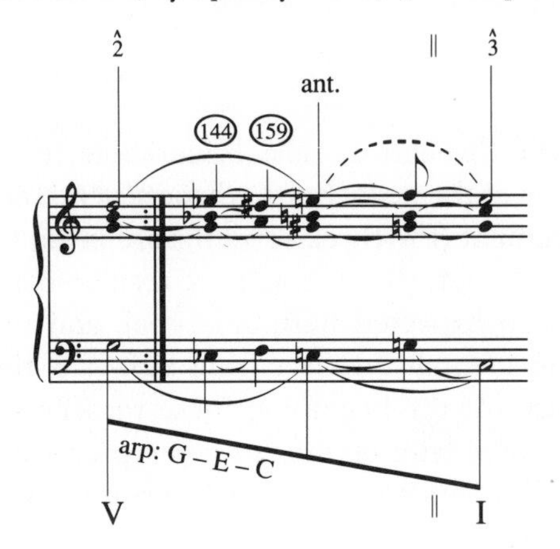

Example 7*b* is a more detailed account of the development up to the arrival on E♭ of m. 144; the reader can complete the picture by referring to Exx. 3 and 7*a*. In the Beethoven, the E♭ major key area appears midway through the development and marks a pivotal point in the design, comparable to the F major 'false recapitulation' in the Mozart.[8] Between the structural V (G major) that closes the exposition and the E♭ arrival of the development occurs a fairly lengthy harmonic transition whose function it is, at least in part, to make the E♭ sould like a goal. This transition is characterized by root progressions falling in fifths—the simplest harmonic device for creating the sense of goal-

[7] This downward arpeggiation (V-III♯-I) occurs frequently in major-mode development sections of the Classical period. See my 'Analysis by Key: Another Look at Modulation', 296–8; see also David Beach, 'A Recurring Pattern in Mozart's Music', *Journal of Music Theory*, 27 (1983), 1–29.

[8] Exactly midway, in fact. The section contains 68 measures (mm. 110–78), and the E♭ appears in m. 144, 34 measures after the beginning and 34 measures before the recapitulation.

EXAMPLE 7*b*. Beethoven, Symphony No. 1, I, development: mm. 110–44

oriented motion. Its first phase begins with the surprising A major 6/3 that interrupts an expected motion from G to C. The chain of falling fifths that ensues does, in fact, bring back G and lead it to C, but to C minor, not major.

A new phase begins with the C minor, continuing the move by falling fifths to B♭ as V of the goal E♭: C–F–B♭ and finally E♭. A long (8-measure) halt on B♭ makes the E♭ an unmistakable goal. The harmonies—C minor, F minor, B♭ major, and E♭ major—constitute a key-defining progression in E♭, in contrast to the triads falling in fifths before the C minor, which do not belong as diatonic elements to any one key. I read the progression as a kind of auxiliary cadence in E♭: VI–(II)–V–I, with the II subordinate to the VI and V.

MOZART: THE RISING FOURTH

Both development sections respond to tonal impulses composed into the music from the opening bars and continued throughout the expositions. Heard in context, the similar passages take on quite different meanings, and these meanings relate to the initial impulses of the movements. In the Mozart, the line of a rising fourth, first heard in the unison triplet sixteenths of m. 1, becomes a basic motivic element; I believe that the huge rising fourth of the development's upper line (as shown in Ex. 5) ultimately derives from it. Of course the mere coexistence of two rising fourths does not necessarily imply a relationship, especially when the first is a mere conventional flourish lasting less than a beat and the second a middleground structure that spans some sixty measures. But the further course of Mozart's exposition, especially in the G major part, reveals the fourth to be more than a cliché used for rhythmic emphasis: it becomes a basic, pervasive, and prominent element of the design, and it already begins to spread over larger spans of time. When the first motivic figure in a piece has exactly the same contour as important design elements later on, I find it counter-productive to disregard the resemblance, despite even considerable differences in rhythm and tonal context.

A fourth from G to C naturally tends to suggest C as a tonic, and it is of course in the context of C major that the motif appears. Mozart's strategy in the second part of the exposition is to repeat these pitches at their original levels—that is as G–A–B–C—but to do so in the local context of G major. The literature contains many instances of basic pitch-successions that persist untransposed through changes of key; and we shall observe two of them in the Beethoven symphony. Because it tends to define its upper note as a tonic, a perfect fourth is a very difficult interval to use in this way, but Mozart succeeds brilliantly.[9] The main melodic motion of the G major section is a descending fifth from D (established over V of V in mm. 49–55) to G (arrived at definitively in mm. 107–11); as often happens, several ancillary fifth-descents branch off from this main one. Mozart reconciles the rising fourth with the G major key in several ways: he expresses it as a motion within IV, as a bass-line rising from I to IV, as a motion out of the inner voice leading to the C of the descending fifth, etc. Example 8 is a graph of the G major part of the exposition (mm. 55–117), showing the rising-fourth motif in its various manifestations.

The first manifestation is more hinted at than expressed literally. The initial G major idea (the 'second theme' of conventional analysis) is composed as a kind of duet, with the bass imitating the fragmentary chromatic line intoned by the violins. As number 1 shows, these measures contain as emphasized pitches G, A, B, and C, though divided between voices and broken up in register. I do not infer a linear continuity in the background here, but only elements of one, waiting to be joined together. Yet hearing at least a potential association among these pitches is less arbitrary than it might at first seem. The violin figure and its imitation in the bass cohere because of their identical melodic and rhythmic shapes. That already suggests a rising third G–A–B. And the C of m. 60, though not connected to the B, would in fact form its most normal continuation, given the V/7 harmony; in the consequent phrase, as we can see, Mozart leads this passage to a 4/2 chord (m. 67), whose bass note (C) does in fact continue the B. This theme is remarkable in many ways, not least of them the tendency of the bass to centre on B, not G, so the local tonic is expressed as a 6/3 chord. At first, the top voice centres on G, as it must if the G–A–B–C motif is to be inferred; the G represents the inner voice of a polyphonic melody. The structural D makes its first appearance in m. 68, and it initiates a rapid preliminary descent to G.

The 'duet' continues into a second strain that sounds at first like a codetta (number 2). D recurs in m. 73, though the cadence in m. 75 permits us to believe for a moment that we are simply reinforcing the G. A varied repetition of this strain, however, makes us

[9] I discuss the technique of retaining the exact pitches of a motif in changed tonal surroundings in my article 'Beethoven's Sketches for the First Movement of Op. 14, No. 1: A Study in Design', *Journal of Music Theory*, 26 (1982), 1–21. Like Mozart in the 'Jupiter', Beethoven tried to incorporate a rising fourth 5–6–7–8 into the V area of this exposition, but he did not succeed to his satisfaction, and he eventually gave up the attempt.

Example 8. Mozart, Symphony K. 551, I, mm. 55–117 (G major part of exposition)

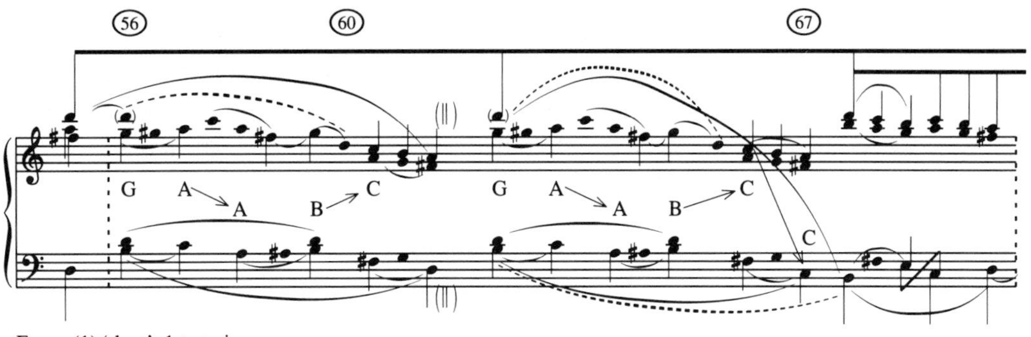

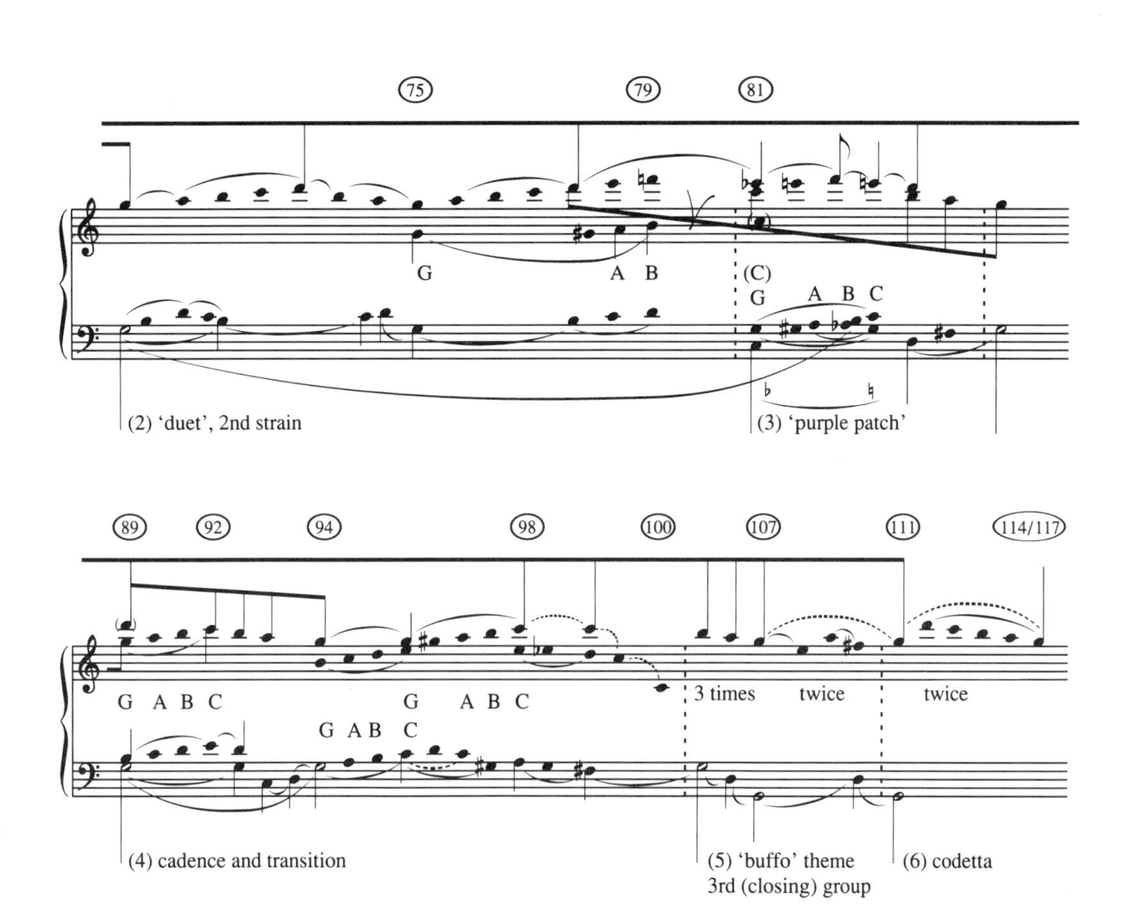

revise that belief and cancels the codetta-feeling, for an ascent above the D in mm. 75–7 shows us that the structural D is once again a point of departure. (The need to revalue past events presses on us at several points in this section, and contributes to its unpredictable, improvisatory character). In avoiding a renewed closure on G, the rising passage in mm. 77–9 seems almost to be drawing back in fear, and little wonder. After the general pause of m. 80, a sudden tutti outburst on a surprising C minor harmony—a 'purple patch'—shatters the lyricism that has prevailed since m. 56, and leads to a cadence (mm. 88–9) that takes the place of the one evaded in mm. 77–9.[10] Although there is a melodic resolution to G in m. 89, it occurs under the shelter of a retained D (from mm. 86 to 87), so that closure is not definitive.

At the beginning of the 'duet's' second strain, there is no hint of the G–C fourth. In the second phrase, however, an inner-voice motion leads from G through G♯ and A up to B (see especially the violas, mm. 75–9). Obviously directed to C, the line breaks off at the general pause and reaches its goal not as a motivic element of the foreground but only abstractly, in the middleground voice-leading. But a powerfully orchestrated and very prominent inner-voice line begins with the C minor of m. 81 (number 3), traversing the same ground but this time arriving on C (mm. 81–5, first oboe, second violins, violas). This is the first really integral G–C fourth of the G major section, and it occurs within a prolongation of IV (minor becoming major), so its C-ishness is very much in place. Note the G♯ of m. 83; like the one in m. 77, it stems from the chromatic passing-tone heard at the beginning of the 'duet'.

The ensuing passage is where the rising fourth really comes into its own (number 4). The first violins lead off in mm. 89–92 with an ascending line whose main notes, G–A–B–C, occur on each down-beat. The line represents a motion out of the inner voice, a kind of tributary to the descending fifth from the structural D of mm. 87–8 through the C, goal of the rising fourth, through B and A to a provisional halt on G in m. 94. In the following phrase, the bass takes the rising fourth (the passage is composed as a simple contrapuntal inversion of the preceding one). The bass executes a linear progression from I to IV; just as it reaches the IV, the upper line again moves from the inner-voice G to C, but now with a rapid rise and a compensating halt on the high C (mm. 98–100). This note—an apparently unresolved dissonance—falls down two octaves and vanishes into the silence of m. 111; but after the intervening rest, the B of the 'buffo' theme resolves the dissonance. The change in character is so remarkable, and the imminence of resolution so palpable, that I must agree with the usual inference of a new ('third' or 'closing') theme—or, better, group here. The new group is at once separated from and connected to the preceding music: separated by the silence in m. 100, and connected by the delayed

[10] William Rothstein uses Tovey's term 'purple patch' to describe this passage, explaining it as a parenthetical insertion that changes the prevailing harmonic colour while forming a rhythmic expansion that delays cadential resolution. See his *Phrase Rhythm in Tonal Music* (New York, 1989), 91–3. Rothstein's description is very apt: one might regard mm. 71–5 and 75–89 as a pair of phrases whose second member is expanded by the insertion of 81 ff.; the resemblance between the first violin parts in m. 77 (or m. 73) and m. 87 confirms this idea, as does the fact that both members contain the same essential bass motion: G–B–C–D–G.

resolution of C over V, which effects a bridge between the groups. There are two further D–G descents in mm. 111–17, but they serve to reinforce the G in the manner of a codetta: structural closure is already confirmed in m. 111; the big line moves down from the D first heard in m. 49, through the sustained C of mm. 98–100, across the rest in m. 100 to the repeated B–A–G of the 'buffo' theme.

When this part of the exposition is recapitulated, the rising fourth will, of course, take the form C–D–E–F (see mm. 277–88). In a literal recapitulation, of course, the G–A–B–C would appear at its original pitch-level only if Mozart had transposed it up a fifth in the exposition. There are two instances of the fourth D–E–F♯–G in the exposition, as it happens, but neither is a very prominent figure. The first one occurs in the second half of m. 61 as part of the link between the antecedent and consequent phrases of the 'duet'; and the other is a cadential flourish in the first violin part of m. 93. One of the few extensive corrections that Mozart made in the autograph of the symphony is in fact in mm. 92–3, and it is not out of the question that he made it to accommodate a transposed version of the motif. This becomes even more plausible when one studies the recapitulation, for the rising fourths in mm. 249 and 281 (the analogues of mm. 61 and 93) are reinforced by doublings that did not appear in the exposition. Far more important, however, is a beautiful event that occurs almost at the end of the movement (Ex. 9). Mozart introduces one measure (304), which has no precedent in the exposition. Its contents delay and enhance the final resolution to $\hat{1}$, and they do so by means of a fourth in its original form, G–A–B–C; and the next bar (305) is changed from its analogue in the exposition to allow the first violins to play a permutation of the same four pitches. This final resolution, therefore, is motivic as well as structural. (The flute plays the structural descending fifth to which the violin line is an inner voice, but its active rhythms and orchestration make it more prominent than the structural upper voice.)

Example 9. Mozart, Symphony K, 551, I, mm. 304–5

In Ex. 10, I try to show the way the rising fourth is deployed throughout the movement, relating it to the large structure of the upper voice. In all of music, I do not know a piece that integrates design, structure, texture, and even affect in a more compelling and beautiful way. The rising fourth—a design element—interacts with the falling *Urlinie*, filling in gaps, and creating emphases at structurally important junctures.[11] As a motif,

[11] This movement shows a kind of top-voice structure first described by Ernst Oster in Schenker, *Free Composition*, 139. The *Urlinie* descends from 5, but without the usual partial descent 5–4–3–2 before the interruption. Thus the D (main top-voice tone over V) comes from E (inner-voice tone of the initial I), and does not

Example 10. Mozart, Symphony K. 551, I: 4th motif and top-voice structure

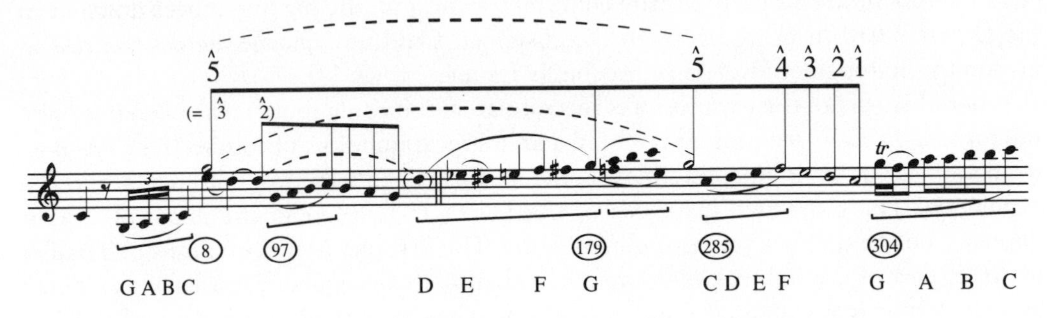

the fourth is associated with tonic harmony, with the massive tutti textures that characterize the first group, and with an energy that is more than personal (even the Beethovenian repeated chords in the big semicadence of mm. 15–23 allude to the motif with reiterated G–C and B–C progressions).

Of course this massive beginning is not monolithic—the tutti is twice interrupted by the quiet, expressive, and contrapuntal string passages of mm. 3–4 and 7–8. Many—maybe most—commentators have called attention to this ripieno/concertino effect and have regarded it as somehow emblematic of the movement as a whole. It would not be anachronistic to think of this contrast as suggesting the 'voices' of a multitude versus those of an individual or group of individuals. Koch, for instance, characterizes the sonata genre (including ensembles like quartets and trios) as depicting 'the feelings of single people' as against symphonies, which, one gathers, express collective feelings. 'The melody of a sonata must present the finest nuances of feelings, whereas the melody of the symphony must distinguish itself . . . through force and energy.'[12] It is characteristic of the 'Jupiter' and of Mozart's late symphonies in general that they integrate energy and nuance of feeling in countless ways.

Nowhere is this more evident than in the second group of the 'Jupiter', which begins in a condition of harmonic fluidity and melodic fragmentation, only gradually achieving stability and integration. Written as a duet, this beginning suggests (to me at least) an intimate conversation carried out in the shadow of some great event. When the voice of the multitude breaks in, it is in the threatening tones of the C minor outburst (m. 81), as if to demand an end to private concerns. The magnificent cadential passage that follows owes not a little of its energy and power to the rising fourths that permeate it. Only after

come directly from the *Urlinie*'s G. As example 11*b* shows, the gap thus created is filled by the rising fourth of the development. Furthermore, the rising fourth of the recapitulation (C–D–E–F) gives special emphasis to F (mm. 286–8) and (by extension) to its resolution to E in the 'buffo' theme (see especially the high register of the flute in mm. 293–5). These are of course the 'missing notes' in the exposition's top-voice structure. And the final statement of the motif at its original pitch-level (m. 304) closes the circle.

[12] Heinrich Christoph Koch, *Introductory Essay on Composition: The Mechanical Rules of Melody, Sections 3 and 4*, trans. Nancy Kovaleff Baker (New Haven, Conn., 1983), 203.

this decisive passage does Mozart permit a sense of emotional resolution with the charming and graceful *buffo* theme.

In the development section, even the tutti passages are polyphonic, and the rising fourth is not associated primarily with massive, homophonic textures. No longer a foreground motif (except in the F major 'false recapitulation'), the fourth withdraws to a higher level—motif has become structure. Its inclusive motion sets a goal for the energetic striving of the upper line, and what a sense of triumph there is when that goal is reached in m. 179! It is in the nature of tonal music that its stratified, hierarchical structure should create different 'temporalities' that unfold simultaneously. But the contrast between the rapid time-scale of the contrapuntal details (imitation at half a measure's distance, for example) and the vast scale of the rising fourth is altogether extraordinary. This is because Mozart's thematic design makes the big fourth take shape with almost as much immediacy as the individual details, as if the rhythms of some cosmic process were brought into the same focus as those of daily human life.

MOZART: CHROMATICISM

The rising fourth of the development's top line is, of course, intensified by chromatic passing-tones, and indeed chromaticism pervades the large structure and many of the details of the section. The most striking and individual chromatic move is the one with which we began our discussion: the E♭/D♯ enharmonic resolving into the E replicates what is perhaps the most striking and individual stroke in the exposition: the C minor eruption of m. 81 with its rising top-voice motion E♭–E–F. Another enharmonic pair that takes on significance in this development is G♯/A♭, and these are also prefigured in this remarkable passage and indeed throughout the G major part of the exposition. Reference back to Ex. 8 will show the close connection between the chromaticism of the development and the prominent chromatic elements in the exposition's second key areas.

BEETHOVEN: THE E–F MOTIF

The course of Beethoven's development section, like that of Mozart's, reflects fundamental attributes of the movement as a whole. The most striking of these attributes is the tendency of the upper voice to move from E to its upper neighbour F. This motion occurs typically in the three-line octave and is most often played by the first flute (though other instruments may join in, usually in lower registers). The E–F motif appears at the very beginning of the Introduction as the top voice of the C/7♭–F chord progression. Though it has surely elicited far less commentary than its accompanying harmonies, the melodic motion is an even more prominent constituent of the movement's design. Ex. 11 shows some of the most important instances, which I shall supplement with a few brief comments.

Example 11. Beethoven, Symphony No. 1, I: examples of the 2-note motif
(*a*) mm. 1–5
(*b*) mm. 11–17
(*c*) mm. 171–9
(*d*) mm. 65–7
(*e*) mm. 90–5
(*f*) mm. 193–8

(*a*)

(*b*)

(*c*)
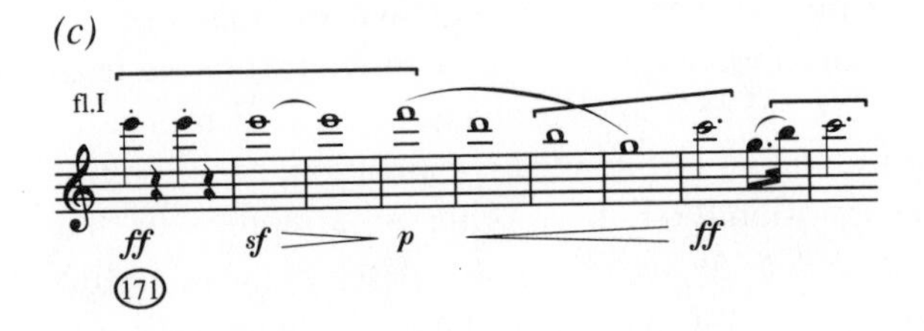

(*d*)

(*e*)

(*f*)
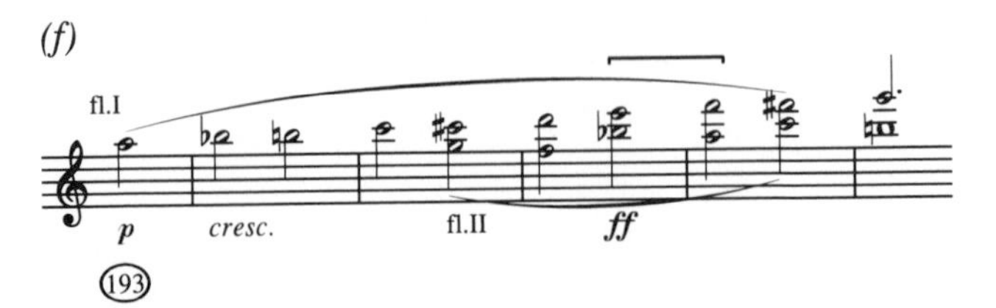

Ex. 11*a* shows the beginning of the Introduction: the F returns to E, but in the inner voice of m. 2, after which the ascending chromatic motion resumes with F♯–G and even G♯–A. In 11*b* we see the end of the Introduction, melodically similar to mm. 1–2, but in a completely new harmonic situation. In Ex. 11*c*, I skip to the end of the development section. The relation to the end of the Introduction is striking, encompassing even the repeated Es. We can see here that part of Beethoven's aim in going from development to recapitulation is to recompose the juncture of Adagio molto and Allegro con brio, but now in the midst of the movement; the long notes create a kind of Adagio within the Allegro. As in the cadence into the Allegro, F is here supported by V/7, but E, of course, is supported by the E major chord discussed earlier.

Like Mozart with the rising fourth, Beethoven also places his basic motif into the G major part of this exposition. We see this in Ex. 11*d*, an excerpt from the initial subject of the dominant group. The F♮s, foreign to the local key, help to tonicize IV and II (C major and A minor). Some thirty measures further on, the exposition's closing section, the E–F again occurs over a tonicization of II (Ex. 11*e*). The placement of the *ff* indication is striking, as is the D♯ before the E, which creates a highly specific relation to the structural contour of the development's top voice. (Is it possible that this passage was inspired by Mozart's 'purple patch' shown in Ex. 8? That is not an answerable question, but it is none the less significant that both passages create a similar bond between exposition and development.) Ex. 11*f* comes from the opening of the recapitulation, where Beethoven fuses the 'first theme' with the bridge. Again note the position of the *ff* at E–F accompanied by harmony that replicates the beginning of the Introduction.

Unlike Mozart's rising fourth, whose last note can easily function as a goal, Beethoven's two-note figure is open-ended, needing a continuation in order to achieve closure. That continuation takes one of a few basic forms: a return to E (neighbour-note function), an ascent to higher pitches (passing-tone function), association with $\hat{7}$–$\hat{1}$ (B–C), the two neighbours ($\hat{4}$ and $\hat{7}$) substituting for a passing $\hat{2}$. All these forms are easy to see in Ex. 11. This fluidity is characteristic of the movement, whose initial tonic occurs in a state of flux.[13] How unlike the Mozart, with its massive and weighty tonic prolongation!

BEETHOVEN: THE RISING FOURTH

In Exx. 11*a* and *b*, we can see how Beethoven's rising fourth G–B–C grows out of the two-note E–F motif. The B–C is a kind of imitation at the lower fourth of E–F; initially, of course, the imitation takes place in the lower 'voice' of a polyphonically conceived line (11*a* and 11*b* before the Allegro). When the Allegro begins, the B is demoted from a harmony note (over V) to a non-harmonic decoration of C (incomplete lower neighbour),

[13] In the light of subsequent events, the chord is revealed as a tonic—and those subsequent events are not more than four bars away from the beginning. From a moment-by-moment perspective, however, it sounds like a V of F. These two perspectives can be reconciled by understanding it as I in the background transformed in the foreground to V of IV.

and the G added to form an arpeggiation. That the two-note figure persists in the 'new' motif is substantiated by the fact that Beethoven tends to use the motif as G–B–C rather than G–A–B–C.

Since it is a derived rather than a fundamental figure, we should not expect the rising fourth to interact with the background structure as it does in the Mozart.[14] But on the foreground, there are wonderful manipulations of the motif, two of which I show in Ex. 12. In 12*a* we see the accompaniment to the main theme of the second group. Here the G–B–C fits into a G major context, but with B as harmony note, rather than C. Not only the three-note figure but also the entire rising arpeggio derives from mm. 16–17, the main tune of the earlier passage now functioning as an accompanimental counterpoint.

EXAMPLE 12. Beethoven, Symphony No. 1, I: transformation of the rising 4th
(*a*) accompaniment to the '2nd' theme
(*b*) recapitulation

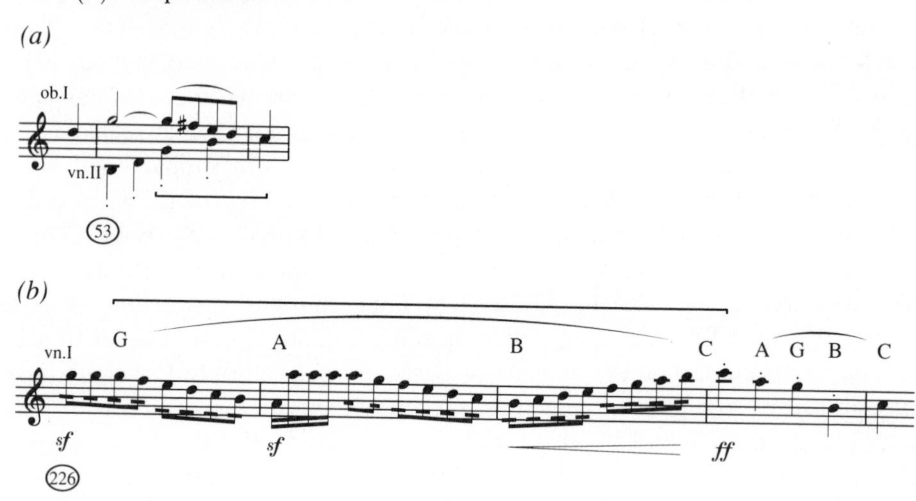

In Ex. 12*b* I show the cadential passage immediately before an improvisatory parenthetical insertion (another 'purple patch', but nothing like Mozart's) that separates the 'second' from the 'closing' group. I quote the passage as it appears in the recapitulation, where the fourth is at its basic G–C level. (In the exposition, Beethoven transposes it into G.) This is the one important passage in the movement where the fourth is filled in by step and somewhat prolonged. Most interesting is the permutation of the four pitches in mm. 229–30, reminiscent of Mozart's final cadence (cf. Ex. 9).[15]

[14] The rising fourth comes into its own in the Menuetto of the Beethoven, where it influences large-scale structure in a most remarkable way. In that movement, incidentally, the fourth has the same stepwise organization (G–A–B–C) as in the 'Jupiter', but its relation to the prominent fourths of the first movement (and the second as well) is undeniable. Connections between movements are very evident in the Beethoven First.

[15] The structural cadence of the Menuetto, obviously related to this passage, is even closer to the Mozart (see mm. 54–7, first violin part).

REMINISCENCE OR RECOMPOSITION?

To summarize the points of resemblance between the two first movements:

They are both in C.

They use similar motifs in their opening themes, and they use them in similar places within the measure and the phrase.

Both development sections contain a modulation from a temporary E♭ tonic to an E major triad approached by an augmented sixth F–D♯. Between the E♭ and the augmented sixth they move to G minor; and the transitions from E♭ to G and from G to the augmented sixth have essentially the same tonal contents. In both movements, the E♭ major represents a motion away from a tonicized structural V of C, though in the Mozart it is a first move and in the Beethoven the provisional goal of a prior transition.

Both expositions contain striking passages that anticipate the large-scale chromaticism in the developments (Mozart, mm. 81–5; Beethoven, mm. 92–5).

Both recapitulations contain important cadences based on similar permutations of the rising-fourth motif (Mozart, mm. 203–6; Beethoven, mm. 226–30).

I find it difficult to believe that this network of resemblances has no cause; surely Beethoven had the Mozart movement in his ear when he wrote. But *how* he had it—whether as an unconscious recollection, a conscious model, or a combination of both—is, I think, impossible to determine.[16] My feeling is that he modelled at least the tonal plan of his development on the Mozart—the relationships seem too specific and detailed to be a mere recollection. And what would be more natural than his going to school, as it were, with a uniquely great master of large-scale structure when planning his own first symphonic work? We know, after all, that he was not above copying out whole pieces or movements by Bach and Mozart. If the modulatory plan was in fact borrowed from Mozart, the passage based on that plan hardly sounds plagiarized. It elaborates a different background from Mozart's (to use Schenker's term somewhat loosely) and it in turn forms the middleground to a very different foreground. It does not take a Beethoven to know that the same underlying chord progressions and voice-leading patterns can occur in countless different realizations—anyone with a mastery of thorough-bass learns it. *Semper idem sed non eodem modo*: Schenker's motto applies to all levels of tonal music, not only to its fundamental structure. Even a feature as seemingly piece-specific as the rather recherché modulation in the 'Jupiter' development can become an integral part of another, and very different, piece.

[16] A particularly valuable study of a great composer's use of a pre-existing piece as a model is Ernst Oster's article, 'The Fantasie-Impromptu—A Tribute to Beethoven', *Musicology*, 1 (1947), 407–29, reprinted in David Beach (ed.), *Aspects of Schenkerian Theory* (New Haven, Conn., 1983), 189–207. Oster gives convincing reasons for his view that the Chopin piece was consciously modelled on the 'Moonlight' Sonata; see especially 204–7 of the reprint. I believe that the Fantaisie-Impromptu presents a stronger case for conscious recomposition than Beethoven's First Symphony, though even there we cannot be entirely certain.

THREE RELATED WORKS

A perspective on the connection between the 'Jupiter' and Beethoven's First can result from looking at other works that share some of their idiosyncratic tonal features. I have chosen excerpts from three orchestral works in C: the Overture to *La clemenza di Tito*, the first movement of Haydn's Symphony No. 97, and the Finale of Schubert's 'Great' Symphony. All three pieces contain modulations from an E♭ tonic to a triad on E; and all of them transform the E♭ to D♯ to facilitate the modulation.[17] I referred to the *Tito* Overture above, and I show a middleground sketch of its development as Ex. 13. Like the 'Jupiter' development, it contains a motion through a chromaticized fourth D–E♭/D♯–E–F–F♯–G, and it derives the D with which the line begins from the structural V that ends the exposition. Unlike the symphony, however, the overture deploys this line in the bass, and this change brings in its train inevitable differences in harmony and counterpoint.

EXAMPLE 13. Mozart, Overture to *La clemenza di Tito*, development

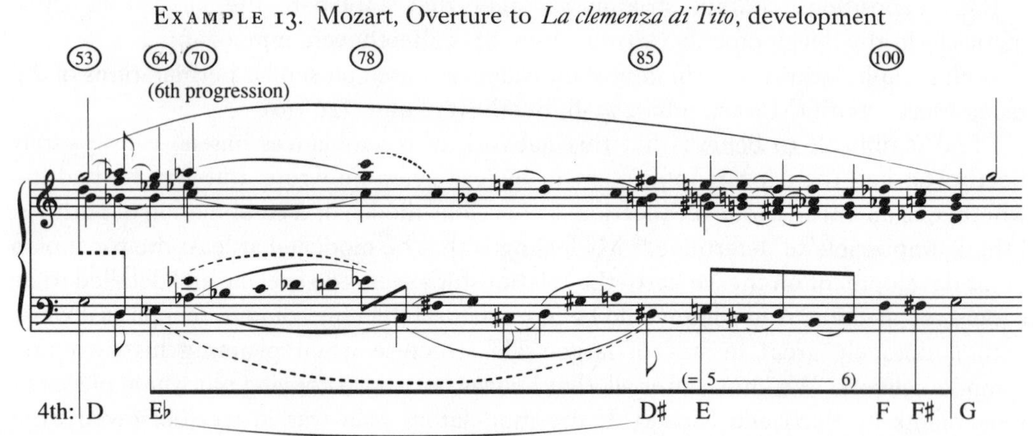

Perhaps the most important change is the necessity of using F♯ rather than F♮ as counterpoint to D♯; Mozart never uses vertical diminished thirds, though augmented sixths are his favourite chromatic intervals. Although the background of this development—a structural V prolonged by a rising fourth-progression—closely resembles the 'Jupiter', its realization has no sustained passage that is as close to it as the Beethoven symphony is. None the less I think that Mozart might possibly have raided the earlier work when writing this one. If we compare mm. 86–90 and 102–10 of the overture with 153–7 and 181–5 of the symphony, we see startling similarities in design and harmony at precisely equivalent points in the pieces.[18] In other respects the two developments have

[17] My colleagues Charles Burkhart and Roger Kamien suggested the possibility of significant E♭–D♯ transformations in two of these works—Burkhart in the *Tito* Overture, and Kamien in the Haydn symphony.

[18] Both Abert and Saint-Foix hear traces of the 'Jupiter' in the *Tito* Overture. Saint-Foix calls attention to a resemblance between the opening themes, and Abert mentions the modulations to E♭ at the beginning of the development sections. See Hermann Abert, *W. A. Mozart*, 2 vols. (Leipzig, 1919–21), ii. 604; and Georges de Saint-Foix, *Les Symphonies de Mozart* (Paris, 1932), 217.

very different foregrounds despite the middleground similarity; if Mozart is recycling here, it is not in an obvious way.

An E♭–D♯ enharmonic also occurs prominently in the splendid first-movement development from Haydn's Symphony No. 97 (Ex. 14). With his characteristic (and unsurpassed) resourcefulness and sense of economy, Haydn derives the chromaticism of the development from the beautiful chromatic progression that occurs at the beginning of the movement's Introduction. Specifically, the E♭/D♯–E and the F♯–G replicate on a huge scale these pitches from the opening's diminished seventh chord and its resolution. As a consequence, Haydn's E chord must be minor, not major; a G♯ would destroy the recomposition of the earlier F♯–G. Like the Beethoven symphony, the Haydn draws a connecting thread from the Introduction to the end of the development—even to the repeated notes in the bass. The background implications are the same, however, as those of the 'Jupiter' development—a prolongation of V—but the middleground has little in common with the other works except for the E♭/D♯ enharmonic. The bass unfolding of the sixths F♯–D♯ and G–E and the registral manipulation of the melodic component D♯–E are of outstanding beauty.

Example 14. Haydn, Symphony No. 97 (Hob. I: 97), I
(*a*) development
(*b*) introduction

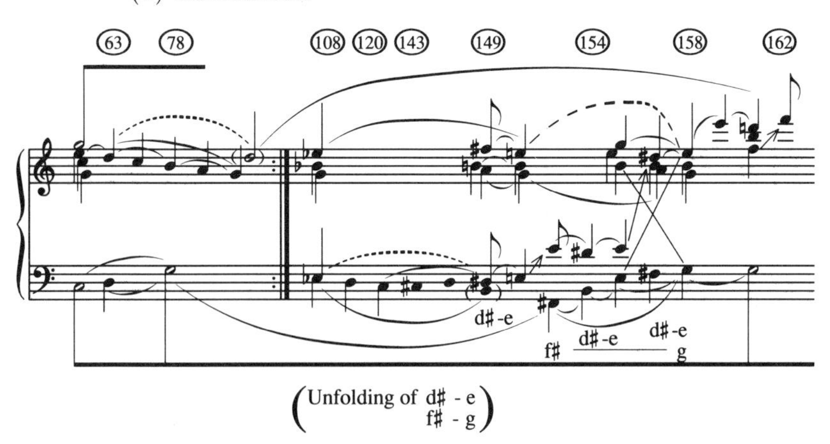

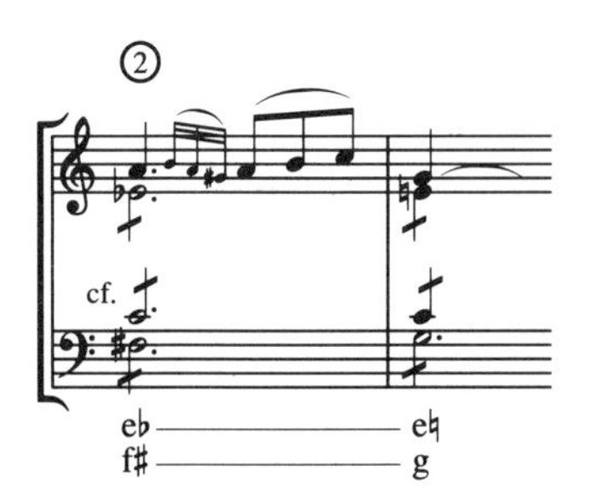

Example 15. Schubert, Symphony No. 9 ('Great'), IV, recapitulation

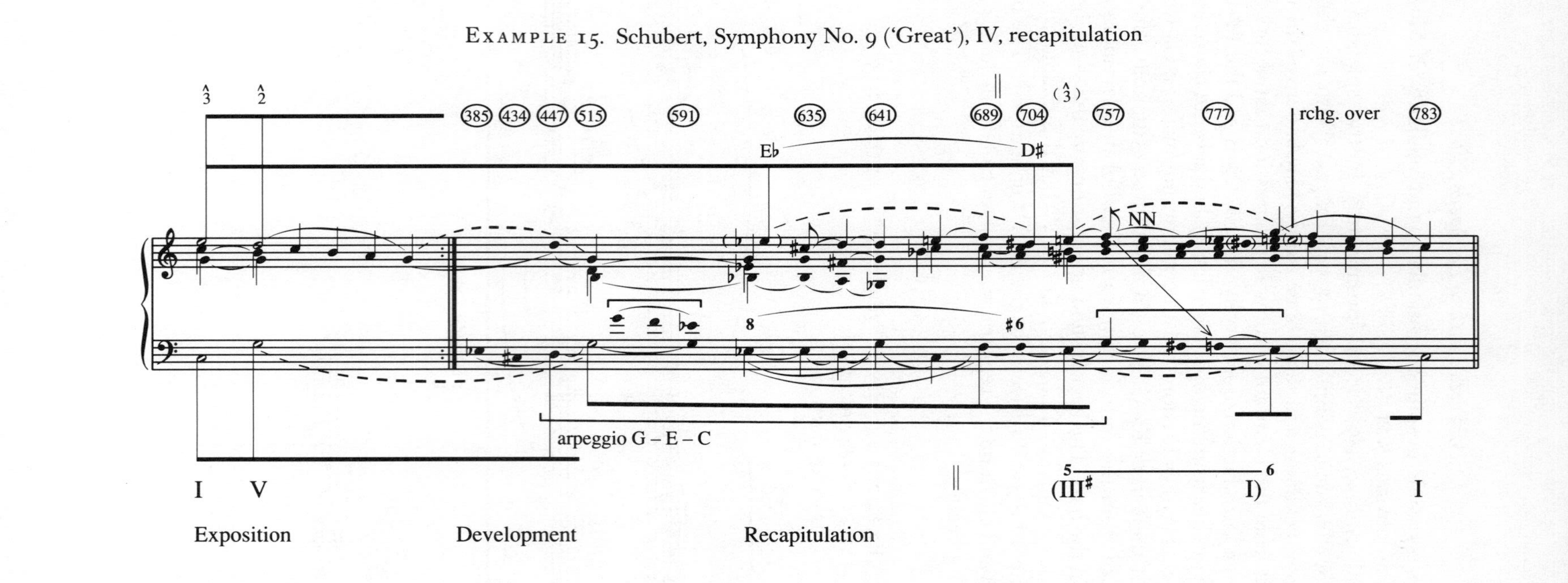

Strangely enough, the Finale of Schubert's 'Great' C major Symphony has structural features that bring it closer to the 'Jupiter' and the Beethoven First than either the *Tito* Overture or the Haydn symphony. I say 'strangely' not only because the Schubert was written a generation after the other works, but also because the similarities in tonal structure coincide with profound differences in form. As in the Mozart and Beethoven symphonies, the Schubert moves from its tonicized E♭ major to a seemingly (but only seemingly) 'dominantized' E major via the augmented sixth F–D♯. These events, however, occur not within the development but within the recapitulation, whose return to the home tonic is delayed until after the onset of the second thematic group (which begins immediately after the E major chord is over).

Recapitulations that begin away from the tonic are far from rare, of course, and Schubert was drawn to them more frequently, probably, than any other composer. This one is especially noteworthy in that it is so unstable and developmental tonally while replicating much of the thematic design of an exposition first group that is almost stubbornly insistent on the tonic. A greater tension, therefore, between the tonal and thematic aspects of a recapitulation would be difficult to imagine. The powerful affirmation of the tonic at the end of the movement sounds so triumphant precisely because that tonic was achieved after such a long and difficult search.

Ex. 15 is a necessarily condensed picture of the recapitulation. Unfortunately, I have had to omit much of the detail that would show how ingeniously Schubert managed to integrate this unique recapitulation into the structure and design of the movement as a whole. But the similarity of the modulatory plan to the Mozart and Beethoven is evident, as are some of the differences. Schubert, too, inserts a G minor area between E♭ and the augmented sixth, but unlike Mozart and Beethoven, he approaches his augmented sixth from F major; all that he needs to do, therefore, is to add the D♯.

I doubt one could maintain that Schubert modelled his recapitulation on the 'Jupiter' or on the Beethoven First, or that Haydn modelled his development section on Mozart's. Although there are striking similarities in the use of enharmonics in all these pieces, the similarities do not extend to other features as they do in the 'Jupiter' and the Beethoven. The specificity of resemblance between the Mozart and Beethoven points to a deliberate act of recomposition or, at the very least, the powerful unconscious recollection of a particular piece. The more general relationships found in the other pieces can be adequately explained by their composers' participation in a shared musical culture. The sharing might conceivably involve the conscious borrowing of compositional devices or their unconscious assimilation through ear and memory. It might also involve the independent discovery of certain technical possibilities that, after all, represent the application of fundamental properties of the tonal system.

The Mozarts' Salzburg Copyists: Aspects of Attribution, Chronology, Text, Style, and Performance Practice

CLIFF EISEN

WHEN Mozart died in 1791, his library, which consisted primarily of his autographs, remained with his widow, Constanze. On several occasions she attempted to sell all or part of the collection—in 1792, for example, eight works were sold to King Frederick William II of Prussia[1]—but it was not until 1799 that she disposed of it (or at least the significant portion that was left) to the Offenbach publisher Johann Anton André.

Although André intended to publish authoritative new editions of Mozart's works, his chief concern soon became the study of the sources themselves and, in particular, the chronological development of the composer's handwriting.[2] He could hardly have foreseen that his pioneering research would leave a permanent stamp on Mozart scholarship. For since the mid-nineteenth century, Mozart source studies have concentrated overwhelmingly, and almost exclusively, on the composer's autographs. What is more, until Alan Tyson's recent work on paper types, scholars from Fuchs, Köchel, and Jahn to Wolfgang Plath, have, like André, been concerned primarily with handwriting and its implications for chronology.[3] Not all of Mozart's compositions, however, and only a few

I am indebted to Dr Wolfgang Plath (*Neue Mozart-Ausgabe*), Dr Ernst Hintermaier (E. B. Konsistorialarchiv, Salzburg), Dr Adolf Hahnl (St Peter's, Salzburg), and Dr Robert Münster (Bayerische Staatsbibliothek, Munich) who generously placed numerous sources at my disposal; and to Stanley Boorman, James Webster, and Neal Zaslaw, who read earlier versions of this material and offered many suggestions for its improvement. Throughout this article, libraries are identified by their RISM sigla. In the text, source locations are given only for non-authentic copies of works by the Mozarts and other composers; the authentic manuscripts are described fully in the Appendix.

[1] Otto Erich Deutsch (ed.), *Mozart: Die Dokumente seines Lebens* [henceforth *Dokumente*] (Kassel, 1961), 386; id., *Mozart: A Documentary Biography* [henceforth *Documentary Biography*], trans. Eric Blom, Peter Branscombe, and Jeremy Noble (2nd edn., London, 1966), 440–1.

[2] André's study of Mozart's handwriting appears in the foreword to his 1833 catalogue of Mozart holdings; a copy, made for Otto Jahn, is in the British Library (GB Lbl, Add. MS 32412). An English-language translation of the foreword is published in Cecil B. Oldman, 'J. A. André on Mozart's Manuscripts', *Music and Letters*, 5 (1924), 169–76. Several of André's other catalogues of Mozartiana are described in Wolfgang Plath, 'Mozartiana in Fulda und Frankfurt. (Neues zu Heinrich Henkel und seinem Nachlaß', *Mozart-Jahrbuch 1968/70*, 356–8.

[3] In particular, see Wolfgang Plath, 'Beiträge zur Mozart-Autographie I: Die Handschrift Leopold Mozarts', *Mozart-Jahrbuch 1960/61*, 82–117 and id., 'Beiträge zur Mozart-Autographie II: Schriftchronologie 1770–1780', *Mozart-Jahrbuch 1976/77*, 131–73. Further, see the relevant discussions in Wolfgang Plath, 'Zur

of Leopold Mozart's, survive in autographs. Many of them, especially works from before 1780, are known only from copies of differing provenance, date, and worth.

At a time when there was little music-printing in south Germany and Austria, and none in Salzburg, manuscript copies represented the chief means by which the Mozarts' works were disseminated. Not surprisingly, copyists are frequently mentioned in the family correspondence. When Mozart was in Augsburg in 1777, Leopold wrote to him:

> You should try to find a copyist ... wherever you stay for any length of time ... The copying should be arranged so that the copyist writes out at your lodgings in your presence at least the *violino primo* or some other principal part. The rest he can copy out at home ... Wherever you are, you must look about immediately for a copyist, or else you will lose a great deal! Otherwise, of what use to you will be all the music which you have taken away? You cannot wait until some patron has them copied; *he would thank you for allowing him to do so* and that is all. It is far too laborious to have your compositions copied from the score, and a thousand mistakes will creep in unless the copyist works the whole time under your supervision. But he could come *for a few mornings*, when you happen to be in, copy out *the principal parts* and then write out the remainder at his house. That is absolutely necessary.[4]

Financial protection was not the only reason the Mozarts sought out regular, reliable copyists. For as Leopold's letter states, unless supervised, copyists were likely to make mistakes. Mozart himself says as much of Viennese copyists, writing to his father shortly after his arrival in Vienna in the spring of 1781: 'I badly need the three cassations—those in F and B♭ would do me for the time being—but you might have the one in D copied for me some time and sent on later, for copying is so very expensive in Vienna; in addition to which they copy most atrociously.'[5] And when the Heilig Kreuz monastery in Augsburg asked Wolfgang for one of his Litanies, Leopold wrote:

> I should prefer to send them a copy of the parts rather than the score in your handwriting ... I could have it copied here much more satisfactorily than they would, if they let their students play about with it and smudge it. Morever, you are aware that to one who is not in the habit of reading your scores, many passages in them are difficult to make out. So I prefer to have it copied neatly and without untidy corrections and possibly fresh errors.[6]

Accuracy of copying was a problem Leopold had identified as early as 1755 in a letter to his Augsburg publisher Johann Jakob Lotter:

Echtheitsfrage bei Mozart', *Mozart-Jahrbuch 1971/72*, 19–36; id., 'Chronologie als Problem der Mozartforschung', *Bericht über den Internationalen Musikwissenschaftlichen Kongreß Bayreuth 1981*, ed. Christoph-Hellmut Mahling and Sigrid Wiesmann (Kassel, 1984), 371–8; id., 'Bericht über Schreiber und Schriftchronologie der Mozart-Überlieferung', *Neue Mozart-Ausgabe. Bericht über die Mitarbeitertagung in Kassel 29.–30. Mai 1981*, ed. Dorothee Hanemann (privately printed, 1984), 69–70.

[4] Wilhelm Bauer, Otto Erich Deutsch, and Joseph Heinz Eibl (eds.), *Wolfgang Amadeus Mozart: Briefe und Aufzeichnungen. Gesamtausgabe* [henceforth *Briefe*] 7 vols. (Kassel, 1962–75), ii. 58–9; Emily Anderson (trans. and ed.), *The Letters of Mozart and His Family* [henceforth *Letters*] (3rd edn., New York and London, 1985), 319. The translations used throughout this article are based on *Letters* but amended in light of *Briefe*.

[5] Letter of 4 July 1781; *Briefe*, iii. 136–7; *Letters*, 749. The Cassations in F and B flat are probably K. 247 and K. 287 (271H); that in D may be K. 334 (320b).

[6] Letter of 1 Dec. 1777; *Briefe*, ii. 157–8; *Letters*, 388–9.

I am really very sorry that you took to Augsburg for nothing the Serenade that I gave you ... Indeed, I believe I told you that I sent it to Herr von Rheling, so it is very believable that Herr Wagner obtained it from him and has already distributed it further ... Why don't you buy things first-hand for the Collegium? ... Isn't it better to have a work from the author himself, well written and without mistakes? Don't the good gentlemen [of the Collegium Musicum] know how bad Herr Wagner's handwriting is?[7]

These letters can be more broadly understood as expressing a concern for authenticity, that is, for ensuring that the manuscripts derived from the authors themselves; otherwise the Mozarts could not secure accuracy of attribution and text or control the dissemination of their compositions. It is therefore surprising that, until now, there has been no systematic study of the Mozarts' Salzburg copyists.[8] To be sure, Salzburg copies have long been recognized as primary sources for Mozart's early works, and virtually the only sources for Leopold's. Their authority, however, does not rest solely on evidence that they were proof-read or owned by the Mozarts, as if they were second-hand autographs, isolated from other, similar sources. As we shall see, their importance also stems from being part of a complex of authentic manuscripts, prepared by trusted copyists who worked for the Mozarts on a regular basis. Like autographs, the authentic copies provide evidence not only for attribution and text, but also for chronology and performance practice and for establishing an authenticated body of works, which has further implications for our understanding of the development of Mozart's style.

SALZBURG COPIES AS EVIDENCE FOR ATTRIBUTION

During the eighteenth century, the Prince-Archbishop of Salzburg governed a territory that included most of the present-day Salzkammergut, and stretched down the Salzach into Bavaria. The court maintained close ties with the numerous monasteries and parish churches in the region, and works by Eberlin, Adlgasser, Michael Haydn, and the Mozarts were widely disseminated in the area, often in copies that derived from the

[7] Letter of [10 Apr. 1755]: 'Es thut mir wirklich recht sehr leid, dass sie die mitgegebene Serenat vergebens mit sich nach Augspurg geführt haben ... ja ich glaube, ich hab es ihnen gesagt, dass ich es dem H: von Rheling überschicket, folglich sehr glaubwirdig mutmasse, der H: Wagner werde es daher etwa erhalten und gar schon weiters verhandelt haben ... warum kaufen sie denn von Seyten des Musikalischen Collegii nicht lieber eine Sache von der ersten Hand ... Ist es denn nicht besser ein solches Stück von dem Autor selbst in guter Schrift und ohne fehler zu haben? wissen die guten Herrn denn nicht wie schlecht des H: Wagners Schrift aussiht?' *Briefe*, i. 1; not in *Letters*. According to *Briefe*, v. 4, Wagner is Jakob Wagner (1719–95), Apostolic and Imperial Notary, from 1763 *Chorvikar* at the Augsburg cathedral. Dr Hilda Thummerer of the Archiv des Bistums Augsburg informs me, however, that the Catholic Wagner cannot be identical with the Wagner cited in Leopold's letter, who was affiliated with the Evangelical Collegium Musicum.

[8] To date, the most important studies to include information on Salzburg copyists are Walter Senn, 'Die Mozart Ueberlieferung im Stift Heilig Kreuz zu Augsburg', *Zeitschrift des historischen Vereins für Schwaben*, 62–3 (1962), 333–68; Manfred Hermann Schmid, *Die Musikaliensammlung der Erzabtei St. Peter in Salzburg. Katalog. Erster Teil: Leopold und Wolfgang Amadeus Mozart, Joseph und Michael Haydn* (Salzburg, 1970); Ernst Hintermaier, 'Die Salzburger Hofkapelle von 1700 bis 1806. Organisation und Personal' (diss., University of Salzburg, 1972); and David Carlson, 'The Vocal Music of Leopold Mozart (1719–1787): Authenticity, Chronology and Thematic Catalog' (Ph.D. diss., University of Michigan, 1976).

composers themselves. Many of these sources survive in collections at Wasserburg, Neumarkt-St. Veit, Tittmoning, Berchtesgaden, Laufen, and Weyarn, as well as Lambach, Seitenstetten, and Graz to the east and south, and Augsburg and Ottobeuren to the north and west.[9] It might be supposed, then, that Salzburg copies are reliable witnesses to attribution, and especially those attributed to the Mozarts, who were well known throughout the region.

This is not necessarily the case, however. Conflicting attributions among Salzburg copies, and other evidence for the deliberate or accidental misattribution of Salzburg manuscripts, can be documented for the Mozarts and other local composers throughout the second half of the eighteenth century. For example, Wagenseil's Divertimento Op. 3 No. 2 (Vienna, 1761), arranged for solo keyboard, two violins, and basso, survives in two early Salzburg copies, one of them attributed to Wagenseil (A Ssp, without shelf-mark), the other, in the very same collection, to Adlgasser (A Ssp, Adl 245.1).[10] And a Mass by Mozart's little-known Salzburg contemporary, the violinist Joseph Hafeneder, survives at Mattsee, a parish church not far from Salzburg, in a copy, dated both 1768 and 1769, originally attributed to Ditters.[11] A striking example from Michael Haydn's works is the

[9] Catalogues have been published or compiled for some of these collections. See Robert Münster and Robert Machold, *Thematischer Katalog der Musikhandschriften der ehemaligen Klosterkirchen Weyarn, Tegernsee und Benediktbeuern* (Munich, 1971); Gerda Lang, 'Zur Geschichte und Pflege der Musik in der Benediktiner-Abtei zu Lambach mit einem Katalog zu den Beständen des Musikarchivs' (diss., University of Salzburg, 1972); and Ursula Bockholdt, Robert Machold, and Lisbet Thew, *Thematischer Katalog der Musikhandschriften der Benediktinerinnenabtei Frauenwörth und der Pfarrkirchen Indersdorf, Wasserburg am Inn und Bad Tölz* (Munich, 1975).

[10] The Adlgasser-attributed manuscript is written on paper from the Hofmann mill at Lengfelden b. Salzburg. The watermark consists of the initials 'ISH' (for Johann Sigismund Hofmann); the counter-mark includes a man with a club in an ornament ('wilder Mann'). The watermark can be found in three different sizes. About 1771 or 1772, the largest size was replaced by a watermark with the initials 'AFH' (for Johann Sigismund's successor, Anton Fidelis). The latest dated manuscripts on large-size 'ISH' paper are the autographs of Michael Haydn's *Der büssende Sünder*, Klafsky VI/13 (dated 15 Feb. 1771), and Mozart's *La Betulia liberata* K. 118 (74c), composed in Mar. and Apr. 1771. Large-size 'AFH' paper makes its first appearance in the autographs of Michael Haydn's Mass Klafsky I/8 (dated 31 Dec. 1771) and in Mozart's symphony K. 114 (fos. 14 and 17 only; fos. 1–13 are on 'ISH' paper) of Dec. 1771; it was also used for *Il sogno di Scipione*, K. 126, and the Regina Coeli, K. 127, both May 1772. Large-size 'ISH' paper continued to be available at least until the middle of 1772; see, for example, the authentic Salzburg Dom-Musikarchiv copy of the Litany, K. 125, composed in May 1772, which includes both 'ISH' and 'AFH' paper. Examples of the large-size 'ISH' watermark are unknown after 1772, just as examples of the large-size 'AFH' watermark paper are unknown before 1771. Manuscripts on paper with the large-size 'ISH' watermark, such as the Adlgasser-attributed concerto copy, can confidently be dated not later than 1772. For illustrations of the 'ISH' watermark, and discussions of its incidence in Mozart's autographs, see Alan Tyson, 'New Dating Methods: Watermarks and Paper-Studies', and id., 'A Reconstruction of Nannerl Mozart's Music Book (Notenbuch)', both in Tyson, *Mozart: Studies of the Autograph Scores* (Cambridge, Mass. and London, 1987), 1–22 and 61–72. The Wagenseil-attributed manuscript is on paper that was available in Salzburg in 1771 and 1772; see also below, n. 72.

[11] A Mattsee, Stiftsarchiv Nr. 143: [wrapper by Mathias Kracher, 1752–1827 or 1830, organist, teacher, and chamber servant at Michaelbeuren from the late 1760s:] *Ex C* | *Missa Solemnis* | *a* | *Canto Alto* | *Tenore Basso* | *Violino Primo* | *Violino Secondo* | *Clarino Primo* | *Clarino Secondo* | *Cornu Primo* | *Cornu Secondo* | *Hoboe Primo* | *Hoboe Secondo* | *Trombon Primo* | *Trombon Secondo* | *Tympano* | *e* | *Organo.* | *Auth:* [*Ditters* crossed out and replaced, in another hand, by:] *Sig Hafeneder* | [Kracher:] *Ad Usum* | *Jos: Math: Kracher* | *Cam: Mich: Buranj* | *ao: 1769*. The *organo* part is dated at the end: *P*[ater]. *M*[athias]. *K*[racher]. | *1768*. Kracher is identical with Schmid's copyist 25. As this manuscript shows, Kracher was active at Michaelbeuern earlier than 1771, as claimed by Ernst Hintermaier, 'Michael Haydns salzburger Schülerkreis', *Österreichische Musikzeitschrift*, 27 (1972), 17.

Te Deum, Klafsky V/2, the autograph of which, signed and dated 9 December 1770, is at the Bayerische Staatsbibliothek, Munich (D-brd Mbs, Mus. mss. 455). There is also a manuscript, by an unidentified Salzburg copyist, originally crediting the work to Joseph Haydn (D-brd TIT, 199). A dating for the false attribution can be fixed to the 1770s: the manuscript, purchased for the collection at St Peter's, has the notation 'comparavit P. Michael Kumberger p[ro] t[empore] Subprior' on its wrapper; Kumberger was Subprior at the monastery from 1767 to 1778.

As for the Mozarts, a Mass by Leopold Mozart (Seiffert 4/1, Carlson IA1) survives in three contemporary Salzburg copies, two of them attributed to Leopold (A Ssp, Moz 10.1 and D-brd Ahk, 77), and one, dated 1753, to Eberlin (A Wn, S.m. 22 247).[12] And in a letter of 4 August 1770 to his sister, Mozart cites the opening bars of the Cassations K. 63 and 99 (63*a*), as well as the March K. 62 (presumably intended to introduce the Cassation K. 100), evidently in response to a now-lost letter, that someone had passed off one of Wolfgang's compositions as his own, adding: 'I find it difficult to believe that it is one of mine, for who would dare claim for himself a composition by the Kapellmeister's son, whose mother and sister are in Salzburg?'[13] By themselves, then, Salzburg copies do not guarantee the attributions they transmit, even if the majority of them are reliable.

In order to be considered a self-sufficient witness to attribution, a Salzburg copy, if it is not directly authenticated by Leopold's or Wolfgang's autograph attribution or corrections in the parts, must be in the hand of a copyist whose immediate connection to the Mozarts and whose reliability can be demonstrated. Four such copyists can be identified: Maximilian Raab, Joseph Richard Estlinger, Felix Hofstätter, and an unidentified copyist, 'Salzburg 1'. In fact, their hands have been known for some time as the hands of important Salzburg copyists. Raab, Estlinger, and Hofstätter were first identified, as anonymous scribes, by Walter Senn in his study of the Mozart manuscripts at the Heilig Kreuz monastery in Augsburg; Manfred Hermann Schmid found the same hands among the holdings of St Peter's. On the basis of archival and biographical evidence, finally, Ernst Hintermaier was able to identify the copyists by name.[14] 'Salzburg 1', whose identity remains unknown, was first described by David Carlson.[15]

[12] A later wrapper for the A Ssp manuscript of Seiffert 4/1 attributes the Mass to Wolfgang: *Missa* | *a* | *4. Voci conc:* | *2. Violino*, [second hand:] *Viola* | [first hand:] *2. Clarini, obligt:* | *con* | *Organo* [second hand:] *2 Cornu, Tymp.* | [first hand:] *e Basso.* | *Del Sige:*[*Amadeo* crossed out by Martin Bischofreiter, *Inspector chori musici* at St Peter's from 1819, and replaced by:] *Leopold* | [first hand:] *Mozart* | *Maestro di Concerto* | *a* | *Salzborgo.* | *Ad Chorum Monasterii S: Petri Salisburgi*. Possibly, then, the wrapper was originally used for a Mass by Mozart, and only later pressed into service for Leopold's. The original title-page agrees with the scoring of the revised version of K. 192 (186*f*); hence Seiffert 4/1 was not necessarily misattributed to Wolfgang, as claimed by Carlson, 'The Vocal Music of Leopold Mozart', 142.

[13] Letter of 4 Aug. 1770; *Briefe*, i. 378; *Letters*, 154.

[14] Consequently, Senn A = Schmid 8 = Raab; Senn B = Schmid 1 = Estlinger; and Senn C = Schmid 31 = Hofstätter. See Senn, 'Die Mozart Ueberlieferung im Stift Heilig Kreuz zu Augsburg', 336–7, 340–1 and 355–7; Schmid, *Die Musikaliensammlung der Erzabtei St. Peter in Salzburg*, 27–8 and 30–1; and Hintermaier, 'Die Salzburger Hofkapelle', 91–3, 182–4, and 333–4.

[15] Carlson, 'The Vocal Music of Leopold Mozart', 113–14 (where the copyist is identified as 'Salzburg 2').

This information has been slow to take hold. Recent descriptions of Mozart sources still identify copyists by Senn or Schmid numbers. What is more, hands that were found first in copies of church music are often not recognized when they occur in manuscripts of secular music; indeed, the same hand is sometimes not identified in different copies of the same work.[16] In short, the exact relationship of these copyists to the Mozarts, and in particular their reliability as witnesses to attribution and authenticity, has never been clearly demonstrated or understood.

Maximilian Raab (*c.* 1720–80) first came to Salzburg in 1748, where he matriculated at the Salzburg Benedictine University. In 1756 he was appointed *Hofvioletist* and in 1762 he was granted an 'Exspectanz auf die Hofcopiatur', a post he took over in 1766, succeeding Johann Jakob Rott. During this time he was also active as *Chorregent* and *Kantor* at Stift Nonnberg.[17]

Raab's hand is occasionally found in copies of Leopold Mozart's works from the late 1750s and early 1760s, and in numerous copies of Wolfgang's works from the 1770s, many of which have autograph corrections in the parts, or title-pages and attributions by Leopold Mozart. A reference in a letter from Leopold Mozart to his wife, written from Milan on 5 December 1772, provides more or less firm evidence that Raab also worked privately for the Mozarts, even when they were absent from Salzburg: 'Concerning the music paper for Herr Rhab, you can give all of it over . . . however, you must hold on to the small[-size] paper.'[18]

Because of his close association with the Mozarts, and because instances of his misrepresenting works by Leopold or Wolfgang are unknown, attributions by Raab can be

[16] See, for example, Josef-Horst Lederer, 'Zur Datierung des Stimmenmaterials der Sinfonie KV 319 aus der Grazer Lannoy-Sammlung, in Christoph-Hellmut Mahling (ed.), *Florilegium musicologicum. Hellmut Federhofer zum 75. Geburtstag* (Tutzing, 1988), 189–95, where Estlinger and Hofstätter are still identified as 'Senn B' and 'Senn C', thereby missing the important connection between these copies and a long-standing tradition of authentic manuscripts of Mozart's works. More striking still is the case of the Concerto for Two Pianos, K. 365, published in *NMA* V/15/2. According to the critical report (ed. Christoph Wolff, Kassel, 1989), the authentic A Ssp copy is by 'Schmid 1'; a second primary source, at CS KRa, is by an unidentified copyist. In fact, both manuscripts are in the same hand, Estlinger's; what is more, the *NMA* fails to note altogether that the title-page of the CS KRa copy is by Leopold Mozart. Further concerning this manuscript, and its importance as evidence for orchestral scoring in Mozart's early concertos, see my 'The Scoring of the Orchestral Bass Part in Mozart's Salzburg Keyboard Concertos: The Evidence of the Authentic Copies', in Neal Zaslaw (ed.), *Mozart's Piano Concertos: Text, Context, Interpretation* (University of Michigan Press, forthcoming).

[17] Hintermaier, 'Die Salzburger Hofkapelle', 333.

[18] *Briefe*, i. 465: 'Wegen dem NotenPapier für H: Rhab, kannst du alles hergeben . . . das kleine Papier muss aber aufbehalten werden.' Not in *Letters*. Presumably the reference here is to the so-called *Klein-Querformat* paper which makes its first dated appearance in Mozart's autographs a few months later, in the Divertimento K. 166 (159*d*) of 24 Mar. 1773. If so, then the paper may have been available to the Mozarts earlier than has generally been supposed, and a number of undated but apparently early autographs on this paper type—including the fugue fragment K. 73*w*, the added wind parts to K. 113, the divertimento fragment K. 320*B*, and Leopold Mozart's cadenzas to arias by J. C. Bach, K. 293*e*—may pre-date the Mozarts' third Italian journey, beginning in late Oct. 1772. See Alan Tyson, 'The Dates of Mozart's *Missa brevis* K. 258 and *Missa longa* K. 262 (246*a*): An Investigation into His *Klein-Querformat* Papers', in Tyson, *Mozart: Studies of the Autograph Scores*, 162–76; and my review of Tyson in *Music and Letters*, 70 (1989), 101–4.

considered reliable. And manuscripts by him, even those lacking title-pages or autograph corrections, can be presumed authentic. Samples of Raab's hand are given as Fig. 1.

Joseph Richard Estlinger (*c.* 1720–91) was an almost exact contemporary of Leopold Mozart (coincidentally, he died in the same year as Wolfgang) and their acquaintance may date from as early as the late 1730s: in 1737 Estlinger enrolled at the Salzburg *Universitätsgymnasium*; Leopold matriculated at the University proper in the same year. From 1760 Estlinger was employed as *Hofviolonist* (court double bassist), and in 1780 he succeeded Raab as first court copyist, although he had been copying for the court at least since 1760.[19]

Estlinger was the Mozarts' preferred copyist. Numerous manuscripts by him of works by Leopold and Wolfgang have the composers' autograph entries in the parts, or title-pages by Leopold Mozart. Like Raab, Estlinger was also entrusted by Leopold with the making of copies during the Mozarts' frequent absences from Salzburg. On 14 October 1767, for example, Leopold wrote from Vienna to his landlord's wife, Maria Theresa Hagenauer:

> I left Herr Estlinger certain symphonies to copy which I hope are now ready. These are the symphonies which I have to send to Donaueschingen. By the next post I shall send you a letter for the Prince which should be enclosed with the symphonies and should be sent off by the mail coach. I hope that Herr Estlinger understood me. The concerto for two claviers should be sent to Herr Gesner at Zurich. The symphonies should go to Donaueschingen, and the keyboard concertos, which Herr Spitzeder gave Herr Estlinger to copy, should, when ready, be delivered by him to Herr von Menhofer, who will then pay him for them.[20]

Until now, Estlinger's hand has been incompletely understood. Because numerous manuscripts by him exhibit two distinctly different forms of the treble clef and two distinctly different forms of the bass clef, Schmid's tacit hypothesis that they are by one and the same copyist was rejected by Carlson in his study of Leopold Mozart's vocal works and by Gerda Lang in her catalogue of the music archive at Lambach.[21] It has gone unremarked that the rest of the handwriting is absolutely identical and that there is a clear chronological division between manuscripts in which the different forms of the clefs appear. All manuscripts by Estlinger dated 1759 or earlier are consistent in their use of the clefs shown in Fig. 2*a*. And all manuscripts dated 1765 or later are consistent in their use of the clefs shown in Fig. 2*b*. What is more, at least three manuscripts, including an undated Litany by Adlgasser (A Ssp, Adl 90.1) and the unique surviving copy of Leopold Mozart's only extant Serenade (A SEI, V 1451), exhibit the 'old' form of the

[19] Hintermaier, 'Die Salzburger Hofkapelle', 91–3.

[20] *Briefe*, i. 241; *Letters*, 74.

[21] Carlson, 'The Vocal Music of Leopold Mozart', 106–12, where Estlinger is identified as Salzburg 1 and Senn B; Lang, 'Zur Geschichte und Pflege der Musik in der Benediktiner-Abtei zu Lambach', ii, pp. cxv–cxvi, where Estlinger is identified as Schreiber 20 and Schreiber 60. Carlson guessed that one of the (what he perceived to be) two different hands was Estlinger's, but was therefore led to conclude that the other belonged to a different copyist. At the time he proposed this identification, however, the hand claimed by him for the 'other' copyist had already been identified by Hintermaier as Estlinger's.

FIG. 1. Handwriting of Maximilian Raab

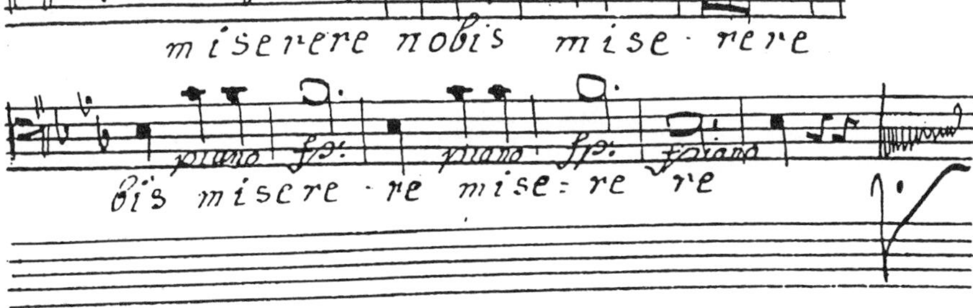

FIG. 2. Handwriting of Joseph Richard Estlinger
(*a*) 'old' style clefs (to *c*.1760)

Del Sig:re Wolfgango Mozart

(*b*) 'new' style clefs (from *c.*1765)

(*c*) Nannerl *Notenbuch*, Nos. 16 ('old' clefs) and 34 ('mixed' clefs)

treble clef and the 'new' form of the bass clef. There is no doubt that each of these manuscripts was copied all at once: they are consistent throughout in their use of clefs, and the paper is invariable with regard both to type and rastrology. Hence it may be concluded that all the manuscripts are in one and the same hand. Because Estlinger has already been positively identified as the 'later' copyist, he must be the 'earlier' copyist as well.

The third manuscript to exhibit Estlinger's 'mixed' clefs, the so-called Nannerl *Notenbuch* of 1759 (Fig. 2*c*), confirms the dating of the changes in his hand to the period around 1760. The first works entered in the book, eighteen unattributed minuets, include ten numbers (1–8, 11, and 16) copied by Estlinger; all of them exhibit 'old' style clefs. Numbers 19 (an unattributed minuet), 39 (an anonymous 'Arietta con Variazioni in A'), and 43 (a presto by 'Sgr. Tischer'[22]), however, also copied by Estlinger, exhibit the 'new' bass clef.[23] Number 19 provides a more or less firm date for the change in Estlinger's bass clef, for at the end of the work is Leopold Mozart's notation, 'Diesen Menuet hat d. Wolfgangerl auch im vierten jahr seines alters gelernt.' Consequently, manuscripts that consistently display 'old' style clefs date from about 1760 or earlier; manuscripts that display 'new' clefs probably date from 1765 or later; and manuscripts with mixed 'old' and 'new' clefs fall in the period 1760 to 1764.

The discovery of these changes in Estlinger's hand has important implications for the dating of otherwise undated works and for the evaluation of copies by him. Some eighteen compositions by Leopold Mozart, for example, including two works at one time thought to have been composed by Wolfgang during the 1770s—K. 115 (166*d*) and 177 + 342 (Anh. C 3.09)—can now be assigned to the 1750s (or possibly even earlier). Similarly, the Serenade manuscript, with its 'mixed' clefs, can be dated 1760–4, which is consistent with other evidence: the fourth and fifth movements of the Serenade are also known as Leopold Mozart's trumpet concerto, the independent autograph score of which is dated August 1762 (D-brd Mbs, Mus. mss. 1275).[24] Furthermore, a tentative

[22] In the foreword to *NMA* IX/27/1 (Kassel, 1982), xiv, Wolfgang Plath identifies the presto as a work by Johann Tischer (1707–74), *Schloss-* and *Stadtorganist* at Schmalkalden, later concert-master to the Coburg-Meiningen court. However, he is not identical, as Plath claims, with the composer of several masses listed in the Lambach catalog of 1768. These are by Joseph Tischer, a local composer active at Lambach during the 1750s. See Lang, 'Zur Geschichte und Pflege der Musik in der Benediktiner-Abtei zu Lambach', i. 46 and ii., pp. lxxxix–xci. During the 1750s, Tischer made copies of several works by Leopold Mozart, including the symphonies D22, D24, G2, G14, and A1; a divertimento for two violins and basso; the Mass Seiffert 4/1; and a Dixit Dominus, Seiffert *deest* (Carlson ID2).

[23] The copyists identified by Plath in his edition of the notebook (*NMA* IX/27/1) as 'Anonymous I' and 'Anonymous III' are therefore both Estlinger. Number 19 is incorrectly given as a copy by 'Anonymous I'; it should have been given as a copy by 'Anonymous III'. In an earlier attempt to sort out the hands in the notebook, Plath had correctly listed all of the Estlinger copies as being in the hand of a single copyist. See his 'Beiträge zur Mozart-Autographie I', 87.

[24] The fact that the Seitenstetten Serenade copy carries performance dates only from 1779–85 need not deter us from proposing 1760–4 as the time of its copying. Other manuscripts in Seitenstetten have dates on their wrappers that are considerably earlier than the earliest documented performance dates: two Masses by Brixi (A SEI, shelf-marks D IV 1a and D IV 1785) are dated 1773 but have performance dates only from 1784 and 1785, respectively; and a mass by Michael Haydn (A SEI, shelf-mark D XV 3a), dated 1772, carries performance dates only from 1791 to 1801. Seitenstetten may not have been the original owner of these manuscripts. Apparently the monastery actively traded with other institutions to acquire works for its library.

chronology for some undated items in the notebook can be established for the first time: the copying of numbers 19, 39, and 43, for example, post-dates the copying of the early minuets. One possible implication of this chronology is that the Mozarts' acquaintance with these compositions stemmed from their first stay in Vienna, where Estlinger accompanied them in 1762. More generally, because Estlinger worked not only for the Mozarts but also for other local composers, the changes in his hand often represent the only evidence for the dating of their works. The Adlgasser Litany described above, for example, can now be dated not later than 1764. Estlinger is probably the most important Salzburg copyist of the second half of the eighteenth century.

The third copyist, Felix Hofstätter (*c.* 1744–1814), was active in the Salzburg court music establishment as early as the end of 1768 as *Hoftenorist* and *Hofviolinist*; from about 1773 he also did copying for the court on an *ad hoc* basis. After Estlinger's death in 1791, Hofstätter was *de facto* in charge of the court copying, although he never received a fixed appointment.[25]

Hofstätter's hand is found in court copies of Wolfgang's works and frequently in copies produced privately for the Mozarts for distribution elsewhere. Samples of his writing are given as Fig. 3. Because there is no evidence that Hofstätter misattributed works by Mozart, copies by him can be presumed to give reliable attributions. Some manuscripts by Hofstätter, however, may represent unauthorized copies produced without the composer's permission or knowledge. On 15 May 1784 Mozart wrote to his father:

> Today I sent with the post wagon the symphony that I composed in Linz for old Graf Thun, together with four concertos. I am not particular about the symphony, only I ask you to have the four concertos copied at home, for the copyists in Salzburg are as little to be trusted as those in Vienna—I am absolutely certain that Hofstetter copied Haydn's music twice—I actually have his three newest symphonies.—since of these new concertos only I have those in B♭ and D, and only I and Fräulein Ployer (for whom they were written) those in E♭ and G, the only way they could fall into other hands is by that kind of cheating;—I myself have everything copied in my room and in my presence.[26]

Although it has been common to assume that Mozart's reference is to Joseph Haydn,[27] there is no evidence to support this identification. More likely, because Mozart names the Salzburg copyist Hofstätter, the reference is to Michael Haydn, whose works are known to have circulated in unauthorized copies. An obituary of Haydn published in the

See, for example, A Gd, Bestand Judenburg 57: *II* | *Gradualia in C et D♯.* | *No I In Festivitate Pentecostes.* | *No II in Festo S. Georgii Mart.* | *et SS. Apost. Philippi et Jacobi;* | *vel de communi tempore Paschali.* | *a* | *4 Voci* | *2 Violini.* | *2 Oboe.* | *2 Corni* | *2 Clarini* | *Tympani* | *Organo et Violone.* | *Del Signor Michele Haydn* | *Chori Seitenstettensis. Sub R. D. P. Carolo.* | [another hand:] *Joseph Prandstetter* | *tauschte gegen duetten*.

[25] Hintermaier, 'Die Salzburger Hofkapelle', 182–3.

[26] *Briefe*, iii. 313; *Letters*, 876–7.

[27] Anthony van Hoboken, *Joseph Haydn. Thematisch-bibliographisches Werkverzeichnis*, i (Mainz, 1957), 117; Dénes Bartha (ed.), *Joseph Haydn: Gesammelte Briefe und Aufzeichnungen* (Kassel, 1965), 131; *Briefe*, vi. 181; *Letters*, 876; H. C. Robbins Landon, *Haydn: Chronicle and Works. Volume II. Haydn at Eszterháza 1766–1790* (Bloomington, Ind., 1978), 489 n. and 602; A. Peter Brown, 'Notes on some Eighteenth-Century Viennese Copyists', *Journal of the American Musicological Society*, 34 (1981), 332 n.

Fig. 3. Handwriting of Felix Hofstätter

Allgemeine musikalische Zeitung lists among his compositions '35 symphonies (three of which were published without his prior knowledge)';[28] presumably these are Perger 18, 19, and 20, issued in Vienna by Artaria in January 1786.

'Salzburg 1', finally, is the copyist of several manuscripts of Leopold Mozart's works, including both church and instrumental music, most of which have Leopold Mozart's autograph entries in the parts. 'Salzburg 1' may have been a court copyist: his writing-style is similar to that of other court copyists, and manuscripts by him are on paper of the same type and quality as other court copies. But his hand is *not* found in copies of Wolfgang's works and he may have stopped copying, or died, sometime in the mid-1760s. Although there is no positive evidence to identify 'Salzburg 1' with Raab's predecessor, Johann Jakob Rott, who died in 1766, such an identification is consistent with the known facts. Samples of Salzburg 1's hand are given as Fig. 4.

The identification of Raab, Estlinger, Hofstätter, and 'Salzburg 1' as the Mozarts' Salzburg copyists helps to resolve several problems of attribution and to identify previously unrecognized authentic copies. In Leopold Mozart's case, the authorship of two well-known compositions that survive with various attributions can now be settled. One of these is the so-called 'Toy' symphony, which is known from numerous contemporary copies with attributions to Leopold Mozart, Michael and Joseph Haydn, and Edmund Angerer.[29] The most important manuscript in this group, formerly at the Bayerische Staatsbibliothek, Munich, is now lost. But its original wrapper, entirely by Raab, survives: it is attributed to Leopold Mozart and includes an incipit.[30] The other work is the *Musikalische Schlittenfahrt*, which is known in at least three different versions: a *Kaiserliche Schlittenfahrt von Wien nach Schönbrunn*, which survives in copies at the Sächsische Landesbibliothek, Dresden, attributed to W. A. Mozart, and in an almost identical version at the Conservatorio di Musica 'L. Cherubini' in Florence, attributed to 'Haydn'; a *Musikalische Schlittenfahrt* at the Staatsbibliothek Preussicher Kulturbesitz, Berlin, with a double attribution, to Leopold Mozart and to Georg Franz Wassmuth, Hofkapellmeister at Würzburg; and in a version at the Bayerische Staatsbibliothek, Munich, attributed to Leopold Mozart (another copy of this version, attributed only to 'Mozart', survives in the Thurn und Taxis'sche Hofbibliothek, Regensburg). There can be little question concerning which version is Leopold's: the Munich copy is by Salzburg 1. In fact, it is probably the copy used at the work's first performance in Augsburg in 1756, for

[28] *AmZ*, 9 (22 Oct. 1806), 60.

[29] For the location of manuscript copies, see Hob. II:47, and Gerhard Croll, *Musik mit Kinderinstrumenten aus dem Salzburger und Berchtesgadener Land* (Denkmäler der Musik in Salzburg, 2; Munich and Salzburg, 1981), 141. Concerning the disputed attribution of the work, see Ernst Fritz Schmid, 'Leopold Mozart und die Kindersinfonie', *Mozart-Jahrbuch 1951*, 69–87 and id., 'Nochmals zur Kindersinfonie', *Mozart-Jahrbuch 1952*, 117–18; Hans Halm, 'Eine unbekannte Handschrift der Kinder-Symphonie', in Joseph Schmidt-Görg (ed.), *Anthony van Hoboken. Festschrift zum 75. Geburtstag* (Mainz, 1962), 101–2; Robert Münster, 'Wer ist der Komponist der Kindersinfonie?', *Acta Mozartiana*, 16 (1969), 76–82; and Croll, *Musik mit Kinderinstrumenten*.

[30] D-brd Mbs, Mus. mss. 5229: [wrapper by Raab:] *Cassatio ex G* | *Due Violini, Due Corni, Trompeterl* | *et Wachtl Ruef, Pfeifferl, Gugu* | *et Corno da Postiglione, Trombl,* | *Rätscherl, Orgel, Windmühl,* | *Basso* | *Del Sigr. L. Mozart.* | [lower left:] incipit.

Fig. 4. Handwriting of the Copyist 'Salzburg 1'

a note tipped into the manuscript traces its history to the eighteenth-century 'Compagna di Musica in Augusta Concordia et Libertate'.

By the same token, some works by Wolfgang which until now have been known only from copies of uncertain authenticity can be shown to be by him, including the aria 'Cara se le mie pene', K. *deest*, which survives in an attributed Estlinger copy in the Salzburg Museum Carolino Augusteum, and the revised version of the motet *Exsultate, jubilate*, K. 165 (158*a*).[31] Also important is the identification of numerous copies as authentic which previously were considered to be of only secondary value or apparently were unknown. These include Estlinger copies of the Mass K. 66 and Offertory K. 117 (66*a*); the only demonstrably authentic manuscript of Mozart's arrangement for keyboard of the minuets K. 103 (61*d*), a Hofstätter copy; copies of the arias 'Se il labbro timido', 'Vanne t'affretto—Ah se il crudel' and 'Sposo mia vita—Ah dove, dove vai?' from *Lucio Silla*; an authentic copy of the symphony K. 338; an Estlinger and Hofstätter manuscript of the internal movements of the Vespers K. 339; and a copy, partly by Estlinger, of the 'Linz' symphony, K. 425, the most important source for the symphony and the only surviving manuscript to derive directly from Mozart's now-lost autograph.

Similarly, some copies considered by the Köchel catalogue and *Neue Mozart-Ausgabe* to justify the attribution to Mozart of works that do not survive in his autograph can now be discounted as authentic sources. Among the most interesting examples is the set of contredanses K. 269*b*. This work, presumed to have been composed in Salzburg about January 1777, is known from a unique, incomplete source discovered in Czechoslovakia in 1956. The manuscript, as described by the *NMA*, is simply a copy.[32] It lacks a contemporary attribution and the title, in the hand of the anonymous copyist, reads *Contradanze del Sig: Conte Czernin. trasposte per il Cembalo*. The work is credited to Mozart by a later notation, 'Von Mozart geschrieben für meinen Vater', presumably in the hand of Johann Rudolf Graf Czernin, who lived in Salzburg and was well known to the Mozarts. Other circumstantial evidence also apparently supports the attribution: the early date of the copy; a document showing that in December 1776 or early 1777 Mozart composed or sold a symphony and other pieces to Johann Rudolf's father, Count Prokop Adalbert Czernin of Prague;[33] and, perhaps most importantly, the fact that the second and twelfth dances are keyboard arrangements of K. 101 (250*a*), numbers 2 and 3, respectively.

On the face of it, the attribution of the contredanses to Mozart is fairly convincing. However, the manuscript is not merely a contemporary copy: it is, in fact, an autograph of Michael Haydn.[34] The relationship between at least some of Michael Haydn's and

[31] For K. 165 (158a), see Robert Münster, 'Mozarts Motette "Exsultate, jubilate". Auffindung einer abweichenden Zweitfassung', *Neue Zürcher Zeitung*, 9–10 June 1979, 67–8. The manuscript of 'Cara se le mie pene' was discovered by Wolfgang Plath; see his 'Der gegenwärtige Stand der Mozart-Forschung', in *Bericht über den neunten Internationalen Kongreß Salzburg 1964*, ed. Franz Giegling (Kassel, 1964), i. 55.

[32] *NMA* IV/13/1/1, ed. Rudolf Elvers (Kassel, 1961), p. vii.

[33] *Dokumente*, 141; *Documentary Biography*, 157–8. Also see Marius Flothuis, 'Problemen rondom Mozart' *Mens en melodie*, 13 (1958), 296–7 and id., 'Mozarts contradans voor Graaf Czernin', ibid., 379–80.

[34] A facsimile of one side of the manuscript is published in Alexander Buchner, *Mozart und Prag* (Prague, 1957), unpaginated.

Mozart's dances is reciprocal in a way that obscures the true authorship of the works. An exchange of letters from 1770 is revealing: Mozart several times mentions minuets by Haydn sent to him from Salzburg; he not only performed them at the keyboard, but he intended to write down arrangements of them as well. And in a note of 19 May he wrote to his sister: 'When I have more time, I shall send you Herr Haydn's minuets. I have already sent you the first one. But, I don't understand. You say that they have been stolen. Did you steal them? Or what do you mean?'[35] Similarly striking is the example of K. 104 (61*e*), numbers 1 and 2. Walter Senn was the first to point out that, with minor changes, Mozart's minuets and Michael Haydn's minuets Perger 79 numbers 1 and 3 are identical.[36] Although Senn gives priority to Haydn, a relative chronology for the works cannot be established. Both are undated—Mozart's autograph appears on the basis of the handwriting to have been written down in the summer or fall of 1770[37]—and their autographs are on the large-size 'ISH' paper that was commonly used in Salzburg until about 1772. And six minuets from K. 105 (61*f*), presumed to have been composed in 1769, survive in a keyboard arrangement copied by Nannerl Mozart, the manuscript of which includes the explicit attribution 'del signore haiden'.[38] It is clear that Mozart and his family were interested in Haydn's dances, that they performed them at the keyboard, and that some of these arrangements were written down. What is true of Mozart's relationship to Haydn's dances is true of his relationship to dances by other composers as well: K. Anh. 109 (135*a*), for example, autograph incipits for a ballet of thirty-two numbers, includes at least six dances by Starzer.

What, then, is to be made of K. 269*b*? Given this new evidence concerning its source, and the relationship between Mozart's dances and those of his contemporaries, several explanations are possible: that both the work and the arrangement are by Mozart and were copied by Haydn; that the contredanses are Mozart's but the arrangement Haydn's; that K. 101 numbers 2 and 3 are by Mozart but not the others transmitted by the source; or even that K. 101, in whole or in part, is also not genuine, for in fact, Mozart's autograph of this work, like his partial or now-lost autographs of K. 104, 105, and Anh. 109, is not signed. In short, it is by no means certain that Mozart is the author of K. 269*b*.

The evaluation of a Michael Haydn autograph as no more than a copy, and the unqualified acceptance and publication of K. 269*b* as a genuine composition by Mozart, provide a clear demonstration of how little has been known about Salzburg copyists and their importance for questions of authenticity in Mozart's works and in the works of other Salzburg composers. Yet the identification of Raab, Estlinger, Hofstätter, and 'Salzburg 1' as reliable Mozart copyists settles only a part of the problem. They were not the only copyists to work for the Mozarts—although they were the only Salzburg copyists to have had demonstrably long-term, reliable relations with them—nor were

[35] *Briefe*, i. 349; *Letters*, 136–7. See also the Mozarts' letters of 18 and 22 Sept. 1770; *Briefe*, i. 390 and 392; *Letters*, 161 and 162.

[36] Walter Senn, 'Die Menuette KV 104, Nr. 1 und 2', *Mozart-Jahrbuch 1964*, 71–82.

[37] *NMA* IV/13/1/1, p. xiii.

[38] Plath, 'Zur Echtheitsfrage bei Mozart', 33.

they the only copyists active in Salzburg during the second half of the eighteenth century. Circumstantial evidence sometimes suggests that manuscripts, or parts of manuscripts, in certain hands may also be witnesses to authenticity, even if the copyists cannot be identified or their exact relationship to the Mozarts clarified. Some of the problems encountered in such copies are illustrated by manuscripts of three works linked, in part, by a common, unidentified copyist: two settings of the Tantum ergo, K. 142 (Anh. C 3.04) and 197 (Anh. C 3.05), and the Litany, K. 109 (74*e*).

Until recently, the most important source for the Tantum ergo settings was a non-authentic copy from the estate of Karl Mozart. No autographs were known for the works, nor copies by any of the scribes normally associated with the Mozarts or the court. Although Köchel accepted both works as genuine, Jahn, Abert, and Wyzewa and Saint-Foix expressed reservations about K. 142. Einstein, in his revision of the Köchel catalogue, removed both from the main chronology, relocating them in the appendix as 'doubtful' works (Anh. 186*d* and 186*e*). Einstein had a low opinion of K. 142 and he argued that since both settings descended from the same source, if K. 142 was doubtful, then so, too, was K. 197.[39] The discovery by Robert Münster of an older, eighteenth-century copy, however, cast a different light on the question of the genuineness of the compositions: because the newly discovered source (D-brd, NT 259) was thought to be of Salzburg origin, Münster, turning Einstein's reasoning on its head, concluded that both works should be accepted as genuine.[40]

Neither of these positions is satisfactory. By themselves, Salzburg copies, except for manuscripts by certain copyists, are insufficient witnesses to authenticity, even if the majority of them transmit accurate attributions. And the fact that the sources have a common origin is of little consequence for the question of Mozart's authorship: they give no indication of what other authentic or non-authentic sources might have preceded them. The upshot of this episode was the discovery of yet another copy of K. 142, attributed to the Mainz Kapellmeister Johann Zach (D-brd Mbs, Mus. mss. 285/5).[41] The Mozart version differed from that attributed to Zach not only in several details, but also by the inclusion of a 42-measure concluding 'Amen'. Münster's revised and more plausible explanation was that K. 142 represented a re-working or arrangement by Mozart of Zach's original.

As for the copyist of the Salzburg source for K. 142 and 197, both Münster and the *NMA* imply that, although he was probably active in Salzburg, his hand is otherwise virtually unknown. The only other manuscripts by him cited in the literature are two copies of Mozart's Litany K. 109, from the collections of Neumarkt-St. Veit and Laufen

[39] Otto Jahn, *W. A. Mozart*, 4 vols. (Leipzig, 1856), i. 687; Hermann Abert, *W. A. Mozart*, 2 vols. (Leipzig, 1919–21), i. 317; Théodore de Wyzewa and Georges de Saint-Foix, *Wolfgang Amédée Mozart: Sa vie musicale et son œuvre* 5 vols. (Paris, 1912–46), ii. 246; K[3] 855.

[40] Robert Münster, 'Mozarts Tantum ergerl KV 142 und 197', *Acta Mozartiana*, 10 (1963), 54–61; *NMA* I/3, ed. Hellmut Federhofer (Kassel, 1963), pp. xvi–xvii.

[41] Robert Münster, 'Das Tantum ergo KV 142—eine Bearbeitung nach Johann Zach?', *Acta Mozartiana*, 12 (1965), 9–15.

(D-brd NT, 253 and D-brd LFN, 268), and a violone part for Joseph Haydn's Mass Hob. XXII:4, also from Neumarkt-St. Veit (D-brd NT, 211).[42] In fact, his hand is far more common than these sources suggest. Copies by him are also extant at Lambach, Munich, Vienna, Tittmoning, Laufen, in the library of the Mozarteum, and, most importantly, at the Salzburg Cathedral archives and at St Peter's. What is more, in addition to works by Mozart and the stray Joseph Haydn part, he also copied works by Eberlin, Adlgasser, Michael Haydn, and Joseph Hafeneder.[43] All of these manuscripts are on paper of Salzburg manufacture, and he was almost certainly a Salzburg copyist.

There is also no doubt that this copyist was active in Salzburg during Mozart's time there. An Adlgasser Litany copied by him is dated 1780, which must represent the date of either acquisition or copying, not composition, since Adlgasser died in 1777.[44] And the quality of his work is high: although manuscripts by him are not always as reliable as copies by Estlinger, Raab, Hofstätter, and 'Salzburg 1', they are nevertheless more accurate than comparable non-authentic manuscripts. These two facts suggest that his sources may have been authentic, or that he had direct access to authentic copies, possibly even court copies. Indeed, a copy by him of the Mass K. 220 (196*b*) not only derives from a primary source, but its title-page is so detailed as to suggest a close proximity to the Mozarts: *Missa | a | 4 Voci: | 2 Violini: | 2: Clarini | Timpani | Violone | e | Organo | [Del] sig[Wolf]gango Amadeo | Mozart: | Academico Filarmonico | di | Bologna e Verona* (A Ssp, Moz 100.1). Arguments in favour of the genuineness of works transmitted by copies in his hand are correspondingly greater.

This brings us to the Litany, K. 109, the attribution of which is not in question: the work survives in Mozart's signed and dated autograph and in an authentic copy by Raab and Estlinger. Salzburg copies include a manuscript in St Peter's (A Ssp, Moz 140.1) and two manuscripts, now at Neumarkt-St. Veit and Laufen, by the unidentified Salzburg

[42] Münster, 'Mozarts Tantum ergerl KV 142 und 197', 55–6; *NMA* I/3/1, critical report, ed. Hellmut Federhofer (Kassel, 1964), 101.

[43] Additionally, the following are known in copies wholly or partly by this unidentified Salzburg copyist: *W. A. Mozart*: Mass K. 220 (A Ssp, Moz 100.1 and A Sm, Rara 220/2); *Ernst Eberlin*: Litany (D-brd LFN, 148); Litany (D-brd LFN, 149), Litany (D-brd, LFN 151); *Anton Cajetan Adlgasser*: Mass AWK 2 (YU Zha, LIX.H), Mass AWK 8 (YU Zha LIX.G), Requiem AWK 10 (D-brd TIT, 109 and YU Zha LV.A), Litany AWK 63 (A Wn, S.m. 13952), Litany AWK 65 (D-brd Po, without shelf-mark), Litany AWK 66 (D-brd TIT, 105), Offertory AWK 22 (A Ssp, Adl 95.1), Offertory AWK 23 (D-brd TIT, 103), Offertory AWK 36 (D-brd TIT, 101), Salve Regina AWK 46 (A LA, 1182), Salve Regina AWK 51 (A LA, 1181); *Michael Haydn*: Mass KL. I/10 (A Ssp, Hay 385.1), Litany KL. *deest* (D-brd Mm 593), Offertory KL. *deest* (A Ssp, Hay 1530.1), Gradual KL. IIa/42 (D-brd TIT, 170), *Der Kampf der Busse und Bekehrung* KL. VI/10 (D-brd Mbs, Mus. mss. 4331); *Joseph Hafeneder*: Cassation (A Ssp, uncatalogued); *J. Haydn*: Mass Hob. XXII:4 (A Ssp, Hay 155.1); *Ferdinando Bertoni*: Chorus de Confessore (A Ssp, Ber 170.1), Chorus Pro Omni Tempore (A Ssp, Ber 171.1); *C. P. E. Bach: Die Israeliten in der Wüste* (A Ssp, Bach 50.1, acquired by St Peter's in 1781). For the identification of Adlgasser's works by AWK numbers, see Werner Rainer, 'Verzeichnis der Werke A. C. Adlgassers', *Mozart-Jahrbuch 1962/63*, 280–91. I am indebted to Christine de Catanzaro for bringing several of the Adlgasser sources to my attention. For a facsimile of a title-page by this copyist, see Münster, 'Mozarts Tantum ergerl', 55.

[44] A Ssp, Adl 55.1: [later hand:] *Ad Chorum Monasterii S: Petri hic Salisburgi.* | [original hand:] *in C dur | Lytaniae | de | B.V.M. | a | 4 Voci, | 2 Violini, | 2 Oboe, | 2 Flauti, | 2 Corni, | 2 Viole, | 2 Fagotti, | Viole ed Organ[o] | 1780. | Del Sig. | Gaetano Adlgasser.*

copyist (D-brd NT, 253 and D-brd LFN, 268). After the autograph and authentic court copy, the Laufen and Neumarkt-St. Veit manuscripts are the best surviving sources for the Litany; probably they were made in Salzburg during Mozart's lifetime. The most striking feature of the Laufen manuscript is that it transmits otherwise unknown parts for trumpets (the Neumarkt-St. Veit copy does not include trumpet-parts). It was common practice in Salzburg and elsewhere for horn-, trumpet-, and timpani-parts to be added later to sacred music: Michael Haydn, for example, added horn-parts to the Graduals Klafsky IIa/26 and IIa/36, and trumpet parts to the Graduals Klafsky IIa/30 and IIa/45; Mozart added horns and oboes to the Mass K. 66 and trumpets to the Missa brevis K. 192 (186*f*). Frequently, however, autographs of such parts do not survive and the authenticity of surviving copies is difficult to establish. Although some of these additional parts are late, or stylistically improbable, in other instances they date from the composer's lifetime and are transmitted by apparently reliable copyists. The trumpet-parts for K. 109 in the the Laufen copy are just such parts. Yet the critical report of the *NMA* edition of K. 109 does not mention these parts, or that the Laufen and Neumarkt-St. Veit sets are Salzburg copies by an apparently reliable copyist whose work is known throughout the Salzburg region during Mozart's lifetime. Nor does it mention an important complication: that the St Peter's copy, which probably dates from the late 1780s or early 1790s, also transmits trumpet-parts, but ones different from those in the Laufen copy.

There is no direct evidence, of course, that any of these additional parts is authentic, and to suggest that they derive directly from Mozart would merely be speculation. Nevertheless, it is clear that some Salzburg copies have a greater claim to consideration than has previously been supposed. What is apparently the case for Raab, Estlinger, Hofstätter and 'Salzburg 1'—that a detailed study of their relationships with the Mozarts has significant implications for problems of attribution and authenticity—may also be true of other copyists active in Salzburg during Mozart's lifetime.

CHRONOLOGY, TEXT, AND CONTEXT

Beyond settling problems of attribution, copies by Raab, Estlinger, and Hofstätter also have implications for the chronology of Mozart's works, for documenting his acquaintance with works by other composers, and, perhaps most immediately, for the texts of his compositions, especially in cases where an autograph does not survive and an authentic copy represents the best surviving source. One striking example is the 'Linz' symphony, K. 425. Because the autograph of this work disappeared before 1800, modern editions of the symphony have been based on other contemporary sources; in the case of the *NMA* these included, primarily, a set of parts sold by Mozart to the Donaueschingen court in 1786 and, secondarily, early copies in the Bentheim library and in the library of the Mozarteum, as well as a keyboard arrangement by Johann Wenzel published in Prague in 1793. The most credible source for the symphony, however, is the Mozarteum copy, which is partly by Estlinger, has an attribution by Leopold Mozart, and, unlike the Donaueschingen manuscript, apparently descends directly from Mozart's now-lost autograph. A comparison of the two authentic copies not only clarifies numerous textual details falsified by modern editions of the symphony, but also suggests that Mozart may have revised the work in 1784 or 1785.[45]

Another example concerns the minuets K. 103 (61*d*), which survive in two versions: the original twenty minuets for orchestra, and an arrangement of twelve of them for keyboard. According to the *NMA*, the primary source for the keyboard arrangement is a copy from about 1829 that, according to a note on its first page, derives from Nannerl Mozart: 'Compositionen von Wolf: Amad: Mozart; aus seinen Kinderjahren. Nach eigner Handscrift. – Von dessen Schwester mitgetheilt' (D-brd B, Mus. ms. 15359).[46] But there is also an authentic copy by Hofstätter that apparently dates from the mid-1770s: Hofstätter was first active as a copyist about *c.* 1773, and the watermarks in the paper suggest a date of *c.* 1774–6.[47] Although the manuscript is not exactly contemporary with the composition of the minuets, which on the basis of the handwriting in the autograph appears to date from the summer of 1772,[48] it nevertheless represents the earliest authentic copy of the keyboard arrangement.

In several passages the Hofstätter copy transmits readings different from those transmitted by the later Berlin copy. Although some of these different readings probably represent copyists' errors, others more closely approximate the orchestral version, or are more internally consistent (Exx. 1 and 2).[49] And in one passage the authentic copy transmits a reading that differs both from the orchestral version and from the Berlin keyboard arrangement (Ex. 3). The fact that this reading differs from the orchestral version does not necessarily mean that it is suspect. There are at least two unquestionably authentic cases among Mozart's other minuets—the trio of number 3 of K. 104, arranged for keyboard as K. 61*g*^{II} (Ex. 4), and the trio of number 14 of K. 176 (Ex. 5)—in which the

[45] Cliff Eisen, 'New Light on Mozart's Linz Symphony, K. 425', *Journal of the Royal Musical Association*, 113 (1988), 81–96; for a new edn., based on a re-evaluation of the sources, see W. A. Mozart, *Symphony K. 425 ('Linz')*, ed. C. Eisen (London, 1991).

[46] *NMA* IV/13/1/1, p. vii. See also Rudolf Elvers, 'Bemerkungen zum Autograph der Menuette KV. 103 (61*d*) und seiner Abschriften', *Mozart-Jahrbuch 1958*, 66–70.

[47] There are two watermarks in the manuscript. One of them, consisting of the letters 'AZ/C' in a crowned shield and three crescent moons of descending size over a bow and arrow, is found with the same total span in the autograph of Mozart's *La finta semplice*, begun at the end of 1774, and in autographs of 1775–6, including *Il rè pastore* K. 208, the church sonata K. 212, the Litany K. 243, and the sonatas K. 279–84 (189*d–h* and 205*b*). The other watermark has the letters 'AZ/C' under a bow and arrow and three crescent moons of descending size. It is found in the autograph of Mozart's incidental music to *König Thamos* K. 345 (336*a*), and in the authentic copy of Mozart's concerto K. 238, composed in Jan. 1776. The first watermark is illustrated in Tyson, 'New Dating Methods', 15. I am indebted to Dr Tyson for the information concerning Mozart's autographs cited here and in nn. 63 and 73.

[48] Plath, 'Beiträge zur Mozart-Autographie II', 151.

[49] The Hofstätter copy also confirms as authentic some readings given as editorial additions in the *NMA*: in minuet 7, pick-up measure, left hand, the editorially supplied A occurs not only in the orchestral version, but also in the Hofstätter copy; similarly, the same minuet, m. 14, inner voice, the editorially supplied *d′* and *c′*, and minuet 9, m. 9, right hand, the editorially supplied *d‴* on the third beat.

EXAMPLE 1. W. A. Mozart, K. 103 (61*d*) no. 4 (compare mm. 2–6)
(*a*) keyboard version
(*b*) orchestral version

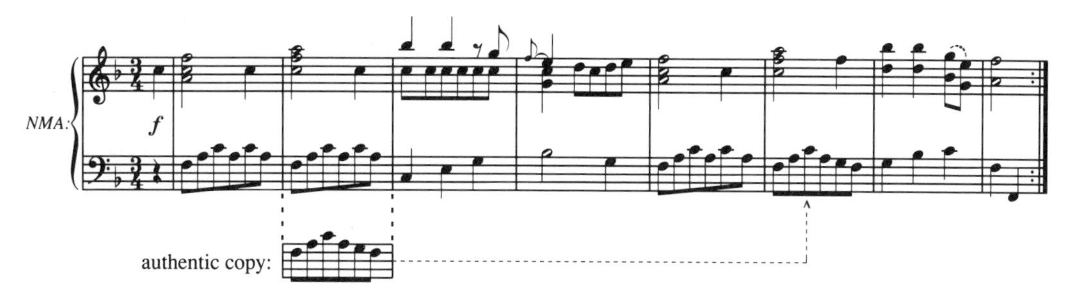

orchestral and keyboard versions differ. In arranging his orchestral works for keyboard, Mozart did not always literally duplicate them.[50]

This raises the question of the accuracy of the authentic copies, and the extent to which their readings can be considered authoritative. By and large, copies by Raab and Estlinger are accurate renderings of the original sources. Estlinger's score copy of the March K. 215 (213*b*), for example, is little short of an exact duplication of Mozart's auto-

[50] This is true of later works as well. See, for example, Douglas D. Himes, 'Mozarts eigenhändiger Klavierauszug zur *Entführung*', *Die Musikforschung*, 39 (1986), 240–5.

Example 2. W. A. Mozart, K. 103 (61d) no. 4, trio (compare m. 3)
(*a*) keyboard version
(*b*) orchestral version

graph. It is somewhat less the case with Hofstätter, who sometimes alters the slurring or obscures the distinction between dots and strokes.

Given the general reliability of the authentic copies, it is surprising that their readings are sometimes ignored. One striking example can be found in the first movement of the concerto for two pianos, K. 365 (316*a*), at measures 30–40, a long orchestral crescendo involving a three-part statement of the idea first heard in the second violins and violas at measures 30–3 (Ex. 6). The crescendo begins in measure 34 with the second statement of the idea, augmented by the oboes, and reaches a climax in the third statement, where the bassoons and basses also participate. In the *NMA* version of this passage, a forte for the entire orchestra—given as a reading from the sources—is reached in the second half of measure 38. In the authentic copies by Estlinger, however, which served as the basis for the edition (at the time, the autograph was lost), the forte for the first and second violins and violas is marked only at the beginning of measure 40, coincident with the re-entry of the horns. The correctness of this reading, which alters the character of the crescendo

Example 3. W. A. Mozart, K. 103 (61d) no. 12 (compare mm. 1, 2, and 4)
(*a*) keyboard version
(*b*) orchestral version

and drives the phrase through to a climax on a dominant-seventh sonority, is confirmed by Mozart's now-recovered autograph, where the forte in the upper strings also occurs on the down-beat of measure 40.

A second example comes from the third movement of the concerto K. 271, at measure 142 (Ex. 7). The passage, beginning at measure 127, is a typically Mozartian gesture: a strong cadence is subverted by a series of deceptive resolutions, in this case at measures 132–3, 138–9, and 141–2, before coming to a substantial resting-point at measure 149. The arrival at B flat is postponed by individual phrases that resolve to G minor, with one exception: according to the *NMA* and, indeed, virtually all other early manuscripts and prints of the concerto, the resolution at measure 142 is to E flat (in first inversion). The

Example 4. W. A. Mozart, K. 104 (61e) no. 3, trio
(*a*) orchestral version
(*b*) keyboard arrangement (K. 61g^II^)

a) K. 104 (61e)/3, trio

possibility for misreading at this juncture is considerable, for in measures 140 to 142 the scoring is reduced to keyboard accompanied only by the oboes; a single misinterpreted note changes the gesture altogether. The authentic Salzburg copy offers a reading that is more consistent with the passage as a whole: at measure 142, the second oboe has the note *d″*, resulting in a cadence to G minor. Again, Mozart's now-recovered autograph confirms the correctness of this reading: it, too, has *d″* for the second oboe.[51] In short, the authentic copies are sufficiently trustworthy to forestall comprehensive editorial intervention. Their readings, especially in cases where autographs are lost or inaccessible, cannot be dismissed out of hand.

Like autographs, the authentic copies also have implications for the chronology of Mozart's works. In the case of the symphony version of the Serenade K. 204 (213*a*), for

[51] The faulty reading occurs in virtually all early manuscript copies, and in numerous editions, including some said to have been edited from Mozart's autograph. Exceptionally, an early copy of the parts in the British Library (GB Lbl, Add. MS 47850) is among the very few sources to give the correct reading. The GB Lbl copy is apparently unknown to the *NMA* and not listed in the critical report to *NMA* V/15/2. Additionally, the critical report does not record the reading of the authentic copy in m. 142.

Example 5. W. A. Mozart, K. 176 no. 14, trio
(*a*) orchestral version
(*b*) authentic keyboard arrangement

example, two hypotheses have been advanced concerning a possible date for Mozart's redaction. One is that the arrangement was made shortly after the work's composition, in August 1775.[52] The other takes as its point of reference a letter of 4 January 1783 in which Mozart asks his father to send copies of his symphonies, including K. 204; he intended to perform the works in Vienna and presumably the redaction dates from that time.[53] The evidence of the authentic copy, however, makes a later date for the redaction unlikely: entirely copied by Estlinger, it is on a type of paper found in dated Salzburg

[52] Hans-Günter Klein, *Wolfgang Amadeus Mozart: Autographe und Abschriften* (Berlin, 1982), 284; *NMA* IV/11/7, ed. Günter Hausswald (Kassel, 1959), pp. vii–viii.

[53] Ernst Hintermaier, critical report to *NMA* IV/12/3 (Kassel, 1988), c/22.

Example 6. W. A. Mozart, K. 365 (316a), I, mm. 30–41

manuscripts only during 1778 and 1779.[54] Hence the symphony version was already in circulation before Mozart left Salzburg.

Other copies can be directly associated with references in the Mozart letters, including a manuscript of the Concerto for Two Pianos, K. 365. This work is the only early concerto by Mozart to survive in *two* authentic Salzburg copies.[55] One of the manuscripts, now at St Peter's, probably dates from 1779 or 1780. The other, at Kroměříž, is slightly later, and has a previously unrecognized connection with performances of the work in Vienna. In June 1781 Mozart wrote to his father asking for copies of the four-hand sonata K. 358 (186*c*) and the two concertos for two keyboards, K. 242 and 365. The concertos arrived in Vienna in October and K. 365 was performed by Mozart with Josepha Auernhammer at his first Augarten concert on 26 May 1782.[56]

Now not only is the Kroměříž manuscript by two of the Mozarts' regular Salzburg copyists, but it is also written on paper that apparently was used in Salzburg only during the autumn of 1781–2.[57] Consequently, it is probably the copy sent by Leopold Mozart to his son in Vienna. This may have some bearing on the question of the origin of the concerto's additional clarinet-, trumpet-, and timpani-parts, the earliest source for which is an edition published by Breitkopf & Härtel in 1881. The Kroměříž copy includes *none* of these additional parts. Hence it seems unlikely, if they are by Mozart, that they were added to the work in 1781, as is sometimes thought.[58]

A more substantial hypothesis concerns the Offertory *Inter natos mulierum*, K. 72 (74*f*). Although there is no question concerning the genuineness of the work—an attributed

[54] The watermark in the manuscript consists of 'REAL / VG' and three stars in an ornament with a crown. Among dated Salzburg manuscripts it occurs first in the autograph of Michael Haydn's Responsory, Klafsky V/9c, dated 4 Apr. 1778. Its last dated appearance is the autograph of Michael Haydn's Symphony, Perger 14, dated 22 Aug. 1779. Alan Tyson generously informs me that the same watermark can be found in the autograph of Mozart's Symphony K. 319, dated 9 July 1779.

[55] A manuscript of the concerto K. 242, now at Stanford University, although it has Mozart's autograph corrections in the parts, probably does not derive from Salzburg. The copyists are otherwise unknown, and the paper types in the copy are typical of south German manuscripts of the period *c.* 1760–80. The title-page reads: *Concerto | per il | Cembalo Principale Primo | Cembalo Principale Secondo | Cembalo Principale Terzo | con | Violino Primo | Violino Secondo | Oboe Primo | Oboe Secondo | Corno Primo | Corno Secondo | Viole | è | Basso* | [to right:] *Del Sig Amadeo Wolfgango Mozart*. Possibly the parts were made during the tour to Mannheim and Paris of 1777–9. Mozart is known to have performed K. 242 in Augsburg on 22 Oct. 1777 and in Mannheim on 12 Mar. 1778. I am indebted to George Barth for a description of the manuscript.

[56] See letters of 27 June and 13 Oct. 1781 and 25 May 1782; *Briefe*, iii. 135, 166, and 209; *Letters*, 748, 772, and 805. Deutsch speculated that K. 365 was also performed on 23 Nov. 1781; see *Dokumente*, 175 and *Documentary Biography*, 197. However, the concerto given on this occasion may also have been K. 242. Mozart's letter of 24 Nov. states only: 'We played the concerto *a due* . . .'; *Briefe*, iii. 176; *Letters*, 780.

[57] The watermark in this manuscript consists of the letters 'AS / C' over the word 'REAL' and three crescent moons over the letter 'Z'. Among Salzburg manuscripts, it occurs in a copy, dated 1782, by Estlinger of a Dixit Dominus by Luigi Gatti, the Salzburg Kapellmeister (A Sd, A 674) and, more precisely, in the autograph of Michael Haydn's Vespers, Klafsky IV/2c, dated 29 Nov. 1781.

[58] Christoph Wolff notes that the now-recovered autograph of K. 365 includes the remark by Nissen 'mit den Stimmen der Fagotti und Klarinetten', which lends weight to the authenticity of the clarinet-parts without, however, suggesting when they may have been composed. See his 'Zur Edition der Klavierkonzerte KV 246, KV 271, KV 365, KV 413–415', *Neue Mozart-Ausgabe. Bericht über die Mitarbeitertagung in Kassel 29.–30. Mai 1981*, ed. Dorothee Hanemann (privately printed, 1984), 40.

Example 7. W. A. Mozart, K. 271, III, mm. 130–49

copy by Raab and Estlinger survives in the Salzburg Dom-Musikarchiv—its date is not certain. Köchel thought the Offertory might have been composed in 1769, a date that was revised by Einstein, following Wyzewa and Saint-Foix, to May or June 1771. In K⁶ it was assigned to the summer of 1771 or 1772, after the first Italian journey. For the most part these datings were based on stylistic perceptions and on an anecdote, reported by Jahn, that the Offertory was composed for the name-day of Pater Johannes von Haasy of Seeon.[59]

The authentic Dom-Musikarchiv copy suggests a speculation of a different sort. Most early, dateable authentic copies of Mozart's sacred vocal music by Raab, Estlinger, and Hofstätter are approximately contemporary with the composition of the works they transmit (Table 1).[60] The only apparent exceptions are copies of K. 65 (61*a*), 195 (186*d*), 257, and possibly 258 and 262 (246*a*), all of which derive from the Heilig Kreuz monastery in Augsburg. But these may represent an atypical case. During his visit to

[59] K¹, 80; Wyzewa and Saint-Foix, *Wolfgang Amédée Mozart*, i. 372–3; K³, 150; K⁶, 126; Abert, *Mozart*, i. 317.

[60] Not all early copies can be accurately dated. Some are written on types of paper that were used in Salzburg for extended periods of time; as such, however, they neither confirm nor contradict the hypothesis that early copies are mostly contemporary with composition.

TABLE 1. *Comparative dates of autographs and authentic copies*

Dateable authentic copies

K1	(K6)	autograph	date	authentic copies	date	basis for dating authentic copies
47	(47)	lost	[1769]	A Ssp	nlt 1772	Work probably composed 1769; A Ssp copy 'ISH' paper (see above n. 10).
				A Gd	1769–72	Wrapper by Estlinger: 'Del Sig:re Wolfgango Mozart Maestro di Concerto' (Mozart appointed third concert-master 14 Nov. 1769), and 'ISH' paper.
66	(66)	D-brd B	1769	A Ssp	nlt 1772	'ISH' paper
				D-brd LAm	nlt 1772	'ISH' paper
				A LA	1772 or later	'AFH' paper
117	(66*a*)	D-ddr B	[1769]	A Ssp	nlt 1772	Work probably composed 1769; A Ssp copy 'ISH' paper.
				A Gd	1769–72	See remarks to K. 47, A Gd copy.
				D-brd LAm	nlt 1772	'ISH' paper
109	(74*e*)	D-ddr B	May 1771	A Sd	nlt 1772	'ISH' paper
125	(125)	D-brd B	1772	A Sd	1772	'ISH' *and* 'AFH' paper.
262	(246*a*)	PL Kj	[? June–July 1775]	D-brd Ahk	*c.*1777	For dating of work, see Alan Tyson, 'The Dates of Mozart's *Missa brevis* K. 258 and *Missa longa* K. 262 (246a): An Investigation into His *Klein-Querformat* Papers', *Mozart: Studies of the Autograph Scores* (Cambridge, Mass. and London, 1987) 162–76. D-brd Ahk copy on paper found in one Salzburg MS dated 1777 (A Ssp. Hay 390.1 = M. Haydn, Mass, Klafsky I/11) and in several copies of works composed 1777.
258	(258)	D-brd B	1775 or 1776	D-brd Ahk	*c.*1777	See previous remarks.
273	(273)	D-brd B	9 Sept. 1777	A Ssp	1777	MS with notation 'Ad Chorum . . . 1777'.
321	(321)	F Pc	1779	D-brd Ahk	1779–80	MS by Raab (†1 February 1780); paper commonly found in Salzburg MSS of works composed 1779–80.
				D-brd Asa	1780–1	Paper found in Salzburg MSS dated 1780–1.
337	(337)	A Wn	Mar. 1780	D-brd Ahk	*c.*1780	See remarks to K. 321 concerning paper.
339	(339)	PL Kj	1780	D-brd Ahk	*c.*1780	See remarks to K. 321 concerning paper.

K^1	(K^6)	autograph	date	authentic copies	date	basis for dating authentic copies
65	(61*a*)	D-brd B	14 Jan. 1769	D-brd Ahk	nlt 1780	MS by Raab; paper found in Salzburg MSS throughout 1770s.
127	(127)	PL Kj	May 1772	A LA	after 1772	'AFH' paper.
195	(186*d*)	D-ddr B	1774	D-brd Ahk	nlt 1780	MS by Raab; paper found in Salzburg MSS throughout 1770s.
192	(186*f*)	A Wn	24 June 1774	A Sd	nlt 1780	MS by Raab; paper found in Salzburg MSS throughout 1770s.
193	(186*g*)	A Wn	July 1774	A Sd	nlt 1780	MS by Raab; paper found in Salzburg MSS throughout 1770s.
194	(186*h*)	A Wn	8 Aug. 1774	A Sd	nlt 1780	MS by Raab (in part); paper found in Salzburg MSS throughout 1770s.
243	(243)	D-brd B	1776	privately owned	nlt 1780	MS by Raab; paper found in Salzurg MSS of late 1770s.
260	(248*a*)	A Wn	1776	A Sd	[nlt 1780]	Lost MS by Raab; see Appendix.
257	(257)	D-brd B	1775 or 1776	D-brd Ahk	nlt 1780	For dating of work, see Tyson, 'The Dates of Mozart's *Missa brevis*'. D-brd Ahk MS by Raab; paper commonly found in Salzburg MSS of works composed 1776–80.
259	(259)	D-brd B	1775 or 1776	A Sd	?1780s	For dating of work, see Tyson, 'The Dates of Mozart's *Missa brevis*'. A Sd MS on paper found in Salzburg MSS dated 1784–5.

Augsburg in 1777, Mozart was asked to present Heilig Kreuz with some of his works, and copies of several of them were made locally. Leopold, however, objected to this practice and arranged for other works to be copied in Salzburg and sent to Augsburg from there.[61] The chronological nonconformity of these copies may therefore be the result of their being a 'special order' of an unusual sort.

Two explanations for the contemporaneity of composition and authentic copies seem likely. One, suggested by the survival of multiple early, authentic copies of K. 47, 66, and 117, is that it was the Mozarts' usual practice to have several copies of sacred vocal works made about the time of their composition.[62] The other is that manuscripts in the Dom-Musikarchiv represent copies of works composed for performance in the Cathedral, the copying of which would have been contemporary with their composition.

If this 'double hypothesis' is correct, then authentic copies by Raab, Estlinger and Hofstätter may provide evidence for the dating of otherwise undated compositions by Mozart, such as K. 72. For although the Offertory is generally thought to have been composed during the early 1770s, the authentic Dom-Musikarchiv copy is on a type of paper that is found in Salzburg manuscripts only during the second half of the 1770s.[63] The most securely dateable manuscripts on this type of paper are Raab copies from before 1780 of Michael Haydn's Masses Klafsky I/10 (dated 4 September 1776) and I/11 (dated 14 September 1777), and of Mozart's Masses K. 257 (composed 1775 or 1776) and K. 275 (272*b*) (composed ?1777), as well as the symphony K. 319 (dated 9 July 1779).[64] All this suggests that K. 72 may date from some years later than has generally been supposed.

A different kind of chronological problem is raised by the authentic copy of Mozart's concerto K. 175, the autograph of which is lost. The manuscript includes orchestral parts for all three movements of K. 175 (A Ssp, Moz 340.1), a keyboard-part with the first two movements of K. 175 and the substitute finale K. 382, composed in 1782 (A Ssp, Moz 340.2), and orchestral parts for K. 382 (A Ssp, Moz 340.3). Five copyists prepared the parts: Estlinger, Hofstätter, and three unidentified Salzburg copyists. One explanation for the copy might be that it represents the original performing parts from 1773, lacking only the finale of the keyboard-part, and a full set of parts for K. 382, which may have been copied from the autograph sent by Mozart to Salzburg in March 1782.[65] However,

[61] See Leopold Mozart's letters of 1 Dec. 1777 and 29 June 1778; *Briefe*, ii. 157 and 381; *Letters*, 398–9 and 555.

[62] See Walter Senn, 'Das wiederaufgefundene Autograph der Sakramentslitanei in D von Leopold Mozart', *Mozart-Jahrbuch 1971/72*, 197. The survival of multiple contemporaneous copies of several works apparently gives the lie to Leopold's hyperbolic assertion in a letter of 10 Aug. 1781 to Breitkopf that 'my son never gives any compositions to be engraved or printed which are already in other hands. For we are very particular about having only one set of copies of every work; for this reason very little by him is known.' *Briefe*, iii. 149; *Letters*, 759.

[63] The watermark consists of the initials 'VG' under two leaves and a crescent moon with face in an ornament under a crown. Apparently it is not found among Mozart's autographs.

[64] A Ssp, Hay 385.2 (Klafsky I/10); A Ssp, Hay 390.1 (Klafsky I/11); D-brd Ahk, 6 (K. 257); D-brd Ahk, 8 (K. 275 [272b]); A Gkh, 40.602 (K. 319).

[65] See Mozart's letter of 23 Mar. 1782; *Briefe*, iii. 199; *Letters* 798.

the parts copied by Hofstätter and one of the unidentified Salzburg copyists, including both K. 175 and K. 382, show that the entire complex orginated at one time: excepting the second trumpet-part to K. 382 they are all on paper with the same watermark, and the total span is consistent throughout. Use of this paper type in Salzburg can be documented only during the period 1782–4.[66]

K. 175 is a concerto that Mozart played often. He took it with him to Munich in 1774, and a later performance, in Mannheim, is described in a letter of 14 February 1778.[67] In Vienna he performed K. 175, with the newly composed Rondo, K. 382, at his Burgtheater concert of 23 March 1782.[68] And it is a work Mozart is known to have revised about 1777 or 1778: there are two authentic versions of the oboe- and first horn-parts.[69] An obvious question, then, is does K. 175 survive in its original form? The earliest surviving authentic source dates from about ten years after the work's composition and may not be identical in every respect with the now-lost original. The distinction is an important one, for authentic Salzburg copies sometimes transmit revised or otherwise different and independent versions of Mozart's works: the symphony version of the Serenade K. 250 (248*b*), for example, includes a timpani-part (in Leopold Mozart's autograph), and a fanfare for winds at the end of the first movement, that are lacking in the Serenade version. What remains of K. 175, then, is the version used by Mozart in the early 1780s.

A further consideration with respect to authentic copies concerns Mozart's acquaintance with works of other composers. It is almost always claimed, for example, that Mozart's earliest symphonies are modelled directly on the symphonies of J. C. Bach, and that his church music stands in a special relationship to the church music of contemporary Salzburg composers.[70] Yet it is often difficult to document exactly which works by other composers Mozart might have known and, accordingly, to establish the plausibility of any possible relationship. One little-known example provides a firm basis for establishing a direct connection between Leopold Mozart's church music of the 1750s and Wolfgang's knowledge of it.

The work in question is Leopold's Litany, Seiffert 4/7–8 (Carlson IB3), which survives in two primary sources: an autograph score (A Sca, Hs. 1900) and the original performing parts (A Sd, A 454). In the autograph, the work is scored for two violins, basso, trombones (with a tenor trombone solo at the Agnus Dei) and four-part chorus. The

[66] The watermark consists of the initials 'A / HF / REAL' and three stars in a crowned ornament. The earliest dated manuscript in which it is found is the autograph of Michael Haydn's Divertimento, Perger 93, completed on 27 May 1782 (D-brd Mbs, Mus. mss. 3105); the latest is the autograph to the same composer's Offertory, Klafsky III/14, dated 27 Oct. 1784 (D-brd Mbs, Mus. mss. 435).

[67] *Briefe*, ii. 282; *Letters*, 482.

[68] See Mozart's letter of 29 Mar. 1783 in which he describes the concerto as 'a favourite here [in Vienna]'. *Briefe*, iii. 261; *Letters*, 843.

[69] Klaus Hortschansky, 'Autographe Stimmen zu Mozarts Klavierkonzert KV 175 im Archiv André zu Offenbach', *Mozart-Jahrbuch 1989/90*, 37–54.

[70] For possible influences on Mozart's early works, see in particular Manfred Hermann Schmid, *Mozart und die salzburger Tradition* (Tutzing, 1976), and the literature cited there.

Dom-Musikarchiv copy, however, includes not only a fourteen-measure introduction not in the autograph, but also several additional parts. It consists of the following:

copied by Estlinger: ripieno canto, alto, two tenors, and bass, violin I and II, viola I and II, violone, horn I and II, and trombone I, II, and III

copied by Leopold Mozart: oboe I and II, a paste-in solo for viola I at 'Salus infimorum', and, on a separate leaf, a transcription for viola of the 'Agnus Dei' trombone solo

copied by Wolfgang Amadeus Mozart: a transcription for oboe of the 'Agnus Dei' trombone solo, on the back of the leaf with Leopold's transcription of the same solo for viola[71]

Much of the manuscript, including the vocal parts and the parts for the violins, violone, and trombones, was copied by Estlinger using 'old' clefs and can be dated not later than 1760. The horn-parts, however, were copied using the 'new' style treble clef; consequently they were written down after *c.*1765—presumably they represent a later addition to the work—but not after *c.*1772, since they are on 'ISH' paper. Because Leopold Mozart was away from Salzburg for most of the period 1762 to 1771, the most likely time for their copying and composition was January to September 1767, February to December 1769, or April to August 1771, when the Mozarts were in Salzburg.[72] No such clear-cut evidence is forthcoming for the dating of the viola-parts not included in the autograph scoring; there are no dateable changes in the form of Estlinger's C clef. Other evidence, however, is helpful: both the horn- and viola-parts (also on 'ISH' paper) use an identical rastrum, which is different from the rastrum of the other parts. Hence it seems likely that the horn- and viola-parts were copied, and presumably composed, at about the same time. The most plausible explanation for the parts copied by Estlinger, then, is that they represent an original set of parts from before 1760, and horn- and viola-parts from 1767, 1769, or 1771.

Evidence for other performances and still more revision of the work is documented by the Leopold and Wolfgang autographs. The two oboe-parts in Leopold's hand are on

[71] Facsimiles of the Leopold and Wolfgang autographs are published in Ernst Hintermaier, 'Zur geistlichen Musik der Mozartzeit', *Mozartwoche 1981 vom 23. Jänner bis 1. Februar. Programm* (Salzburg, 1981), 141–2.

[72] Because the precise date of the change in Estlinger's treble clef is not certain, it is not out of the question that the horn-parts were written down as early as 1761. But they could not have been copied much before this: not only does Estlinger consistently use 'old' style clefs before 1760, but according to Leopold Mozart's own testimony, in 1757, oboes and flutes were seldom used in the Salzburg Cathedral, and horns not at all. See [Leopold Mozart], 'Nachricht von dem gegenwärtigen Zustande der Musik Sr. Hochfürstlichen Gnaden des Erzbischoffs zu Salzburg im Jahr 1757', in Friedrich Wilhelm Marpurg (ed.), *Historisch-kritische Beyträge zur Aufnahme der Musik*, iii (Berlin, 1757), 195: 'Die Oboe und Querflöte wird selten, das Waldhorn aber niemals in der Domkirche gehöret [Oboes and transverse flutes are seldom heard in the Cathedral, horns never].' According to Schmid, *Mozart und die salzburger Tradition*, 257, Leopold's Litany in D, Seiffert *deest* (Carlson IB2), the autograph of which is dated Apr. 1762, may be the earliest work composed for the Salzburg Cathedral to include horns. Other early works by Leopold, however, all of them from before 1760 (Estlinger, 'old' clefs), also include original horn-parts: the Mass, Seiffert 4/2 (Carlson IA2b); the Offertories *Omnes hodie coelestium*, Seiffert *deest* (Carlson IC1), *Jubilate Deo omnis terra*, Seiffert *deest* (Carlson IC2), and *Convertentur sedentes*, Seiffert 4/13 (Carlson IC5); and the *Confitemini Domino* Seiffert 4/15 (Carlson ID4). Some of these works may have been intended for the Cathedral.

paper with no visible watermark; consequently their dating is uncertain, although it was probably later than the writing down of the autograph score. The oboe and viola transcriptions of the Agnus Dei trombone solo, however, can be approximately dated: they are on a type of machine-ruled, possibly Italian, paper used by Mozart *c.* 1771.[73] A possible explanation for the transcriptions is that, during the early 1770s, there was no trombonist in Salzburg capable of adequately performing the solo. This ties in well with the biography of the trombonist Thomas Gschlatt, who was highly thought of by Leopold;[74] Gschlatt had been active at Salzburg from 1756, but left the court in 1769.

Although it is possible that all of these changes represent a single performance, it is more likely that they represent *two* later performances, for Mozart's handwriting in the oboe solo is *not* consistent with his handwriting in other manuscripts on this paper type, and apparently dates from the mid-1770s.[75] The earlier of the two solos, then, is the viola solo by Leopold, and it may be concluded that the viola- and horn-parts were all composed for a performance given during the summer of 1771. Leopold's oboe-parts, and Wolfgang's oboe solo, represent a still later performance.

In sum, a detailed evaluation of the Dom-Musikarchiv copy of Leopold's Litany does more than identify the manuscript as authentic: it documents the new use of horns and violas in works composed for the Salzburg Cathedral; it provides evidence that, contrary to received opinion, Leopold Mozart continued to perform his works and to engage in compositional activity even in the later 1760s;[76] and it identifies a composition, a representative of the 'Salzburg tradition', with which Mozart was unquestionably familiar.

ATTRIBUTION AND STYLE

Beyond the evaluation of individual sources and their content, or even groups of manuscripts and their importance for chronology and text, establishing criteria for authenticity also has broader implications for Mozart's output in general and for his development as a composer. For it is now possible to establish exactly what constitutes the authenticated repertory of works composed by Mozart before about 1780. The genre most suitable for such an investigation is the symphonies.

[73] Because the Leopold–Wolfgang autograph is a single leaf, the precise configuration of the sheet watermark is not certain; only the letters 'FV' and parts of two stars are visible. Alan Tyson informs me that a similar, probably identical watermark, with the same total span, is found in the autographs of Wolfgang's Litany K. 109, dated May 1771, in the first four leaves of the symphony K. 129, dated May 1772 but possibly begun the year before, and in *Il sogno di Scipione* K. 126, also from 1771.

[74] [Leopold Mozart], 'Nachricht von dem gegenwärtigen Zustande der Musik', 189: 'Posaunist ... Hr. Thomas Oschlatt [*recte* Gschlatt] aus Stockerau in Unteröstereich. Ist ein grosser Meister auf seinem Instrumente, dem es sehr wenig gleich thun werden [Mr Thomas Gschlatt, from Stockerau in Lower Austria. He is a great master of his instrument, whose equal is hardly to be found].'

[75] I am indebted to Wolfgang Plath for his opinion concerning the date of the Wolfgang autograph.

[76] In general, see Cliff Eisen, 'The Symphonies of Leopold Mozart: Their Chronology, Style and Importance for the Study of Mozart's Early Symphonies', *Mozart-Jahrbuch 1987/88*, 181–93.

According to the Köchel catalogue, Mozart composed twenty-five symphonies between 1764 and 1771 (K. 16 to K. 112). Although many of them do not survive in his autograph, there is general agreement that the works *are* by Mozart: they continue to hold their places in the standard Mozart literature and in the main bodies of the Köchel catalogue and the *Neue Mozart-Ausgabe*. More than half of these works, however, lack authentic sources of any sort.

The attribution to Mozart of most of the unauthenticated symphonies derives from the so-called Breitkopf & Härtel manuscript catalogue, an early nineteenth-century attempt to list titles and incipits of all works attributed to Mozart.[77] In part, the catalogue was based on manuscript holdings inherited from the original Breitkopf, whose firm was taken over by Härtel in 1796; other listings derived from printed editions by well-known publishers such as André and Artaria, or from manuscripts acquired through the Hamburg music dealer Johann Christoph Westphal, the Salzburg Kapellmeister Luigi Gatti, Mozart's sister, Nannerl, and the composer's widow, Constanze.

None of the sources used by Breitkopf & Härtel is above suspicion. The provenance of the manuscripts inherited from Breitkopf is entirely unknown, and some of the printed editions include demonstrably spurious works. Nor was Constanze Mozart, or her future second husband, Nissen, whose attestation of authenticity appears on many of Mozart's scores, always certain which manuscripts in her possession transmitted works by Mozart or even which were his autographs.[78] And while the derivation of manuscripts from Nannerl Mozart has generally been considered reliable evidence that the works they transmit are genuine, the manuscripts did not, in fact, originate with the Mozart family. As her correspondence shows, many of the copies she sent to Breitkopf & Härtel originated with the Salzburg Kapellmeister, Luigi Gatti. There is little reason to suppose that Gatti was reliable. Evidence for his apparently deliberate falsification of attributions survives in a thematic catalogue of the Salzburg Cathedral holdings from the late 1780s drawn up under his direct supervision: included in the catalogue are Vesper Psalms by Johann Baptist Sternkopf, organist at Metten, a Benedictine monastery not far from Salzburg, that are credited to Gatti himself.[79] Consequently, attributions to Mozart in the Breitkopf & Härtel catalogue that derive from Salzburg or elsewhere are insufficient as evidence for authenticity.

Several of the uncertain symphonies survive only in editions published by Breitkopf and Härtel in 1881, including K. 75, 76 (42*a*), 95 (75*n*), 96 (111*b*), and 97 (73*m*). Other contemporary sources for these works are unknown and no documentary evidence ties

[77] Although the original of this catalogue is lost, copies made for Jahn and Köchel survive in the Staatsbibliothek Preussischer Kulturbesitz, Berlin, and the Gesellschaft der Musikfreunde, Vienna, respectively. The Breitkopf catalogue is discussed in detail in Neal Zaslaw, *Mozart's Symphonies: Context, Performance Practice, Reception* (Oxford, 1989), esp. 130–2, and Cliff Eisen, 'Problems of Authenticity among Mozart's Early Symphonies: The Examples of K. Anh. 220 (16*a*) and 76 (42*a*)', *Music and Letters*, 70 (1989), 505–16.

[78] Plath, 'Zur Echtheitsfrage bei Mozart', 29.

[79] Walter Senn, 'Der Catalogus Musicalis des Salzburger Doms (1788)', *Mozart-Jahrbuch 1971/72*, 182–96 at 183; Eisen, 'Problems of Authenticity among Mozart's Early Symphonies', 508–9.

them directly to Mozart. K. Anh. 215 (66*c*), Anh. 217 (66*d*), and Anh. 218 (66*e*) are known *only* from incipits in the Breitkopf & Härtel manuscript catalogue; otherwise they are entirely lost. Yet the Köchel catalogue boldly includes them among Mozart's genuine works and gives their place and date of composition as Salzburg, 1769. K. Anh. 222 (19*b*) is similarly lost; it, too, is included among the genuine symphonies and said to have been composed in London in 1765.

Some symphonies do survive in eighteenth-century sources, although there is no evidence to connect them directly with Mozart or his circle. A recently discovered manuscript of K. Anh. 220 (16*a*) apparently derives from the Westphal,[80] and K. Anh. 214 (45*b*) survives in two contemporary copies, one in the Staatsbibliothek Preussischer Kulturbesitz, Berlin (D-brd, Mus. ms. 15305) and another, apparently unknown to the *NMA*, at Einsiedeln (CH E, 819/1,12). The Berlin copy of K. Anh. 214 dates from *c.* 1800 and is probably south German in origin; the Einsiedeln copy, possibly from the 1770s or 1780s, is local.

A particularly difficult problem concerns the symphonies said to have been composed in Italy in 1770. Although documents show that Mozart gave orchestral concerts, including symphonies, in Verona and Mantua in January, the earliest reference to newly composed symphonies comes from a letter of 25 April, written at Rome: 'When I have finished this letter I shall finish a symphony which I have begun . . . A[nother] symphony is being copied (the copyist is father, for we do not wish to give it out to be copied as it would be stolen).' And in a letter of 4 August, written at Bologna, Mozart reported to his sister: 'In the meantime I have composed 4 Italian symphonies.'[81]

According to the Köchel catalogue and the standard Mozart literature, these four symphonies are K. 81 (73*l*), 84 (73*q*), 95, and 97. None of them, however, is known in Mozart's autograph or authentic copies. It has already been noted that the earliest references to K. 95 and 97 are their listings in the Breitkopf & Härtel manuscript catalogue, and that the earliest surviving sources are Breitkopf & Härtel's editions of 1881. As for K. 81, the unique surviving eighteenth-century copy of this symphony (A Wgm, XIII 20026 (Q 18464)) has the notation 'In Roma 25 April. 1770' on its cover, which squares well with Mozart's letter of the same date. However, the source cannot be exactly contemporary with the supposed place and date of composition. The wrapper describes Mozart as 'Knight [of the Golden Spur]', an honour conferred on him by the Pope only later, in July. And it is certainly not authentic, as has been claimed,[82] for it derives from the area around Prague and has nothing to do with the Mozarts, their Salzburg copyists, or the normal dissemination of his works during the 1770s. The same may be said of the Gesellschaft der Musikfreunde copy of K. 84, which is by the same copyist, and on the same kind of Bohemian paper (A Wgm, XIII 20027 (Q 18465)). There

[80] Neal Zaslaw and Cliff Eisen, 'Signor Mozart's Symphony in A-minor, K. Anhang 220 = 16*a*', *Journal of Musicology*, 4 (1985–6), 191–206; rev. and repr. in Zaslaw, *Mozart's Symphonies*, 267–81.

[81] *Briefe*, i. 342 and 377; *Letters*, 131 and 153.

[82] Ernst Fritz Schmid, 'Zur Entstehungszeit von Mozarts italienischen Sinfonien', *Mozart-Jahrbuch 1958*, 71.

are conflicting attributions for both symphonies: K. 84 survives in another contemporary copy attributed to Ditters (CS Pnm, Pachta XXII C 18), and K. 81 is attributed to Leopold Mozart in Breitkopf's 1775 thematic catalogue.

In short, while it has been common to assume that Mozart composed at least twenty-five symphonies between 1764 and 1771, more than half of them lack authentic sources and there is no convincing evidence that any of them is by him. The authenticated repertory consists of K. 16, 19, Anh. 223 (19*a*), 22, Anh. 221 (45*a*), 43, 45, 48, 73, 74, 110, and 112.

These observations have significant implications for our understanding of Mozart's development as a composer of orchestral music. A commonly held view has it, for example, that the symphonies composed in 1771—usually said to be K. 73, 75, 96, 110 (75*b*), 112, and 120—show that '[Mozart's] symphonic development at this time had not reached any new creative phase.'[83] Yet the repertory cited in defence of this notion cannot be entirely justified as either contemporary or authentic: two of the symphonies, K. 75 and K. 96, have no authentic sources; another, K. 73, dates from late 1769 or early 1770;[84] and K. 120 is a finale composed for the overture to Mozart's opera *Ascanio in Alba*. Consequently, there are only two complete, independent, and certain symphonies from this time, K. 110, composed in Salzburg in July 1771, and K. 112, composed in Milan in November.

In several respects, both works represent important new directions in Mozart's symphonic thinking. The first movement of K. 110, for example, is longer than any previous symphonic first movement by him, and tends towards an uncharacteristic monothematicism; the recapitulation, unusually, hints at further development. The contrapuntal writing for the bass and inner voices, which is prominent not only in the first movement but also in the slow movement and especially in the canonic minuet, is a novelty. And in the slow movement, Mozart, for the first time in a symphony, writes independent parts for the bassoons.[85] As for K. 112, this symphony has the first sonata-form slow movement by Mozart to include some genuine development, not just a re-transition to the recapitulation. Both symphonies explore new tonal relationships between Menuet and Trio. Prior to 1771, Mozart's trios were exclusively in the sub-dominant; the Trio of K. 110, however, is in the submediant, while that of K. 112 is in the dominant.

The most striking aspect of the symphonies, however, is that they break down the previously strictly adhered-to association of thematic or motivic material with function. In K. 110, the stable opening gesture returns as a concluding motif at the end of the exposition (measures 53 and following). And in K. 112, the beginning of the transition is obscured by the re-use of the symphony's stable opening bar as a jumping-off point for the modulation (Ex. 8). What makes this passage particularly effective is the structure of

[83] Jens Peter Larsen, 'The Symphonies', in H. C. Robbins Landon and Donald Mitchell (eds.), *The Mozart Companion* (London, 1956), 165.

[84] *NMA* IV/11/1, ed. Gerhard Allroggen (Kassel, 1984), p. xiii.

[85] See also Zaslaw, *Mozart's Symphonies*, 211–12.

EXAMPLE 8. W. A. Mozart, K. 112, I, mm. 1–14

ob.
hn.
I
vn.
II
p f p
p f p
va.
p f p
b.
f

the opening idea. For in earlier symphonies with similarly constructed openings—an idea that consists of two parts: an aggressive, forte, and often unison, triadic idea, and a softer motif with stepwise activity, as in K. 16, 19, and 22—the first idea is more or less literally repeated. In K. 112, however, the repetition of the first part of the gesture, measures 1–2, is lacking; measure 1 does not recur at measure 6. Consequently, measure 10, the equivalent of measure 1, functions not only as the conclusion of the statement, bringing the phrase to a symmetrical five-measure plus five-measure conclusion, but also as the first element in a two-measure phrase at the beginning of the transition, which is marked not only by the forte dynamic and repeated eighth-notes for the violas and basses, but especially by the transition-like texture of the repeated sixteenth-notes for the first violins beginning in measure 13. The first time through the exposition, then, measures 10–11 are without decisive functional identity. The reinterpretation of previously heard material creates not only the illusion of unity, but also of ambiguity, and it was to become a standard feature of Mozart's symphonies, and of his style in general, during the 1770s and later.

AUTHENTIC SALZBURG COPIES OF THE 1780s

It is well documented that Mozart regularly received music from Salzburg after his permanent move to Vienna in 1781. In March 1782, for example, he asked Leopold to send his scores of the *scena* 'Misera, dove son!—Ah! non son' io che parlo', K. 369, as well as some masses, and in January 1783 he wrote for copies of the symphonies K. 204, 201 (186*a*), 182 (173*dA*), and 183 (173*dB*); the next month he asked for the oboe concerto K. 314.[86] It is less widely appreciated, however, that Mozart also continued to send his new works back to Salzburg, where some of them were copied and performed. In December 1781, for example, he sent his scores of *Idomeneo*, the sonata K. 448 (375*a*), some cadenzas, and a copy of the printed sonatas K. 296 and 376–80 (374*d–e*, 317*d*, 373*a*, and 374*f*). In March 1782 he sent the Rondo for piano and orchestra, K. 382, and in July scores of *Die Entführung* and (piecemeal) the 'Haffner' Symphony, K. 385.[87] A substantial parcel, sent in May 1784, included the sonata K. 333 (315*c*), the symphony K. 425, and the concertos K. 449, 450, 451, and 453; Mozart's letter includes the further cryptic remark: 'Well, I don't know what it was that you were thinking about and did not want to mention in your letter; and therefore to avoid all misunderstanding, I am sending you herewith all my new compositions.'[88]

The copyists employed by Leopold Mozart during the 1780s to produce parts from Mozart's scores, or to make later copies of earlier works, were not entirely the same as

[86] See Mozart's letters of 23 Mar. 1782 and 4 Jan. and 15 Feb. 1783; *Briefe*, iii. 198–9, 248, and 256; *Letters*, 798, 835, and 840.

[87] See Mozart's letters of 15 Dec. 1781, 23 Mar., and 20 and 27 July 1782; *Briefe*, iii. 179, 198–9, 212–13, and 214; *Letters*, 782, 798, 808, and 809.

[88] Letter of 15 May 1784; *Briefe*, iii. 314; *Letters*, 877. See also Alan Tyson, 'The Date of Mozart's Piano Sonata in B flat, K. 333 (315*c*): The "Linz" Sonata?', *Mozart: Studies of the Autograph Scores*, 73–81.

they had been in the 1760s and 1770s. Estlinger's hand continues to appear regularly in post-1781 Salzburg copies of Mozart's works, including manuscripts of K. 259, K. 365, K. 382, K. 425, and K. 427 (417*a*). Raab, however, had died on 1 February 1780 and Hofstätter appears to have become Michael Haydn's preferred copyist during the 1780s (what is more, Leopold may have been influenced by Mozart's accusations concerning Hofstätter's dishonesty).[89] Other hands, however, are consistently found in the manuscripts, although none of the copyists can be identified by name. One scribe, described by Senn as *two* copyists, E and F, helped produce manuscripts of the Masses K. 220 (A Sd, A 709), K. 258 (D-brd Ahk, 7), and K. 275 (D-brd Ahk 8), the Offertory 222 (205*a*) (D-brd Fulda, Kasten M 11/229), and the Concertos K. 175 + 382 (A Ssp, Moz 340.1–3) and K. 246 (A Ssp, Moz 235.1), while the handwriting of another, Schmid's copyist 9, is found exclusively among the concerto copies now at St Peter's, including K. 175 + 382, 271, 449, 451, and 466 (A Ssp, Moz 340.2, 240.1, 265.1, 270.1, and 275.1, respectively).[90] The most important manuscript among this last group is the authentic copy of the D minor Concerto, K. 466.

One problematic reading in the concerto concerns measures 267–8 in the first movement, a sustained, sequential build-up, beginning at measure 262, to the brief orchestral outburst in measure 269 (Ex. 9). At the climax of this passage, Mozart in his autograph uncharacteristically writes a rest for the orchestral basses in measures 267 and 268, which surely needs correcting; otherwise the triplets for the cellos are left hanging in mid-air and much of the cadence occurs without an effective orchestral bass part. This passage was understood as faulty by even the very earliest copyists and editors of the work, all of whom 'completed' the missing orchestral bass-part.

The solution provided by the *NMA* has the violoncellos taking over the left hand of the piano for both measures, a reasonable conjecture if this were a tutti passage, in which the piano was playing *col basso*. However, although it leads to a brief orchestral outburst, the passage itself is part of an extended solo section and the orchestral basses cannot be expected necessarily to duplicate the piano left hand. The authentic copy offers a different reading: the violoncellos double the piano left hand only in measure 267; they drop out for the second and third beats of measure 268—where the violas effectively take over the bass function—re-entering, in dramatic fashion, with the double basses for the climactic triplet on the last eighth of measure 268. This is also the reading given by early manuscript copies and editions of the concerto.[91]

A more substantial issue raised by the St Peter's copy of K. 466 concerns the periodic reduction of orchestral forces. Mozart's concerto autographs often include the notations

[89] See Schmid, *Die Musikaliensammlung der Erzabtei St. Peter in Salzburg*, 30 ('Schreiber 31'), and the list of Michael Haydn copies there. Numerous other manuscripts from the 1780s of Michael Haydn's works, including many copies in libraries outside of Salzburg, are also by Hofstätter.

[90] Concerning the provenance of the concerto copies, see Manfred Hermann Schmid, 'Nannerl Mozart und ihr musikalischer Nachlaß: Zu den Klavierkonzerten im Archiv St. Peter in Salzburg', *Mozart-Jahrbuch 1980/83*, 140–7.

[91] Although the St Peter's copy of K. 466 is given as a primary source in the critical report to *NMA* V/15/6, ed. Horst Heussner (Kassel, 1986), this reading is not listed there.

Example 9. W. A. Mozart, K. 466, I, mm. 265–9

Tutti and *Solo*, which are generally thought to indicate the entire string body versus a reduction in the number of players. Until now, the chief evidence for this hypothesis has been a contemporary copy at Melk of the Concerto K. 175 + 382, which includes separate ripieno parts.[92] The Melk parts, however, are not demonstrably authentic, and may not reflect Mozart's practice.

The authentic Salzburg copy, on the other hand, apparently confirms Mozart's practice of reducing the orchestra. For alone among authentic copies of Mozart's concertos, it includes additional parts for first and second ripieno violins ('Violino Primo Rip:no' and 'Violino Second Rip:no'). The breakdown of *Tutti* and *Solo* is as follows:

first movement

1–77	full orchestra (ritornello)
78–111	reduced orchestra (beginning of solo)
112–14	full orchestra (cadence on dominant)
115–72	reduced orchestra (solo)
173–92	full orchestra (medial ritornello)
193–253	reduced orchestra (development)
254–87	full orchestra (beginning of recapitulation)
288–355	reduced orchestra (recapitulation of dominant material)
356–end	full orchestra (final ritornello)

second movement

1–39	full orchestra (ritornello)
40–75	reduced orchestra (solo)
76–83	full orchestra (ritornello)
84–134	reduced orchestra (central episode and return of main theme)
135–41	full orchestra (ritornello; cf. m. 25)
142–end	reduced orchestra (recapitulation of dominant material)

third movement

1–62	full orchestra (ritornello)
63–179	reduced orchestra (solo, including return of rondo theme)
180–95	full orchestra (ritornello; cf. m. 13)
196–336	reduced orchestra (solo)
337–88	full orchestra (ritornello, including cadenza and beginning of D major coda)
389–411	reduced orchestra (beginning in mid-phrase)
412–end	full orchestra (beginning in mid-phrase)

Among other things, the copy highlights the fact that full and reduced textures are not tied exclusively to the soloist's taking on a continuo function. In the final movement at measures 139–46, for example, the ritornello-like gesture of the orchestra, following a prominent trill and cadence for the soloist in measure 137, who then plays *col basso*, is given out by reduced forces (the parallel passage, measures 302–9, is similarly scored).

[92] *NMA* V/15/5, ed. Eva and Paul Badura-Skoda (Kassel, 1965), pp. xi–xii.

The final coda, with its turn to the tonic major, provides another good example of scoring used to emphasize a cadence, although not necessarily where expected: after the aggressive orchestral build-up of measures 370–6 and 382–8, the texture is reduced as the movement moves to its conclusion; the full orchestra re-enters only in mid-phrase, at measure 412, with the double- and triple-stops in the first and second violins, respectively.

Differences in full and reduced texture are also used to draw attention to one of the soloist's special tasks in concertos, the giving-out of a new theme. In the first movement, the orchestra is reduced from the very beginning of the first solo—it has only a short outburst in measures 112–14—and the new theme stands out for being in the dominant. In the recapitulation, however, where the theme will appear in the tonic, the orchestra is reduced only at measure 288, the restatement of the new, formerly dominant-area, theme; its continued special nature is thereby emphasized. Colouristic effects are even used to create dramatic links between movements. The *Romanze*, from measure 142 on (the second half of the recapitulation), is exclusively for reduced orchestra; there is no *Tutti* again in the movement. How much more dramatic, then, is the orchestral outburst at the beginning of the Allegro assai, beginning at measure 13?

The evidence of the St Peter's manuscript of K. 466 is striking not only because it is the only authentic copy to include ripieno violin parts, but also because it can be associated, even if only indirectly, with Mozart's performances of the concerto in Vienna. As several autograph entries show, the copy was made under the supervision of Leopold Mozart, who, according to a letter of 16 February, heard the first two performances of the concerto in Vienna:

> On [11 February] we drove to his [Wolfgang's] first subscription concert, at which a great many members of the aristocracy were present ... The concert was magnificent and the orchestra played splendidly. In addition to the symphonies, a female singer of the Italian theatre sang two arias. Then we had a new and very fine concerto by Wolfgang, which the copyist was still copying when we arrived, and the rondo of which your brother did not even have time to play through, as he had to supervise the copying ... Yesterday, the 15th, there was again a recital in the theatre given by a girl [Elizabeth Distler] who sings charmingly. Your brother played his new grand concerto in D [minor] most magnificently.[93]

In December, Mozart sent the score to Salzburg, where Leopold had it copied and performed.[94] At the very least, then, the St Peter's copy of K. 466, like the Kroměříž copy of K. 365, represents one of the relatively few surviving manuscripts that can with some confidence be associated with a documented performance by Mozart, albeit only indirectly.

An overwhelming reliance on Mozart's autographs does not do full justice to the wide range of authentic and potentially authentic sources of evidence for the attribution,

[93] Letter of 16 Feb. 1785; *Briefe*, iii. 373–4; *Letters*, 886–7.

[94] See Leopold Mozart's letters of 2 Dec. 1785 and 23 Mar. 1786; *Briefe*, iii. 461 and 518; *Letters*, 894 and 896.

chronology, text, and performance practice of his works. Indeed, it could not be otherwise, even if every composition by Mozart survived in his score. For while autographs may be primary sources, they represent only one element in a complex web of evidence. Even a few examples—revisions written directly into the performance copies, as in the symphony version of K. 250, or the added wind-parts, lacking in the autograph, to the Mass K. 66—show that the composer himself did not always consider his autographs the sole authentic sources for his works. There is a considerable gap between conception and its commitment to paper, on the one hand, and realization and dissemination, on the other.

For the period before 1781, and indeed for several years after Mozart's permanent move to Vienna, that gap is filled in by those sources closest to the autographs, the authentic copies made under the Mozarts' direct supervision. In cases where the autographs are lost, they often represent the best surviving sources for his works; and in several instances they provide apparently unequivocal testimony concerning Mozart's own performances. As such, they are of primary importance in the complex of sources upon which our direct knowledge of Mozart and his works depends.

Appendix

Authentic Copies, in Whole or in Part, by 'Salzburg 1', Raab, Estlinger, and Hofstätter of Works by Leopold and Wolfgang Amadeus Mozart

I: LEOPOLD MOZART

(* = manuscript with title page or autograph corrections by Leopold Mozart)

Seiffert (Eisen)[a]	Work	Source	Copyists	Remarks
1/11	*Schlittenfahrt*	D-brd Mbs, Mus. mss. 5306	'Salzburg 1'	Probably copy used at first performance, 1756; MS inc. several parts by ?local Augsburg copyist.
3/2 (C2)	Symphony	*D-brd HR, 4°534	Estlinger	MS not later than 1760 (Estlinger: 'old' clefs).
3/8 (D6)	Symphony	*D-brd HR, 4°518	'Salzburg 1', Estlinger	MS not later than 1760 (Estlinger; 'old' clefs); inc. duplicate Basso part by unidentified copyist.
3/11 (D9)	Symphony	*D-brd HR, 4°522	Estlinger	MS not later than 1760 (Estlinger: 'old' clefs); inc. duplicate Basso part by unidentified copyist.
3/12 (D11)	Symphony	*D-brd HR, 4°536	'Salzburg 1'	MS inc. parts by Johann Ferdinand Pater (*c.*1745–93), court musician in Munich. Copy sold to Wallerstein in 1751; see G. Haberkamp, *Thematischer Katalog der Musikhandschriften der Fürstlich Oettingen–Wallerstein'schen Bibliothek Schloss Harburg* (Munich, 1976), p. x.
3/18 (F1)	Symphony	*D-brd HR, 4°535	Estlinger	MS not later than 1760 (Estlinger: 'old' clefs).
3/20 (F3)	Symphony	D-brd Mbs, Mus. mss. 4758	Estlinger	MS not later than 1760 (Estlinger: 'old' clefs).
3/23 (G3)	Symphony	*D-brd HR, 4°540	Estlinger	Only Vn. I, II by Estlinger; others by unidentified copyist. MS sold to Wallerstein in 1751; see Haberkamp, *Thematischer Katalog*, p. x.
3/25 (G5)	Symphony	D-brd Asa, MG II 24	Raab	MS not later than 1768.
3/27 (G7)	Symphony	*D-brd HR, 4°525	Estlinger	MS not later than 1760 (Estlinger: 'old' clefs); inc. duplicate Basso part by unidentified copyist.
3/29 (G9)	Symphony	A Wgm, XIII 23533	'Salzburg 1'	MS inc. several parts by unidentified south German copyist.

deest (G16)	Symphony	*D-brd Asa, MG II 59	Estlinger	'New Lambach'. MS probably 1767; presented by Leopold to Lambach on 4 Jan. 1769.
3/33	*Bauernhochzeit*	D-brd B, Mus. ms. 15005	Estlinger	Only Vn. I, basso, and oboes by Estlinger, not later than 1760 ('old' clefs); other parts by 3 unidentified copyists.
3/35	Concerto (2 hn.)	*D-brd HR, 4°421	Estlinger	MS dated 1752; solo horn-parts and wrapper by Leopold Mozart.
3/36	Minuets	*A Sca, Hs. 659	Estlinger	Composed for the wedding of Francesco Spangler, 4 Jan. 1755. MS lacks hn. II; wrapper by Leopold Mozart.
deest	Serenade	*A SEI, V 1451	Estlinger	MS *c.* 1760–4 (Estlinger; 'mixed' clefs); mvts. iii, iv = Leopold Mozart, Trumpet Concerto (autograph D-brd Mbs dated 1762).
deest	Cassation	D-brd Mbs. Mus. mss. 5229	Raab	'Toy' Symphony. MS 1772 or later ('AFH' paper). Incomplete; only wrapper extant.

Seiffert (Carlson)	Work	Source	Copyists	Remarks
4/1 (IA1)	Mass	*A Ssp, Moz 10.1	Estlinger	MS not later than 1760 ('old' clefs).
		*D-brd Ahk, 76	Estlinger	MS not later than 1760 ('old' clefs); inc. parts by 3 unidentified ?Salzburg copyists; ripieno tenor and basso parts (*not* by Estlinger) dated 1753.
4/2 (IA2b)	Mass	A Ssp, Moz 15.1	Estlinger	MS not later than 1760 ('old' clefs).
lost (IA3)	Mass	*A Sd, A 450	'Salzburg 1'	
4/7-8 (IB3)	Litany	*A Sd, A 454	Estlinger	MS not later than 1760 ('old' clefs) except va. I, II, hn. I, II *c.* 1771; additional ob. I, II (L. Mozart autograph), mid-1770s; va. solo (L. Mozart autograph) *c.* 1771, ob. solo (W. A. Mozart autograph, on verso of va. solo), mid-1770s. MS also inc. later *Dubletten* by Joachim Fuetsch (1765–1852), court violoncellist from 1791, Kapellmeister at Salzburg Cathedral 1824–41.

I: LEOPOLD MOZART (*cont.*)

(* = manuscript with title page or autograph corrections by Leopold Mozart)

Seiffert (Carlson)	Work	Source	Copyists	Remarks
4/9 (IB4)	Litany	A Sd, A 453	Raab, Estlinger	Part copied by Estlinger after 1760 ('new' bass clef). MS inc. later hn. parts (probably not authentic) by Mathias Kracher jun. (1752–1827 or 1830), organist and chamber servant at Michaelbeuern from late 1760s.
4/10 (IB5)	Litany	*A Sd, A 452	'Salzburg 1', Raab, Estlinger	MS not later than 1760 (Estlinger: 'old' clefs); inc. L. Mozart autograph vn. I part and later hn. parts (probably not authentic) by Kracher.
4/13 (IC5)	Offertory	*A Ssp, Moz 35.1	Estlinger	MS not later than 1760 (Estlinger: 'old' clefs); inc. duplicate soprano, alto parts by Joseph Tremml (*c.* 1800–67), active at St Peter's from at least 1830. Copies A RB, Wgm, D-brd FW, B, Mbs attr. W. A. Mozart (K^6 Anh. C 3.09).
4/14 (IC4)	Offertory	*A Sd, A 451	'Salzburg 1'	
deest (IC1)	Offertory	*D-brd TIT, 49	Estlinger	MS dated 1757.
		*D-brd Asa, MG II 52	Estlinger	MS not later than 1760 (Estlinger: 'old' clefs).
deest (IC2)	Offertory	*D-brd Asa, MG II 53	Estlinger	MS not later than 1760 (Estlinger: 'old' clefs).
4/15 (ID4)	Confitemini	A Ssp, Moz 40.1	Estlinger	MS not later than 1760 (Estlinger: 'old' clefs).
4/16 (ID2)	Tantum ergo	A Ssp, Moz 45.1	Estlinger	MS not later than 1760 (Estlinger: 'old' clefs). Inc. later duplicate vn. I by Martin Bischofreiter (1762–1845), *Praefectus chori figuralis* at St Peter's from 1794, *Inspector chori musici* from 1819; and soprano and alto parts by Joseph Tremml.
deest (IE3)	Cantata	D-brd Asa MG II 51	Estlinger	MS not later than 1760 (Estlinger: 'old' clefs).
deest (IE2)	Cantata	D-brd TIT, 54	Estlinger	MS not later than 1756 (wrapper: 'ad Chorum San-Petrensis Ecclesiae in donationem oblata, Anno 1756').

II: WOLFGANG AMADEUS MOZART

(* = manuscript with title-page or attribution by Leopold Mozart, or with autograph corrections by Leopold or Wolfgang Amadeus Mozart)

K[1]	(K[6])	Source	Copyists	Remarks
42	(35*a*)	*D-brd Mbs, Mus. mss. 1281	Estlinger	*NMA* I/4/4 (critical report), *deest*. MS 1772 or later.
–	(45*a*)	*A LA, 2073	Estlinger	*NMA* IV/11/1, pp. xi–xii; copyist not identified. MS *c.* 1767.
47	(47)	*A Gd, Mariazell 333	Estlinger	*NMA* I/3 (critical report), source B. MS with performance dates 1777–1814 but copied not later than 1772.
65	(61*a*)	*D-brd Ahk, 1	Raab	*NMA* I/1/1/1 (critical report), source B.
66	(66)	*A Ssp, Moz 80.1	Estlinger	*NMA* I/1/1/1 (critical report), source B. MS acquired by St Peter's 1776 (organo: 'Ad Chorum Monasterii S. Petri 1776') but copied not later than 1772 ('ISH' paper); inc. ob., hn., 'tromba' I parts written by L. and W. A. Mozart, not in autograph.
		D-brd LAm, 91	Estlinger	*NMA* I/1/1/1 (critical report), *deest*. MS not later than 1772; inc. hn. parts.
72	(74*f*)	*A Sd, A 1123	Raab, Estlinger	*NMA* I/3 (critical report), source A (autograph unknown). Work traditionally dated early 1770s but MS copied later 1770s.
103	(61*d*)	A Sm, Rara 103/2	Hofstätter	*NMA* IV/13/1/1, *deest*. MS copied mid-1770s.
109	(74*e*)	*A Sd, A 1124	Raab, Estlinger	*NMA* I/2/1 (critical report), source B. MS copied 1771–2.
110	(75*b*)	D-ddr LEm	Raab	*NMA* IV/11/2, *deest*; see Plath, 'Mozartiana in Frankfurt und Fulda', 334. MS incomplete, only vn. I, II, basso extant; basso by unidentified copyist.
117	(66*a*)	A Gd, Mariazell 332	Estlinger	*NMA* I/3 (critical report), source C. MS not later than 1772.
		D-brd LAm, 88	Estlinger	*NMA* I/3 (critical report), *deest*, MS copied not later than 1772; apparently based on A Ssp, Moz 185.1 (authentic copy by unidentified Salzburg copyist, with L. Mozart corrections in parts).
125	(125)	[formerly A Sd]	Raab, Estlinger	*NMA* I/2/1 (critical report), source B. Description based on *NMA* (MS could not be found in A Sd as of June 1990).
127	(127)	*A LA, 1639	Hofstätter	*NMA* I/3 (critical report), source A (autograph formerly lost but now D-brd B). MS 1772 or later.
135[10]		*YU Zha, Algarotti XLVI 2F	Raab	*NMA* V/7/1, *deest*. MS dated 10 January 1777.
135[11]		*A Wgm, VI 31595	Raab	*NMA* V/7/1, *deest*. MS 1773–4.

II: WOLFGANG AMADEUS MOZART (*cont.*)

(* = manuscript with title-page or attribution by Leopold Mozart, or with autograph corrections by Leopold or Wolfgang Amadeus Mozart)

K1 (K6)	Source	Copyists	Remarks
135[21]	D-brd Asa, MG II 136	Hofstätter	*NMA* V/7/1, *deest*. MS 1773–4.
	YU Zha, Algarotti XLVI 2G	Hofstätter	*NMA* V/7/1, *deest*. Score copy with date obliterated and replaced (by ?Mozart) with 'Carnovale 1786'.
141 (66*b*)	[formerly A Sd]	Raab	*NMA* I/3 (critical report), source A (autograph unknown). Description based on *NMA* (MS could not be found in A Sd as of June 1990).
146 (317*b*)	*D-brd Mbs, Mus. mss. 1280	Estlinger	*NMA* I/4/4 (critical report), source [A] (autograph unknown). MS 1772 or later.
165 (158*a*)	*D-brd WS, 1162	Estlinger	*NMA* I/3 (critical report), *deest*. Transmits revised version; see Münster, 'Mozarts Motette "Exsultate, jubilate"'.
182 (173*d*A)	*D-brd B, Ms. mus. 15271	Raab, Hofstätter	*NMA* IV/11/4 (critical report), source B (copyists not identified). MS inc. parts from 1773–4 and 1776–8.
192 (186*f*)	[formerly A Sd]	Raab, Hofstätter	*NMA* I/1/1/2 (critical report), source B. MS inc. later hn. parts (probably not authentic) by unidentified Salzburg copyist.
193 (186*g*)	*A Sd, A 1125	Raab, Estlinger, Hofstätter	*NMA* I/2/2 (critical report), source C (copyists misidentified).
194 (186*h*)	*A Sd, A 710	Raab, Hofstätter	*NMA* I/1/1/2 (critical report), source B.
195 (186*d*)	*D-brd Ahk, 13	Raab, Estlinger	*NMA* I/2/1 (critical report), source B. MS inc. ripieno vocal and trombone parts by unidentified Salzburg copyist.
204 (213*a*)	*D-brd B, Ms. mus. 15333/4	Estlinger	*NMA* IV/11/7 (critical report), source A (copyists not identified). MS *c.*1778–9, not *c.*1775 or 1783 as usually assumed.
215 (213*b*)	I Mc, Noseda L-45/1	Estlinger	*NMA* IV/12/3 (critical report), source B. Score copy. Described as 'Sekundärquelle' in edition, p. vii; correctly described as authentic copy in critical report, ed. E. Hintermaier (Kassel, 1988).
220 (196*b*)	*A Sd, A 709	Raab, Estlinger	*NMA* I/1/1/2 (critical report), source A (autograph unknown). MS later 1770s.
222 (205*a*)	*D-brd Ahk, 20	Raab, Estlinger, Hofstätter	*NMA* I/3 (critical report), source B (parts by Hofstätter not identified). MS inc. parts by three unidentified local copyists.

238 (238)	*A Ssp, Moz 230.1	Estlinger	*NMA* V/15/1, p. x (copyist not identified).
242 (242)	D-brd B, Ms. mus. 15468	Hofstätter	*NMA* V/15/1, p. ix (copyist not identified). Only kbd, I, II by Hofstätter; other parts by unidentified ?Viennese copyist.
243 (243)	*privately owned	Raab, Estlinger, Hofstätter	*NMA* I/2/1 (critical report), source B. Description based on *NMA*.
246 (246)	*A Ssp, Moz 235.1	Estlinger	*NMA* V/15/2 (critical report), source D (copyist not identified). MS probably *c.* 1778–9. Only kbd. by Estlinger; other parts by unidentified Salzburg copyist.
250 (248*b*)	*D-brd B, Autogr. KV 250	Raab	*NMA* IV/11/7 (critical report) source A (copyist not identified). Parts by Raab copied 1776–8; MS inc. *Dubletten* by 3 Viennese copyists, *c.* 1785. MS used by Mozart to perform work in Vienna?
257 (257)	*D-brd Ahk, 6	Raab, Estlinger, Hofstätter	*NMA* I/1/1/3 (critical report), source B. MS inc. duplicate ob. parts by unidentified copyist.
258 (258)	*D-brd Ahk, 7	Estlinger	*NMA* I/1/1/3 (critical report), source B. MS 1780–1; inc. several parts by unidentified Salzburg copyist.
259 (259)	[formerly A Sd]	Estlinger	*NMA* I/1/1/3 (critical report), source B. Description based on *NMA*; MS could not be found in A Sd as of June 1990. MS included oboe parts by W. A. Mozart not in autograph.
262 (246*a*)	*D-brd Ahk, 5	Raab, Hofstätter	*NMA* I/1/1/2 (critical report), source A (primary source for *NMA*; autograph formerly lost but now PL Kj). MS *c.* 1777 inc. autograph timpani part; duplicate ob., tbn. I and timp. parts local.
273 (273)	*A Ssp, Moz 195.1	Estlinger	*NMA* I/3 (critical report), source B. MS acquired by St Peter's 1777; inc. later hn. parts, not in autograph (probably not authentic), copied by Kracher.
275 (272*b*)	D-brd Ahk, 8	Raab, Hofstätter	*NMA* I/1/1/4, pp. xi–xii; MS inc. parts by unidentified Salzburg copyist.
318 (318)	*D-brd F, Hs. 208	Raab, Estlinger	*NMA* IV/11/6, p. viii. See Plath, 'Mozartiana in Frankfurt und Fulda', 360 (but copyists not identified). MS inc. *Dubletten* by 2 Viennese copyists; parts used by Mozart to perform work in Vienna?
319 (319)	A Gk(h), 40.602	Estlinger, Hofstätter	*NMA* IV/11/6, p. ix (copyists not identified). MS inc. parts by 3 unidentified Viennese copyists; used by Mozart to perform work in Vienna?

(* = manuscript with title-page or attribution by Leopold Mozart, or with autograph corrections by Leopold or Wolfgang Amadeus Mozart)

K^1 (K^6)	Source	Copyists	Remarks
320 (320)	A Sm, Rara 320/2	Hofstätter	*NMA* IV/12/5 (critical report), source B. MS 1779–80.
	*D-brd F, Hs. 209	Estlinger	*NMA* IV/12/5 (critical report), source C. Mvts. iii, iv (*Concertante*) only. MS inc. additional Viennese parts; copy used by Mozart to perform work at Burgtheater on 23 Mar. 1783?
321 (321)	*D-brd Ahk, 15+16	Raab, Estlinger, Hofstätter	*NMA* I/2/2 (critical report), source B. MS 1779.
337 (337)	[formerly D-brd Ahk, 9]	Estlinger	*NMA* I/1/1/4, p. xvi. MS lost; description based on Senn, 'Die Mozart-Überlieferung im Stift Heilig Kreuz zu Augsburg', 368.
338 (338)	A Gk(h), 40.570	Hofstätter	*NMA* IV/11/6, *deest*. MS inc. parts by 2 unidentified Viennese copyists; used by Mozart to perform symphony in Vienna?
339^i, vi	*D-brd Ahk, 17	Estlinger, Hofstätter	*NMA* I/2/2 (critical report), source B. *NMA* uses as preferential source score from Köchel's library, A Wgm (autograph formerly lost but now PL Kj).
339^ii–v	*D-brd Ahk, 18	Estlinger, Hofstätter	*NMA* I/2/2 (critical report), *deest*.
364 (320*d*)	D-brd Mbs. Mus. mss. 6843	Estlinger	*NMA* IV/12/2, p. xiii. See R. Münster, 'Eine Salzburger Handschrift der Sinfonia concertante KV 362 [*sic*] aus Mozarts Zeit', *Mitteilungen der Internationalen Stiftung Mozarteum*, 15 (1967), 3–6, with the proviso that excepting the violone part copied by Estlinger, MS is of Viennese origin.
365 (316*a*)	*A Ssp, Moz 245.1	Estlinger, Hofstätter	*NMA* V/15/2 (critical report), source C.
	*CS KRa, II G 65	Estlinger, Hofstätter	*NMA* V/15/2 (critical report), source D. MS 1781, inc. autograph cadenza for mvt. i and several parts by unidentified Viennese copyist; MS used by Mozart to perform work in Vienna. Critical report fails to note title-page by Leopold Mozart. See Eisen, 'The Scoring of the Orchestral Bass Part'.
381 (123*a*)	?	Hofstätter	*NMA* IX/24/2 (critical report), *deest*. MS auctioned at Sotheby's (London), 17 May 1990; incorrectly described in auction catalogue as Leopold Mozart autograph.
382 (382)	A Ssp, Moz 340.3	Estlinger, Hofstätter	*NMA* V/15/1, pp. vii and ix (copyists not identified). MS 1783.

425 (425)	*A Sm Rara, 425/1	Estlinger	*NMA* IV/11/8, p. viii. MS 1784; inc. several parts by unidentified Salzburg copyist. Attribution by L. Mozart and copyist not noted in *NMA*; see Eisen, 'New Light on Mozart's "Linz" Symphony, K. 425'.
427 (417*a*)	*D-brd Ahk, 10	Estlinger, Hofstätter	*NMA* I/1/5, p. xv. Possibly *not* copy used to perform work in Salzburg on 26 Oct. 1783, as claimed in *NMA* and H. C. Robbins Landon, 'Mozarts Mass in C Minor, K. 427', in Eugene K. Wolf and Edward H. Roesner (eds.), *Studies in Musical Sources and Style: Essays in Honor of Jan LaRue* (Madison, Wisc., 1990), 419–23; paper in MS suggests date of mid-1784 to mid-1785.
deest	A Sca, Hs. 1747	Estlinger	Aria 'Cara se le mie pene'; see Plath, 'Der gegenwärtige Stand der Mozart-Forschung'. *NMA* II/7, p. xiii (copyist not identified).

[a] The only catalogue of Leopold Mozart's complete works remains the now badly out of date thematic listing in Max Seiffert, *Ausgewählte Werke von Leopold Mozart* (Denkmäler der Tonkunst in Bayern ix/2; Leipzig, 1908). For a modern catalogue of the vocal music, see David Carlson, 'The Vocal Music of Leopold Mozart (1719–1787): Authenticity, Chronology and Thematic Catalog' (Ph.D. diss., University of Michigan, 1976); and for the symphonies, Cliff Eisen, *Leopold Mozart. Ausgewählte Werke I. Sinfonien* (Denkmäler der Musik in Salzburg, 4; Bad Reichenhall, 1990).

General Index

References to illustrations and musical examples are indicated by **bold** type.

Works by Wolfgang Amadeus Mozart

References to illustrations and musical examples are indicated by **bold** type.

Köchel numbers are given routinely from first edition listings (followed by sixth-edition numbers, where applicable, in parentheses). Entries with the indication K⁶ reverse this procedure.